MELOME

Dumarest lo... constellations which formed patterns holding the likeness of men and beasts, women and creatures of the sea. The signposts of Earth — wherever that might be.

He looked up and felt again the surge born of the sudden realization that, at last, his search could be over. That the answer he had hunted for so long was at hand.

Melome could find it.

She *had* to find it!

ANGADO

"Go to the field," he ordered. "I want all details of every vessel movement from Baatz from the time Tron landed here."

Effort and expense with little hope of reward, but Avro was beyond counting the cost. If Dumarest was dead, he must be certain of it. If, despite all the evidence, the man had managed to survive, then he must know that too.

The future of the Cyclan depended on it.

Also in Legend by E. C. Tubb

MELOME
and
ANGADO

DUMAREST SAGA 28 and 29

E. C. Tubb

A Legend Book
Published by Arrow Books Limited
62-65 Chandos Place, London WC2N 4NW

An imprint of Century Hutchinson Limited

London Melbourne Sydney Auckland
Johannesburg and agencies throughout
the world

MELOME first published 1983 by Daw Books, Inc.
ANGADO first published 1984 by Daw Books, Inc.
Legend edition 1988

Printed and bound in Great Britain by
Anchor Brendon Limited, Tiptree, Essex

ISBN 0 09 957230 3

MELOME

To ROY and DAPHNE MORTIMER

CHAPTER ONE

Dumarest heard the scream of a tortured child and turned, eyes searching, relaxing as it came again and he recognized the source. A hundred yards to his right, raised high above the decorated surface of the boulevard, a painted crone lolled on a gilded throne standing on a platform of massive timbers supported by a dozen stalwarts. They, in turn, stood on another platform, larger, borne by twice their number. Overseers lashed them on with whips which left carmine streaks on naked, sweating flesh.

A show as false as the screams; a mature beauty lay beneath the masking paint and the massive timbers were thin cladding over buoyant rafts. Props for the actors demonstrating their skills; the grimaces, the fatigue, the grunts of pain. The whips were thin tubes containing dye but the men wielding them were clever as was the woman with her screams.

She shrieked again as Dumarest watched, the cry now accompanied by the clash of beaten metal, the harsh tintinnabulation prolonged by the chime of tiny bells. A score of girls ran from the shelter of the lower platform, weaving among the spectators, one coming to a halt before Dumarest.

"My lord—do I please you?" She was young, lithe, radiating unabashed femininity. Bells circled her ankles and wrists, more caressing the column of her throat, the narrow cincture of her waist. The long skirt, slit to the hip, displayed naked, slender legs, the hint of unclothed loins. Paint accentuated the luster of

5

her eyes, the soft fullness of her lips. Curled hair the color of gold held the glint of metal and gems. "My lord?"

A girl demanding his attention as the screams of the crone had caught it. The girl smiled as he nodded, chiming as she moved, the bound of unfettered breasts an enticing invitation.

"You are gracious, my lord." Her eyes were frank in their appraisal. "It would pleasure me to serve you. At the circus of Chen Wei. A spectacle of marvels culled from a thousand worlds. Things which will amaze you, amuse you, puzzle you, fill you with rapture. A feast for the eye and ear and mind and one not to be missed. The circus of Chen Wei. And, if you should be in a mind for dalliance—" Her face became lewd with unspoken promise. "My name is Helga. Ask for Helga."

A smile and she was gone leaving nothing but the scent of perfume and the fading tinkle of bells. Things which belonged on Baatz, and Dumarest took a deep breath as he looked at the sky, the hills, the boulevard on which he stood. It ran arrow-straight from the landing field to the market, the surface tesselated in abstract designs, curlicues, broken rainbows. Triple-tiered buildings edged the wide road, dwellings, shops, businesses, the verandas gaudy with bright hangings, the roofs with bloated lanterns. On the flanking hills the mansions of the rich and influential rested like a scatter of gems.

A good world, one of balm, of warmth and gentle breezes, of golden sunlight and rounded hills. A place of tranquility; the exudations of massed vegetation filling the air with subtle vapors which took the edge off violence and aggression and induced a tolerant lethargy.

A danger he recognized but could do nothing about and it was good to relax, to enjoy the sun, to become one with the crowd. To feel wide expanses around him instead of the cramping confines of a hull. And Baatz, with its transient population, was as good a place as any for him to be.

But caution remained and before he moved on, Dumarest made sure that none had lingered for no apparent reason, that he wasn't the object of covert interest. All seemed innocuous, most had followed the spectacle advertising the circus, others were intent on their own affairs, the rest headed toward the market, the sights, sounds and smells it contained.

"My lord!" A woman dressed in the barbaric apparel of a warrior-amazon gestured with an imperious arm. "Fine weaves from Kirek, strands as tough as steel and as soft as silk—nothing can beat spider-webs for utility. I have fifteen bales of it—you offer?"

A scowl marred the mannish face as Dumarest moved on, the voice yielding to another.

"High quality grain proof against bacterial molds and virus infestation. Strains from the biolabs of Lengue and Femarre. Fifteen kobolds a measure. Buy! Buy! Buy!"

A man stepped forward, another catching at his arm.

"Wait, Krasse. It could be cheaper deeper in the market."

"And less trustworthy. I've dealt with Chamile before and I don't trust you among the stalls. Best to buy here and now and get back to the farm before you've spent all we have."

Brothers or partners—they fell behind as Dumarest moved on. Booths and stalls stretched on all sides, some bearing a profusion of items, some only a few. Many held examples of goods housed in the holds of the vessels which had carried them. Others showed goods yet to arrive or dealt in future harvests, the samples on display examples of earlier yields. Stalls bearing gems of price were set next to those heaped with the cheap glitter of rubbish.

Businessmen, traders, thieves, entrepreneurs—the market of Baatz catered to all.

The jangle of a bell and the echo of a gong announced an operation in progress and Dumarest halted at the booth of a transient healer. The man was old, his robe not as spotless as it could have been, but he was deft and practice had augmented his skill. The patient was seated, eyes wide, the milky orbs already anesthetized. A woman in middle age attended by a young girl who watched with horror as the needle was applied. Within seconds it had been done, the cataracts removed and the eyes bandaged. The assistant had been generous with the prophylactic spray.

"Here, my dear." The healer handed the girl a phial. "All done and nothing to worry about. Give your mother this draught, as soon as you get her home."

A strong sedative with a touch of slowtime; the woman would sleep while her accelerated metabolism speeded the healing process. She would wake rested, hungry—and cured.

Another booth housed a dentist, another a dealer in charms, yet another a man who promised a cure for all the afflictions of the heart.

7

A fortune teller sat staring into a bowl of sand, the fine grains spurting in a random pattern of plumes.

A man swallowed flame.

A boy lay screaming on the ground, held by four men while, over his naked chest crawled the insect whose bite would cure him of the epilepsy which controlled him.

"Earl!" Evan Luftman waved from where he stood chewing at a mouthful of meat. "Enjoying the sights?"

"Just looking around."

"Baatz holds everything a man could need." Luftman wiped his mouth and looked at the skewer he held. On it fragments of meat lay beside succulent vegetables, the whole flavored with spice. "Good food, amiable women, diversions of all kinds. Going to the circus?"

"Maybe."

"They say it's good. Something special." Luftman licked at his skewer. "If those girls are anything to go by they weren't lying."

Dumarest made no comment. Luftman had been a fellow passenger on the journey to Baatz. They'd killed time over the card table and the man had talked more than he had wanted to listen. A roving entrepreneur dealing in what came to hand. A man past middle age with a face creased and blotched by the passage of time and dissipation. The meeting was one he could have done without.

"I've finished my business," said Luftman. "A quick profit, small but a man can't be too greedy. Now I'm looking for a couple of healers willing to travel to Jardis. They have a lot of eye trouble in the mines and it costs money to ship in regular doctors. Working on a profit-sharing basis I figure three months should make us all a comfortable pile."

"It could."

"It will if—" Luftman looked at his skewer then threw it aside. "I could use someone to take care of things, Earl. Muscle in case it's needed. Those miners can get awkward at times. Refuse to pay after treatment or gang up and demand a refund. You know how it can be."

"You can handle it."

"Once, yes, not now. I can't face them down, not like you could. One-fifth the profit, Earl. Maybe three months' work. A deal?"

"For a fifth?"

8

"Make it a quarter. An even share, Earl, you, me, the two healers—after expenses, naturally."

Which would be high. Dumarest said, "When are you leaving?"

"On the *Yegor*. It leaves at midnight. Be on the field an hour before then."

A rendezvous Dumarest hadn't made and wouldn't keep. Luftman's scheme held little appeal, and the only one to gain would be the entrepreneur himself. If he · could find willing healers—even on Baatz trusting fools were rare.

On the ground the writhing boy shrieked, twisted, shrieked again as the mandibles of the insect fed healing venom into his blood. A convulsive heave and he slumped. Head tilted to one side, lips parted to bare the teeth, the rod clamped between them.

In the comparative silence Dumarest heard the rattle of clashing ceramics, the whine of a female voice broken by the brittle sound.

". . . gather to hear . . . *clash* . . . the ancient . . . *clash*. . . songs of . . . *clash* . . . *clash* . . . Terra."

Terra?

Earth!

She stood in a ragged circle of semi-curious spectators, a girl little more than a child with long, straggling hair the color of sun-bleached bone, eyes like bruises, a mouth of bloodless lips and down-curved corners. Her skin matched the color of her hair, pale, waxen. The limbs were brittle appendages, nails of hands and naked feet rimmed with dirt. A frayed skirt hugged boyish loins and a halter shielded nascent breasts. Her waist, bare, was circled by a metal belt from which hung strands ending in spooled grips.

"Melome!" The woman standing beside her rattled her cluster of ceramic shards. "Who dares to test her powers? What man is brave enough to yield to her skill and taste the acid burn of remembered fears? What woman has the strength to shred the veil hiding her secret dreads?" Again the brittle chiming. "You, sir? You? You, my lady?"

A grifter and a good one; gaining attention, building a pitch, selecting the marks even as she spoke. A boy, blushing, looked at the spooled grip she thrust into his hand. A woman frowned as she was given another. Two men, grinning, took their places.

"Guaranteed entertainment for a mere five kobolds and your money back if dissatisfied. You, sir? Here, my lord!"

9

Dumarest felt the spool thrust into his hand and held it as he stared at the woman. She was no longer young, raddled beneath her paint, the body shapeless, the eyes hard.

He said, "You spoke of Terra."

"Terror, my lord? Aye, that and more for those with the courage to face it. Here you will find the ancient and dire songs of fear and hate and abject terror. Threnodies to chill the blood and numb the mind. A unique experience and one not to be missed. You there, sir! And you!"

A mistake, one born of noise and confusion, and natural enough to make. The twist of a vowel—yet for a moment there had been hope. The hope died as Dumarest looked again at the girl, the older woman, the two men squatting to one side. Ragged, both old, one with a drum, the other holding a pipe. Its wail rose as the woman returned to halt before him.

"The last place, my lord. Take it and we can begin."

A market-spectacle, born of illusion and the circumstance of the moment; it could be little more than that. But curiosity remained, why the belt, the connecting strands? How did the woman hope to prevent those who had not paid from enjoying what she had to offer?

"My lord!" The woman smiled as she took his money and handed him the spool. "Be seated. All be seated and let the entertainment commence!"

The spool was spring-loaded, the strand remaining taut as Dumarest sat on the ground, forming a connection between his hand and the belt the girl wore against her naked flesh. Connections repeated by all who had paid to join the circle. Like a spider in the center of a shimmering web the girl stood, motionless.

The tap of the drum joined the wail of the pipe, a throbbing, monotonous beat which seemed too loud for the instrument, as the wail of the pipe seemed too loud, the sudden hush drowning normal sounds too strong. A moment in which his eyes followed the glinting strand, moved to others, returned to his own and then, without warning, the girl began to sing.

A song without words.

One which filled the universe.

Dumarest had known the Ghenka-art which took vocal sound and used it to gain a hypnotic compulsion in which the mind was opened to flower in a profusion of mental images. He had heard the song of a living jewel and would never forget the awesome tonal effects of Gath. But this diminished them all.

10

A song—no, a dirge—no, a paen—no, a threnody, a lilting cadence, a sobbing, sighing, heart-wrenching murmur which created sympathetic vibrations from the thin strands so that they, too, sang in metallic harmony. A quivering which seemed to cloud the air and mask the slender figure in writhing strands of light and darkness. A chiaroscuro which blurred and changed to become a face snarling in anger.

One Dumarest had seen before.

It swelled to fill his vision, small details becoming plain; the eyes with their yellow tinge, the thinned, cracked lips, the nostrils rimmed with mucous, the ears tufted with hair. The face of a man who intended to kill.

One without a name on a world far distant in a time long forgotten, but Dumarest felt again the shock he had known then; the sudden realization that he had been duped and what he'd thought was a practice bout was the stage for his public butchery.

The shock and the terror. The fear and pain as edged steel cut a channel across his torso and sent blood to stain the floor of the ring. The lights, the weight of his own blade, the ring of avid faces but, above all, the terror of being maimed, crippled, blinded, turned into a mewling, helpless thing.

The face promised it all, the man, the knife he held, the profession he was in. A trained and savage killer amusing himself with an inexperienced boy. One who had no choice but to learn fast.

To move, to dodge and weave, to cut and slash and rip and stab and to find speed and use it. To be fast . . . fast . . . fast . . .

But the terror remained and would always remain if only as a whispering echo in the dim regions of his psyche. A weakness which strengthened his iron determination to survive.

He blinked, aware of the spool in his hand, the sweat dewing his face. To one side a man rocked, wailing, tears falling over his cheeks. Another shuddered, quivering. A woman appealed to invisible ghosts.

"No! Dear God, please! Please!"

Facing Dumarest the young boy looked sick, one of the two laughing men stared blankly at his clenched hand, his companion had a blood-smeared chin from a bitten lip.

Only the girl seemed unchanged. She stood as Dumarest remembered, head lowered a little, eyes blank, hands limp at her sides. A sensitive, he guessed. Someone with an unusual attri-

11

bute which she barely recognized and had paid for with physical penalties; weakness, poor development, lethargy, stunted growth.

"Wine, my lord?" The woman was beside him, a tray of brimming cups in her hand. "A kobold only."

A high price for weak liquor but of them all he was the only one to refuse. And none had asked for a return of their money.

Dumarest heard the clash of the ceramics again as he moved away. Unnecessary advertising; the spectacle of how the song had affected the initial group would be attraction enough but, he guessed, the girl would need a little time between performances to gain strength. Even a normal singer would need that.

He heard the wail of the pipe as he bought wine at a booth, sipping it slowly, hearing the pulse of the drum merge with the wail, the peculiar distortion which seemed to muffle the sound. Of the song he heard nothing.

"Clever." The vendor wiped his hands on his apron as he nodded toward the place where the girl operated. "She sings but unless you're in contact you hear nothing. An electronic barrier, I guess."

"Have you tried her?"

"No. I've no love for terror and the sight of those who've tasted it is enough to tell me I'm right. Still, I can't complain, it's good for business if nothing else."

Dumarest looked at his glass. "I guess it is. Has she been here long?"

"I wouldn't know. I only relieved my partner a week ago. She was here then."

"Alone or—"

"With the woman. Kamala's hard in her way but I guess she's fair enough. Someone has to look after the girl and Kamala knows how to take care of a valuable property. She could do worse." The vendor wiped his hands again. "More wine?"

A hint, even on Baatz information had to be paid for, but the wine was good and helped to dispel the chill induced by remembered terror. Or had it been simply remembered?

Dumarest recalled the face, the details he had noted, the pain he had experienced. Real pain as the lights had been real, the knife in his hand, the avid faces. A montage of isolated incidents? A possibility but he doubted it; somehow the song had opened a door in his mind. Touching a node and triggering a total recall of an emotion-loaded incident. One unique to himself.

To one side a juggler wafted a dozen glittering balls into the

12

air, keeping them spinning as he danced on a floor spiked with points. Next to him a girl undulated in an erotic rhythm while beyond a man with a stall loaded with hoes frowned his displeasure. Dumarest ignored them all, seeing nothing but the trembling of his own hand, feeling nothing but the surge which warmed his blood. Luck—it had always been with him, but now it seemed overwhelming.

The girl, Melome, could give him far more than a song.

Kalama said, "My lord, it is not wise. You should not—"

"Here!" Dumarest cut her short, thrusting money into her hand, snatching a spool from the fingers of another. "Let us begin."

Impatience rode him, displayed in the small act of violence which made him the center of attention, a thing he ignored as he sat, looking at the metallic strand, the girl standing within her web. One who seemed to blur as the throb of the drum merged with the wail of the pipe, to become a focus, an instrument he sought to use.

A key to explore the past.

He concentrated, narrowing possibilities, honing his mind to a single thought and then the terror came, the fear, the sick and hollow feeling in his guts.

The wind like a razor on his cheeks.

The cold, the hunger, the feel of the gritty soil, the desperation.

The conviction that he would die.

Before him the bulk of a ship rested in a strange and enigmatic beauty. The first he had seen but, young though he was, he knew it held the warmth and food he needed if he hoped to survive. He edged toward it, a child older than his years, one who had killed and was ready to kill again. The crew were careless, not seeing the small shape which darted from point to point, freezing, moving again with frenzied urgency.

To reach the port, to dive inside, to find a nook in which to crouch. To wait, dozing, as the unaccustomed warmth gave a false security, to jerk to awareness, to doze again.

To wake heart pounding with terror at the touch of a hand, the sight of a startled face, another which scowled.

"By God, look what we have here! A damned stowaway."

"A kid."

"Still a stowaway. That's what you are, boy. Know how we treat scum like you? Into the lock and out, that's how. Dumped into the void. Your eyes'll pop out and your lungs will become

13

balloons frothing from your mouth. You'll look like raw meat—ruined but still alive. A hell of a way to go.''

"Don't make a meal of it." The other man was uneasy. "You don't have to gloat. Anyway, it's up to the skipper to decide.''

The captain was old, his face lined, graced with tufted eyebrows, his nose pinched and set above a firm mouth.

"How old are you, boy? Ten? Eleven?''

"Yes, sir.''

"Yes, what? Eleven?''

"Twelve, I think, sir. I'm not sure." The face before him blurred, jarred to clear focus. "Sir?''

"I could dump you but I won't. You can ride with us, working your passage. A hard life but better than what you've known.'' Again the blurring. "Food, warmth, security—but you'll earn it all.''

"Sir? I—sir?''

But the face had gone and he looked at a glittering strand and the girl to which it led while, from the circle of which he was a part, came the groans and wails of those who had tasted an evil fruit.

"Wine?''

Kamala was beside him with her tray of beakers and Dumarest bought and sipped while retaining his place. The moment had been too short; memories revived and speeded by subjective time so that he had lived an hour, more, in a few minutes. Or was it simply that? Did the moment of terror, once experienced, form the whole of the incident?

He had been a boy again, back home on Earth, and only the ship and the captain's kindness had saved him from death. But there had been other moments of terror; times when through ignorance he had known the fear of a trapped animal. One augmented by the threats of sadistic members of the crew who had taken a perverse delight in relating stories of dreadful punishments inflicted for small wrongs.

Of burnings, beating, maiming, blinding—things which his experience had told him were all too possible.

Time had negated them; the savagery he had known had no place in any civilized community, but, until he had learned, terror had been a close companion.

"My lord?'' Kamala again, looking at his barely touched wine, the spool still held in his free hand. "Is something wrong?''

Dumarest realized that he alone was left of the circle. Finish-

14

ing the wine, he handed the woman the empty beaker. He followed it with coins.

Kamala refused them with a shake of the head.

"No, my lord, it would not be wise. I warned you against hearing the song again so soon. Yield again to terror and—"

"I won't go mad."

"So you say and it could well be true but others have made the same boast and failed to live up to it. I want no trouble."

Dumarest said, flatly, "I've the money and I'm in position. Rattle your chimes, woman, and stop wasting time."

"No."

"You want a higher fee? Double, then. Triple. Damn it, name your price!"

"No!" She backed from the anger blazing in his eyes, one hand lifting, steadying, the massive ring she wore on the index finger glowing with a metallic sheen. A weapon he recognized. "Baatz is a peaceful world," she said. "But a woman would be a fool to be without protection on any world and, my lord, I am not a fool. It would be best for you to leave now."

Advice he was reluctant to take. Pressed, he could negate the threat of the weapon, moving before she could discharge its darts, reaching her, twisting hand and wrist so as to obtain the ring. But if he used his superior speed and strength he would ensure her enmity. It was better to master his impatience.

"My lady, I must apologize." A smile replaced the anger which had frightened her. "I mean no harm and want no trouble. It was just that—well, I'm sure you understand."

"You're holding the spool."

"Is that bad?"

"Release it."

"Of course." He let it fall and watched as it moved toward the girl, the reel climbing the strand to hang at her belt. "I would like to talk business." He added, as she frowned, "At least let me make the offer."

"Melome sings no more today." Kalama was adamant. "She is tired and soon it will be dark. Not even for two hundred kobolds will she sing."

Twice what she would earn in a session; a score of spools hung at her waist. But if he should offer more? Dumarest decided against it; as Kalama had said, the girl was tired and the sky held the hint of coming darkness. In the softening light Melome stood like a broken animal, one which had been ridden

15

too hard and too far. The lowered face was ghastly in its pallor, the bruised eyes ugly smears.

He said, "I understand, but I want her to sing for me again. A private performance—it can be arranged?"

"Perhaps." The lifted hand wavered a little, fell as, again, he smiled. "You want to buy her?"

"Hire her."

"For an hour, a day, a week?" Her lips twisted in a cynical lewdness. "It will not be as you hope. Those in the grip of terror make poor lovers."

Dumarest said, patiently, "I want her to sing and that is all. To sing to me alone and to keep on singing if I ask. Once may be enough. One song—two hundred and fifty?"

"Not tonight," she said quickly. "One song, you said. If you should want more?"

"Five hundred for as many as I want. For a session to end when I say so."

"Five songs only—and she stops if the strain is too great." Again her mouth displayed cynical distrust. "You have no objection to me being present?"

"None."

"And my instrumentalists?"

"I want her to sing," said Dumarest. "Nothing else." He jingled coins from one hand to the other. "Here is fifty as proof of my good faith. At dawn?"

"At midday. Be at the house of the Broken—no, better we visit you." Kalama nodded as he gave the address of the room he'd hired. "At noon then, my lord. Be patient in your waiting."

Patient but not foolish and it was dark by the time Dumarest left the market. Even at night the place was still alive; lamps burning with swaths of red and gold, blue and umber, the scent of cooking meats and vegetables hanging in the air together with writhing plumes of incense, sparks from torches, beams from shimmering orbs of kaleidoscopic hues. Mundane trading had ended, the vendors of hoes and seeds and domestic items giving way to others who filled the night with a different allure. Drummers and pipers together with dancers, the thin whine of strings, the drone of flutes. Gamblers who called from tables set with cards, dice, hollow shells. Women with snakes, spiders, crawling beetles. The tellers of fortunes and artists who created glowing picture on living skin.

Men who fought with knives.

16

Practice blades; edges and points shielded and capable of dealing little more than bruises and scratches. And the bouts lacked the savage intensity normal to any good fighter—the magic of Baatz had robbed them of serious intent so that the crowd laughed at bad play instead of jeering and the loser accepted defeat with a grin and a shrug.

"Sir!" The promotor had spotted Dumarest, noted his height, his stance, the hilt of the knife riding above his right boot. "A bout, sir? You look like a man used to the arena. A little harmless sport to entertain lovers of the art. A demonstration of skill, the winner decided by popular acclaim. No?" His voice held a philosophical shrug. "Then how about you, sir? Or you?"

Dumarest walked on. Ahead the lights of the boulevard matched those of the stars now illuminating the sky; clusters of vibrant colors, sheets and curtains of luminescence, nebulae like smoke. Too many stars and he longed for an emptier sky. One illuminated by the swollen bulk of a silver moon blotched in the likeness of a skull. Of constellations which formed patterns holding the likeness of men and beasts, women and creatures of the sea. The signposts of Earth—wherever that might be.

A world lost in distance and time so that even its name had become a legend.

But one now so close. So very close!

Dumarest halted, leaning against a wall, looking up at the sky and feeling again the surge he had known in the market. One born of the sudden realization that, at last, his search could be over. That the answer he had hunted for so long was at hand.

Melome could find it.

She *had* to find it!

Waking that moment in the past when, as a child, he had stood in the captain's cabin and stared uncomprehendingly at the volume on the desk. A book which had meant nothing at the time and he had turned from it in sudden terror as footsteps came from the passage. If discovered, he could be accused of prying or stealing, be beaten, maimed, tormented—his sadistic mentors had taught him well.

But that terror, stimulated by the song, would bring the book again before his eyes, the data it contained. All he had to do was wait.

Then noon passed and the girl did not appear and when he went searching he learned she had been sold to the circus of Chen Wei.

17

CHAPTER TWO

—•◆•—

The man was a grotesquerie; a thing of extended limbs, massive ears, lumps, bumps, protrusions. A clown cavorting on stilts, the painted face ludicrous above a padded torso. The hair was like a brush touched with a dozen hues. The voice was like an organ.

"Why hesitate? The circus of Chen Wei waits to entertain you. See novelties, marvels, impossibilities. Wander in realms of mystic enchantment. Thrill to the impact of exotic stimuli. The chance of a lifetime. Not to be missed. Hurry, now. Hurry! Hurry! Hurry!"

A bell clanged, three acrobats spun in a confusion of sequins and satin, a woman sold tickets.

"Ten for transport and the same for initial entry. Twenty, kobolds—thank you, sir. Keep the stub for your return."

A dwarf guided Dumarest to where rafts waited in line urging him into the first where he sat on a bench next to the rail. A girl came to join him, another at her side. She was young, eager to enjoy her day, hopeful for masculine company but after one glance at his face she turned to her friend leaving Dumarest to stare at the ground below.

It fell away as the raft lifted, streaming beneath in an unbroken expanse of curled and matted vegetation dotted with delicate flowers. The afternoon sun touched them, turned them into scraps of gold, of ruby, of smoking amber. Flecks which looked like eyes and all of them mocking.

Why had he been such a fool?

Melome had been in his hand—he should never have let her go. Never have trusted Kalama to keep their bargain. What had made him so careless? He had quested the market and gained her address, verifying it from more than one source. An elementary precaution, but why hadn't he done more? Why had he been content to wait until it was too late? The woman had cheated him but the money was nothing; he would willingly give ten times as much to correct his stupidity.

"Mister?" The girl at his side pointed over the rail. "Is that the circus?"

"No—I don't know."

"Sorry. I thought maybe you'd been before. My friend thought you might have done. A lot of people have done. That is—" He wasn't listening and she knew it. "Sorry."

An apology Kalama would never have to make. She was gone, probably on the *Yegor*—he had seen the ship head for space wreathed in the blue cocoon of its Erhaft field. Robbing him even of revenge. Leaving Melome—his hand tightened as he thought about it. Closed in anger more against himself than Kalama. What use to blame another for his folly?

One caused by the wine or the shock of the song or the emotional impact of realizing what Melome could give him. Like a climber reaching a summit, confident of success, hurrying a little—and taking that one false step which led to destruction. Thinking more about that moment when, in the captain's cabin, he had seen the book on the desk. A journal, perhaps, or the ship's log he had brought up to date. But both would have held the details of his journeys.

Both would have held the coordinates of Earth.

"There!" The girl at his side, excited, rose as she pointed. "There it is!"

Froth cupped in a fold of the hills. Bubbles laced and striped with gaudy candy colors; vivid purples, reds, greens, blues, sickly yellows, lambent violet. Spires bearing floating pennants. Twisted towers topped with flags. Walks and slides and curving spirals. Peaked roofs graced with undulating crests.

The circus of Chen Wei.

Dumarest studied it as the raft dropped to the landing. Much of what he saw had to be mirage; illusions created with paint and fabric, using distorted perspective to give the impression of buildings and space where none existed. A spire vanished as he looked at it, became a blur of lines and blotches, became a spire

20

again as he turned his head. An optical illusion repeated on all sides as cubes, stairs, landings shifted and took on other dimensions.

"Welcome to the circus!" A clown like a ball bounded toward them, another on stilts stood, beaming, as a man with a crested headpiece took their tickets, tore them, returned the stubs. "Enter and enjoy! Hurry! Hurry! Hurry!"

Entry was through a giant, laughing mouth, the passage forming the throat set with a series of spongy rollers; air traps which kept the internal pressure high. Dumarest pushed his way through them to emerge in a playground filled with seats, stalls, niches holding bizarre statues. A fountain shone with shifting luminescence while filling the air with crystalline merriment. Sideshows ran to either side, barkers shouting their spiel. A place of fun and games and assorted entertainment.

All that the initial entry ticket would buy.

Dumarest checked the sideshows and moved on, paying for admission to a curving gallery set with tableaux depicting a variety of horrific torments. Whispering voices gave graphic details while informing him that, for an extra fee, he could take advantage of the sensatapes which would allow him to experience the agonies of the victims.

A popular entertainment; each bench held customers, heads wreathed with silver bands, faces twisted as they suffered on a subjective plane. A place where Melome could have been but the tableaux were static models and Dumarest moved on.

To a hall where mirrors reflected his image in a thousand grotesque distortions.

To a misted cavern filled with invisible forces which caused him to sweat, to shiver, to feel the heat of passion and the chill disgust of self-contempt. To sigh and laugh and, with sudden fury, to scream curses.

A place yielding to another filled with drifting balloons which chuckled and cried, pleading, fuming, groaning, whimpering, tittering, sneering. Voices of suggestive intent and others mouthing abrasive insult. Hit, they burst to dispel sweet scents or acrid vapors. One clung, stinging, to his hand, the memory-plastic shriveling to mould itself into a plaque.

STUPID! The word it bore glowed with golden flame. It was followed by others, smaller; *"This token entitles you to a free gift."*

21

A blank-faced doll which he gave to a child gawking at a caged clown who mimicked the antics of a fierce and savage beast.

A gift easily disposed of but the accusation remained. Stupidly compounding his initial mistake—Melome would not be found by a frantic searching of public areas. She would need to be groomed, taught the finer arts of showmanship, tested to gauge her powers. Things he had overlooked in his urgent need to find her.

Dumarest slowed, turning at the sound of a bell. A girl with long raven hair, alabaster skin, a body shaped like an hourglass came slowly toward him. Her legs and arms were bare, a sequined dress hugging her figure with ebon brilliance. The bell was silver, its tone no sweeter than her voice.

"Get your tickets for the big show. Available at all barriers and booths. Half-price for children. Take your places for the most exciting, unusual, entertaining and overwhelming spectacle ever to be seen on Baatz. The performance will commence within the hour. Hurry! Hurry! Hurry!"

She halted as Dumarest touched her arm.

"I need help," he said, and swayed a little as he smiled; a man bemused a trifle but harmless enough. "I'm looking for a friend. She works for the circus but I can't seem to find her."

"Maybe she's off-duty, sir. Resting."

"I doubt it. She said to ask for her." He frowned, searching for a name. "Hilda. She said to ask for Hilda—no, Helga. That's it. Her name is Helga. Young, gold hair, nice smile. She was in town. On the boulevard. Advertising the circus. She said to be sure to ask for her and, well, here I am. You know her?"

She said, coldly, "Not personally. Ask an attendant to direct you to the information desk. They will send for her. If she's free she may meet you there."

She came after an hour, smiling, eyes searching his face. A mechanical smile and a look devoid of recognition; she must have spoken to more than a hundred men on the boulevard—he was just one of a crowd. Then, as she studied the neutral grey of his clothing, the lines and planes of his face, the smile changed, became warmer, more genuine.

"So it's you. I'm glad you came."

"That makes two of us. How long are you free?"

"For as long as you want—if you can pay."

22

"That's no problem." He smiled as he looked into her eyes, projecting his personality, his obvious admiration. "I've money and I'm in no hurry. But I am hungry and I guess you are too. Something to eat, maybe?"

"That would be nice."

"You'll make the food taste twice as good." He looked at her clothing, a simple dress belted at the waist, one devoid of ornamentation as was her throat, her wrists, her fingers. The bells and chains and displaying garment she had worn on the boulevard were for a different kind of work. "I've been lucky," he said. "And I like to share my good fortune. I'd also like you to remember me. Let's buy something to make sure you do that."

Smiling, she led him to a booth where he bought a bracelet of precious metal set with scintillant gems. An item worth the cost of a High passage but one he could afford. As he could afford the expensive meal, the wine, the liqueurs. Bribes augmented by his charm, his attention and courtesy so that later, in the privacy of her cubicle, she clung to him with genuine passion.

"Earl, my darling! Hold me! Hold me!"

She writhed in the circle of his arms, the warmth of her nudity burning against him, the softness of her flesh triggering his own desire so that it grew to dominate the universe, to flower, to fade in soft murmurings as her fingers searched his face, his naked body.

"A man, Earl. God, you're a man!"

"As you are a woman."

"Do you mean that? Do you really like me?"

"More than like you." He touched in turn and she sighed her pleasure, snuggling close to him. "You are a beautiful woman, Helga."

"Your woman, Earl."

"Mine."

She sighed again and walked her fingers over his torso, soft pads which traced the pattern of scars marring the skin. Old cicatrices; the medals of wounds won in the arena and visible proof of his skill and ability to survive.

"A fighter," she said. "Is that how you won your money?"

"Have you known many fighters?"

"A few."

"Here?"

23

"No," she was scornful. "Baatz is too soft. How did you get your money?"

He said, blandly, "How did you get to work for the circus?"

"Luck." She stretched against him, her hand sliding over his chest to the muscled plane of his stomach. "I developed fast and had a friend who told me to use what I had. The circus gave me an opportunity. I worked a dance routine for a while then settled for this." Her hand began to move in small circles. "And you?"

"I had a stake in a ship and sold out."

"A good deal?"

"The best." His arm closed around her. "Who buys for the circus?"

A question she ignored as her hand moved faster, lower, her chest heaving as her breath accelerated to a sudden, unaccustomed wave of desire.

"Earl!" Her lips found his own, pressed, fell moistly away. "You're wonderful. Such a man. A hero. So satisfying. Take me, darling. Take me!"

Mechanical words used in an automatic response but beneath them was something more. A feeling expressed by the movement of her body, the hunger of her lips even as she spoke the ritual of commercial love. Dumarest recognized it, knew that she was hampered by lack of true experience, unable to do more than use words and phrases learned by rote. A woman basically a stranger to love but learning and learning fast.

"Darling! Darling!" She heaved against him in demanding fury. "Hold me! Hold me, Earl! Hold me!"

Against the fears and terrors of the unknown; the frightening abyss which lay beyond the boundaries of mechanical sex. A region which demanded emotional surrender and gave in return a hint of paradise.

After, when again the fires had died and she lay snug in the crook of his arm, she said. "Did you mean it when you said you loved me?"

"Yes."

A moment then, as a statement, she said, "You've known a lot of women. You know too much not to have done. Did you love them?"

"Does it matter?"

"You loved them. You had to love them. Some men are like that; with them it's all or nothing. Others are like machines.

24

They aren't interested in you as a person but simply as a body to be used. There's a difference—God, what a difference!" She reared to lean over him, breasts hanging like succulent fruit. "Am I really your woman?"

For answer he stroked her hair.

"I'd be all you could ever want," she said. "I promise that. And I wouldn't want anyone else but you, ever."

A lie though she didn't know it; her own nature and intense femininity would drive her along the path she had chosen. To love and be loved—even the facsimile of true affection would govern her life.

Dumarest said, "It's nice to think about, but don't you have commitments? A contract?"

"It can be broken. If you've enough money they'd let me go."

The moment he'd been waiting for. He said, casually, "It's a thought. Who would I have to see to make the deal?"

"I could arrange it."

"No, things like that are best done personally." A smile made the remark innocuous, a smile he retained as he said, with equal casualness, "How does it work? I mean, if someone's sold to the circus what happens to them?"

"They have to be trained. Washed, fed, dressed, healed sometimes and taught to walk and stand and smile." Her eyes narrowed a little. "Why the interest?"

"Curiosity. I guess they must be kept in a special place. That dome with the false stairs?"

"That's the infirmary." She stooped to trail her breasts across his face. "Kiss me, lover."

He obliged. "The one with the spirals?"

"You're close. Again."

"Tell me."

"It's next to the one you said." Straightening, she frowned. "Why the interest?"

Dumarest shrugged. "There could be money in it. A man I met in town has lost his daughter and thinks she may have been sold to the circus. He's willing to pay well to get her back."

"His daughter?"

"That's what he said. She's young, bleached hair, thin, washed-out, half-starved. Her name's Melome. Maybe you've seen her."

"No."

"You could find out about her. Find out where she is. Fix it to buy her back."

Dumarest felt his anger rising as Helga shook her head. "Why not? Damn it, woman, why not?"

His anger betrayed him, was reflected in her face, her eyes, the rising tempo of her voice.

"You came here looking for her. Your girl. Lying to me. Using me. Making me feel I was something special. Promising—you bastard! You dirty bastard! Out! Get out! Out!"

"The girl!" Dumarest reared as she came at him, hands extended, fingers hooked, nails aiming at his eyes. "Melome! I—"

His hand thrust out in a defensive blow to save his eyes. The blow slammed against the woman's jaw and sent her rolling from the bed to lie shrieking on the floor.

"Rube! Rube! Hey Rube!"

The warning carny cry which spelled trouble and the need for help. Any circus worker within earshot would answer on the run.

Dumarest snatched at his clothes, found his knife, rose with it in his hand as men burst into the cubicle. Three of them armed with clubs. They halted as they saw the gleam of the blade, the man holding it in a fighter's stance. Their leader, a man with close-cropped hair and the massive bulk of a weight-lifter, glanced at the girl.

"Helga?"

"A pervert! The bastard hit me!"

"She's lying," said Dumarest. "If I hit her where's the mark?" The pad of his hand had cushioned the blow. "I'll leave but when I do I'll be dressed and walking." He turned the knife, light from the overhead lantern splintering from the steel, fuzzed on the edges and point. "Anyone have other ideas?"

"I'll handle this." The big man lowered his club as his companions left. To Dumarest he said, "I'll take you to a raft and, mister—don't ever try to come back!"

The shop was a cave of wonders; of ruffles and flounces, leather, plastic, feathers, belts glowing with filigree, garments heavy with fictitious gems. In the dim lighting the owner was a snuffling wasp who stared and shook his head in disapproval.

"A clown?"

"A clown." Dumarest was patient. "Nothing too elaborate. I

26

want to crash a party," he explained. "It's a fancy dress affair and I'm not too popular with the host. His wife, you understand." He saw the thin face crease in a frown and quickly adapted the story. "She doesn't like the plans I've made for her sister. If she hadn't interfered we'd have been married by now."

"An affair of the heart?" The costumer beamed, mollified. "But a clown?"

"It seems appropriate—all men in love are fools."

"True, but there is an art in these things. A soldier, now, or a great lord or a captain from space—you have the look and bearing of such. But a clown—who can take such seriously?"

"Exactly. You can supply me?"

"Of course. But you had better strip." The costumer gestured at the tuin Dumarest wore, high-collared, tight at the wrists, falling to mid-thigh. The pants and high boots. "The art of costume is to dress from the skin—only then can you really slip into the part."

"I'm not acting, just pretending, and I won't be wearing the costume for long. Could we hurry?"

Minutes later Dumarest left the shop, stooping, his head and face hidden by a grotesque mask, his clothing by a loose garment of ragged tatters. One which led to flared pants trailing the ground and all in blotches of vibrant color. He swayed as he moved toward the area where the circus rafts were kept, using a bottle to daub himself with alcohol.

It was past midnight and the area was apparently deserted, but as he reached it a shape loomed from the shadows.

"You there! What do you want?"

"A ride." Dumarest halted, swaying, lurching closer to the guard. "Gotta get back to the cus . . . cir . . . gotta get back."

"You're drunk." The guard wrinkled his nose at the reek of spirit. "Stinking. Why don't you sleep it off?"

"Gotta get back."

"Sure. Tomorrow at first light." The clown was of the circus and the circus looked after its own. "Bed down in a raft." He gestured toward the grounded vehicles and laughed. "Pick a soft one."

Dumarest picked the one farthest from the light falling over the rail, muttering, changing the mutter to a snore. He heard the crunch of boots as the guard came to check and sensed the impact of the man's eyes. Satisfied he turned away and Dumarest

27

relaxed, unclenching his hand, opening his eyes to look at the stars. They were blotched by patches of cloud but clear enough to check their wheeling. A clock which measured time for the guard to relax and fall into a doze. For the circus to bed down for the night.

The raft was locked, the key missing, as Dumarest had expected. The knife whispered from his boot and eased away the casing over the control panel. Wires lay exposed, black in the starlight, and he traced them with his fingers to select two pairs. Insulation shredded beneath the edge of the blade. A twist and the vehicle became alive.

Dumarest sent it upwards, rising like a shadow, soundless save for the hum from the antigrav units. A good vehicle and well-maintained—the circus could not afford accidents. When the town had fallen far below and the boulevard was a thin streak of brilliance he sent it toward the place where Melome would be waiting.

A short journey but one longer by night and he strained his eyes, searching the hills, grunting his relief as, far to the left, he saw the glow of massed bubbles. Poor navigation and he corrected it, swinging wide so as to approach from the far side. The lights were dim, the glow a pearly sheen which hid sharp detail, and he halted the raft as he examined his target.

Where had Helga said?

He thinned his lips as he remembered the woman, the incident her jealousy had caused. His own fault—he should have remembered the double standard of those who followed her profession. The sudden tempers and demanding passion. The brittle emotions and fierce possessiveness, but his own urgency had made him careless.

Where had she said?

A dome moved before him as he touched the controls; one daubed with lozenges of color now dulled by starlight. A walk which wasn't real, a sweeping arch, a winding path, a spire—all the products of illusion. A minaret circled with a staircase. . . .

Stairs?

The infirmary, Helga had said—would Melome be there? The woman hadn't said and, at the time, she'd no reason to lie. There, perhaps? There?

Again the raft moved and Dumarest narrowed his eyes. Starlight and shadows altered perspective and robbed colors of distinctive hues. Was that dome white with red spirals or black with white? Close, Helga had said; the place he wanted was close to a spiraled dome. But which?

He had to take a chance. To drift was to invite discovery. The raft dropped as he made his decision, softly, lightly, coming to rest on taut membrane, indenting it, the plastic rising as he adjusted the lifting units. A delicate balance but shielding domes would protect it from any wind and those same domes would keep it hidden from the ground.

Dumarest left the raft and looked around. He'd landed on the roof of what he assumed to be a gallery; part of a convex web lying between soaring domes. One close to him was ridged in a pattern of fluted columns, another, smaller, bore snarling beast-masks, the mouths ugly with fangs. He left them behind as he walked to where the web branched, halting as he reached the target he had chosen; a cone which held a steady rustling, one set with a ladder that was real.

A vent, he guessed, or an induction tube feeding the pumps which maintained the internal pressure. The gilded summit would hold filters and the ladder was to allow access. The place should have a door yielding to inner mechanisms, and he found it on the far side, a narrow panel which jerked open to reveal a dimly lit interior filled with a louder murmuring and the scent of dust.

From below came the sound of voices.

". . . had about enough. If Zucco pushes me much harder I'll quit."

"That's your privilege, but he's not so bad."

"He's an animal. Well, to hell with him. Playing tonight?"

"I'm bushed and the luck's against me. I'm for the sack."

Odd scrapings rose above the murmuring; tools being set in their place, Dumarest guessed, or cans being moved. The men could be roustabouts on cleaning or maintenance duty, tired now, careless, but it would be a mistake to take that for granted. Yet to find another entry would take too much time. The external membrane was too tough to slit and, even if he slashed an opening, air loss would register.

Dumarest stripped off the clown's mask and costume; if the circus had bedded down it would arouse attention and would hamper quick movement. Stairs led down from where he stood and he moved down them, freezing as something moved at their foot. His face was in shadow, the grey of his clothing blending with the wall behind him—only movement would betray him.

29

He saw the blur of a face looking upwards, the hand which reached for the rail.

"Leave it, Brad." The other man, invisible, echoed his fatigue. "We'll sweep out tomorrow. Come on—I've had enough."

The face vanished, the hand, and Dumarest heard the pad of boots, a sighing rustle, then silence. Cautiously he moved to the floor below. The air-vent passed through it and from the vibration he guessed the pumps were below. Brooms, cans, dusters stood racked against a wall together with loose coveralls and peaked caps. He donned one, slipped a loose coat over his shoulders and picking up a broom, pushed his way through the rollers of an air-trap.

Beyond lay the curve of a gallery, another door, a room holding tables, chairs, people.

Circus folk at recreation.

Men for the most part though women were among them, all casually dressed, none in costume though some bore the traces of makeup. Cards, bottles, plates of small cakes stood on the tables and, on the far side, a man swore as he rolled dice.

"Six again—damn the luck! Three times down in a row!"

A woman said, "Give it up, Sakai. Lose more and you'll be paying to work."

"That'll be the day—there's always the punters."

"Try lifting their cash and you'll be out on your butt." The woman, a hard-eyed, hard-faced brunette with skin raddled beneath her paint, poured more wine into her glass. To Dumarest she said, "Hey! Come to sweep us out?"

He grimaced, lifting the broom, pointing ahead.

"Swamping, eh? Rather you than me. Say, you new here?"

He nodded, gesturing with the broom again, acting the mute. To talk would lead to conversation which could betray him.

A man called, "Guide him right, Zulme."

"Sure." She pointed to a door to the left. "Through there, swamper. Then the first door to your right. Clean good, now, or Draba will be after your tail."

Laughter followed Dumarest as he left the room. A short passage lay before him and he passed the door to his right. Then one led to something he chose to avoid—the laughter had lacked true humor and he guessed the woman had made him the butt of a joke. An air-trap ended the passage and he squeezed through it, scenting the sudden acridity of the air. An odor which strength-

30

ened as he reached a door, cracked it open, passed through into a soft dimness.

"Melome?" She could be asleep, resting—the place was where he judged she might be. "Melome?"

Then, suddenly, he was fighting for his life.

CHAPTER THREE

It came from the shadows, a blow which tore the peaked cap from his head, raking downwards to shred the loose coat from his shoulders. One which would have torn the scalp from his head had Dumarest not acted with unthinking speed. A stir of the air warned him, a gust of fetid odor, the sense of movement and he was moving forward and down to cushion the blow which slammed against his back. Feeling the impact of it. The grate, as claws ripped into his tunic to meet the protective mesh buried in the plastic.

The metal saved him from crippling lacerations but he felt the bruising fury, the shock, the force driving him to the floor.

He rolled as he hit, rolled again as something struck close enough to sting his eyes with wind. Something looming monstrous in the gloom, a shape of hair and limbs and a squatly huge body. One with claws and fangs gleaming with a greenish phosphorescence.

A beast spawned on some radiation-lashed world now snarling with a killing rage.

It lunged forward, foot raised to kick, taloned nails to rip out Dumarest's stomach and spill his intestines. A blow which would kill even if the mesh held, rupturing the spleen, pulping liver. A blow which missed as he flung himself over the floor, rising to back, almost falling as his foot hit the broom.

A weapon he snatched up and poised, bristles forward, the points aimed at the back-sloping face, the eyes. A thrust and he dodged the reaching claws, darting to one side as the thing

33

pawed at its sockets. A minor irritation and it snarled as again Dumarest attacked, snatching at the broom, snapping off the head to leave him with a splintered stick.

A broken spear less than five feet long.

One he lashed upwards, feeling the tug of a claw in his hair as he hit the crotch, the genitals resting between the massive thighs. Ducking to stab at the same target. Backing as saliva and stench gushed from the fanged mouth.

After a moment of respite Dumarest checked the area. The door by which he had entered the room was barred by the thing facing him but another lay to one side. The room itself was illuminated by a single glowing plate set in the ceiling. A mass of straw lay in one corner, a trough in another. One containing water, he guessed, a bowl, now empty, could have held food.

A snarl and the creature lunged toward him. Clearly it had learned; the long arms hung protectively over the crotch, one lifting as it came close, the clawed paw missing as Dumarest darted aside. A move which gave him a choice of either door, but the one by which he had entered led only back the way he had come.

He spun, dropping to one knee, the wooden shaft in his hands whining as he sent it in a savage blow to the creature's leg. A blow which hit the kneecap, shattering the wood, but hampering the beast long enough for Dumarest to reach the other door. To duck through it. To slam it fast.

He leaned his back against it as he fought for breath.

Before him stretched a chamber, narrow, set with a guard rail before flanking cubicles with raised floors. Rooms like cells but without the bars. In the nearest something stirred.

At first he thought it a large bird then it turned and Dumarest saw the undoubted humanity behind the elongated jaws which gave the impression of a beak, the rounded, avian eyes, the double-orifice where a nose should have been. An illusion heightened by the extended column of the neck, the lack of ears, the backward slope of the forehead. Vivid tattooing supplied an artificial plumage.

As he stepped forward the creature retreated, hopping on distorted feet, thin, curved fingers lifting in futile protection. A quasi-human, naked, slight, unmistakably female.

"Don't touch her!" The voice was a deep gurgle coming from a cubicle opposite. "Leave her alone. You frighten her, Gora, and I'll—" The voice paused. "Gora?"

34

"No." Dumarest turned to face a bloated obscenity; a man so gross as to be repulsive. Like the bird-girl he was naked. "Who is Gora?"

"Someone I'll kill one day. If he gets within reach of my hands. If I can get my teeth in his throat. Come closer—I can't see so good. Who are you? Your aura's strange."

"It's mine. Who are you?"

"Rastic Alatabani Seglar. Call me Ras. Would you believe I was handsome once?" The massive bulk shook with either laughter or tears. "A traveler. A kid with stars in his eyes. I had the universe to rove in but I chose the wrong world. Got contaminated. Began to swell. Money would have saved me but I had no cash. Now I can't move. If I wasn't with the circus I'd die."

A product of disease, disfigured, almost blind. Dumarest looked at the caricature of a face, the filmed orbs. A freak as the bird-girl was a freak, and the man tufted with feathers in the next cubicle, and the woman lower down—the one with two heads.

"I'm Olga," said one. "My, you're handsome. Tall and strong and a real man. More than Ras ever was, I'll bet. He lies, you know. Lies all the time."

"Like you," said the other head. "I'm Inez. Pay no attention to her. She's jealous. She thinks everyone who comes to see us is interested only in her. Tell the truth, now, aren't I the prettiest?"

Dumarest said, "Maybe you can help me. I'm looking for a friend."

"A girl! I bet it's a girl!"

"Shut up, Olga! You talk too much!"

"And you eat too much! You're making me fat! Soon I'll be as ugly as you are!"

"Bitch!"

"Cow!"

"Shut up!" A harsh voice roared from the end of the chamber. "Cut that babbling or I'll do it for you! You hear me? Cut it out!"

"Gora!" Olga sucked in her breath. "Inez—do as he says."

"I'm not afraid of him."

"I am. Now be quiet."

Their voices faded to twitterings as Dumarest walked to the far end of the chamber. Past a cubicle from which something stared at him, faceless, sexless beneath the thick mat of hair covering it from scalp to toes. Feeling the eyes of a woman with multiple breasts, another with a hump topped by a squinting, elfin face. A man with scales and vestigial wings. One thick with warty encrustations. A score of distorted human shapes.

Gora looked like a dog.

He sat in the far cubicle, lips sagging, jowls, the pouches of his eyes. Pointed ears added to the resemblance and his hair, fine and russet, covered forehead, neck, face and body. Pointed teeth gleamed as he bared his lips.

"Artificial," he said. "But the customers like it."

"You in charge here?"

"I try to keep some sort of order. I've the voice for it." He deepened his tone to a snarling growl, one terminating in a bark. "That's acting—the rest is real. Genetic disorder, myasthenia, myopathy—you a doctor?"

"No."

"Then you wouldn't be interested. A freak-nut, then? Come to indulge yourself? Wanting to see how we behave when not performing?" The liquid eyes studied Dumarest. "No, I guess not. What, then? Grag wouldn't have passed you unless you were straight." He looked at the door through which Dumarest had come. "Conditioned to stay in his room," he explained. "But without the whistle he'll kill without warning."

"A watchdog?"

"Something like that. Keeps us in and others out. Too rough for showing but he has his uses. Which is more than you can say for the rest of us."

"Including you?"

"I do what I can. I'd go crazy if I didn't. At times I think I'm crazy anyway and it gets worse when we're not on show. Then, sometimes, it's possible to think of the marks as freaks and us as normal. Their eyes, the way they goggle, grin, act. Talking as if we were deaf, acting as if we couldn't talk, poking with sticks, making suggestions, speculating how we come to be as we are." The artificial fangs gleamed as Gora snarled. "Throwing us bones, candy, filth. They must be sick in the head."

Dumarest said, "Is this all there are of you?"

"Freaks? Why be afraid of the word? That's what we are— freaks. Some born that way, some growing, others made. You think I'm joking?"

"No," said Dumarest.

"That spider-man over there. Can you guess how his arms and legs got that long? Babies are malleable. Tissue can be stretched, bone too when you're young and mostly gristle. They rested him

36

on a plank and tied weights to his wrists and ankles. Heavy weights left for years. Something to see when he was ready." Gora spat his disgust. "People!"

Dumarest made no comment.

"So we sit here," continued Gora. "Amusing the normal. Taking their insults, sometimes their pity. At times I don't know which is worse."

"I do," said Dumarest. "One freak bullying another, for example."

"I don't bully them."

"Ras wants to kill you."

"Ras wants to die," corrected the dog-man. "At times we all want to die. How else can we escape this hell?"

"You're fed, housed, kept warm," reminded Dumarest. "So you have to earn it—but who else would employ you? Some would think you are lucky. And if you want to die you can do it whenever you want."

"How? Without a gun? A knife?" Gora looked at the hilt riding above Dumarest's boot. "You could do it. Give me an easy way out."

"No, I won't do that. Any edge will do. Teeth if you've nothing else. Just bite through a vein."

"That all?"

"That's all—if you've the guts." Dumarest watched as Gora lifted his wrist to his mouth, the fangs lowering, biting, indentations showing on the hair, the flesh beneath. Before blood could flow he said, quickly, "You've the courage but you're not ready yet. When you are you'll do it fast. But you know the others need you."

An out the other accepted. "Yes," he said, lowering his wrist. "Yes, I guess they do."

"You help them all the time."

"That's right."

"And you can help me. I'm looking for a girl named Melome. She was sold to the circus last night."

"A freak?"

"A sensitive." Dumarest added, "Some would call it the same thing."

"They could be right." Gora shook his head. "I haven't seen her. Try the infirmary." He gestured at the door close to his cubicle. "You'll have to go out that way." As Dumarest reached for the knob he said, "Would it hurt?"

"Just the sting of the bite. After that you'd just drift into sleep."

Into sleep and death and final oblivion. An easy way out—but one Dumarest would never take.

Reiza snapped, "Up, Chang! Up!"

He was slow to respond, snuffing the air, lambent eyes shifting in the sleek perfection of his skull. Small signs others might have overlooked or ignored but to her they were beacons of danger. Attention diffused when it should have been concentrated solely on her. The crack of her whip demanded attention.

"Stay!" The animal had moved a little. "Stay, Chang! Stay!"

A beast troubled by unaccustomed stimuli; during the last performance some fool had chosen to use a klaxon. A trick which had raised a laugh but which had almost shattered the delicate balance of command she held over her charges. An unthinking gesture, perhaps, or maybe one with a sinister intent; placid though Baatza was yet there were always those yearning for violence and the sight of blood.

"Up!" The crack of her whip again. "Up, Chang! Up!"

Again the obedience was slow though others wouldn't have noticed the delay. The mating season? Had the stir of hormones made the beast restless? A possibility and one she would check using drugs to gain tranquility if they were needed. A procedure she would rather avoid; drugged animals lacked the sharp edge which enhanced the performance.

"Reiza?" Zucco spoke from the shadows, the seats behind him rising in a tiered array to circle the ring. "Will you be much longer?"

A question which irritated her; rehearsals and training took as long as was necessary.

"You're tired," he said, stepping forward. "It's been a long day and—"

"Stay clear!" The crack of her whip emphasized the command. "Damn it, Jac, you know better than to interfere at a time like this. Chang's edgy enough as it is. That fool with the klaxon—"

"I threw him out."

"But the damage was done. Now leave me." She saw the movement of the beast's eyes, the tensing of muscle beneath the ebon fur. "Leave me!"

He obeyed and yet still something was wrong. Not just her fatigue or the drifting attention of the animal but something else.

A conflict of wills on a primordial level, one Hayter had warned her about before he had died, his face ripped from the bone beneath, intestines spilling from opened bowels.

"Never take them for granted, Reiza. Cats look calm and placid but always they are a danger. A whim and you could be dead. The blow might be struck in anger or for sport—but you are still dead."

Just as he was dead, as were others she had known, but she would not be one of them.

"Chang!" An animal to be dominated and she felt the surge of anger rising within her. A radiated determination which eliminated the possibility of disobedience. "Down! Down!"

The crack of the whip, showmanship when giving a performance but in reality signals the creature obeyed. The punctuation of her verbal commands, repeated as, dutifully, the animal dropped from the stool, mounted another, stepped through a hoop, squatted like some ancient deity.

And, again, snuffed at the air.

"You!" Reiza turned, saw a glimpse of white, the hint of movement. "You there!"

"Me?" Dumarest halted, shifting the bundle beneath his arm; a mass of paper and rag he'd wrapped close to form a package. One which a casual glance would assume he was delivering. "You want me?"

"Come closer!"

She stood waiting as he approached, straddle-legged, the whip dangling from her right wrist. Tall, strong, a mane of black hair cut to reach her shoulders. A color matched by the halter she wore, the shorts, the boots which rose to mid-thigh, accentuating the creamy whiteness of her skin. Above the naked midriff her breasts bulged against the thin plastic of their prison.

She said, "You're new here, right?"

"Yes, but—"

"You smell wrong. Chang noticed it. Weren't you warned about coming into the main ring?" Her eyes searched his face, his clothing, her own nostrils flaring. "You stink."

The saliva sprayed by the ape-thing guarding the freaks. A scent caught now by the woman as it had disturbed the beast. As Dumarest watched it moved, sickle-claws gleaming from velvet pads, fangs showing between lifted lips.

A black leopard; rearing, it would be as tall as a man. A killing machine holding the beauty of functional design.

39

He said, "I shouldn't leave that animal alone too long."

"You're teaching me my business?"

"Giving you some advice. You—"

"Keep it." She was scornful. "Who the hell are you, anyway? A swamper? What are you doing here?"

Questions he'd so far managed to avoid. A man with a package, moving with purposeful determination—those he'd met had assumed he belonged. But the infirmary had been empty and Melome had still to be found.

"It's my sister," he said. "I'm bringing her a few things."

"Your sister?"

"That's right. She joined the circus last night and forgot to take a few essentials." He gestured with the package. "Maybe you know her? A sensitive. If I could just have a word with her?"

"You're lying!" Reiza was curt. "If you don't belong you've no right to be wandering around. What's in that package? Stuff you've stolen? Is that what you are; a lousy thief? And that smell—what the hell have you been up to?"

"Nothing." Dumarest backed away. "Nothing at all. I'll just get away, now. Leave you to it."

He turned and took three steps toward the shadows when he heard the woman's sharp command.

"Chang! Hold!"

One which sent the leopard hurtling from where it squatted.

Dumarest turned, jumping to one side, the package lifting, lancing toward the snarling mask. A distraction the leopard ignored, landing, springing again as Dumarest reached for his knife, feeling his foot slip on something in the sand, toppling, feeling the slamming impact of the animal as he went down. Pinned, helpless, he stared into the snarling mask.

And froze.

Reiza said, "At least you've the sense not to move. A hunter?" As Dumarest made no reply she added, "You're playing dead. Hoping Chang will get bored and move away. In the wild that might work if you aren't bleeding and the beast isn't starving." She leaned over him, nostrils flared, sniffing. "You stink but not of fear. That's good. All right, Chang, back now." Her tone hardened. "Back, Chang! Back!"

Dumarest sat upright as the beast left, seeing it lope toward the shadows, its caged den. He climbed to his feet as the woman turned to face him.

"A thief," she said. "Certainly a liar." The lash of her whip tore at the package. "A few things for your sister? It holds nothing but rubbish." The lash cracked an inch from his cheek. "Talk, damn you!"

"I came looking for someone. A girl. Melome. That's all."

"Your sweetheart?" The whip cracked again and he felt a sting on his cheek. Touching it, he saw blood on his fingers. "You like her?"

As she liked what she was doing, the whip, the questions, the usage of power. Dominating him. Playing with him as a cat would torment a mouse. And there was more than a little of the feline about her. In the slant of her eyes, the set of her mouth. The whip was a claw she sent to sting.

"Thief! Liar! Why are you here?"

"I told you. I'm—" Dumarest looked at the welt she put on the back of his hand. It burned like fire. "Be careful with that whip."

"I could take out your eyes. Have one lying on your cheek before you knew it." Already she had proved it to be no idle boast. "Cut off your ears. Flay you. Slice open your face. Do you think I wouldn't?"

"I think you'd enjoy doing it."

"So?"

"Don't touch me with that whip again!"

A warning rejected. Dumarest saw the widening of her eyes, the movement of her hand and was moving before the lash could strike. A spring toward her, his right hand snatching at his boot to rise weighted with nine inches of pointed, razor edged steel. His left arm shot out, the hand gripping the lash as the blade sliced upwards to sever it inches from the stock.

"You!" Startled, she looked at the knife, the ruined whip. "Bastard!" Anger replaced the amazement. The stock parted in her hand, became a falling sheath and a foot-long stiletto which she held like a sword in her hand. Its point lanced toward his eyes.

Dumarest parried it with a clash of metal, attacked in turn, air whining as his blade slashed in a vicious arc. One aimed at the throat, the jugular it contained, the life-blood it carried. A blow dictated by reactive instinct. One changed almost too late to send the point of the knife slashing downwards. Leather parted as it sliced through the halter to free her breasts and leave a shallow gash on the creamy skin.

41

Then she was his prisoner, his left arm rising beneath her right, his fingers locked in the mane of her hair. Pulling back her head and exposing her throat to the prick of his blade.

"You—"

"Shut up!" The point dug deeper, almost breaking the skin. "You had your fun and now it's my turn. I could blind you," he said, mimicking her threats. "Slash your face. Cut off your nose. Do you think I wouldn't?"

She swallowed. "What do you want?"

"Melome. Take me to her."

"The girl? I don't know where she is."

"Then find out." Impatience edged his voice with the raw note of anger. "Someone bought her. Someone must know where she is. Now move. Move!"

He shifted to stand behind her, his hand still locked in her hair, the knife still at her throat. A position maintained as he urged her over the sand of the ring toward the tiered seats.

The passage, the men who were waiting, the gas which sent him spinning into oblivion.

Zucco had given her a lamp; a thing of delicate artistry depicting a woman locked in a feline's embrace, the whole illuminated from within. By its light Reiza examined herself in a mirror.

She was nude, skin still damp from a scented bath, the thick mane of her hair framing her face and edging her shoulders. A good body, one still firm, muscles clothed by softening fat which enhanced her unabashed femininity. One untouched by claw or fang—luck and skill had seen to that; the costume she wore was for show and not concealment. But now she had been marked and her hand lifted to touch the gash on her breastbone. One about an inch long, shallow; healed it would leave no trace. But, always, within her mind she would bear the scar.

The scar and the man who had injured her.

Closing her eyes she could see him again. The face hard, cold, the mask of an animal. A creature determined to survive. One ready to kill to avoid being killed. Like Chang and Ahrda and Torin. Like all the great cats she had trained—his eyes had matched theirs. His reflexes had been as fast. Faster—never had she known a man move so quickly. Death had been very close.

And, again, she felt the thrill of it.

42

A moment Hayter had mentioned when, satiated, he had lain beside her in a place redolent of the cats they both loved.

"It's the power," he'd said. "The dominance. To rule over creatures which could kill you without hesitation if the mood took them. But over that is the thrill of danger. Each time you train or perform you risk your life. Take a gamble—your skill against their instincts. It's like a drug which, for a moment, makes you more than human. Makes you come really alive. And, always, there is the temptation to push your luck a little harder. To tempt fate a little more. Don't do it, Reiza. When it comes to that, quit the game."

Advice he hadn't taken—had he welcomed the claws which had ripped out his life? The attack which had saved him from descrepit old age?

She hoped it had been like that. He had been too full of life to waste and fade. Too proud to be other than the best in his field. And, when her time came, would she feel the same as when death had come so close?

The knife slashing at her throat—time had seemed to slow to extend the moment and, against her lids, she could see the glitter of steel, the edge and point. Feel again the constriction of her stomach, the anticipation. Then the burn, her breasts falling free, the sting of the knife at her throat.

And the face so close to her own.

A chime and she opened her eyes, swaying a little. The effects of the gas had been neutralized but traces lingered and she caught the edge of the mirror to steady herself.

"Reiza?" Zucco's voice and, again, the chime. As always he was impatient. "Reiza? Are you all right?"

"A moment." A robe lay close and she donned it, yellow silk, rich in the diffused illumination. Material which held a sensuous appeal and it clung to her body as she tied it around her waist. "Enter!"

He walked like a cat, light on the balls of his feet, his body slender, lithe, bright with scarlet and gold. Garments modeled on those worn in the ring lacking only the cheap glitter of sequins and artificial gems. His face, thinned, held the sharp awareness of a predator. His eyes held the darting flicker of a serpent's tongue.

"My dear!" He halted before her, tall, showing an outward concern. "Are you sure you're all right? The gas—"

"Did you have to use it?"

43

"There was no other way. Shot he could have killed you as he fell. Threatened—" His shrug was expressive. "Your life was too valuable to risk."

And so the gas kept by for use in emergencies against animals running wild, men, crowds.

"A madman," he said. "Deranged. He could have killed you."

Would have done had he really wanted. Zucco, watching from the shadows, had not seen the initial lethal aim of the blade, the sudden withdrawal.

She said, "Did you find out who he is?"

"Dumarest. Earl Dumarest. He was at the circus earlier and Ruval had to throw him out. Some trouble over a girl. One of Tusenbach's. It could have been settled but he drew a knife and left Ruval no choice."

"Melome?" She saw his frown. "He spoke of a sister he'd come to see. Melome. Was that the girl?"

"He lied."

"About the girl?"

"She isn't his sister. He asked after her before and then she was the daughter of a friend. Forget her." He stepped closer, hands reaching, his intention plain. As she stepped back he said, impatiently, "What's wrong?"

"Nothing."

"Then why avoid me? Or do you want to play a game?" His eyes glowed with a new fire, his face taking on a feral expression, a gloating anticipation. "You want to be mastered, forced, made to yield to the whip? Dominated? Treated like you treat your cats? Given a taste of pain."

Things he enjoyed but her needs were not governed by a sadistic nature. One he possessed, now rising to be mirrored on his face as he stared at her, stimulated by her femininity, her reluctance.

She said, quickly, "What about the girl? Melome. Is she with the circus?"

"I told you to forget her."

"Something special?"

"That isn't your business. Just worry about your cats and leave the rest to me. Ask questions and Shakira won't like it. Now let's stop wasting time." He frowned as she shook her head. "No? Why not?"

"Be sensible, man. I'm tired. I've been gassed and am still

44

groggy. And I've had a hell of an experience. All I want now is to be left alone to sleep."

A lie and he sensed it as he sensed her heightened sensuality: emotions inflamed and sharpened by recent events. As he moved purposefully toward her she stepped to one side, reaching her spare costume, the flat pistol normally worn in a holster beneath the shorts. A gun she hadn't bothered to carry when dealing with a single animal. One she lifted to point at Zucco's face.

"I said no, Jac."

He halted, staring at the twin muzzles of the over and under; wide orifices which could spout a leaden hail.

"You'd use that? Against me?" Her eyes gave him the answer. "Bitch! I thought we were friends."

"We are," she agreed. "That and more. But you don't own me. I don't dance to your tune. We'll get on better if you remember that." Lowering the gun she added, casually, "What happened to Dumarest?"

"He's safe enough."

"Dead?"

"Would you care if he was?" His eyes searched her face, his own hardening as they moved to the gap in her robe, the wound lying between her breasts. "He cut you, remember. Marked you."

Branded her—there was a difference.

She said, "I'm curious. He acted strange. He's safe, you say?"

"Safe." Zucco's smile held malice. "He's down in the sump."

CHAPTER FOUR

Dumarest woke to the stench of it, the dirt, the noise. The circus was a closed world of inflated tents, domes, galleries, compartments. One holding animals, workers, a continual flow of visitors. A close-packed consuming society—the sump took care of the waste.

A place of dimness in which sewage and garbage was dumped to be fed to machines which churned it and fed the slurry to pipes leading outside. There was leakage, accumulations, pools of slime. Maintenance workers wore enclosing suits and breathed tanked air.

Dumarest, naked, was chained to a wall.

His head ached from the effects of the gas and thirst burned throat and mouth. In the gloom things looked blurred, out of focus, and he closed his eyes, palming them, feeling the tug and clank of restraining links. Manacles circled each wrist, the chains from them running through a circlet on the metal belt locked around his waist. Another chain at the rear led to a ring on the wall.

He could stand, take a step forward, lie on the crusted floor and that was all.

A prisoner sentenced without trial to a period of isolated confinement. One which could be the prelude to execution. It was possible, the circus was a law unto itself. A hostile world in which he was a stranger. For now he could do nothing but wait.

Squatting, he examined the links. They were too strong to break, welded, made of high-grade steel. The manacles were too close fitting to slip and prevented him reaching the chain holding him to the wall. A futile exercise; it too would be strong.

Something ran over his foot and he saw a blur of chiton as a multilegged insect scuttled toward a patch of crusted slime. Food and water for the thing but only vileness for himself. Yet the creature was food and could be eaten if starvation threatened. But, before that, he would be dead of thirst.

The wall behind him was of metal and he touched it, feeling the dew of condensation. Moisture he collected on the flat of his hand, licking it, wiping the metal to gain more. It held a flat, unpleasant taste but it moistened his lips and eased his thirst a little. Relaxing he leaned his back against the wall.

Waiting, dozing, conserving his strength. Jerking to full awareness as metal clanged and a light shone into his eyes.

"So you're awake." Zucco, his finery protected by a plastic film, lifted the wand he carried. One tipped with metal. Dumarest jerked at the sting of it against his flesh. "Hurts, doesn't it." The voice held a feral purr as it came through the diaphragm of the helmet. "A thing we use on beasts to teach them to obey." It stabbed again. "Like this. And this. And this."

A series of nerve-jarring shocks as the current tore at his body. Through a red haze of pain Dumarest twisted, fought the restraint of the chains, the instinct which urged him to snatch at the wand. Even if he gained it he would have won nothing. Not until the man himself was within reach dare he act.

"Why did you come here?" The wand hit again before Dumarest could answer, touching his knee, his stomach, dropping to his loins. "Answer, you scum. Answer!"

Crude interrogation; questions followed by pain and then more questions with no time given for answers. A technique designed to break the spirit and induce unthinking responses.

Cowering, Dumarest said, "Melome! I came for the girl!"

The cowering was an act, the answer genuine; one he had given before.

"Why?" Again the wand. "Why? Why? Why?"

"A job." Dumarest gagged, pointing at his mouth. "Water! Give me water!"

"After you talk." The wand seared nerves and filled the universe with pain. "The truth, now! Damn it, I want the truth!"

"You've had it. I wanted a job. I figured Melome could give me an introduction to the boss. Someone who could hire me."

"So you came here, sneaked into the circus, crept about like a

48

thief, attacked Reiza and would have killed her—just to get hired?" Zucco sneered his contempt. "Do you take me for a fool?"

"No—a sadistic bastard!"

Zucco tensed with anger, face taut, as he raised the wand, holding it like a rapier, the metal tip circling inches from Dumarest's eyes.

"Now we're getting somewhere," he whispered. "I knew you couldn't be broken so easily. But you will be broken. Made to beg. To crawl." The wand jabbed forward, touched, touched again. Bruising impacts which lacked the previous searing energy; Zucco had deactivated the instrument. "Odd," he said. "Reiza said you were fast. Fast enough to have dodged but—" This time Dumarest jerked as Zucco fed power to the wand, sent the tip to jab a shoulder. "Talk!"

"Water!"

"Talk, damn you! Talk! Talk! Talk!"

A man beside himself with rage, converting it to pleasure, enjoying the pain he caused, the anguish. One who would kill unless satisfied; his need justification enough for any action he chose to take.

Dumarest jerked, slumped to the floor, feeling the bite of nails in his palms as he clenched his fists. Screaming to vent his rage at the pain which consumed him, a sound Zucco mistook for terror, the signal of his victory.

Panting he stepped back, lowering the wand, looking at the slumped figure before him. A man sprawled in a faint and beyond any further pain he could inflict.

"I'll be back," he said. "And, when I do, you won't escape so easily. Ruval!"

Dumarest heard the pad of boots as Zucco moved away. More footsteps came close, heavier, accompanied by a metallic clinking. He gasped as a flood of water drenched head and shoulders. Another and he rose upright to stare at a massive body, a close-cropped head. One he had seen before.

"Here!" Ruval handed him a beaker of water. "I warned you not to come back but you had to be smart. Crazy to do what you did. Now you're paying for it."

Dumarest handed back the empty container. "Your doing?"

"Zucco's. The one who questioned you. Reiza's his woman. You made a mistake going up against her."

"And you?"

49

"I just work here." Ruval refilled the beaker and handed it to Dumarest. "Gas makes you thirsty and you've enough trouble as it is."

"Thanks." Dumarest sipped, looking at the big man. Less kind than he seemed; Zucco must have given him orders to take care of his charge. To get him in condition for another session with the wand. "Is Zucco the boss?"

"The ringmaster."

"But not the owner?" As Ruval shook his head Dumarest added, "You said something about paying. I can pay. A thousand kobolds if you help me get out of here."

"Forget it."

"Why? All you need is the key. A file if you can't get it. I've money on deposit in town. It's yours if you'll help. A thousand in cash." Money which would buy luxury. Dumarest watched as the man's interest grew. "What can you lose?" he urged. "Think of what you could buy."

Ruval said, "How would you pay?"

"I'll give you a note. The money will be put aside. You can see it, check that it's there. When I sign the transfer it'll be yours."

"Sign?"

"Countersign. Of course, I'll have to be with you at the time. A thousand kobolds." Dumarest emphasized the figure. "How long would it take you to earn that much?"

Too long, but there were problems.

"I don't know," said Ruval. "I'm just not sure."

"Afraid of Zucco? You could break him in half with one hand. Doubt my word? Talk to Helga, she'll tell you I've money. I didn't hurt her, you know. I wasn't lying."

"I didn't figure you were. A push, a slap, touch them in the wrong way, even, and they scream murder." Ruval sucked at his cheeks. "A thousand?"

"That's right."

"Just for bringing you a file?"

"For getting me out of here," corrected Dumarest. "I want to be free and clear."

He sipped at the water as the man thought about it. Ruval was dressed in good clothing; pants of good weave and boots of fine leather. His blouse was ornamented by a cluster of brilliant stones held to the fabric by a long pin. His belt was carved in elaborate designs. A chain around his neck held a massive lucky

50

charm. A dandy despite his bulk. One who would always need money.

"Well?"

Ruval shook his head. "I daren't risk it. Zucco would have my hide."

"Two thousand then. Double."

"No."

"Coward!" Dumarest blazed with anger. "You stinking freak! You've no guts!"

He flung the beaker into Ruval's face.

It hit above an eye, shattering, breaking the skin to mask the face with blood. Ruval snarled and lunged forward, fists clenched, slamming like hammers at Dumarest's face and body. Blows he tried to divert, dissipating their force as he grappled with the big man, but enough landed to make him grunt with shock and pain. To fall and lie slumped in a limp heap.

"Scum!" Ruval drove his boot into the naked body. "I treat you decent and what do I get? To hell with you!"

He stormed away leaving Dumarest lying bleeding, semiconscious, the gemmed pin he had stolen clutched tightly in his hand.

It was going all wrong.

Reiza, standing in the brilliant circle of light, alone with her animals, sensed it with the instinct which made her what she was. Chang was too slow to obey, Ahrda too edgy, Torin flexed his claws too often, Kiki bared his lips too wide. Small details which warned of danger and she met it, mastering the beasts as a matter of survival more than art. Quashing all trace of fear, feeding her anger so as to radiate an aura of seething rage and determination.

Even so she had to cut short the performance, giving the signal which brought the clowns running, tumbling, distracting attention while the handlers wafted tranquilizing vapors at the cats before guiding them from the ring. As they vanished from the area her cheeks burned to the yelled annoyance of the audience.

A hard crowd; mostly new arrivals and as yet uncalmed by the soothing atmosphere of Baatz. Rock-miners, mercenaries, hunters from nearby planets hungry for entertainment and free with lewd advice, suggestions, open invitations.

They quieted as the gymnasts began to spin in complex patterns of incredible dexterity; lithe bodies like living flames adorning the struts and poles with practiced grace.

"You were terrible." Old Valaban faced her in the tunnel beneath the stands. In the light from the ring his face was creased, worn, the livid scars which ran from scalp to chin on his left side a barred chiaroscuro. "An amateur couldn't have done worse and you know it. Hayter—"

"He's dead!"

"Sure—as you could have been a couple of times out there. But he died because of pride. You would have gone down because of stupidity."

She saw the change in his eyes and looked at her raised hand, loaded with the stock of her whip, heavy with its concealed blade.

"Sorry." He was a genius with animals and the claws which had ripped his face had paid the dues for a free tongue. "Val—I'm sorry."

"Something's wrong, girl. You should know what it is."

Tiredness. Turmoil—her brief sleep had been haunted by dreams. A face which dominated her universe. The glitter of a knife—the thought of what it would have felt like as it sheared home. At first nothing, the blade like a cat's claw too sharp to register. Then the sting, the burn, the horror of impending death.

The face—why couldn't she wash it from her mind?

Valaban said, "Women don't make good tamers as a rule. Nature's against them; at times their scent is too strong and makes the cats restless. You're lucky in that way but other things can be as bad as blood."

She said, curtly, "I'm not a fool. I bathe before each performance. I don't smell."

"But you sweat." He was blunt. "And I'm talking about scents, not smells. You're in rut," he accused. "A bitch in heat. I can't smell it but the animals can. They're males—do I have to spell it out?"

"You're sick! Perverted!"

"I'm alive." A hand rose to touch the scarred cheek. "I've had time to learn. To realize that you, me, all of us are just the same as any other animal. We all share the same hungers, the same fears. If you think you're special then you should quit the ring before it's too late. I'd hate to see your face look like mine."

He was trying to frighten her; such scars could be healed but

52

he wore his like a badge. Would she have such courage? She knew the answer, knew too that such wounds would break her spirit. Even if the damaged tissue was repaired the trauma would remain and, once a tamer radiated fear, it was the end.

"Think about it," said Valaban. "I'll do what I can with the cats but the rest is up to you."

He vanished among the activity beneath the stands, Zucco taking his place. He was resplendent in his uniform; scarlet and gold flashing with scintillance. The king of a small world that he handled well.

He shook his head as he met her eyes. "Bad, Reiza—but you know that."

"It happens." She added, in an attempt to lessen her guilt, "The crowd didn't help."

"We've had worse. Maybe you should take a rest. Lacombe—"

"Isn't ready!" She was sharp in her rejection. Once let the man take her place and he would fight to keep it. "The cats would tear him apart."

"Maybe that's what they want." Zucco looked toward the mouth of the tunnel, the seats beyond, the faces blurred in the distance. "At least it would revive interest. We could do with something to fill the empty seats."

"The gate still falling?"

"Not fast, but falling. Well, it happens."

A tobey running out of tap. Soon would come the time to break up and move. To find another world and set down in another place. One which could only be more violent than Baatz.

And Dumarest?

"I told you, he's safe," snapped Zucco when she asked the question. "Why worry about him?"

"Is he still in the sump?"

"You know a better place?" He shrugged when she made no answer. "He'll keep. Just forget him. Now, as to your own problem, we'd better talk about it later." His head tilted as a roar came from the audience. "I'm due out there. Irina! Spall! Pryor! The rest of you! Stand ready!"

Fire-dancers assembled, almost nude, garish in paint and tinsel. On the ring flames would be leaping in a dancing pattern of red and gold, orange and scarlet. A furnace tinged with smoke into which the waiting dancers would throw themselves, merging with the searing fury, spinning, seeming to be burned to be reborn and rise again.

A spectacle to add to the rest. The life of the circus and one she had always enjoyed but now, oddly, she felt no elation. First Valaban and now Zucco. The first was genuinely concerned but the ringmaster would have his own motivations. Refused, he would turn ugly, promote Lacombe to her spot, find her a lesser place. Once she lost her status the descent would be inevitable. On another world she could have sold her skill to others but, on Baatz, that was impossible.

"No," she said. "By, God, no!"

A clown stared at her and moved quickly on. One she ignored as her hand closed on the stock of her whip. Zucco thought he held the master hand; her poor performance the weapon she had given him to justify any decision he might choose to make.

The victory in the war between them—one she determined he would never enjoy.

Dumarest stirred, feeling the sharp sting of teeth in his leg, seeing a small rodent dart away into the shadows. A scavenger of odorous waste and the creatures which fed on it. His blood and sweat had attracted it to a more wholesome feast.

He looked at his hand and the gemmed pin clutched in the fingers. His escape if he could use it, a weapon if he could not. If Ruval or Zucco came again to torture him he would not be so defenseless. One or both would lose an eye if not more.

He sat upright, fighting a wave of nausea. His mouth was dry and small tremors ran over his limbs. Bad but not as bad as he had been when shocked nerves and the beating made it impossible to stand or exercise control. Time in which he had drifted on the edges of oblivion wrapped in a red-shot nightmare of pain.

Now, ignoring the small shape which watched from the gloom, he bent over the manacle on his left wrist. A narrow band, closed tight, held by a simple lock. One into which he slipped the pin, moving it with practiced care as he searched for the tumbler. It slipped free and he drew in his breath with a sharp hiss before trying again. His hands were clumsy, quivering, the pin seeming to have a life of its own. At the third attempt it held and he applied pressure, easing it as the slender probe bent, trying to hit a workable compromise. Too much force and the metal could snap, too little and it wouldn't throw the tumbler. Sweat stung his eyes before the catch yielded with a click.

The other followed and Dumarest stretched his arms to ease

the ache in his shoulders. The belt still held him chained to the wall but it too yielded to the pin. A few moments and he stood upright, breathing deeply as the released circlet fell to clash against the wall.

A sound which produced echoes; small scurryings in the dimness, vibrations which quivered and died as he stepped toward the door to his right. One Zucco had used and Ruval after him but it was locked as was another facing it. Strong catches against which the pin was useless and he slipped it into his hair as he turned to study the pounding machine.

It held a pulse like that of a heart; an irregular throbbing as it churned the detritus from above and fed it into the pipe. Masses fed from a hopper yielding its contents when full. Accompanied with water so as to make a liquid sludge. If he could open the pipe it offered a chance of escape.

If he could breathe while traveling along it. If he didn't get jammed in a bend. If he didn't drown in the filth of the lagoon into which it emptied.

A gamble he couldn't take; the room was devoid of tools, the pipe impossible to open.

Back at the door Zucco had used he examined the hinges then tensed, ear to the panel. A moment and he backed, flattening himself against the wall, the gemmed pin gripped sword-fashion in his right hand.

The door opened and Reiza stepped into the sump.

"Earl? Earl Dumarest?" She spun as he stepped behind her, flattening his shoulders against the thrown-back panel of the door. "My God!" Her eyes widened as she looked at him. "What the hell have they done to you?"

"They?"

"You don't think I had anything to do with this." She looked at the blood on his face, the blotches on his body. "The swine! I should have guessed."

She wore a robe of blue touched with silver. This she untied and slipped from her shoulders to reveal the white nudity of her body, loins and breasts embraced by silver lace.

"Here." She handed him the robe. "Put this on and let's get out of here. It stinks!"

Dumarest said, "Is anyone out there? Ruval? Anyone?"

"No." Her nose wrinkled again. "Hurry up and put on that robe. You need a bath."

It was scented, warm, a place of luxury in which to wallow as the dirt and smell was washed away. More water replaced the soiled and he felt the sting of medications and the easing of strained muscles. Tissues knotted by the charge of the wand but the red mesh of broken capillaries remained together with the purple of ugly bruises.

"They'll go," said Reiza. She stood beside the bath, her skin dewed with condensed vapor. "I've got a salve which will help. Something for your eyes, too."

They were puffed, swollen from the impact of Ruval's fists as his ribs ached from the impact of his boot. Pain caused by cracked bone but the toe had slipped to prevent more serious damage. Dumarest sat as the woman checked his torso with surprisingly strong fingers.

"This will hurt a little." She reached for a syringe from among a litter held in a wooden box bearing a name burned in the lid. Valaban's kit, the contents more suited to the treatment of animals than men. "Hold still, now."

A hypogun would have been more efficient but the needle was sharp enough and the hormone-enriched bone glue better than bandages.

As she finished Dumarest said, "You've done this before."

"On animals, yes."

"And men?"

She straightened without answering to stand before him, hands on hips, legs straddled. In the glow of the lamp her skin held a nacreous sheen, small gleams coming from the silver lace marring her nudity. A woman displaying herself and Dumarest looked at the long columns of her thighs, the swell of hips, the narrow waist, the contours of her breasts. The body of a magnificent animal and one matched by the face.

She said, bluntly, "If you like what you see it's yours."

"Just like that?"

"For me, yes." Her breath came faster as she stared at his own nudity. "It happens and no one knows just how or why. A person in a crowd, a single glance, and it's done. A need. An obsession. Call it love or madness it's just the same. You've got to have that person. For me it happened with you."

"Is that why you came to rescue me?"

"No." She was blunt in her honesty. "You were in my mind—I can't deny that, but I had another reason. I still have it. "Zucco—" She broke off, looking at his face. "You know Zucco?"

Dumarest nodded.

"He wants to use me, degrade me, but I'm damned if I'm going to let him do it. You can give me something to use against him."

"Such as?"

"Melome. You know her. You asked after her. Why?"

He said, dryly, "That's what Zucco wanted to know."

"But you didn't tell him. You—" She broke off as she realized what he was thinking. "No, Earl! No! It isn't like that. I'm not working with Zucco. I didn't rescue you just to gain your trust. Please! You've got to believe that!"

An easy path to take but his caution warned him against it. The rescue, the bribe of her body, the relaxing waters of the bath—all could be the steps of a master plan.

He said, "Zucco is the ringmaster. Surely he would know why Melome was bought."

"Not necessarily. Shakira has his own methods. A lot goes on which only he knows about."

"Shakira?"

"The owner of the circus." She handed Dumarest a pot containing a clear jelly. "Use this salve. Rub it in all over. The gymnasts use it and it works." Her eyes lingered on his face before she turned away. "I'd better get dressed and find you something to wear."

The salve stung a little, the momentary discomfort yielding to a warm glow as it dried. Alone Dumarest examined the chamber, the bed, the few furnishings it contained. A cabinet held costumes and other garments; mementoes of earlier roles of those used in different performances. Like all circus-folk on the way up Reiza would have had to be versatile. A shelf held packages of cosmetics, threads, sequins, a photograph edged in black. One of a man.

He smiled as Dumarest picked up the portrait, the surface shimmering to give an illusion of life. As the warmth of his hand triggered the cycle, Dumarest heard the whisper of a low, intimate voice.

"I love you. My darling, I love you. Reiza, my dearest, always be mine. I love you. I . . ."

The voice ended as Dumarest replaced the photograph and continued his examination.

A table bore a glowing lamp, a shelf beneath it the weight of a decanter and goblets. The bed was covered with an ornate creation of fine threads woven on silk; pictures depicting dragons, felines, couples in exotic embraces. A rack held books. A vase a cluster of crystalline flowers.

A small place, cramped by necessity, a box which held the appurtenances of a life. One which held the sense of lonely isolation.

The bath lay in an adjoining chamber, the tub still half-full of water. A curtain, now drawn back, closed the opening. A whip lay coiled on a second chair. The gemmed pin he had used to free himself lay beside the lamp. The door leading to the passage outside was masked by a curtain of vividly colored plastic tubes and balls threaded on strings ending in copper bells.

Dumarest heard their chime as Ruval thrust his way into the room.

CHAPTER FIVE

He was dressed as Dumarest remembered, a tear now in the blouse where the pin had been, a white patch of bandage resting over one eye. Halting, he stared, air rasping through his nostrils as he drew in his breath.

Dumarest said, "You've come for the money. Good. Give me pen and paper and I'll write that note."

Words which could have been silence for all the notice the big man took.

"You," he said. "I guessed that bitch might have you here. Sneaked down and let you out, did she? And I might never have known if I hadn't missed my pin." His eyes moved to where it lay. "So you found it. Maybe took it during the fight. Well, no matter. I'll take you back now."

"No," said Dumarest.

"You going to stop me?" Ruval smiled as he looked at Dumarest's naked body, his empty hands. "No knife now, friend."

"No knife," agreed Dumarest. "But I've got your pin. You want it?" He moved forward, snatched it up, threw it. "Here."

Ruval was fast, batting at the spinning glitter arcing toward his eyes, sending it to fall to one side. A distraction he had mistaken for an attack and Dumarest had reached him before the bauble had fallen, left hand sending stiffened fingers jabbing at the face, right hand rising, the heel of the palm forward, slashing upwards at the nose as the big man threw back his head.

A blow which would have killed had it landed, shattering the

59

nasal septum and sending splinters of bone up into the sinus cavities and the brain.

But it missed as Ruval twisted his head, landing instead on the cheek, creating surface bruising and internal damage.

Ruval snarled, twisting away, his foot rising to lash out in a savage kick. Dumarest dodged, felt the brush of the boot against his knee, dodged again as the big man sent a fist at his stomach. A hard and vicious fighter careless if he killed or maimed so long as he won. One now maddened with rage.

"You scum! Making a mock of me! Laughing at me! I'll make you laugh—the next time you go into the sump it'll be as garbage!"

Talk wasted energy but the big man could spare it as he could the wild blows which ruptured air. Strength Dumarest lacked; weakened by his ordeal he knew the fight had to be ended soon or he would go down.

He weaved to one side, his left arm stabbing, the fingers like a blunted spear as they thrust into the fat and muscle over Ruval's heart. A blow followed by the edge of his right palm slashing lower down and to the side. As it hit his knee jerked up toward the groin as he jerked his head forward to slam his skull against the other's nose.

Ruval cried out, staggering backward, blood from his broken nose masking his mouth and chin. Minor damage; his massive bulk had protected his internal organs and Dumarest had missed the small target of the genitals. He backed to gain room to maneuver; his speed would be useless once clutched in Ruval's crushing grip.

"Now!" The big man wiped a hand across his face smearing its back with vivid carmine. "Now, you scum!"

He came in a rush; a living mass of bone and muscle, powered by hate. A killing machine intent on destruction. Dumarest sprang toward the adjoining chamber, felt his foot turn beneath him, staggered and, before he could regain his balance, Ruval was on him.

Dumarest felt the pound of a fist against his cheek, another at his jaw—and gagged as a third found his throat.

A blow to the larynx which blossomed into searing agony filled his mouth with the taste of blood, blocking the passage of air to his lungs. A killing blow—unable to breathe—death was scant minutes away.

He dived within the circle of Ruval's arms, his own lifting, elbows spread to keep the other's hands from his eyes. His own darted toward the thick neck, thumbs searching for the carotid arteries pulsing beneath the surface. Finding them. Closing them with pressure to cut off the supply of blood to the brain.

Waiting, fighting to remain calm, to maintain the pressure until Ruval sagged and he slumped unconscious. Falling toward the bath as Dumarest released his hold, splashing into it and coming to rest face-down in the water.

Dumarest left him there. He was dying, blackness edging his vision as he lurched toward the whip now lying on the floor. A twist and the blade came free of the stock; twelve inches of flattened steel, pointed, edged to a third of its length. Bells jangled as he tore down the masking curtain, slashing a strand free, catching one of the thin plastic tubes.

Tilting back his head he drove the blade into his throat.

A calculated thrust; the point guided by the fingers of his left hand, piercing the trachea just above the breastbone and well below the larynx. A stab which opened the windpipe between two ridges of cartilage, the cut widening to the drag of the blade. As it came free Dumarest forced the plastic tube into the opening.

And breathed.

Falling to his knees in a welling darkness as he sucked air through the narrow tube; the entire universe diminished to the stream of oxygen which was his life.

After the fifth blatant error Valaban snapped, "Get hold of yourself, Reiza. You're confusing the beasts. Keep on like this and you'll make them useless. Lose your reputation too, but that's your business. The animals are mine."

"You tend them—I work them!"

"Then do it. Damn it, I've seen tyros do better!"

A harsh rebuke but she deserved it and Valaban knew his trade. As she knew hers too well not to know he was right.

More softly he said, "Get a shower. Some sleep. Go into town for a while. Give the cats a rest until you've settled down. You know what I mean."

Good advice but even if she took it the torment of waiting would still remain. Irritably she strode from the ring, seeing Zucco standing in the passage, his normal finery subdued under a cloak of black trimmed with yellow. A means to remain inconspicuous in the shadows? A possibility and if true meant that he had been watching her. More ammunition to feed his intentions, but now she had weapons of her own.

"Reiza!" He fell into step beside her. "You have my sympathy. It was a dreadful thing to have happened. You were lucky Dumarest didn't hurt you."

He knew—there was little that went on he didn't know about, but some things had to remain speculation. Now it suited her to be ignorant.

"Dumarest?"

"A murderer. I sensed it from the first. Now we have proof."

"Ruval? He drowned in my bath."

"With bruises on his face and throat. We know who must have put them there. Dumarest—"

She halted and turned to face him, her eyes matching the hardness of her voice.

"Yes, Dumarest. The man you gassed then stripped and chained in the sump. One you tortured and Ruval must have helped. Well, Ruval has paid. It could be your turn soon, Jac."

"You think he could beat me?" His amusement was genuine. "That scum? Have you forgotten what I was before I became ringmaster?" Abruptly he smiled. "We quarrel for no purpose. You have chosen to care for Dumarest as another would care for a sick dog. A weakness I deplore but I am willing to let you indulge yourself. Simply be aware of what he is. A liar. A cheat. A thief. A murderer."

"A man!"

One such as Zucco could never be. His strength was built on the weakness of others, his power the fruit of pandering to decadent tastes.

He said, quietly, "A man who will use you as he used Helga. I suggest you remember that, my dear. And, when you are sane again, I shall be waiting."

Smoothness coupled with the vicious barb of a subtle tongue. Why else mention Helga if not to make her jealous? And why no mention of what must have been foremost in his mind? The details Dumarest could have told her about Melome and which he had wanted so desperately to know? And why had he made no move against Dumarest?

The answer waited in the infirmary where the doctor greeted her with a smile.

"He's fine." He answered her question before she could ask it, jerking his head toward where Dumarest sat in a chair sipping from a beaker. "Basic laced with brandy from Shakira's own store. His orders. All to be of the best."

"He knows?"

"Of course. I sent him a full report. We don't get many patients who've given themselves a tracheotomy. A good one too, I must admit, but he almost left it too late. Of course there was other damage; the larynx, cellular disruption, dehydration, nervous degeneration—used to excess those wands can be nasty things. The gas didn't help either."

'But he's all right now?"

"Fine."

Healed by the drugs and skill of the doctor, the magic of slowtime. Dressed now in a drab robe of dull puce which was a little too short for his height. He smiled as she came toward him.

"My lady, it seems I must thank you for my life."

The formality stunned her then she understood; such a man would be accustomed to moving among those to whom procedure was paramount. To be less than punctilious would be to invite retribution.

She said, "This is the circus, Earl. We're ordinary people. You don't have to crawl on your knees."

"Ordinary?" His eyes studied her, bringing a flush of pleasure to her cheeks. "Whatever you are, Reiza, you're not that. And you did save me."

"I found you," she corrected. "But you'd already saved yourself. Unconscious but breathing steady. We've just patched you up and speeded the healing. Now, I'll bet you're hungry." She saw him glance at the empty beaker which had held a fluid rich in protein, sickly with glucose, laced with vitamins. And Shakira's brandy—that had been an extra. "For real food; meat and richness and things you can get your teeth into. Come on—I'm buying." To the doctor she said, "Can't you find him something more decent to wear?"

Dumarest said, "Where are my own clothes?"

"God knows—we'll find them later. Please, Doc, can't you hurry?"

He produced pants and a blouse in faded blue together with soft shoes tied with thin laces. The legacy of a dead man, perhaps, but they fitted well enough and Reiza was satisfied. Delaying only long enough to change from her costume into a gown of lilac ornamented with jet she led the way to the outer galleries, to a restaurant Dumarest had used before.

"The best," she said. "You'll like it here. Voe!" She saw the waiter's glance of recognition as he approached her companion. "You order, Earl." She added, with a touch of malice, "Let's have the same meal you had before."

"No. This should be special."

"True." She was glad he hadn't tried to dissemble. "The best, Voe. Red meat and all the trimmings. Some wine too—this is a celebration!"

But it was shared with an invisible companion. Had Helga used this very glass? Sat at this very table? Seen his smile as he looked at her? Felt the same acceleration of her heart?

Foolishness and she knew it. Knew too that she was talking too fast and laughing too loud. Eating too little and drinking too much.

As she reached for the decanter Dumarest leaned forward and caught her hand.

"It's none of my business," he said. "You can drink yourself stupid if you want. I've no right to interfere. But do it for the right reasons."

"Such as?"

"That's for you to decide. Most do it for escape. Is there anything you need to run from?"

"No."

"Zucco?"

"No. I—" She shook her head and lifted the decanter as he released her hand. Wine filled her glass in a ruby stream. Looking at it she said, "I guess I'm running away from myself. Have you ever wanted to run?"

"Often."

"I find that hard to believe."

"It's the truth." Dumarest helped himself to some of the wine. Scarlet, the hue of a cyber's robe, the Cyclan which hunted him from world to world. "Were you born in the circus?"

"No. I was sold. Twenty years ago now when I was ten. On Tsopei."

"A harsh world."

"You know it?"

"I've heard of it."

"If you're smart you'll leave it at that." She was bitter. "If there are worse places I've yet to find them. Burn during the day, freeze at night, fighting insects, rot, mildew and, if you

64

don't eat what walks, crawls or flies they'll eat you. Like they did my parents. My kin.''

"It happens."

"Too often," she agreed. "But I guess I was lucky. The man who took me in intended me for something else but an agent of the circus landed and offered a good price. I guess he could see more than others. He had me taught, trained, and—well, that's about it." She swallowed some of her wine. "And you, Earl?"

"Much the same as yourself. I ran away."

"From home? Your world? Which was it?" She frowned at his answer. "Earth? That's an odd name. I've never heard of it. And now?"

"I move around."

"Just that? Don't you do anything else?"

Managing to stay alive. Dodging the hunters. Searching for clues which would guide him back home. Things he left unsaid.

"I'm looking."

"For what? Happiness?" She shrugged as she lifted her glass. "Isn't that what we're all doing? Hoping to find that elusive something which will make everything wonderful? Sometimes you think you've found it then, when you feel most secure, everything falls apart." As it had when Hayter had died. As it threatened to do now—why was he so cold? "Earl!"

Dumarest said, "I haven't forgotten what you said before Ruval attacked."

"Then—"

"I'm honored. More than that—overwhelmed." He paused, sensing her inner turmoil, conscious of the danger it created. A proud woman who, rejected, could become a vicious enemy. The only ally he had in the world of the circus and even now he wasn't sure if she worked for Zucco or not. "Reiza, I—"

"Don't say it!" Wine slopped over her hand to stain the cloth with the color of blood. "If it's a rejection I don't want to hear it. Just get up and leave."

Her, the table, the circus, Melome, his chance of finding Earth.

Dumarest said, "When I leave we go together. I was going to suggest we do it now."

"Earl!" Happiness sparkled in her eyes. "Earl, darling, you—" She broke off, frowning as a man halted at the table. He held a parcel and wore a sigil on his blouse. The mark of Chen Wei. "What do you want?"

"The man." He looked at Dumarest. "You are to accompany me at once to the office of Tayu Shakira."

It was a place filled with an indefinable scent which hung like a ghostly emanation in the air. One composed of subtle spices, of flavors, smokes, blooms, the taint of flesh, the hint of seas. The perfume of a thousand worlds which the circus had known inhaled by the man who sat behind a wide desk. He gestured toward a chair and waited until Dumarest had seated himself and the guide had left them alone.

"You are well, I trust?"

"Well."

"And comfortable?"

"Very."

The truth; the parcel the guide had carried had contained his clothes, refurbished and as good as new. Only the knife had been missing and, as he watched, Shakira lifted it from somewhere behind the desk and set it down before him.

"A fine blade," he said. "One worth studying."

As he was himself and Dumarest, ignoring the knife, searched the man with his eyes.

Tall, slender, a skull topped with raven hair sweeping back from a point between and above the eyes. High brows sheltered deep-set orbs in slanted sockets. The nose was thin, predatory, the mouth a gash. The skin, olive, held a mesh of tiny lines which added to the mask-like appearance of the face.

"You are a fighter," he said. "And have used this knife to kill. Often?"

"Only when necessary."

"Of course." A thin hand reached from the wide sleeve of a blouse marked with an arabesque of gold on a background of lavender. "And yet you drew it here in the circus. An unusual thing to happen on Baatz where violence is rare."

Dumarest said, dryly, "My experiences hardly justify that statement."

"You miss the point. The air within the circus is filtered and those who work here are sheltered from the enervating influence of the outside atmosphere. Visitors carry their apathy with them. You did not. Either you are proof against the external vapors or are able to rise above their influence. I suspect the latter. Tell me, now, and be honest. Have you made no errors since landing?"

Too many and Dumarest admitted it.

66

"Good." Shakira was pleased. "If you had been immune it would have proved nothing. As it is you have adapted to a potentially dangerous environment. Dangerous for you, that is, and for all who have enemies. Think of a snake," he urged. "A master of movement over sand and rock. But set it on a sheet of oiled glass and it is helpless. It can only writhe and squirm, easy prey for any predator. So, for a while on this world, you were at a disadvantage. Here!" The knife spun glittering through the air. Dumarest caught it an inch from his face. "Fast too," mused Shakira. "The reports did not lie."

"Reports from whom?"

"Those who need to make them." Shakira dismissed the subject with a small gesture. "There are questions you wish to ask?"

Only one of importance but if the owner knew as much as he claimed then he would know of Dumarest's interest in Melome. He hadn't mentioned that and subtlety was a game two could play.

Dumarest said, casually, "I'm surprised the circus is so large. I wouldn't have thought Baatz capable of supporting it. But I guess you rely on the concessions."

"You've worked in circuses?"

"Carnivals."

"It is not the same."

"Maybe not," agreed Dumarest. "But I've never known a circus which doesn't have sideshows. Basically it's all the same. When you come down to it what else is a circus but entertainment? So, logically, everything goes. It all belongs."

"Not in the circus of Chen Wei."

"But—"

"We move," said Shakira. "We travel from world to world and with us, like those small limpets which cling to the leviathans of the deep oceans, come the purveyors of common entertainment. They are mere appendages—if lost the circus would not suffer."

"And the circus itself?"

"A compilation of the unusual. Of the rare and particular. The ordinary has no place among us. Each represents the apex of his art."

Dumarest said, "Like Zucco?"

"He has his skills."

"I think I can guess what they are. And you?"

"I have my talent. I have it as you have it as every living

67

creature has it. That special attribute which sets it above its fellows. The ability to sing sweeter, run faster, see more clearly, swim farther, dive deeper, kill faster—always there is something. Usually it is a small advantage and one negated when set against a greater development but, always, it is there. Here, in the circus, are those who have learned what they are good at and have excelled beyond all others in doing it. Others have yet to train and develop their skills; buds swelling toward full bloom. As for myself?" Shakira made a small gesture. "My skill lies in recognizing the potential of others. Your own, for example."

"You flatter me."

"That would be stupid. It would be even more stupid to refuse to recognize the obvious. It is a mistake I never make." Again Shakira made the small gesture, lifting both hands in an upward movement. "You have more questions?"

"One." It was time to get to the point; the gesture had held connotations of dismissal and he was tired of the fencing. Dumarest said, flatly, "How much for Melome?"

"So we come to it—the girl."

"As you've known all along. I want her."

"So it would seem." Shakira's thin lips formed a smile. "Enough to break into my circus, hurt one of my people, threaten another, kill a third—"

"In self-defense."

"True, and Ruval deserved all that happened to him. But the rest?"

"I came for Melome."

"You say that as if it gives you justification for all you did," mused Shakira. "Had you forgotten she is mine?"

"No."

"But it didn't matter, is that it? You would have willingly stolen the girl."

"I wanted what I had paid for. A deal had been arranged and money paid in advance as a token of good faith."

"Fifty kobolds," agreed Shakira. "It was that which decided my agent to act. Too often things of value are lost because of delay and he knew I would not be gentle had he failed. Kalama cheated you. Be thankful it was not for more."

"To hell with the money!" Dumarest fought to remain calm. He found it hard. The air held the traces of too many distant worlds, Shakira himself too like a serpent in his subtle deviations.

A man enjoying the situation. Yet here he was the master and he had the girl. "How much for Melome?"

"Would you be willing to pay a hundred thousand kobolds?" Shakira lifted his hands as Dumarest made no answer. "A ridiculous sum, I agree, but you don't really want to buy the girl. Think of the problems owning her would create. Let us decide on a price, then, for your original agreement."

"That was done."

"But I own the girl now and my values are not the same as Kalama's. There are only two things you could give me which I don't already own. One is your skill. The other is the knowledge you carry in your brain. The skill can be purchased but the knowledge must be freely given." Shakira's voice hardened a little. "Why do want to use the girl?"

"You know what she does."

"Of course, but few willingly seek the terror she induces. Some men will do it once for an act of bravado but rarely twice. Yet you wanted more and more of her song. The action of a desperate man or a stupid one as was your later pursuit. I do not think you to be stupid and am curious as to why you are so desperate. So willing to risk your life to get the girl."

"There is something I want and she can help me to find it." It was not enough and Dumarest knew it. Bluntly he added more. "She can help me find my way home to Earth."

"Earth?" A veil filmed Shakira's eyes. "You believe in legends?"

"Earth is no legend."

"And you claim it as your home world. I find that interesting. We must discuss it in greater detail." Shakira rose from his chair. He was taller than Dumarest had estimated, the golden arabesque of his blouse continued over the pants of matching color, the garments blending so that he seemed to be a creature of lavender laced with gold. "But later. Now we must settle the question of price."

"I offer to share my knowledge."

"Which will be valuable, true, but it isn't enough. You could learn nothing and how would I profit? I want your skill. You must agree to work for me." Shakira added, "If you want the girl, my friend, you have no choice."

CHAPTER SIX

Melome had changed. The waif of the market with the dirt and thinness and ghastly pallor had gone as had the ragged clothing, the belt holding the reeled spools, the lank straggle of the hair. Instead Dumarest looked at a pubescent girl dressed in a neatly belted gown, the long hair braided and set in shimmering coils, the nails trimmed and polished. When she smiled she held the glow of inner health.

A miracle wrought with expensive and intensive therapy, but some of the earlier traces remained; the almost luminous waxen appearance of the skin, the bruised and haunted eyes. Windows which held secrets, unchanging as she lifted her hands, a strand of woven metal between them, as bright and coldly gleaming as her hair.

"Touch it," said Shakira. "Sit and hold the metal."

The contact which would open the door to the past.

Dumarest sat, cross-legged, the metal pliant and cool in his hands. The strand was long, reaching in a double line halfway across the chamber to where Melome now stood against a wall. At Shakira's touch an instrument came to life filling the air with the wail of pipes and the throb of a drum.

Music recorded, refined, filling the room with a relentless pulsing. Closing around Dumarest, enfolding him in a web of silence broken only by the throbbing beat, the nerve-scratching wail, rising, demanding—

The ship!

He must concentrate on the ship. The cabin. The precious book.

The book!

Melome began to sing.

Sound which dominated, directed, engrossed—and became a scream of rage.

"You bastard! You've been stealing again!"

"No!" Dumarest cringed, backing away, sick with the terror which knotted his stomach. Vomiting the scrap of food he'd taken from the pot, the first in two days. "No! Please, no!"

The lash of a belt and pain to add to his fear. Another and the heavy buckle tore at flesh, breaking the skin, sending blood to mingle with the dirt coating his buttocks and legs. The single garment he wore ripped as a hand snatched at his shoulder, the belt lashing at his nakedness, beating him down to the tamped dirt of the floor, sending him in a foetal huddle.

A child of eight years terrified for his life.

"Bastard!" The man, drunk, gloated in his sadistic pleasure. "You no-good bastard! Eat without asking my permission, eh? Stuffing your guts without getting my say-so. I'll teach you. By, God, I'll teach you!"

With the belt, his hands, boots, charred sticks from the fire. Augmenting the hell of normal existence into a dimension of screaming terror. Standing now, beating, beating, beating until his arm grew tired. Staggering away at last to gulp raw liquor from a bottle, spitting a mouthful into the fire. In the sudden flame his shadow loomed against a wall like a grotesque creature from nightmare.

One which blurred to become a girl with braided, silver hair.

"Earl?" Shakira was at his side. "Here."

The wine was rich, pungent, held in a goblet of hammered brass. A warmth which eased his throat and comforted his stomach. Dumarest swallowed it all; if Shakira intended harm he'd had time enough to have done it by now.

Sitting, he looked at the metallic strand, now lying in a loop before him. The goblet held decorations of men and beasts chasing each other in an eternal circle. The carpet was woven from fine materials in a blend of barred and chevron designs. The light came from an overhead dome as if from a luminous pearl.

Things noted with a strange detachment while, deep inside of him, terror remained.

72

Keil, the man had been Keil, one of a succession who had governed his formative years. Beasts shaped like men lacking any generosity, charity or understanding. Using him for the labor he could provide. Working him like an animal as they worked their women. Lusting in violence and the dealing of pain.

"Earl?" Shakira again, his face close, eyes bright and questing. "Tell me, quickly before the impression fades. Was it stronger than before?"

Too strong—such terror should remain buried.

"Her talent is unimpaired." Shakira beamed at Dumarest's nod. "I had fears it might have diminished. Too often sensitives seem only to work their best when subjected to physical hardship but this does not seem to be the case with Melome. And the intensity? The detail? How was that?"

"Clear." Dumarest held out the goblet for more wine. "Too damned clear."

The beating could have been a second ago—his body burned from recollected blows. He could smell the dirt, the vomit, his own excreta and sweat. Taste the blood from his bitten lips, the acid bile of cringing terror.

Terror!

Her song was well-named.

"It could be a matter of sharpened ability or one of concentration," mused Shakira. "In the market she was dull, spiritless, the effort must have drained her vital energies. Now, rested, she is reenergized. Couple this with the fact you are alone—but, no. I doubt it. Does a fire care how many warm themselves at its blaze? The song induces a reaction in those in contact. One or more it could be the same. And yet?" He broke off, thinking.

Dumarest said, "I failed. I missed my target."

"By much?"

Minutes would have been too much but he had missed by years. Her strengthened ability? His own lack of concentration? What must he do to ensure success?

He said, "I want to try again. Now."

"It would not be wise."

"I'll be the judge of that." Dumarest reached for the metal strand, looked up as Shakira kicked it beyond his reach. "We have an agreement."

"That you work for me until such time as you have gained what you want from Melome. An unfair bargain; you could have

73

achieved success at your very first try. But I accepted the gamble and you must do the same."

"Must?"

"You have no choice." Shakira lifted his hands as if demanding attention. "I mean that quite literally. To think that you could use violence against me would be madness. To try it would be to commit suicide. You could leave now and I will stand the loss. A broken agreement—these things happen and the fault would be mine for having misjudged you. But stay and you will have no further option. You will do what I command when I command it. To work for me is to obey."

To be beaten, burned, starved, made to grovel, to beg—the memory of the past was too recent. As was the lesson it had taught. To yield was to die and to do it slowly. And Dumarest was no longer an eight-year-old tormented child.

"Earl!" Shakira stepped back as Dumarest rose to his feet, reading the emotions he saw, recognizing the determination. "Think, man! Attack me and you die!"

"Perhaps." Dumarest took one step closer. "But you will go first."

"Wait!" The thin hands lifted in a gesture of defense or warning. "You are disturbed. Affected by your recent experience. I should have remembered that. Remembered, too, that you are no ordinary man. You have heard of the Band of Obedience?"

"A slave-collar, you mean?"

"The name is unimportant; they are the same. A circlet which is locked around the neck. It contains a device which can be activated from a distance to cause excruciating pain leading to death. It also contains explosives which can be detonated. That same charge will blow if the collar is cut or the lock tampered with. A barbaric device but one which has its uses. Refined it can be most useful."

"To persuade others to keep agreements?"

"Exactly." Shakira lowered his hands. "While you were being treated in the infirmary I thought it best to take certain precautions. Leave now and they will be negated. Stay and you will obey me—or die!"

Reiza stirred, mumbling in sleepy contentment, pressing herself against Dumarest like a kitten seeking warmth. A woman who moved her arm to hold him close while whispering in half-wakeful awareness.

74

"Earl, my darling. You've made me so happy. I love you. I shall love you forever."

This he doubted; passion swift to bloom could fade as quickly.

"Earl?"

She sighed as he stroked her hair, lapsing again into sleep as he stared at the ceiling of her chamber. One adorned with lacelike traceries, black against the nacreous glow shining through the plastic membrane. Artificial moonlight which dimly revealed the furnishings of the room, the mane of her hair, the stark whiteness of her naked arms and shoulders. Against it the traceries took on shape and form.

Bars illustrating the trap he was in.

One baited by Melome.

Shakira's property now and his price had been high. Dumarest's hand rose to his neck as he remembered the weight of the slave-collar he had worn on a world far distant. One he had managed to shed but that had been obvious and Shakira's threat was not.

A bluff?

A possibility and Dumarest considered it as his fingers probed at his neck. They found no lumps or foreign masses but that meant little; a capsule could have been implanted within an inner organ or a time-poison administered. There were a score of ways it could have been done by those skilled in the ways of death.

And, to be sure Shakira was bluffing, he had first to know the man.

He grew on the traceries as Dumarest painted a mental picture of the head, the body, the face, the hands. These details held a subtle oddness as did his clothing, his very walk. A glide rather than punctuated steps which together with the arabesque markings over the matching pants and blouse gave the man an ophidian appearance. A snakelike resemblance accentuated by the slant of the eyes, the thin mask of the face. Yet the hands did not match and he remembered the lifting gesture. One of dismissal, then of defense and warning. Again as a shrug but, always, the same double lift of both appendages. An idiosyncrasy which could mean nothing like the rest of the details; to know the man he must learn more.

"Earl?" Reiza stirred under his hand. "Darling, you want—"

"To talk," he said. "Wake up."

"Talk?" She laughed and pressed herself closer to him.

75

"Darling, you must be joking." Then, as she saw his face with clearer eyes, she said, "You mean it. You really mean it!"

"Tell me about Shakira. What do you know about him?"

"Not much." She reared upright, white in the dim glow, the mounds of her breasts tipped with areolas of darkness. "He owns the circus and gives the orders. If you're wondering about the name forget it. The circus of Chen Wei has existed for over a hundred years. It has a good reputation and I guess Shakira thought it worth keeping."

Profit before pride. Dumarest said, "Did you ever meet the previous owner? No?" Which meant Shakira had run the circus for at least twenty years. "Has anyone?"

"Valaban, maybe. He handles the beasts. You've met him." On the tour of inspection Shakira had insisted he take with Reiza as his guide. "He might know. I'll ask him."

"Anyone else?" Then, as she hesitated, Dumarest said, "Never mind. I'll find out for myself. But about Shakira. Have you ever crossed him or know of anyone who has?"

"What are you getting at, Earl?"

"I need to know."

"And don't intend saying for why." Reiza fell silent then, with an abrupt movement, rose from the bed, standing naked as if a statue carved from alabaster before slipping on a robe. "I thought we'd grown close enough for me to be trusted."

"I trust you."

"Then—"

"I want facts," he said. "Small things, maybe, but enough to build the picture of a man. If you don't want to cooperate then I'll find out some other way but I'd rather not attract his attention." He paused for a moment then added, "When we first met he hinted that he wasn't gentle with those who failed him. True?"

"Are you in trouble, Earl?"

"I could be."

"And you want my help, is that it?" She smiled at his nod. "Well, it isn't much. Shakira's a hard man. A cold one and, yes, he isn't gentle with those who fail him. Do your best and he'll be fair even though he may want your best to be always better. Slack and he comes down hard. Keep slacking and you're out."

She was talking from the viewpoint of an artiste; her opinion conditioned by her work. Dumarest wanted finer data.

"Do you know of anyone who defied him and got away with it?"

"No. Zucco likes to give the impression he had but he's lying. He might act the boss but Shakira is the one who cracks the whip. When they are together there is no doubt who is the real master."

"What does he eat?"

"What?"

Dumarest was patient. "What kind of food does Shakira eat? How often? Does he have any unusual habits? Any personal dislikes? Things like colors," he explained. "Loud noises. Certain kinds of music. Smells. Does he play cards? Gamble? Encourage others to take risks? Has he ever struck anyone? Lost his temper in public? Is he easily amused? Does he—"

"No," said Reiza. "He isn't amused, I mean. I've never seen him appear happy. Even when he smiles it's more like a grimace and I've never heard him laugh. As for the rest—" She shrugged. "I don't know," she admitted. "When young I was too busy working to take any notice and, later, well minding your own business gets to be a habit. I've no time for gossip and rumor."

Two things which would have helped the most.

Dumarest said, "When you guided me around there was a part of the circus we didn't enter."

"Shakira's private quarters," she explained. "They're strictly out of bounds."

"To everyone? Cleaners? Servants?"

"Everyone." She frowned. "At least that's what I thought. Come to think of it someone has to do the cleaning."

And someone had to take care of the other sensitives. There had to be others; why else had Shakira bought Melome if not to add to his collection? But why did he want such a collection at all? Circuses were for the display of trained animals and skilled people before a large audience. Sensitives were unable to entertain more than a few at a time and, like physical freaks, their attraction was limited. An expensive luxury—and a man who retained the old name of the circus because of profit would not waste money.

"Earl?"

"A moment, Reiza."

He wanted to look at the pattern from a different viewpoint and, suddenly, the pieces fell into place. If Melome was alone then she must have been set as a lure; one he could never resist.

77

Following her he had walked into the trap and now it had snapped tight around him.

Did Shakira know the value of what he held?

If so he had been cunning even to the extent of offering a free choice. Dumarest wondered what would have happened had he decided to leave. An academic point now and he wasted no time considering it. Set against what he hoped to learn from Melome the risk had been acceptable. A gamble that Shakira was what he seemed and would keep his word. That his threat had been a bluff. That the luck which had turned sour would become sweet again.

"Earl!" Reiza was impatient. "What's the matter with you? You wake me up, get me to talk, then forget I'm alive."

"Sorry." Dumarest lifted himself in the bed. "I was thinking."

"About us?"

"Of course."

"Of our future together?" A smile banished the last of her irritation. "Darling, why didn't you say? What had you in mind? Shall—no!" She snapped her fingers. "Why guess when there's no need? Krystyna can tell us."

From somewhere came a low snuffling, the sound of a laugh quickly suppressed, a rumble which could have been a snore. Sounds Reiza ignored as she led the way through narrow passages flanked with doors. Living quarters little better than cubicles but cheap and acceptable to those inside.

"She's good, Earl. Really good. She even foretold the way Hayter would die. I didn't believe her then and now I wish I had. Not that it would have made any difference."

Dumarest remembered the talking photograph.

"You were close?"

"Hayter and I? Yes." Her tone ended the subject. "I saw her again recently. I was having some trouble with my act and she gave me some good advice. She even mentioned a stranger coming into my life. It must have been you, Earl. If nothing else I owe her for that."

The weakness of her kind; to confuse prediction with performance. A trait of all who were superstitious and those who lived on the razor-edge of danger were always prone to become that.

Dumarest said, "What does she do? Stare into a crystal ball?"

78

"Don't scoff, darling. She's clever. You'll see."

She pressed on, through the rollers of an air-lock, down a gallery, into the outer section dominated by booths and sideshows. The place was empty now; the circus had yet to come to life. Beyond a flap painted with garish symbols a candle flickered in a crested bowl. In its light the cowled figure sitting hunched in a chair behind a table looked shrunken and dead.

"Krystyna?" Reiza stepped closer to the table. "Are you asleep? I know it's a bad time but—"

"Step aside, child. I know why you are here."

An elementary trick of the trade; why else should people come to a fortune teller but to have their fortunes told? One augmented by others; the candle with its flickering, disguising flame, the tang of incense with its misting fumes, arcane symbols and mysterious objects. The woman herself.

She was old, gnarled with passing years, her face seamed and scored deep with a mesh of lines. The cowl framed it with kindly shadows and provided a setting for her eyes. Small, deep-set, palely blue and as penetrating as a tempered blade.

"Sit!" The hand matched the face, twisted, a blunted claw marred with lumps. Her voice was the thin rustle of dried leaves in a winter's gale. "Sit!" Again the hand stabbed at the chair facing her across the table. "You hesitate, young man. Do you doubt my powers?"

"No, Mother." Dumarest sat in the proffered chair. "I know you are expert at what you do."

"A sly tongue. Do you mock me?"

"No." Dumarest was genuine in his denial. "I would never do that."

A woman, old, twisted with crippling infirmities, fighting the hampering effect of her afflictions. One alone or with a youngster to whom she would teach her trade. Paying her way and giving her clients what they expected. For that, if nothing else, she deserved respect.

"There is truth in you," she said. "And kindness. And, I think, some mercy."

"And love," said Reiza. "That too."

"Love," said the old woman. "Always they want to be loved. To find love and be given it. Well, I tell them what they want to hear and more often than not things they would be better not knowing. A fault, but I grow old and impatient. Why peer

79

into the future if you are afraid of what you might see? Death, despair, pain, betrayal—such things are inevitable. But I try to be kind. Always I try to be that.''

Conning the punters with slick words and facile phrases. Quizzing them by indirection, milking them of details to be fed back later in different words and subtle suggestions. Using misdirection, hesitation, ambiguity and guile to weave the client into a mesh of self-betrayal. An art at which Dumarest guessed she was an expert.

"You know too much," she said. "And, at the same time, not enough. For those I choose I give genuine service. But, you understand, I cannot be precise as to moments of time. Nor as to exact means of action. Events take their own time and operate in their own manner. For example, that you will die is inevitable. But just how and when—''

"You warned of Hayter's death," said Reiza. "You said how he would end.''

"A man plays with fire—what are the chances of his getting burned?" A shrug moved the fabric of the cowled robe. "Some things are obvious and cast their shadow before them. Others—'' Again the shrug. "Give me your palm.''

Dumarest felt the twisted fingers grasp his own as he obeyed. A nail traced a path, paused, traced another.

"No." She released his hand. "For you there is a better way. Here!''

Dumarest looked at the stack of cards she set before him. Old, the backs a mass of complex lines, cracked but bearing the gleam of applied polish. The size was wrong for a normal deck.

"Shuffle them," said Krystyna. "Run them through your hands. Impregnate them with your personal magnetism. Their order will illustrate your fate.''

"Do it," urged Reiza. "Please, Earl.''

Dumarest picked up the cards, riffled them, shuffled with a gambler's skill.

The old woman said, "You handle them well. You know what they are?''

"Yes.''

"Then cut them into two piles. Rest a hand on each and concentrate on your present situation. Then shuffle again and hand them to me.''

She waited until it was done then sat with the deck poised in her hands.

"Once, so legend has it, these were the only cards known. Men depicted gods and natural hazards thinking that the symbol gave dominance over the thing and that, by controlling a part of the universe, they could govern the whole. They were wrong but later, perhaps because men grew afraid of alien places and needed something to guide them, the original pack was enlarged to what it is today. Every hazard and circumstance which could affect a person was isolated, compacted and illustrated to form the Arcana Universalis. Fire, flood, storm, war, space, bursting suns. Of course each symbol has extended meanings. For example space does not just mean the void between the stars but a gap, a distance, a setting apart. The art lies in the interpretation. I could set out these cards and you would see things of personal import but because you have intimate knowledge of your life your vision would be narrowed against the wider implications. And you, child—" She glanced at Reiza. "You know even less and so would look for what you wanted to see. Love, fecundity, happiness. I?" The eyes closed, opened again. "I read the truth."

Her twisted fingers slid a card from the top of the deck and laid it face-down on the table before Dumarest.

"Your card," she told him. "Your significator."

She spread others around in a ritual pattern, face-up, bright symbols glowing in the guttering light of the candle. Reiza drew in her breath as the skeleton appeared.

"Earl—"

"Death," said Krystyna. "The fate which waits us all. But also it is a transformation. Here it signifies an end; the cards before it carry your fate."

She gloomed over them, a finger touching, passing on, her withered lips pursing, moving as if she mumbled esoteric incantations. Dumarest watched with inward amusement. Beside him Reiza was a coiled spring.

"Earl," she whispered. "I'm frightened. I shouldn't have brought you here. If the reading is bad—God! How can I bear to lose you?"

He said, "There's nothing to be afraid of. It's just a game."

"A game?" Krystyna lifted her head with a sudden motion and sat poised like a snake about to strike. "Aye," she said after a moment. "A game as all life is a game. One I can read—or would you prefer not to know the things which wait?"

"Let's go, Earl." Reiza tugged at his arm. "It was a mistake to come. Please, Earl."

81

"No." He freed his arm, his eyes holding those of the old woman. "When you're ready, Mother."

Again she brooded over the cards.

"First the beginning for the child is father to the man and as the twig is bent so the tree will grow." Her finger touched a card next to the significator. "The Egg, symbol of life and fertility but also of change for from the egg springs a different form. And this is touched by conflict, desolation, catastrophe." The finger moved from card to card, pausing at the depiction of a man dressed in tattered garments, smiling, a staff bearing a bundle resting on one shoulder. "The Rover. Restless, always moving, ever seeking the unknown beyond the horizon. A fool, some would say, leaving reality in pursuit of a dream. A man without faith and faith is not for him." The finger moved to the symbol of a priest, the card reversed. "The comfort of spiritual assurance is absent and he lacks the support of the church. But it does not work against him for it lies on the dexter side. A neutrality. This is not." The finger moved, came to rest. "The Cradle. Also reversed and therefore empty. There will be no fruitful issues or successful outcomes."

"No." Reiza dug her fingers into Dumarest's arm as she whispered the denial. "She's wrong, Earl. She has to be."

He rested his hand on hers, giving her the comfort of his touch as the old woman droned on. Looking at the cards she touched, the Wheel, the Ship, the Pylon. Reiza drew in her breath as the gnarled finger came to rest on the Skull.

"Deceit," said Krystyna. "Poison of the mind and even of the body. Threats of a secret nature. Associated with knowledge." Her finger tapped the Book, moved to a card meshed with a web and an eight-legged creature. "The Spider. Already you are deep in the snare of its spinning and the danger of the skull warns of its intention. But the Book?"

She fell silent, brooding over the cards, checking their association. Reiza was too impatient to wait.

"Tell us," she blurted. "Krystyna—what do you see?"

"Death." The old woman leaned back, her eyes winking points of brilliance in the guttering light as she looked at Dumarest. "You are enmeshed in danger and deception which can have only one end. How it will come and from what source has yet to be revealed." Her hand reached for the face-down card which represented Dumarest then, abruptly, she drew it back. "No. You do it. A man should find his own destiny."

Dumarest reached out, took the card, turned it. In the dim lighting the figure it depicted seemed made of blood. Tall, thin, the scarlet robe it wore emblazoned with the Cyclan Seal.

"Logic." Krystyna added, "The fifteenth card. Fifteen—the number of your fate."

CHAPTER SEVEN

———•——•——•———

Master Marle, Cyber Prime, woke to stare into darkness broken only by a single point of light which relieved the stygian gloom of the chamber. A matter of efficiency; total darkness would prove hampering in case of emergency; time wasted as eyes grew accustomed to the light, movement disorganized. Now he lay supine as his body geared itself to a higher degree of function. Minutes which grew longer as the years progressed for no matter how efficient the basic mechanism the aging process took its toll.

"Master." The voice followed a bell. "Time to wake, Master."

A summons repeated, dying as his finger touched a control. Another and the light strengthened to reveal the bleak outlines of the room. One devoid of all but functional units, lacking decoration, cell-like in its Spartan simplicity.

Marle rose, swinging his legs over the edge of the bed, sitting and waiting as his body accepted the higher demand. The clock showed it to be night on the surface but here, in the caverns sunken deep, the divisions of light and darkness held no meaning. Time was governed by the segments of hours. He had slept four of them, waking minutes before the alarm. Once, not long ago now, he would have woken seconds before the bell.

A thought he took with him as he showered, feeling no pleasure from the lash of water against his flesh. To bathe was a matter of hygiene, a necessity as were other functional demands. As was the food he ate when, cleansed and dressed, he sat to a frugal meal.

Prolo bowed as he entered his office. "Master, I have placed—"

"A moment." The aide was new, replacing Wyeth who had gone to his reward. A good man and a dedicated servant of the Cyclan, but as yet a little unaccustomed to his new position. "Any news from the laboratories?"

"As regards the affinity twin? None, Master, all negative as before."

"Matters of prime importance should always be given precedence," said Marle. "And to repeat the obvious is to be inefficient. Any news of Avro?"

"None." The rebuke had stung even though deserved yet the aide's face remained passive. "His condition is as before."

A statement of the obvious and another demonstration of inefficiency—if there was no news the condition could not have changed and so to have mentioned it was a waste of both words and time. Prolo would learn, and soon, or the aide would be replaced. And, if he was, an investigation would be held to discover why a man so flawed had been allowed to rise so high.

Marle glanced at his desk where reports rested in a neat pile. Prolo had stacked them and if his judgment was at fault it was the last mistake he would make.

Alone Marle studied them. The first required his immediate decision and he gave it into a recorder.

"Report XDB 13572. Prince Tyner must be deposed. Arrange his death before the Omphale Festival. Throw blame on the Kaspar faction. Cease all imports of penka from Nemcova."

A classic situation; Prince Tyner, young, idealistic, wanted to free his people from their dependence on expensive imports. Dead, his friends accused, trade threatened by the lack of penka, confusion would be accelerated by the festival. From the chaos an older ruler would rise to seize power. One aided and advised by the Cyclan.

The next report was of lesser urgency and Marle gave thought to the most efficient way of resolving the problem. A matter of trade dependency which could yield to the impetus of a new discovery.

The number then, "Instruct the resident cyber on Chroneld to release the formulae for the synthesization of ondret to the Smyslov Laboratories."

Within two years the farms of Chroneld would be ruined as the artificial product rendered their crops superfluous. Desperation would induce civil war and to retain their power the rulers would need help. The Cyclan would give it—at a price. And one more world would fall to the domination of logic and reason.

Quickly Marle ran through the rest of the reports. Prolo had done his job and earned a remand. His previous errors could have been the result of too great a desire to appear efficient, but with time he would learn. Learn and take his place at the side of the most powerful man the galaxy had ever known.

Marle recognized the error and corrected it. Not the man but the organization which he served. The Cyclan which dominated a host of planets, working always from positions behind established authority. Ruling cadres and princes who, desperate to maintain their hold, had turned to the Cyclan for advice.

The service had been given for a fee, but the initial payment was merely the beginning. Once the client had tasted the power at their disposal they wanted more, more. For a cyber, any cyber, could take a handful of facts and from them extrapolate the most probable sequence of events. Not true prophecy but calculated assessment of available data and a prediction of what most likely would happen. Predictions so accurate that they seemed like actual announcements of what was to come. With such information a ruler could maintain his power, a trader grow rich, a mercenary always win or, if not win, never lose.

Then, once their need was recognized and relied on, the Cyclan moved to formulate its own purpose.

Marle rose and touched a control, the chamber darkening as, within it, a simulacrum of the galaxy flared to life. A host of minute points, blurs, streamers of luminous gas. At such a small scale details were lost; individual planets, rogue moons, wandering asteroids. But the stars remained and a wide scatter of them were marked in red.

The scarlet of the Cyclan—the color marking their conquests.

Soon the scarlet would have spread to engulf entire areas of space. Eventually it would dominate all and then there would be an end of waste, of futile effort, of wasted resources. Logic and reason would replace the idiocy of emotional response. The old, sick, crippled and nonproductive would be eliminated. The inefficient. The maladjusted. The human race would become a smoothly functioning machine, each ability and mind directed to the solving of all the problems of the universe.

And he, now, was at the head of the Cyclan.

Power such as no one had ever hoped to attain before. At his decision men died, worlds were ravaged, others urged into the fruitfulness which was their potential. But all flecked with the scarlet touch, even though unknowingly, obeyed, without question, himself as their ruler.

A power which would last as long as he proved himself capable of using it.

"Master?" Prolo calling on the intercom. "Master?"

His face appeared as Marle touched a control.

"What is it?"

"Avro, Master. There has been a positive response."

Tyzach met him as Marle entered the laboratory. The place held a variety of instruments, a bed surrounded by monitors, assistants who stood at a respectful distance. They, like the physician, wore laboratory clothing. Only Marle warmed the chamber with his scarlet robe.

"Master." Tyzach's nod was acknowledgment of superior rank. "There has been no improvement."

"But you did obtain a positive response?"

"Ten minutes ago."

It had been minor and inconclusive but the first obtained since Avro had been brought back to Cyclan Headquarters from the world named Heaven.

Marle moved to where he lay on the bed. He was naked, wires wreathing his emaciated body, his shaven skull. A corpselike creature, old, withered, the skin taut over prominent bone. Stripped, Marle would have looked his twin.

But Avro had failed while he had not.

To Tyzach he said, "We know that Dumarest injected him with the dominant half of the affinity twin. The host was a local life-form. Is it possible, now that there is evidence the bond is weakening, for you to isolate the portion of the affinity twin within his brain?"

"No." Tyzach was positive. "In theory it should be possible but the affinity twin nestles deep in the cortex and, as far as we can determine, changes its nature once activated by the host. A deeper examination than we have as yet made would lead to inevitable death."

A small loss; Avro's failure had merited his extinction. Not for him the reward Wyeth had obtained, his body reduced to ash, his living, thinking brain now sealed in a capsule and a part of

Central Intelligence. The reward all cybers enjoyed unless they proved themselves inefficient.

Yet to dig into the brain would be to kill all hope of potential knowledge.

A dilemma resolved as soon as recognized. Avro would live, yield whatever knowledge he possessed and then, if the action was promising of added knowledge, would be dissected.

Nothing must stand in the way of obtaining the secret of the affinity twin.

The secret stolen from the Cyclan and passed on to Dumarest.

Marle turned and paced the laboratory, thinking of those who had failed and what had happened to them. A punishment directed as example, not revenge. To regret the past was a waste of time. Such emotion was alien to any cyber as were love and fear and hate and physical pleasure. An operation performed on the thalamus when young together with rigorous training had freed them of the poison afflicting the human race. Replacing it with reason and cold logic. Tools with which to reshape the universe.

But which, as yet, had failed to capture the one man who held the secret. The sequence in which the fifteen biomolecular units forming the affinity twin had to be joined.

"Master." Tyzach was beside the bed checking the monitors. "Another response."

"To applied stimuli?"

"Yes. I'm shortening the period."

Stabbing the brain and body with demanding current. Shocking the system into a reaction other than that of the autonomous process which had kept the heart beating, the lungs breathing, the body moving in a self-preserving pattern. Raised to his feet Avro would stand, would move if pushed without falling. Would void his system of waste and ingest food and water. A mindless vegetable of less worth than an insect.

At such times it was hard to remember that the sharp intelligence Avro possessed was not dead but merely absent. Lodged in another brain belonging to a creature far distant on another world.

"Quickly." Tyzach called to an assistant. "Raise stimulating power one degree."

A stronger thrust of energy rewarded by the kick of a needle, the movement of pens tracing lines on a rolling sheet of paper. An encephalogram, another record to add to the rest. In the

89

search for the affinity twin no scrap of data could be overlooked or ignored.

"Again." Marle broke the silence as the body on the bed remained inert. "There should be some muscular reaction by now. Increase the stimulus."

"That would not be wise." Tyzach was firm in his objection. "For the bond to be broken the host-body must die. If the released intelligence has nowhere to return then it will dissipate. A stronger stimulus, applied now, might destroy those few cells within the cortex which could be of paramount importance."

A guess but a good one and, failing all concrete evidence to the contrary, might well be true. If Marle insisted his suggestion be followed, and the result should be less than successful, his own efficiency would be thrown into doubt.

He stepped back, arms folded, hands thrust into the wide sleeves of his robe. A gaunt and watchful pillar of flame. One who noted every detail as his mind expanded to engulf a vast section of the cosmos. The world on which Avro's intelligence was lodged—how did he see it? How did he assess it? How easily did he manipulate the host body? How efficient was the transfer?

The early studies had been staggering in their implications, the data promising incredible powers. The affinity twin could give the old a new, a young and virile body. A bribe no man or woman could resist. But it went much further than that. The mind of a cyber could be placed within the brain and body of a ruler. Gone would be the need for tedious manipulation of events. Decisions, once made, could be acted on without delay.

The Cyclan could rule the entire galaxy within a matter of decades.

A dream of power soon to be regained and Marle felt the euphoria of it. The glow of mental achievement which was the only pleasure he could know.

"A positive increase in neurological activity." One of the assistants reported to Tyzach. "Synaptic time-lag decreasing."

"Muscular response?"

"Improving."

"Apply vibro-massage to extremities." Tyzach added, "Note muscular contraction rate and build up of fatigue toxins."

Marle said, "The encephalograph?"

"Functioning on both prime and secondary levels of cortical activity. Scintillometers are tracing neutron paths within the cortex."

"Electronic scan of the basic area?"

"No, for the reason already given. The dominant half of the affinity twin must not be influenced. Once the subject has woken a full scan can be made."

"Heart-beat accelerating." The voice of the assistant maintained the even modulation devoid of any irritant factors, the vocal hallmark of all cybers. A moment then, "Master! He wakes."

Avro opened his eyes.

The bowl held a nourishing soup scientifically composed so as to give the maximum of energy-potential together with essential minerals. With it had come a portion of bread with a high percentage of roughage. Fuel for the engine which was his body, but even as he ate it Avro remembered other foods, unfamiliar tastes.

A time in which he had been an angel.

He leaned back, closing his eyes, recalling the rush and pressure of air, the strain of outspread wings as he had ridden the uprising thermals. A thing which had happened in a flash, his mind leaving his body as it fell from the prick of a needle. For a long moment he had been disorganized, the host body failing, wheeling as it fell to the rocks below, then its autonomous system came to the rescue and the pinions carried it up and safely away.

Flying.

Flying as no man had ever flown before.

Now it was over and he was back in his own body among his own kind. They had fed him, bathed him, checked his body and mind, questioned him with probing efficiency. Now, fed again, he was to learn his fate.

Marle looked up from his desk as Avro entered the office remaining silent until the aide had left them alone.

Without preamble he said, "It is the decision of the Council that you failed in your mission. Do you agree with their finding?"

"No."

"You claim to have succeeded?"

"Not wholly." Avro continued, "There are degrees of success. I went to find Dumarest and I found him. That was not failure."

"You went to capture him," corrected Marle. "You elected to do so and the Council met your every demand as regards supplies and men. A special ship. A special crew. The entire resources of the Cyclan placed at your disposal. Yet you returned with nothing. Dumarest eluded you and retains the secret of the affinity twin. We still lack the correct sequence in which the fifteen units must be assembled. The Council has determined that your lack of positive results illustrates your inefficiency and merits the penalty of failure.''

Total extinction, both body and brain reduced to ash. His personal awareness, his ego, destroyed along with the rest.

Avro felt an inward chill as he considered it. An unusual reaction; as a cyber he should be a stranger to fear. And the punishment was normal; the penalty paid by all who failed. Marle himself would suffer the same end should he demonstrate his inefficiency.

Avro said, ''I failed to effect Dumarest's capture, that is true, but even in defeat things can be learned.''

''Not to underestimate your opponent?''

''I did not underestimate him. But his luck, the factor which seems to play such a prominent part in his like and which I suspect stems from some paraphysical source, saved him yet again. But I am not wholly to blame. The crew failed to operate with the expected efficiency. No matter what happened to me they should have taken Dumarest.''

A mistake—explained by the debilitating effects of the journey, bluff, fear of losing their quarry, of killing their superior.

Dumarest was clever, Marle had never doubted it, but only now had he come to appreciate how elusive the man had made himself. Was it because of some paraphysical power he possessed? Certainly his luck seemed incredible at times. A trap set, sprung—and still he had managed to escape. Using the dedication of the servants of the Cyclan to their master to aid his plan.

What had it been like to fly?

Avro had done his best to tell them; spools of tape were filled with his report, but none of them could convey what he must have really known. Dead that knowledge would be lost. Alive it could be used to spur him to greater efforts.

Avro said, as if following the other's thoughts, ''I know Dumarest now better than before. I've met him face to face, talked with him, tested his resolution. Incorporated into previous data the experience could be the turning point. The next time I shall not fail.''

''Are you asking for another chance?''

''Eliminating me will gain the Cyclan nothing. If I try and

92

again fail what would have been lost? To discard a useful tool is both illogical and inefficient."

Arguments bolstering Marle's own conviction. Avro had lived too long, had served too well not to have value. His failure must be punished but total extinction need not be the answer. Not now. Not when he could be of use.

The depiction of the galaxy blossomed into life as Marle touched a control. It expanded as he operated another, stars streaming outward from the center to cast swaths and streaks of transient brilliance over their faces and robes, the utilitarian furnishings of the office. As it settled he indicated a glowing point, a tiny speck beside it.

"There," he said. "Heaven."

A world of soft winds and soaring hills, of rolling plains and wide-stretching seas. Of crystalline nests hugging precipitous faces. Of winged figures which rose to wheel and dive and rise again.

And, suddenly, Avro was an angel again.

He felt the lash of wind against his face and body, relived the euphoria induced by the thrumming pulse of blood through veins and arteries, the drumbeat of his heart loud in his ears. Rising to soar, to glide while beneath him the terrain shrank to the dimensions of a toy. To lunge at others of his own kind, to drive off arrogant males, to circle the females, ushering them back to the nest.

"Avro." Marle was facing him, his eyes questing. "Is something wrong?"

"No." Avro drew air deep into his lungs. "It is nothing."

"The report on your physical condition stated that you are close to optimum function. There has been some loss of tissue, but that was to be expected despite the intravenous feeding during your journey back and the period here before your intelligence returned. And yet then, for a moment, you seemed about to collapse."

"A slight nausea." Avro corrected the statement, to be sick was to prove the inadequacy of the body. "A lack of immediate coordination of mind and eye." He gestured at the depiction. "The retinal musculature has been at rest too long. Exercise will correct it."

Marle nodded, dismissing the subject, Avro was the best judge of his condition. Again he faced the depiction and the planet he'd indicated.

"Heaven," he said again. "A world of little value even though the dominant avian life form holds a certain interest. From it Dumarest travelled to Aumont."

"When?"

"Shortly after you were stricken. The captain of your vessel did his best to make the most of the situation in which he found himself. He could not attack for fear of destroying Dumarest and he had also to safeguard your person. Leaving the world, he headed far out into space and there hung in a position to monitor the other ship. A chance which succeeded; his instruments were of a superior quality. He could register the other vessel but the reverse did not apply. He waited long enough to track their direction of flight."

"They could have altered course."

"A possibility but of no importance. Dumarest landed on Aumont. Word had been sent ahead to our cybers and agents in the area and he was spotted. He left before action could be taken, first to Kreuz then to Tolen and then to Ceruti. There the ship was seized by our agents."

"And Dumarest?"

"Missing. He had left the ship either on Kreuz or Tolen. Both are busy worlds with many vessels offering a choice of routes and directions." Marle's tone did not change as he added, "Which ship would he have taken? To which world would he have gone?"

A test; Marle would already have made the prediction and was now examining his ability. On the outcome could hang his fate. Avro studied the data which flashed on a wall; details of ships, cargoes, destinations, times. Dumarest would have been aware of his danger; a man on the run doing his best to delude his pursuers. Shifting in a random pattern and avoiding the obvious. But no pattern could be wholly random; each choice had to be dictated by the man himself and each would be governed by personal and subconscious idiosyncrasies. A dislike of the color red—and a ship so painted would be avoided. A dislike of cold, of mountains, of roaring winds. A reluctance to share a cabin. A fondness for warm climes. A host of minor spurs unsuspected by the quarry but glaring signposts to the hunters.

And Avro had studied every aspect of Dumarest's behavior known to the Cyclan.

"Schike," he said. "Dumarest would have traveled on the *Hoyland* to Schike."

"And then?"

"The *Vladek* to Caltoon." A small world on the edge of a busy cluster, one on which no cyber would find a use for his services but where a man could lose himself in a crowd. "And then to Ostrogoth."

And from there?

Avro checked the data. A normal man, even though aware of pursuit, would follow a predictable path, but Dumarest was far from ordinary. A man to take the obvious because it was just that, to bluff and counter-bluff, to do the unsuspected. Like traveling to Vanch with its continual rain. Or Leasdale with its icy seas. Bad worlds both and Dumarest would not want to be stranded. Where then?

Where?

"Baatz." Marle supplied the answer. Avro had demonstrated his ability, to continue the test would be inefficient. "Dumarest is on Baatz at the circus of Chen Wei. Cyber Tron is on his way to ensure his capture or to take possession of him should the capture have been made."

"And if he should escape?"

"He will not."

"The possibility exists," said Avro. "Nothing can be one hundred percent certain. Always there is the unknown factor. Tron is a stranger to Dumarest, he has yet to learn of his wiles. He could be overconfident. It has happened before."

Too often and with too many dead cybers to add to the failures. A fact Marle knew as he was aware that, should Dumarest escape again, the blame would be his.

He said, "I place you in charge of Dumarest's capture and return. You will leave immediately." He added, in a tone bleak despite its even modulation, "You failed once, Avro—do not fail again."

CHAPTER EIGHT

Valaban said, "Settle down, Earl. The way you pace about is making me nervous. Quit it before you disturb the beasts."

Good advice and Dumarest took it, taking his place beside the old man on a bench. Around him stretched the cavernous area beneath the stands, one split and sectioned to avoid waste, the part reserved for the animals thick with smells.

He drew them into his nostrils, recognizing the tang of sweat, dung, oils, embrocation, urine. An odor too similar to another he knew but this, at least, was free of the reek of blood.

"You're restless," said Valaban. "I can sense it and so can the animals. Here." He held out a bottle. "Take a drink of this—it will calm you."

"Thanks." Dumarest took the bottle, held it to his lips, threw back his head and pretended to drink. Handing it back he said, "So you never met Chen Wei. Who owned the circus before Shakira?"

"Damned if I know." Valaban frowned at the single lamp which illuminated the area. A pool of light in a darkness edged with cages and gleaming, watchful eyes. "It was a long time ago now. Maybe Chen Wei did, I only said I'd never met him. Burski hired me. He got himself killed on Daleth—a fight over a woman as I remember, then Shakira took over. That must be, oh, close to thirty years ago."

A long time in a transient society and if Valaban lacked the answers they weren't to be found.

He stiffened as noise came from a cage, relaxing as it died.

"The klachen," he grunted. "The damned thing's more trouble than it's worth. Zucco must have been crazy to take it on."

"Maybe he likes its rider?" A lithe young girl with a rounded face and slanted, enigmatic eyes, she danced on the platform of the creature's back with stunning agility. "Is he like that?"

"What man isn't if he gets the chance?" Valaban shrugged. "But Kiki's too tame for him, too docile. He likes strength in a woman, something he can beat down, use, conquer. I guess you know what he is."

"I know."

"Then you know enough to be careful. Stay away from him. Maybe he'll forget you're around."

A warning? Dumarest looked at Valaban, studying the seamed face, the sunken eyes. An old man with an inner wisdom who would see more than he admitted and know more than he was willing to tell. But some information had been gained; small details which added to build a picture. Zucco, for example, a man who had joined the circus some five years earlier and who seemed to possess no special skills. One who had climbed fast and high. Dumarest wondered why.

"You're good, Earl," said Valaban. "I appreciate you helping me out. You've a way with animals. Some have it and some don't and no one knows just what it is. Trust, maybe, or just an absence of fear. You don't scare them." He frowned as, again, the klachen kicked at the bars of its cage.

Dumarest said, "When the circus moves do the beasts go with it?"

"Not all. We sell them off for breeding stock mostly, that's why none of the males has been neutered. Most can easily be trained but some can't. The cats, for instance, they come from Flyte. Special mutated stock bred for guardians. You know Flyte?"

"No."

"It's a prison world. Jungle and cleared areas ringed with wire. Outside the cats are allowed to roam free. Sometimes a prisoner tries to escape and when he does the authorities write him off. The cats get him," Valaban explained. "Use him for sport. If he's lucky he dies fast."

"Has Reiza had them long?"

"Since they were kittens. Shakira bought them for her. I cut their claws and blunted their fangs and she used to sleep with them. To build an affinity, you understand. Before they will

98

obey they must accept her as one of themselves.'' Valaban paused then added, ''Maybe she became more like them than she realized. A creature of whims and fancies and sudden impulses. Hayter said that once.'' He glanced at Dumarest. ''You know about Hayter?''

''Her dead lover? Yes, I know. The cats killed him, didn't they?''

Valaban took a sip from his bottle and lowered it to stare at the lamp.

''Hayter was a good man and I liked him. The cats ripped out his life but I figure he was dead before he entered the ring. His mind wasn't on the job which was bad enough but I think there was something more. An animal,'' he said. ''But walking on two legs like a man.''

Zucco? A possibility, he had become Reiza's lover and Hayter's death had been a convenient accident. If it had been an accident.

Dumarest said, casually, ''I've heard of such things. Used them at times when hunting for a living. A special mix which attracts the prey. A scent they can't resist and I suppose you could make one which would induce an attack. Was it something like that?''

''Maybe.''

''You didn't spot it?''

''Hayter was covered in blood and his stomach was a mess. The stink was enough to cover all others but I remember, just before he went into the ring, he dabbed at his face with a cloth. To dry the sweat, I guess, but he could have been putting something on as well as taking it off.''

''Did you tell any of this to Shakira?''

''I tried but he didn't seem to want to listen. And who am I to go up against his man? Not that I give a damn for any of them. With my skills I can go anywhere. Every farmer will want a man who can handle his beasts and this isn't the only circus in the galaxy.'' Valaban used his bottle again. ''Maybe it's time to quit the way it's being run.''

''Zucco?''

''It's not just him. Every circus needs a strong ringmaster but there are other things.''

''Like too many empty seats?''

''You've noticed,'' said Valaban. ''The take's too low. We've been here too long and lost our novelty. We should be up and moving to greener fields. In the old days this place would be on its way by now. The animals sold, acts thinned, half the tents deflated and packed. We even started—'' He broke off, rearing to his feet as the klachen screamed its rage. ''What the hell's going on?''

Metal clanged and, suddenly, the creature was before them.

It was the size of a horse, scaled, the head like that of a lizard. A vestigial tail ended in a knotted mass of bone and spine, the feet tipped with round and blunted claws. Beneath the hide and across the broad platform of its back muscle rippled in smoothly coordinated motion.

''Freeze!'' Valaban's voice, while gentle, held the snap of command. ''Something's scared it. Move and you'll make it worse. Leave this to me.'' He faced the animal, talking as he moved slowly toward the creature. ''Easy, now. Easy. Just rest easy, now. Easy.''

Words which became a soothing drone directed at the lifted head, the orifices of the ears. A demonstration of his skill, the talent which gave him mastery over the majority of animals. Dumarest remembered a man he'd once known who could calm the most frenzied horse by whispering in its ear. Valaban had the same attribute but the klachen wasn't a horse and, if it charged, the old man would be dead.

And Dumarest knew it would charge.

Knew it with the instinct which had served him so often before. Even as Valaban stepped closer Dumarest was on the move. A lunge which closed the space between them, sent his shoulder slamming into the other man, hurling him down and to one side.

Falling beside him as the beast tore past where he had stood.

''Earl! I—''

''Your bottle!'' Dumarest climbed to his feet. He didn't look at the other man. ''Give me your bottle!''

His knife was in his hand ready to slash and stab but used it would fill the air with the scent of fresh blood. An odor which would madden the other beasts within the area into a destructive outburst. Already they deafened him with their snarls and growls, the metallic clash as they fought the confines of their cages.

''Leave it to me, Earl.'' Valaban, shaken, was on his feet beside Dumarest. ''I know how to handle it.''

''Get close and it will kill you.'' Dumarest pointed to where the klachen stood, head weaving, nostrils dilated as it snuffed the air. "You can't move fast enough to dodge. Now give me that bottle and your blouse. Or something to hold the liquid. Move!"

Time was against them. The creature, disturbed, could run amok. But to wait was to allow its fear to build, to explode in a killing fury.

"Here!" Valaban handed over the bottle and a blanket. He watched as Dumarest tore loose the cork and spilled the fluid over the material. "You going to blind it?"

"I'm going to try." Dumarest sheathed his knife. "Stand ready. Once I get this over its head it'll start to rear. When it calms run forward and do your stuff."

He edged forward before Valaban could answer, the blanket in his hands, booted feet silent on the floor. As the scaled head turned toward him he froze, standing motionless until the ruby eyes had moved away. Closer, he froze again, the blanket held high before him, the smell of the fluid masking his scent. As the head turned away he was running, jumping high to land on the broad back, the blanket falling to wrap around the head, blinding the eyes.

As it settled the klachen exploded into violent action.

Dumarest felt the surge and lift of muscle, the jarring impact as the creature landed. He slipped, almost fell as the beast reared, clamped his legs tight as it darted forward and came to a sudden halt. A moment in which he tasted blood and felt the strain on nerve and sinew then the animal was rearing again, the tail lashing to free itself of the rider on its back.

"Earl! Watch it!"

Dumarest heard Valaban's yell of warning and felt the blow which scraped over his spine. One which would have knocked him to the ground with a shattered back if he hadn't heaved himself forward to lock his thighs around the base of the klachen's neck. A hold he maintained as the creature threshed beneath him, stooping forward to wrap the blanket over the jaws, twisting to clamp them shut. Locking the fabric with his left hand he pressed his right over the nostrils, blocking the passage of air and filling the beast's lungs with the fumes of Valaban's bottle.

Choked, near to asphyxiation, the creature slowed its wild lungings, came at last to a quivering rest.

"You've got it," said Valaban. "You can leave the rest to me." He came close, moving the blanket as Dumarest released his grip, his voice low as he stroked the scaled head.

Dumarest watched, waiting, then as the old man looked up

and nodded he slid from his position to land softly at the side of the klachen. As Valaban continued to soothe the beast he stepped over to its cage.

The lock was simple but far too sophisticated to ever be released by an animal. Dumarest checked the cage and the area around it. The rear was masked in shadows which blurred detail and he stood among them looking toward the bench and the single lamp. Someone with a stick could easily have opened the cage without being seen. He moved farther back to where a wall rested close to the bars. The smooth surface gaped in a long, vertical cut. Dumarest fingered the material; thin plastic meant only for a flimsy screen. At the base of the cut a silken scarf rested like a smear of yellow.

One bearing a perfume he recognized.

"Reiza's." Valaban snuffed at the fabric. "That's her perfume."

"You certain?"

"She wears it like a brand. It's hers all right." Valaban glowered at the scarf. "Expensive stuff. Zucco bought her a bottle once and she's worn nothing else since. But why would she want to open the cage?"

Dumarest said, dryly, "One reason might be to kill you."

"Not Reiza. Why should she want that?"

"Someone opened the cage," said Dumarest. "That same person must have tormented the klachen. Whoever it was knew that you'd come running when it screamed."

"And if it hadn't been for you I'd be dead by now." Valaban drew in his breath, the scarf ripping between his hands. "Cats," he said bitterly. "You can make a fuss of them, spoil them, talk to them and make them purr. They'll let you stroke them and scratch their ears and roll over all as friendly and nice as you could want. Then, as you turn, they'll rip out your spine." The shredded scarf fell to lie at his feet. "Cats and women—you can't trust either."

In the crowd a girl was crying; big tears running over rounded cheeks, a fuzzy-haired doll clutched to the faded dress she wore. She seemed lost and afraid and looking at the adult world with brimming blue eyes.

"Hello, there!" Dumarest knelt before her. "Can't find your way?"

"I turned," she sobbed. "And when I looked back they were gone."

102

"Your mother and father?"

"And Ingred and Uncle Mac. I've looked and looked but they've vanished. They've left me!" The tears ran faster over her cheeks. "I'm all alone!"

A small tragedy and one easily resolved but, to the child, a frightening experience.

"We'll find them," promised Dumarest. "Would you like to ride on my shoulder? Could you hang on?" He straightened as she nodded. "Right then. Ready? Up we go!"

A lift and she was perched high, the doll firm beneath one arm, the other locked around his neck. A clown called to her and waved, another whistled; novelties which dried her tears as Dumarest walked down the gallery toward the information desk. The woman on duty smiled.

"Another lost one? Well, set her down." She waved to where a cushioned area held a few stuffed animals, a ball, some scattered toys. "What's your name, dear? Celi? That's a nice name." She looked at Dumarest. "I can take care of this now. Thanks for bringing her."

He nodded and walked on. The crowd was thin for the time of day; late afternoon was prime for those on vacation or with a day off from work. Later would be better but if it was like the pattern of others, it would be far from what was desired. Poor attendances led to bad performances from those operating the sideshows. Already most would be grumbling.

Krystyna would be one of them.

Only a couple of clients waited outside her booth instead of the normal dozen and they were a pair wanting a joint reading. They dived through the flap as a woman emerged to stand, looking vaguely about, blinking as she saw Dumarest.

"Tall," she murmured. "All in gray—how did she know?"

A glimpse caught from a mirror reflecting the external scene and Dumarest could guess what the woman had been told. A stranger, waiting, who could guide her on her way. One who would steer her decision.

She said, "Pardon me, but could you—I mean, would you help me? She," a hand lifted to gesture toward the booth, "She said you would."

"How can I help?"

"Give me a color. Black or blond. Quickly now."

"Black." She was a brunette, young, and it was easy to guess torn with indecision over an emotional affair. Two suitors—which

103

should she choose? The old woman had craftily avoided any chance of being placed in the wrong.

"Black—that's Marek. I'm glad. So glad!" Her smile was radiant. "Thank you. Thank you so much!"

For telling her what she had wanted to hear. Dumarest watched her move away then thrust himself into the booth as the couple left. It was as he remembered; a shadowed dimness lit by a single, guttering flame. In her chair the cowled figure waited, silent as he slipped into the chair.

"Give me your hand."

He extended it, frowning, the voice though dry was not as he remembered. He caught the hand which moved toward his palm, gripped it, held it as he threw back the shielding cowl.

"Where's Krystyna?"

"Please!" The girl was young, her face marred by furrows which had torn her cheek and ruined her nose and upper lip. "The cowl."

Dumarest watched as the face disappeared into kindly darkness. An apprentice or someone filling in. The former, he guessed, for someone so scarred and lacking the funds to have the damage repaired opportunities of earning a living would be few.

She said, "If you want a reading give me your hand."

"No, give me yours." He heard the sudden intake of her breath as he ran a coin over her palm. "You've been badly taught, girl. Always have your hand crossed with silver before doing anything else. Here." He dropped the coin into her palm. "Where's Krystyna?"

"Resting."

"At this time of day?" He guessed the reason. "Is she just tired—or sick?"

He knew the answer as soon as he stepped into the cubicle she called home.

"The doctor," he snapped at the girl who had guided him. "Run to the infirmary and get medical aid."

Alone he stooped over the narrow cot and the supine figure it contained. Devoid of her shielding cowl the old woman looked like a mummified corpse. The skull was bald but for a few wisps of straggling white hair, the skin crèped and looking like leather. The eyes opened as Dumarest touched the scrawny throat.

"Water! I thirst! Give me water!"

A plea couched in a whisper which he barely heard. A small table stood beside the bed containing a decanter of water, a glass, a small bottle of some volatile liquid. A few crumbs lay scattered on a scrap of brightly colored paper; the remains of a snack bought at one of the stalls.

Dumarest poured the glass half-full, sniffed at it, held it to the parched lips. She drank as he supported her, lifting her almost upright, laying her back as she finished the water.

"You shouldn't be alone," he said. "I've sent for help."

"Which I don't need—and my own company's good enough."

"I'll pay for it." Dumarest guessed the reason for her objections. Quietly he added, "Who put you up to it, Mother?"

"What?" Her eyes were suddenly bright, wary. "I don't know what you're talking about."

"Yes you do."

"No, I—" She licked her lips. "My head hurts and I've a burning in my stomach. Leave me. I must sleep."

"The reading," he said. "Reiza brought me to you, remember? Who told you what to say?"

"A reading? You want a reading?" Her hand fumbled beneath her pillow and returned bearing the familiar deck. "Shuffle. You have to shuffle."

Dumarest said, harshly, "Quit trying to con me. I've handled an arcana deck too often not to know when one has been stripped. The pack I shuffled was too thin. You'd selected the right cards and made the switch after I'd finished with them." He leaned closer to the withered face. "Who told you to do it? Who told you what to say?"

The skull-like head rolled a little as, again, Krystyna licked her lips.

"Water! God! I burn!"

Dumarest could feel the heat of her as he lifted the thin body with his left hand. Water dribbled from the glass over her chin, spattering as it fell to her chest.

"Help's coming," he said as he put her down. "The girl is getting the doctor." And taking too long about it or the man was hard to find. "Now tell me who gave you the orders."

"Orders?"

"About the cards." Dumarest forced himself to be patient. The woman, old, afflicted by what ailed her, could be finding it hard to concentrate. "The reading. Reiza brought me to you. Who arranged with you to make the switch?" A thing easily done in the guttering candlelight; cards placed on the pack he'd shuffled from where they'd been kept hidden in a wide sleeve of the robe. "Who told you what to say?"

"Eh?"

"Who told you what to say?" The important question, one he repeated. "Who told you what to say? Tell me, damn you! Tell me!"

She responded to the raw anger in his tone, trying to rise in the bed, gasping as he supported her. Cards riffled from the gnarled hands to lie in a scatter on the bed, the floor. One lay face-up on her chest. The depiction of an hourglass.

Time—for him it was running out.

"Krystyna!" Dumarest leaned over her, fingers searching, finding no movement beneath the dry texture of her skin. "Krystyna!"

She was dying, already dead, showing no sign of a pulse in neck or wrist. Dumarest lowered his hands, thrust his clenched fists hard beneath the breastbone in a series of impacts against the heart. As again he made to check her pulse the doctor burst into the cubicle.

"Here, let me!"

He was skilled, fast and efficient, working with drugs, a hissing hypogun, trained massage. For long minutes Dumarest could do nothing but stand and watch.

Then, as the doctor straightened, shaking his head, the girl who had followed him into the cubicle said, "Will she be all right now?"

"No, I'm afraid not. She's dead."

"Dead?" Her voice rose a little. "But she was just tired and wanted to rest for a while. How can she be dead?"

The doctor glanced at Dumarest then at the girl. Gently he said, "It happens, my dear. Krystyna was very old. She could have gone at any time."

"But—"

"There's no more I can do." At the door the doctor paused, turning to look back at the dead woman. "I'll send men to take care of things. The best thing you can do, my dear, is to get back to work."

To the booth and the anodyne of effort. Dumarest caught her by the arm as the girl headed toward the door.

"Do you know if she was close to anyone in the circus? Or if anyone had a hold over her?"

"Krystyna? No." Her eyes were moist, soon the tears would flow. "Everyone loved her."

"That food." Dumarest nodded at the crumbs and paper. "Did you bring it to her?"

"No." Her lower lip began to tremble. Her head turned from him, hands rising to mask the ruin of her face. "Let me go now. Please let me go!"

He heard the fading noise of her running feet and turned for a last look at the cubicle, the body it contained. One surrounded by the cards she had used, one still held in her stiffening fingers.

Dumarest pulled it free and looked at the coils, the raised head, the iridescent scales. The Snake—the symbol of lies.

CHAPTER NINE

Dumarest heard the roar from the crowd, the following, pregnant silence and guessed that Reiza was heading for the grand finale of her act. A moment of tension in which Chang would rear before her, poised with claws extended, then to drop, one paw lashing out, the razor claw shearing through the fabric of her halter to release the confined breasts.

A dangerous trick requiring split-second timing and fine precision but one the crowd loved. As the roar came again, men yelling their appreciation, Dumarest moved quickly beneath the stands. Next would come the clowns, then, the ring cleared, the final procession. A time in which the artists would be engaged as would most of the roustabouts, the musicians, Zucco himself.

The best time for him to act.

He pressed on, heading toward Shakira's private quarters, with a deliberate economy of movement. A man dressed in functional blue glanced at him, recognized him and turned away. A guard or technician and Dumarest passed two others. In a secluded corner he had chosen from previous examinations of the area he knelt and produced rags from beneath his tunic, a bottle of volatile spirit from a pocket, a package of chemicals from another.

Fire fumed from his hand, caught the spirit-soaked rags and leaped in consuming hunger. As it grew he threw the chemicals on the flame and, as smoke billowed in thick, dark clouds from the fire, rose and ran down a curving passage.

The fire was harmless; the plastic membrane would not burn

but it would sag and shrivel in the heat. A true blaze would have been dangerous, the smoke was merely to give the impression of a holocaust.

"Fire!" Dumarest shouted as he ran. "Fire! Fire! Fire!"

The smoke followed him, filling the air with an acrid stench and blocking vision. A man, running, cannoned into Dumarest and reeled to one side. Another cursed and dived back into a room. Within seconds alarms sounded, adding to the confusion.

But that would not last. Trained, the circus personnel would soon isolate the source of the smoke, deal with it, have things returned to normal. Bare minutes in which Dumarest had to complete his plan.

A door opened beneath his hand. A panel ripped open to reveal a mass of printed circuits. The knife in his hand lifted to slash across the complex tracery, sparks arcing, fretting the edge. Damage which killed the lights and he hoped would negate Melome's protection.

The forces which could kill him if Shakira hadn't lied.

A gamble and luck was with him. The girl rose from her chair as he burst into her room, mouth opening to scream. Sound muffled by the hand he clamped over her mouth.

"Sing and I'll kill you," he snapped. "Scream and I'll do the same." A meaningless threat but she wasn't to know that and he felt her sag in the circle of his arm.

A length of fabric was tucked under his belt, one bearing a knot the size of an egg. He thrust it into her mouth, tied the gag firmly behind her head, and lifting the slight body threw it over his shoulder. As he left the room he heard a peculiar wailing scream from deeper in the secluded area. Another which followed it and which could have come from no human throat. As it died a burst of maniacal laughter jarred his ears and dewed his face with sweat.

"Easy," said Dumarest as the girl stiffened under his arm. "I'm not going to hurt you. I'm just going to take you for a ride. A trip to town. Just relax now."

He ran down the passage and back into the smoke. Men, invisible in the reeking, chemical fumes, shouted above the hiss of extinguishing sprays. Dumarest avoided them, racing along a remembered way, reaching the rollers of an air-trap, thrusting his way through them and halting at the door beyond. It was locked, the catch yielding to the pressure of his blade with a snap of broken metal. As it swung wide he dived through it, slammed it

110

shut and wedged it with a bin half-filled with a fibrous mass. The detritus of the filters above.

He raced past them, taking the stairs three at a time to reach another locked door at their summit. One which proved more stubborn than the last and he thinned his lips as he fought the catch. Time was against him. Already the fire must be under control, the ruse discovered and Melome missed. Unless he escaped soon he would not be able to escape at all.

The door yielded and he passed through to stand on the roof of the circus. All around reared the spires, towers, pinnacles of illusive spaciousness, the whole illuminated by the glow of the night sky. The starlight altered colors and he stood fighting to orient himself. That way? This? Beyond that minaret? That dome?

Long seconds in which he mentally reviewed what lay beneath the surface of the roof then, deciding, Dumarest loped over the firm covering. A twist, a turn and a long, curving convexity. A striped creation and there, nestling in a spot between rearing protrusions, he saw it. The raft he had stolen to reach the circus, apparently undiscovered and unharmed.

Placing the girl within its body he said, "Lie still now. Don't move and don't try to run. I'd rather not hurt you but unless you obey I'll knock you out. Understand?"

He saw her eyes, wide and terrified, limpid pools in the starlight. A creature tasting the terror she had so often aroused in others. One deserving of pity but his need was too great to allow of gentleness.

Dumarest swung himself into the raft and reached for the controls. They were slow to respond and he snarled, anger turning his face into the savage mask of a killing beast. Then the vehicle lifted, rising higher as he fed power to the antigrav units. Only when the circus had fallen far behind and below did he relax.

The girl stiffened as he touched her, gasped as he removed the gag.

"Don't sing," he said quickly. "Talk if you want but in a normal tone."

"What do you want of me?"

"You know what I want."

"But Tayu was giving it to you."

Dumarest said, harshly, "As and when he decided but it wasn't enough. I haven't the time to play his game."

111

"And you think I'll play yours?"

She had grown in more ways than one and Dumarest studied her in the starlight. A little more rounded and far more self-assured. She had called Shakira by his first name—how close had they become? How often had they talked and how often had he accelerated her growth? Each time she slept drugs could have shortened the months. Was he hoping to speed the development of her talent?

Dumarest said, "I need to find out one thing. When I have found it I'll have no further use for you. I'll give you money and you can go your own way. Return to the circus if that's what you want or move to another world. But I can't afford to wait."

"Because you are afraid?"

She paused then, as Dumarest made no answer, said, "You are afraid. But Tayu said it was a fear which made you strong. A challenge you'd accepted and, by accepting it, proved your courage."

"Did he tell you more?"

"The cause of your fear? No. But I think it has to do with something out there." Her hand lifted to point at the stars. "Something coming close."

Avro moved, a mind suspended in darkness as his body was immersed in the amniotic tank of his ship. A special vessel which he had used before when on a similar mission. The product of the Cyclan workshops and incorporating new techniques and discoveries which gave it an incredible velocity.

But, as fast as it was, for him it was still too slow.

Baatz was distant and Tron would be there before him. The cyber had been sent his orders and would obey them but the unknown factor could negate even the most carefully laid plan. If the agent proved less than reliable or made the fatal mistake of underestimating Dumarest. If an engine should fail or a generator develop a fault. If an animal should escape confinement and run wild in a killing frenzy—the possibilities were endless and, even though of a low order of probability, they had to be reckoned with. Only when Dumarest was safe and fast in his care would Avro be satisfied.

In the meantime he could do nothing but wait.

But to wait did not mean to be inactive.

Avro concentrated his mind. Already devoid of sensory irritations, it was only a moment before the Samatchazi formulae completed total detachment from reality. Only then did the engrafted Homochon elements become active. Rapport was immediate.

Avro expanded into something unique.

Each cyber had a different experience. For him it was as if he were a bubble moving in continuous motion in a medium of light interlaced with other bubbles. Minute globes which interspersed but never touched. Each, like himself, the living parts of an organism which stretched across the galaxy. All moving toward and coming from the glittering nexus which was Central Intelligence.

It absorbed his knowledge as if it were a sponge sucking water from a pool. Relaying orders in turn with the same efficiency. Mental communication which was almost instantaneous.

The rest was sheer intoxication.

Always, after rapport, was this period in which the Homochon elements returned to quiescence and the machinery of the body realigned itself to mental control. Avro drifted in a vast emptiness in which he sensed strange memories and unfamiliar situations; the scraps of overflow from other intelligences. A strange, near-telepathic affinity with things he would never see and men he would never meet.

A time of mental euphoria but, as he sobered, his mind pondered certain oddities.

The communication itself—had there been hints of illogic? Everything was proceeding as to the predetermined plan, but had he sensed a trace of irony? The disturbing suggestion of fanciful speculation?

Things unsuspected by any ordinary cyber but Avro knew what they did not. The degeneration of the brains which formed a part of the gestalt of Central Intelligence threatened the stability and very existence of the Cyclan. The rot had been checked, the affected brains reduced to atomic dust, but unless the basic cause was isolated and removed the degeneration would continue.

Had it already gone too far?

He concentrated, trying to isolate impressions, sifting through the mass of imposed data to find specific details. The disposition of agents revealed no fault but their placement was a matter of basic logic. The movement of ships with attendant instructions— why did Cyber Boyle need to go to Travante? A moment and he had the answer and with it a reassurance that the brains compris-

113

ing the organic computer at the heart of the Cyclan was not at fault. And yet still the nagging doubt remained.

Avro moved, feeling nothing in his amniotic tank, likening his existence to those who had gone before. The fortunate ones now sealed in their capsules, minds released from all physical irritations, free to think, speculate, extrapolate—was boredom the answer?

A question answered even as thought; no intelligent mind could ever get bored while problems remained to be solved. Those presented by the Cyclan would be minor in comparison to the greater questions governing the basic construction of the universe.

Had they, as he suspected, drifted into the construction of their own frames of reference? Building universes based on subtle alterations of present reality? The degenerated brains, perhaps, their observed insanity had been classic examples of aberrated thinking. Or had they been judged by too harsh a standard? Destroyed without due thought?

Questions already considered and certain answers had been found but only Dumarest could provide the concrete proof. Once the identity of an encapsulated mind could be transferred to a host-body real communication could be established. That and more—each mind could enjoy a surrogate life. Reward heaped on reward; potential immortality in a succession of young and virile bodies.

Virile?

Why had he thought of that?

A body was a machine and it was enough that it be functional. Beauty, agility, grace, charm were all unnecessary components. Youth was desirable because it extended the period of useful performance. The rest had no place.

And yet?

Avro spun in his tank as his mind became suffused with burning images. The mountains. The crystalline glitter of nests. The sheen of wings and the glow of sunlight warming pinnacle and crag. The moonlight which bathed the world in a silver, nacreous glow. The stars. The rain and cloud and gentle winds. The taste of crisp, morning air. The smell of grass. The soft impact of another living, breathing shape.

Madness!

A roiling succession of images, memories, accumulated data which tore at his mind and stability. Frightening, bursting in a crescendo which left him limp and gasping like the victim of a vicious attack. As he had been a victim but his enemy had been himself and it had been a foe without mercy.

Avro closed his hand and hit the emergency button set in the palm of his glove. Waiting as the fluid was drained from the tank and attendants came to strip him and restore him to an awareness of true reality. They had aged, paying for scientific achievement with their disturbed metabolism, unprotected as Avro had been in his tank. He watched them leave and, alone, sat and pondered his future.

He would be eliminated—that had been obvious from the first. Marle was using him as a prop in the barely possible event of failure. Should he succeed and bring Dumarest back to Cyclan Headquarters he would still be eliminated. His task done he would be expendable and used as an example to others. In Marle's place he would do the same.

And, as a servant of the Cyclan, he should acknowledge the punishment deserved and accept it.

Instead he had used his persuasion to gain his present mission; arguments based on irrefutable logic but had his main motivation been only to serve?

Or had he wanted to survive?

He leaned back, closing his eyes, conscious of the quiver of the ship as it hurtled through space but unable to feel it. As he was unable to feel hate and fear and love. But once, as an angel, he had known a new and different world.

One filled with smells and music. With taste and touch and physical reactions. Of wanting in biological heat, of concern and, yes, of hate and anger too. Emotions which had been strange and disturbing in their mind-unsettling effect. Now, sitting, he wondered what it would be like to live continuously with such things. To know the insanity of emotion as against the calm exercise of logical reason.

And why, during the interrogation, he had minimized his experience.

A precaution, followed with basic instinct, applied with calculated skill. Waking he had recognized his danger and done his best to guard against it. Now he was a living proof of Marle's inefficiency but, alone, that wasn't enough.

He had to capture Dumarest.

To win the secret he held.

The one thing which would ensure his potential immortality.

And he would win it. The man was boxed in a trap which

115

would shortly be surrounded by a cage. It was only a matter of time before he would be held and the secret obtained.

And Avro would be the master.

He opened his eyes and again pressed the button set into the glove now lying beside him. It was time for him to return to the tank. There to drift and dream and anticipate the power to come.

Melome said, "Earl, I'm cold. You're flying too high and I'm cold."

Dumarest turned from the controls and looked at her. She sat huddled in the body of the raft, small, pale in the starlight, knees drawn up to her chest, arms wrapped around her body. Her eyes followed him as he rose and came close.

"Cold? But the night is warm."

"I'm still cold." Her tone was petulant. "Look if you don't believe me." She held out an arm and he could see the goose-pimples marring the smoothness. She shivered a little as he touched her. "Please! Can't we go lower?"

"We aren't that high."

"Then land and build a fire or something. I'm freezing!"

Landing would waste time and to build a fire would be to advertise where they were. Did she want that? Dumarest touched her again and felt the chill of her skin. To one side lay the clown's disguise he had discarded and he lifted the fabric and wrapped it around her slim body.

"It won't be long," he soothed. "Once we hit the town I'll buy you some hot food and some new clothes. Gems too if you want them. Just be patient."

"I'm still cold."

A child or a stubborn young girl. It was hard to tell for even if the body matured the mind still retained its youth. Yet she seemed mentally alert and he guessed she wanted to exercise her power. To reassure herself that she held some measure of dominance. An attitude he encouraged; to beat her down would be to lose her cooperation.

Beneath him the raft tilted a little and he adjusted the controls, leveling it against the thrust of a vagrant wind. Rising he tried for clearer air and looked behind as the altitude increased. If there was pursuit it was invisible; the rafts riding without lights and staying low so as not to occlude the stars. A fault he was making but he was unfamiliar with the terrain and to ride too low was to invite destruction.

"Earl!"

"All right, Melome. We're going down."

The upper regions held chill winds which held an edge and he dropped the raft to its former level. Hunched in the clown's disguise the girl remained silent and, struck by a sudden suspicion, Dumarest went to kneel beside her.

"Listen to me," he said. "Do you feel ill? Odd? In any kind of pain?"

"I'm just cold."

"Did Shakira ever tell you what would happen to you if you ran away? Did he?"

"No."

"Be honest now."

"I told you. Tayu was good to me. Better than that bitch Kamala. Better than you—he didn't make me freeze."

"It won't be for long."

Dumarest frowned as he returned to the controls. He'd gambled that Shakira's threat had been a bluff and it seemed he'd guessed right. The girl was further proof; if anything, the owner would have safeguarded his property but apparently he'd made no effort to hold her. Nor to follow her; even if rafts had raced ahead to town they would have no idea from which direction he'd arrive.

And yet it seemed too easy.

The raft tilted again and he evened its flight. Below, silvered by the starlight, he could see massed vegetation broken by rearing outcrops of stone. Jagged masses which could rip the bottom from the raft if they dropped too low and he lifted the vehicle to allow for any sudden change in the terrain.

"Earl! Can't we land? Walk around for a while?"

A good suggestion if the girl was really cold but not if she was hoping for rescue. Dumarest looked at the stars but failed to gain a clear direction. The points were too many and he had taken an erratic course since leaving the circus. The wise course would be to rise high in order to spot the lights of the town. To delay too long would be to risk missing it altogether.

"Hold tight," he said. "We're going up."

"Earl!"

He ignored the protest as he sent the raft rising toward the stars. Up, beyond the layer of chill winds, higher to where the air stung like knives, higher still as breath plumed from his lips and, behind him, the girl wailed her anguish.

117

And still he couldn't spot the town.

Something was wrong and he sensed it as he lowered the vehicle. The distance between circus and town wasn't all that great and with the distance he had covered and the altitude he'd gained the lights should have been visible. Instead he'd seen nothing but endless, silvered darkness.

Crouching, he fingered the wires behind the control panel, touching the steering control, the direction indicator. A simple gyro-compass but one which seemed to have unusual additions. He jerked free a wire and watched as the needle kicked across the dial.

From where she sat Melome said, "Is something wrong?"

"No."

A lie—Shakira had been smarter than he'd thought. The controls had been tampered with and, instead of heading toward safety, the raft had swung in a wide circle and was now level with or behind the circus. Dumarest sent it wheeling toward the left, straightened as he watched the needle, fed power to the engines as the vehicle cut through the air. A velocity increased as he tilted the nose, gaining the pull of gravity in a long, downward slope. One reversed as the silvered darkness came too close. An extended seesaw motion which would baffle any observer.

Melome whimpered as the air tore at her hair, the covering she held wrapped tightly around her.

"Lie down," snapped Dumarest. "Roll against the side and keep below the rail. You'll feel warmer out of the wind."

But the wind increased to a whining drone as he fought for speed to cover distance. To rise again as the ground loomed beneath him, to reach his apex, to dive again toward the rock-studded vegetation.

To double in agony as it came close.

The pain was a fire tearing at nerve and mind and sinew. One which struck without warning to blur his vision and turn the world into a hell of screaming torment. Dumarest sank, quivering, sweat dewing face and neck and body with a liquid film. A time in which he was helpless, conscious only of the agony which dominated every cell of his body.

Then, as Melome screamed, it eased to vanish as quickly as it had come.

"Earl! Earl!"

The raft leveled as he grabbed at the controls, juddering, metal grating from one side as it glanced off an upthrusting finger of stone. Then it was riding clear and Dumarest gasped for breath, tasting blood, aware of the jerking quiver of his hands.

The pain had gone—but why had it come at all?

Shakira?

He had gambled the owner had been bluffing—had he lost the wager?

For a long moment Dumarest kept the raft riding scant yards above the ground, eyes narrowed as he followed a clear path. Distance covered while he gained time to think and then, again without warning, the agony returned.

To send him doubled, writhing, the raft slewing to one side, the nose lowering to hit the ground, the rock half-buried within it.

CHAPTER TEN

There were rustles and squeaks and small scampering noises as rodents foraged in the vegetation. Sounds as harmless as the wind but which caused Melome to quiver in fear. Like most who clung to urban places, for her the open at night was filled with imagined terrors.

"It's nothing," said Dumarest. "Just the wind and creatures hunting for food. Small creatures," he added quickly. "Things like mice. There's nothing big or harmful on Baatz."

"How can you be so sure?"

"It's the air. It leads to pacifism. A predator needs to stalk and kill in order to survive. It can't do that if it just wants to lie down and dream."

A facile explanation but it had elements of truth and Melome relaxed, leaning back to look at the sky.

"I'm not used to the open. It's too big, too empty. You could get lost and wander and starve and die and no one would ever know." She shivered a little. "And it's cold."

The truth—the air held a pre-dawn chill. Dumarest paused in his task of gathering twigs and rose, stretching. Behind him the raft lay on its side, the nose crumpled, the controls useless. They had been lucky. The impact had flung them from the open body to land on cushioning fronds and, aside from minor bruising, neither was hurt.

"Earl?"

"We'll have a fire before long." He stooped and ripped free another mass. Most was green but enough had dried to feed a

121

blaze. "Why don't you help? Pick some fuel and choose the lightest. Come on, now!"

She obeyed the snap in his voice and came toward him with a large bundle of fibrous strands. Dropping it she went for more while he arranged the fire, siting it before the raft so as to gain its protection against the wind. The open body would act as a reflector.

Fire winked as he stooped over a small heap of finely whittled twigs. It grew as he fed it with thicker pieces to steady into a red and glowing comfort topped by a rising plume of smoke.

"That's nice." Melome held out her hands to the warmth. She sat beside him, one shoulder touching his, the firelight touching the pale blondeness of her hair with dancing, russet glows. She looked less pale, more animated, her eyes holding a sharper expression. "Shouldn't you do something about the smoke?"

"No."

"They'll see it. If they come looking for us it'll guide them right here."

"I know."

"You want that?" She turned to look at him. "I don't understand. You stole me from Tayu and yet now you want them to find me and take me back to the circus. Why, Earl?"

He said, "The raft's wrecked and I don't know where we are. We've no supplies and this is hard country to make out in. Walking takes energy and we've no food to supply it. No water, either."

"So, unless they find us, we'll die. Is that it?"

"They'll find us."

"But I still don't understand why you stole me. I thought—" She broke off then, in a different tone, said, "I guess you just wanted me to sing for you. Is that it?"

The truth but he took his time admitting it. The firelight which gave her vivacity had also given her an unsuspected maturity. The pubescent girl had developed into a young and mature woman, one now touched by the magic of the night.

"Melome, I need—"

"I can give you what you need," she said. "I'm as much a woman as Reiza." Then, as he shook his head, "Why doubt it? Look at me. Touch me if you think I lie. Stop thinking of me as a child." She added, with a petulance which denied her claim to maturity, "Kamala kept me looking young. She thought a skinny girl would arouse sympathy and denied me certain things essential to my development. Tayu explained it all. I'm a certain physical type with a delayed pubescence but when it comes I catch up fast.'' The deep breath she took inflated her chest. "I've had drugs and hormones to help. Tayu wants me to be a real woman.''

"Did he tell you why?''

"It's something to do with my talent. That or—'' she shrugged. "Does it matter? I wanted to grow fast for you, Earl. Now you want to send me back.''

"I've no choice.''

"We could hide,'' she said. "Take a chance on finding our way. We might even spot another raft. One not from the circus. And I'll sing for you if you want. We'd be together and alone and I'll sing for you. Earl?''

He looked at her, a young, infatuated girl, and dangerous because of that. One who would deny him the use of her talent if he was curt in his rejection. Who could still withhold it should she doubt his intentions.

He said, "When you sing do you know what happens?''

"Those listening relive old terrors.''

"But can you control the reaction?'' He saw the shift of her eyes. "In a sense they move back in time,'' he said. "Become young again or not so young. Does the song govern that? And do you govern the song?''

"Earl! Look! A falling star!''

He ignored the arm she lifted, the finger she used to point at the bright streak against the sky.

"When you sang for me in the circus did you obey Shakira's orders as to how far to send me back?''

"Earl! Look! Another!''

She gasped as he caught her arm and turned her to face him. Her eyes widened as she saw his face, read his expression, the turmoil of his emotions.

"No! No, Earl! Please!''

A child caught in a web despite her protestations of maturity. Obeying orders, delaying him, keeping him locked in the prison of his own making.

One on which Shakira had turned the key.

The threat had been no bluff—the pain had proved that. Agony which had left him helpless and which would return should he attempt to escape. He remembered the card Krystyna had let fall toward the last. The Hourglass, the symbol of time.

123

How long did he have?

"Earl! Don't hurt me! Please don't hurt me!"

Who was the Snake?

"Earl!" Melome's voice rose as fear robbed her of confidence. Tears filled the luminous eyes and her lips trembled as he reached for her. "No! Don't! Please don't—"

She fell silent as his hand touched her hair, followed it over the curve of her head and shoulders. A soothing caress to which she responded, coming closer, resting her head against his shoulder as his arm closed around her shoulders.

He said, "You don't have to fear me, Melome. I'd never hurt you. I want you to believe that."

"I do." Her voice was muffled against his tunic. "It was just the way you looked at me. You were so savage."

"I was thinking of someone else."

"Tayu?"

"No."

"Zucco? Reiza?" Her voice took on a note of jealousy. "Who do you hate so much, Earl?"

"It doesn't matter."

"No," she said. "As long as it isn't me." She snuggled a little closer. "You're strong," she murmured. "So strong. I felt it from the very first. In the market when you made the deal with Kamala. I wanted to sing for you and then she told me. Well, you're here now and that's all that matters. Together we're safe."

"Yes." Dumarest fed more fuel to the fire. "Who else lives where you do in Shakira's private quarters? Have you seen them? Talked to them?"

"One. Elagonya's nice."

"What does she look like?"

"I don't know. I've never seen her. She wears a cloth over her head."

"Old? Young? How does she sound?"

"Like music. I asked Tayu about her once and he said she had a very special talent. He didn't tell me what it was but I think she makes dolls. I saw some in her room."

Dumarest said, "Did they look like anyone you know?"

"No, they were just dolls. Small, about that tall." Her hands measured a distance. "Some of them were very old."

"And her room, was it decorated with strange signs? Like those the fortune tellers used in the market."

"I didn't see any." Melome twisted in his arm to look at him. "Why so interested, Earl? What's Elagonya to you?"

"Nothing, but I knew someone once who made dolls. She tried to use them to hurt people."

"Not Elagonya." Her tone was emphatic. "She's too nice."

To her, perhaps, but to strangers she could be different. A sensitive, hidden away, unwilling even to reveal her face—what hatred could such a creature harbor against normal people?

"Earl, you're worried. I can tell it." Against him Melome stirred, relaxing as she yielded to the pressure of his arm. "Maybe I can help. Tell me why you're so worried."

"Forget it now. Just listen to the wind." It sighed as it caressed the silvered fronds, a susurration which filled the air. "And the crackle of the fire. It's like music, isn't it. And watch the stars. Perhaps more will fall. When one does you're supposed to make a wish. Did you know that?"

She muttered, sleepily, "Will the wish come true?"

"It might. So make sure it's a good one." His voice droned on, soothing, hypnotic in its comforting reassurance. He felt the weight of her slender body as she slumped against him, the sound of her deep, regular breathing. "Melome? Melome, are you asleep?"

A sigh was his answer and he fell silent looking at the fire, the smoke, the wheel of the paling stars.

The raft came two hours after dawn arrowing from the horizon directly toward the rising pillar of smoke. Dumarest watched it from where he lay buried in the vegetation far to one side of the fire. Melome, still asleep, lay where he had placed her close to the shelter of the wrecked vehicle.

She woke as the raft landed, rearing upright as Zucco strode toward her. He was tall, arrogant, wearing yellow and black, cruel colors which matched the expression on his face. The wand in his hand reached out, touched her arm, drew back as she screamed.

"Hurts, doesn't it, you bitch. Think of it the next time you're tempted to run from the circus. Where's the scum who helped you?"

"I didn't run! I—" She screamed again as the wand touched her body. "No! Don't hurt me! Please don't hurt me!"

"Where's Dumarest?"

"I don't know! I was asleep!"

"Where's Dumarest?" The tip of the wand hovered an inch from her face. "Why is he so interested in you? What can you do for him?" A sneer thickened his tone. "Aside from the obvious, that is. Talk, damn you! Talk!"

From where he sat at the controls of the raft Valaban said, "Take it easy, Jac. This isn't the way to handle the situation. The girl isn't to blame."

"Stay out of this!"

"I'm in it. Shakira—"

"Never mind him. I'm in charge and I don't intend wasting time. If you don't like it then you know what you can do." Zucco returned his attention to Melome. "Well, bitch, are you going to talk?"

"We crashed. I fell asleep. When I woke he had gone." Her arm waved at the surrounding vegetation. "He must have tried to make it on foot."

"In which case we can spot him." Valaban jumped down from the raft, staggered a little, regained his balance. "He must have left tracks and couldn't have got far. Let's load the girl and go looking."

"I told you to stay out of this." Zucco's voice was cold. "The next time you open your mouth I'll shut it for good."

"You could try." Valaban took a step closer, one hand buried beneath his blouse. "But it'll earn you a ruined face. I may be old and slow but this makes us equal." His hand appeared holding a flat gun, a twin to the weapon Reiza carried in the ring. "Now let's load the girl and lift. For all you know Dumarest could be within yards of us. Maybe hiding under the wreck and waiting his chance to jump us."

The truth but he had realized it too late. As he had guessed wrong as to the location. Like an animal, Dumarest had moved silently through the vegetation, taking advantage of the argument to get close, rising to lunge forward as Zucco turned to face the girl.

Valaban fell as Dumarest slammed against him, snatching the gun to level it as Zucco turned, snarling, the wand lifted in his hand.

"Drop it!" Dumarest fired as the man hesitated, the shot whining inches to one side of Zucco's body. "The next one you get in the face. Now drop that wand!"

He stepped forward as it hit the ground, thrusting back the

126

man with the heel of his left hand, the muzzle of the gun held steady in his right.

"Melome! Get up and get over here. Move!" He didn't look toward her as she obeyed. "Take hold of his hand, girl. Grip it tight."

"No. I don't want to touch him."

"He won't hurt you." Dumarest stepped back as he heard a rustle to his rear. "Stay out of this, Valaban. Move over to the fire and lie face down. And you," he snapped at Zucco as the old man obeyed. "Down and kiss the dirt."

"Go to hell!"

"You've a choice." Dumarest tightened his finger on the trigger. "You've three seconds to make it."

A moment and Zucco was down, lying with his face to the dirt, trembling with the helpless rage which consumed him.

"Right, girl, put your hand on his neck." A glance at his face and she obeyed. "Now sing, Melome. Sing!"

Dumarest jammed his hands against his ears as the air filled with the wailing cadences of her song.

It was different, driving through the bone and flesh and muscle of his hands, without the wail of pipe and pulse of drum and yet still it caught at his mind and sent it wheeling in a succession of phantom images. An effect lacking its true power because of the lack of contact. From where he lay beside the fire Valaban groaned and cupped his ears with veined and blotched hands.

Zucco lay as if dead.

A man lost in terror—a captive of the song.

Bound and helpless by the fantasies of his mind and suffering a greater punishment than any physical torment. Dumarest watched him and then, as Melome looked toward him, dropped one hand and sliced the edge across his throat.

An unmistakable signal and he lowered the other hand as she broke off her song.

"Into the raft, girl. Quickly!"

He followed her into the vehicle as Valaban sat upright, shaking his head. It rose as Zucco twitched, climbing as the man rolled over to sit with his face buried in his hands. Figures which dwindled as the craft soared into the sky.

"You did it!" Melome came to sit beside him. "You got us away."

"For now."

"You had it planned," she said. Her voice was excited; a

youngster enjoying a treat. "You left me asleep to act as bait and then, when they didn't expect it, you attacked. But what if there had been more?"

"Your song would have taken care of them."

"A weapon," she said. "You used it as a weapon. But I wasn't in contact so—" She answered her own question. "Zucco. You had him helpless. They would have had to obey." She laughed with pure delight. "Earl! You're so clever!"

Lucky would have been a better word. Had Zucco not given way to his spite, pandered to his sadism, the plan would have failed. As it could still fail.

Dumarest checked the controls. The raft was moving as it should in the direction indicated on the instrument but he sensed something was wrong. Why had Zucco come for them at all? Why had Valaban come with him? Any crew would have done and the circus had rafts and men to spare.

Questions lost in a sudden blast of pain.

As before it came without warning, a red tide of agony which doubled him over the controls and filled the universe with screaming torment. An eternity which lasted for seconds for when he could see again the raft was still on an even path, the ground below no different from what he remembered.

"Earl?" Melome was beside him. "Is something wrong?"

"Can you handle a raft?" A stupid question; how could she have learned. "Listen," he said urgently, "if anything happens. If I should fall sick, touch nothing. Understand? Stay away from the controls."

"Yes, Earl, but—"

The rest was lost as again fire caressed him, acid burned every nerve, vises crushed bones and sinew. A man flayed and set unprotected in the sun. As if smeared with honey and covered with ants. Boiled, broken, seared—all the torments ever devised inflicted in a wave of utter torment.

"Earl!"

Sweating, he reached for the controls. The escape had been an illusion, the trap Shakira had constructed still held him fast. More pain would come and more after that until he was helpless to do more than breathe. And Melome was in the raft, frightened, liable to do anything in her panic.

"Please, Earl, talk to me. What's happening?" She caught at his arm as the raft began to turn. "What are you doing? Where are we going?"

128

"To the circus," he said. "Back to Shakira."

He sat in his office of a dozen scents; odors and tangs echoing strange and alien places. Again he wore lavender, this time ornamented with a tracery of black which gave the appearance of somber scales.

"Be seated, Earl." A hand gestured toward the chair facing the wide desk behind which he sat. "I'm sure there is no need to warn you of attempted violence. You have had time enough to realize its futility."

Too much time. Hours during which he had been locked in a cubicle, given food, water, allowed to sleep after bathing. Time enough for Melome to be swallowed into the circus, for Zucco and Valaban to be rescued.

Dumarest said, "Why did you send them to recover the girl?"

An unexpected question and Shakira paused before replying.

"Someone had to go and they were best suited."

"An old man and a sadist?"

"Coincidence."

"No," said Dumarest. "Not coincidence but intent. Did you want them both out of the way at the same time? Or did you hope I would do what you seem to lack the courage to do?"

"And that is?"

"Zucco is ambitious. He yearns for power and intends to get it. Resents having to take orders. You are old. Need I say more?"

"You imagine he thinks of killing me and taking over the circus?" Shakira lifted his hands in the sudden, upward gesture. As he lowered them he said, "Do you really think it would be as simple as that? For a barbarian, perhaps, but we are not barbarians. There are considerations of finance, administration, loyalties, contracts. Those who work for the circus of Chen Wei would not be eager to follow a murderer. Would you?"

"If I had the choice, no."

"You are bitter," said Shakira. "You are thinking of the pain. The agony you had to bear as the price of your disobedience. But why blame me for that? I warned you what could happen and you chose to disregard that warning. Or you thought it a bluff. A mistake—I never bluff. Those who know me would have told you that."

"Reiza, for example?" Dumarest watched as Shakira made no movement. "Krystyna? Valaban? Helga, even? Melome? Who

129

knows you, Shakira? Who really knows you? Elagonya? Your tame sensitive. Does she know what you are?"

"Shrewd," murmured Shakira. "I sensed it from the first. Shrewd and cunning and with a primeval instinct for survival which operates on an intuitive level. Which is why I was glad when you agreed to work for me."

"Work," said Dumarest. "As yet I've done nothing but walk around and let myself be seen. You didn't want me for that."

"You are wrong, but there is more."

"What?"

"You will learn soon enough." Shakira rose and stepped from his desk. "But first let me introduce you to Elagonya."

She sat in a cubicle thick with the fumes of aromatic incense but despite the pungent smoke the air held an acrid stench. One based on corrosive acids, alien exudations and warning odors. A blend which caught at his nostrils and Dumarest wondered why Melome hadn't mentioned it.

Shakira gave the explanation.

"You are a stranger," he said. "A hostile intrusion into her environment. For the sake of your life, I warn you not to be violent. Do not even think of extracting revenge. Before you could act you would be dead."

"A telepath?"

"No, but with you she has a rapport. One built on fragments of your blood, tissue, muscle, bone. A focal point for her directed thought. Sometimes she incorporates it into a doll."

Small artifacts which Dumarest could see lying around. Crude things with vacuous faces and oddly distorted bodies. The product of unskilled hands or hands so disfigured that they were incapable of normal dexterity.

"I found her on Tomzich, a world in the Bannerheim Cluster. She was living in a cave at the edge of a village living on scraps and hiding from the light of day. A mutant, hated by those from whom she had sprung. At times she cursed them and, at times, those cursed would die. They called her a witch and would have killed her had they been able." Shakira stepped forward and rested one hand on the rounded hump of a shoulder. "My dear," he said gently. "Have I your permission to reveal your face?"

The masked figure turned to face Dumarest, the covered head seeming to tilt as if to question.

He said evenly, "As you wish, my lady. Here, at this time, I am at your command."

Shakira lifted the cloth.

Elagonya was a parody of what a woman should have been. The victim of cruel nature which, tormented by the blasting radiation which had distorted the pattern of genes, had taken a vicious revenge. The face was a jumble of features, one eye higher than the other, the mouth a twisted gash, the chin cleft so that it was forked, the nose the grotesque appendage of a clown. Lank hair hung like worms from a peaked skull and the eyes, muddy brown, flecked with yellow and red, looked like the dusty windows of an empty house.

"No surgery can aid her," said Shakira. "No drugs or treatment alleviate her condition."

It must have been a living hell. Dumarest looked at the warted encrustations on the skin, the puffed cysts marring the lines of the scalp. The gown she wore came high up the throat and covered the arms and legs to touch the floor but he could guess at the condition of the body it covered.

The whisper of her voice was the thin grate of a nail on slate.

"You look at me and do not cringe. Are you so accustomed to horror?"

"That is not what I see, my lady."

"You mock me?" For a moment tension stiffened the air and Dumarest heard Shakira's sharp inhalation, the touch of something like a feather against the naked surface of his mind. And then, as if he had been tested and had passed the test, the tension vanished. "No," she whispered. "You do not mock. Yet I do not need your pity."

"Something else, then?" A question to which she gave no answer and Dumarest continued, "We are what we are, my lady, and have no hand in our making. Therefore we should not be blamed for what we cannot help. Nor derided. Nor abused. But to deny pity is to reject what is good in a person. And there are those who, if they were you, would beg for more than pity."

"A quick and merciful end—you offer me that?"

"If I did, would you accept it?"

"No." The denial was sharp. "I live and while I live I serve. I can help those who have been kind." A sleeve lifted to reveal a knotted appendage which touched Shakira's hand. "Save your pity for those who need it. I do not."

Dumarest bowed, lowering his eyes.

"Yet you have been kind and merciful in your fashion. Tayu!" He lowered the cloth to hide the ravaged features, the fabric

131

softening the harsh timbre of the whispering voice. "Therefore, from me to you, something to remember."

The touch came again, a feather on the mind followed by a wave of pleasure so intense as to send his mind spinning in a vortex of indescribable ecstasy. One which blinded him to the journey back and left him shaken and gasping in Shakira's office.

"Her talent, Earl." The owner offered him a glass of wine. "The reverse of the coin she can spin at will. Pleasure and pain. Reward and punishment. Ironic, isn't it, that such power should be housed in such a frame."

The price paid by most sensitives for their talent; physical weakness and deformity, but Elagonya had paid higher than most. How many others like her did Shakira keep in his private quarters? And how to break the hold she had over him?

Dumarest said, "In order to function she needs a focal point."

"That is so." Shakira lifted his own glass of wine. "You had no choice but others are more cautious. Also her ability is limited." He sipped and swallowed and, looking at his glass, added, "I wanted you to realize how helpless you are, Earl. Run and pain will torment you. Attempt violence against me and you will be rendered helpless. Elagonya's talent has fabricated an affinity between you. In a sense you are an extension of her body."

"And?"

"That makes you mine, Earl. A part of the circus of Chen Wei."

CHAPTER ELEVEN

———•—•——•—•———

In a gallery a man was protesting, his voice high, edged with anger, "You cheated me! Sold me rubbish! That's bad enough but you took me for a fool. No one does that and gets away with it!"

"Easy, mister." The grafter, small, wizened, spread his hands in an age-old gesture. "There's no need for temper. You got what you paid for, right?"

"Wrong! A liquid which turns metal into gold—the damned stuff wears off after a day!"

And he had spent more than its cost in coming back to complain. An awkward one. A noise. He turned as Dumarest touched his arm.

"I'm an assistant market-inspector attached to the circus from the main office, sir." A lie the man was willing to accept especially when Dumarest continued, "As I see it you have a good case. You can prosecute or come to some settlement. Naturally we'd prefer you to prosecute; thieves like this mustn't be allowed to rob honest people. Are you willing to place charges?"

"Well—"

"Of course if you prosecute you'll have to attend court and pay certain charges which you can later claim against the defendant should the verdict go against him. And it will take some of your time. The preliminary hearing, the depositions, witnesses and their statements—naturally you have proof of purchase?"

"No." The man scowled. "Look, must I go through all that? It's time and expense I may never recover."

"You'd rather settle without formality?" Dumarest registered his disapproval. "Well, it is your right, of course, but hardly fair to others. But if that's the way you want it go ahead."

"A creep." The grafter scowled as the man, his purchase price refunded, moved away. "What the hell did he expect for a lousy kobold? Thanks for taking care of it, Earl."

"Forget it. How's trade?"

"Bad and getting worse. Why doesn't Shakira up stakes and move?"

"Ask Zucco—he's the one dragging his feet."

A suggestion he'd sown and which would spread like wildfire and if it created discord between the owner and the ringmaster Dumarest would be satisfied.

The gallery ended and he entered another familiar in its scenes of torture and pain. A woman stood before a tableau dimmed with shadows which shrouded the depicted figures in brooding menace. Tall, robed figures in scarlet watching the victim as he strained against his bonds. One lying supine on a bench, face contorted, bulging eyes fastened on the razor-edge of the curved blade swinging above him. A pendulum which lowered by degrees until it would slice through skin and fat and flesh and inner organs.

"Horrible!" She shuddered as Dumarest halted beside her. "The things people imagine! Could a thing like that really have happened?"

Too often and in too many places and he said so, not softening his words.

"But those men. They're cybers. The Cyclan doesn't operate like that."

"Those aren't cybers."

"No?" She turned to face him and Dumarest saw the glint of amusement in her eyes, the quirk of lips artificially enhanced. A matron on the prowl knowing the erotic stimulus of depicted agony and willing to respond to any advance he might choose to make. "They look like them."

"What do you know of the Cyclan?"

"Me? Not much but I've a cousin who tried to join them. That was on Pikodov—my home world. Then I married and we settled here. A mistake, I was widowed within five years."

"And Juan?"

He was really involved. That's how I know what they look like. Cybers, I mean. One used to come to the house to give initial instruction or make tests or something. Odd me seeing these." She gestured at the tableau. "I saw one only this morning in town."

"A cyber?"

"That's right. At the Dubedat Hotel. I'm staying there." Her voice was suggestive. "A big room and I'm all alone and I hate not having company."

"If I'm free we'll have dinner tonight," said Dumarest. "Had the cyber just arrived?"

"No. Someone told me he'd booked in a day or so ago."

When he'd run with Melome from the circus. When Zucco and Valaban had been sent after him. Coincidence—or design?

A question Dumarest pondered as he moved on to the shadowed area beneath the stands. It was between performances, the ring holding the dilapidated, slightly tatty air such places always did when the lights dimmed and the stands were empty. Some men raked the sand, smoothing and cleaning the surface while others worked in the tiers. Routine tasks which would soon be completed.

Citizens of a world of which Shakira had made him a part.

A close, snug, normally safe world but a prison to a man used to the spaces between the stars. Dumarest moved on, conscious of the partitions which reared too close, of passageways too narrow and ceilings too low. They lifted as he moved deeper beneath the stands but still the sense of confinement remained. That and the warning prickle of danger which he had learned never to ignore.

"Hi!" Valaban lifted a hand in salute as Dumarest came toward the cage in which he stood. "Be with you in a second, Earl."

He stooped over the limp body of a feline, hands deft, fingers probing, grunting as he jerked a splinter from the thick, black fur. A slender shaft, pointed, tipped with a tuft of wool at the thick end.

"Nice." He handed it to Dumarest and slammed shut the cage. "Some bastard wanted a little fun and used a blowpipe. I've warned Reiza about that trick of hers but she won't listen. She'd be crazy to try it anywhere else."

135

Dumarest turned the dart in his fingers. "Do you get much of this?"

"Not on Baatz. Other worlds are different. You'd think people would have more sense but they want more than entertainment. They want blood."

"Maybe they should be catered to," Dumarest handed back the dart. "Fights," he explained. "Open bouts and championships. Mixed pairs, even. Bets on first blood, third or to the death. There's money in it. I'm surprised you aren't running them."

"Shakira wouldn't hear of it."

"How about Zucco?"

"Maybe, but Zucco isn't the boss." Valaban looked at the limp body in the cage. "But he's good at his job. He saw the cat twitch and gave the signal without delay. Before it could jump the clowns went in with gas and knocked it out. It'll recover soon."

"And Reiza?"

"Lucky—but mad as hell."

"About the cat?"

Valaban hesitated then said, "Look, Earl, maybe it's none of my business but it wouldn't do any harm for you to be careful. When we got back she spent some time with Zucco. They were talking and she didn't like what he said. I guess you haven't seen her since you left?"

"No. I've been busy."

"And she's been alone. Thinking, brooding—remember what I told you about cats and women? You can't trust either. And she's handy with that whip."

Too handy. Dumarest felt the bite of it as he turned. The raw sting as again the lash touched his cheek.

Facing him Reiza said, "You bastard! This time you lose your eyes!"

She wore a gown of yellow edged with black, draped so as to bare one shoulder, belted at the waist, the fabric taut over the mounds of her breasts, the swell of her hips and thighs. A garment designed to enhance her femininity but there was nothing soft or gentle about her face or eyes. It was the mask of a tiger illuminated by the narrowed, blazing slits of rampant jealousy. Her voice carried the echo of the crack of the whip she held in her right hand.

Backing, Dumarest said, "Reiza! Be careful!"

"Like hell I'll be careful!" The lash tore the air before her. "I trusted you! Wanted you! Loved you more than I'd ever loved anyone before. And you run off with that pallid freak. Spent the night with her under the stars. How was she, Earl? Did you lie to her too? Tell her you loved her? Use her as you used me!"

He said, "Reiza! Shut up and listen!"

"I've listened to all I want. I've heard how you were found snuggling close. How she clung to you and cried when you parted. The state she was in. You dirty swine! You filth! To prefer that bitch to me!"

Jealousy bordering on madness. Dumarest dodged as the lash tore at his face, feeling the wind of it, the heat of its passing. Leather moving at supersonic speed and able to slice flesh as if it had been a knife. To kill a fly without disturbing the sweat it was drinking—or to tear out an eye as a man would thumb a pea from its pod.

A threat he had faced before and from the same source but now there was a difference. Then she had been playing, teasing him as a cat would tease a mouse, enjoying the game and the demonstration of her skill. Now she wanted to hurt, to maim and blind—and she had the ability to do it.

"Reiza, listen to me." Again Dumarest dodged, the whip slicing the plastic of his tunic at one shoulder. "Damn you, woman, listen! To Valaban if not to me. He was there. He'll tell you what he saw."

"I know what he saw. If he says different he'll be lying. You were with that girl. That freak Melome. You slept with her. You chose her over me. Me!"

A woman too much like a cat. One who had suffered imagined insult and who now wanted nothing but a savage revenge.

Dumarest backed as the lash whined toward his face, felt the bars of the cage slam against his spine, moved quickly to one side the thong hitting metal. A grab and he had it in his hand, a twist and it was around his knuckles. A moment in which each faced the other as she pulled and then, with a sudden jerk, he had thrown her off balance, to stagger, to trip over his foot, to sprawl in an ungainly heap on the littered floor.

She screamed in fury as he slammed his foot hard on the hand holding the whip.

"Jac! Kill him, Jac! Kill him!"

137

Dumarest stooped, snatched up the whip and rose with it in his hand. Zucco stepped from the shadows as he turned, tall in his ringmaster finery, his own whip lifted before him. One he lost as Dumarest sent his lash against the tall stock, ripping it from the other's grasp and sending it flying to one side.

"Jac!" Reiza almost sobbed in her rage as she rose to her feet, one hand nursing her bruised wrist. "Kill him! Kill him and I'm yours!"

"You have always been mine." Zucco looked at Dumarest. "Do you understand, you poor fool? She went with you for a whim. A momentary passion which I permitted for reasons of my own. Later, perhaps, we shall laugh at your ineptitude."

"As you laughed at Hayter's death?" Dumarest saw the cold, sneering mask of the ringmaster change a little. "You did kill him, didn't you? You wanted the woman that badly. So you made sure he carried a scent which would turn the cats into a fury. The act of a coward—but what else are you?"

"Your better," said Zucco tightly. "Your superior. Now and at any time."

"As you demonstrated in the sump." Dumarest shrugged and half-turned toward Reiza, the whip dangling in his hand. "If you want revenge," he said, "pick yourself another champion. Only a man has the guts to fight for a woman he wants. Zucco hasn't got what it takes."

"You think not?"

"He's a murderer, a liar, a cheat and a thief. Things once said about me. Maybe the accusation holds an element of truth. But I'm not a coward."

"Neither is Jac." Reiza looked at Zucco. "Please, don't shame me. Kill him and take me in any way you want—but kill him. Kill him!"

"He can't," said Dumarest. "Not in the open. Not when I'm unchained and he hasn't got a gun and some bullies like Ruval to back him up. Scum like Zucco work in the dark with poison and hired assassins. Take him for what he is if you want him so badly. Let him own you, use you, beat you as he wants. But never make the mistake of thinking him a man."

Her laughter surprised him. "You think that? You believe him helpless? Afraid? Jac!"

"A challenge," he said, and smiled, standing relaxed, arrogant in his confidence. "Us facing each other on equal terms.

138

Armed with knives and battling to the death. Is that what you have in mind?''

From where he stood Valaban said, urgently, "Don't listen to him, Earl. Don't let him goad you. Let him have the bitch and good riddance. She isn't worth fighting over." ~

"Shut up, you old fool!" Reiza snapped her anger. "Stay out of this."

Dumarest ignored them both. To Zucco he said, "I don't fight for nothing. If we meet what is the prize?"

"The girl. I win and she is mine. If you beat me—"

"I gain nothing," said Dumarest. "I don't want her."

"The pleasure of killing me then—if you can."

"I can do that now." Steel glimmered as Dumarest jerked free the blade from the stock of the whip he held. "In fact I'd be a fool not to. So—"

"No!" Shakira stepped forward from where he had stood watching from the shadows. He wore emerald traced with silver, ornamentation which caught and reflected the light to clothe him in the semblance of shimmering scales. Gleams Dumarest had spotted before Zucco had made his challenge. "There will be no murder. A fair fight is another matter."

Dumarest shrugged and lowered the blade. "Why give an enemy the chance of killing you?"

"You think he could?"

"All fights are gambles."

"And all gamblers need a wager. For what would you risk your life?"

"Unlimited access to Melome," said Dumarest. "The end of a certain inconvenience. Money and freedom to travel and medical aid should I need it. The aid to be given without charge."

"Agreed. And for you." Shakira turned to Zucco. "What you have always wanted. The control of the circus of Chen Wei."

"And me," said Reiza. "In any way you want." Then, to Dumarest, she said, "Think of that when he's killing you."

"You're sure he can do that?"

"I'm certain of it." Her voice was high, triumphant. "You're a fighter, Earl, but so is Jac. He was a champion before he joined the circus—and he bears no scars!"

Valaban filled his palm with a pungent oil and, as he rubbed it over Dumarest's naked torso, said, "This is crazy, Earl. I tried to warn you. Why the hell didn't you listen to me?"

"How good is Zucco?"

"You heard Reiza." Valaban rubbed harder. "The bitch," he said bitterly. "I tried to tell her he was lying but she wouldn't listen. She didn't want to listen. Just like a cat. You think you own one then it up and leaves for someone else. No loyalty. No gratitude."

"She was upset."

"Sure, but would a normal woman have acted that way? At least she'd have given you the chance to explain. She didn't even turn a hair when you mentioned Hayter. Did you notice that? It's my guess she's known all along. Maybe that's what attracted her to Zucco—a pair of animals together. Well, to hell with her. Just watch out for yourself." Valaban scowled at the noise coming from the seats beyond the tunnel. "Listen to them! They should be in a cage!"

They filled the rows closest to the ring, cramming tight for the sake of a better view. Entrepreneurs abandoning their concessions, grafters, dancers, spielers, shills all able and willing to relinquish a profit for the sake of witnessing a bloody entertainment. And others from the circus proper; roustabouts, artists, clowns, technicians. Their voices droned like a swarm of bees.

Dumarest watched them from the mouth of the tunnel as he wiped his body free of surplus oil. A trace remained on his hands and he stooped to rub them in the sand; oil which would prevent an opponent from getting a hold had no place on fingers needing to grip a hilt. Straightening he heard a shout and saw Zucco step from the mouth of a tunnel opposite.

"Right, Earl," said Valaban. "I guess this is it. Go out and gut the bastard!"

A sentiment echoed in a roar as Dumarest stepped into the ring.

One he had heard too often before.

The cry of a beast scenting blood, mindless, unthinking, eager only to witness battle and agony. To see the spurt of crimson, the writhing of lacerated flesh, the screams of the maimed and dying, the final convulsions. To know the euphoria of vicarious combat. To bet and gloat if they won and to curse the vanquished if they lost.

A sound as familiar to Zucco as to himself.

Dumarest knew it as the man came forward, naked aside from shorts, his body bearing the sheen of oil. He ignored the crowd as he trod the sand, smiling, eyes narrowed as he summed up the opposition. And Reiza had told the truth—Zucco bore no scars.

The sign of a novice or of a victor who had never known the ice-burn of a razor's edge. One too fast to be touched, too deft, too cunning. An unmarked champion. A thing so rare as to be almost unknown and Dumarest wondered how Zucco had managed it. Bribes, fixes, special blades which oozed red but did not cut could provide a show and safety for those involved. Things common in booths where men offered to fight all comers for cash or put on spectacles for gaping yokels. But the cognoscenti of the arena would never be so easily deluded—and no man could become a champion without their support.

"You fear." Zucco halted, facing Dumarest, the space of yards between them. "I can smell your sweat. Yet the crowd is with you." His smile turned into a sneer. "Let them shout— soon they will have cause to regret their mindless braying. As you will have cause to regret your temerity."

Dumarest made no comment, standing poised on the balls of his feet, ready to move in any direction. Zucco seemed more at ease, relaxed, the knife in his right hand hanging at his side. Ten inches of curved and pointed steel, burnished to a mirror brightness, honed and tempered to cut through bone. An inch longer than Dumarest's own blade but it was one he was accustomed to and this was no time to change.

"Yield," said Zucco. "I give you the chance. Throw down your knife and admit defeat. Better to serve than to die and, if you obey, I'll let you have the woman."

"Does she know that?"

"What she knows or wants is of no importance. Soon I shall be the master. Then—"

He broke off as Dumarest lunged, darting to one side, his blade rising to clash against the one Dumarest thrust toward him. An open attack and an easy feint but the speed at which Zucco acted was illuminating. As was the quick move he made to one side away from a second attack.

"You are impatient, my friend." His smile held no humor. "And clumsy, too—your attack had no grace. A tyro would have done as well. I wonder you managed to survive so long."

"Talk," sneered Dumarest. He stumbled as he moved to one side, as clumsy as Zucco had said. "Is that how you win? Bore your opponents to death?"

"No." Zucco crouched a little, knife held forward like a sword, point slanted upward. "I cut them, my friend. I slash their veins to make them bleed and their tendons so as to leave them crippled. I blind them and watch as they grope in the dark. I nick their jugulars and hamstring them and, at times, I ruin them as men." The point dropped, darted toward Dumarest's groin. "I offered you mercy—now I shall teach you the meaning of pain."

He came with a flash of steel, metal ringing as Dumarest parried, attacked in turn, his own blade swept aside as Zucco diverted the cut to slash in turn.

An exchange which left Dumarest with blood streaming from a gash on his side and the crowd, roaring, on its feet.

"First blood to me." Zucco bared his teeth in a smile. "And a taste of what is to come. Don't delay, my friend. Show your admirers how skilled you are. See? I offer you a target."

He spread his arms to expose his body, still smiling, light catching the blade he held and turning it into a gleaming star. A man radiating a supreme confidence and Dumarest searched for the reason why.

Zucco was quick, lithe, agile, moving with a dancer's grace. Things essential to any good fighter but not enough on their own to account for his victories. His lack of scars. There had to be something more.

"You're cautious, my friend." Zucco lowered his arms. "Too wary to take what was offered. A pity. But why don't you attack?"

A question to match the invitation and Dumarest sensed he was close to the answer. To attack was to precipitate the action, to score if the attack was fast enough and the opponent slow. To force his reaction if neither and so to still retain the advantage. One lost if the party was unexpected and the return unusual. But if both could be predicted?

Dumarest weaved, slowly, edging forward, knife a gleaming sliver in his hand. It turned so as to catch and reflect the light, to catch the eye and to narrow the concentration. Tricks Zucco must know but even so his head moved as he followed the blade. Moved then steadied as Dumarest lunged in a feint, drew back, lunged again, the blade in his hand sweeping up and forward in a thrust which would have opened the other's abdomen had it struck home.

A gamble lost and he felt the lack of resistance, following the lunge with a blur of speed as Zucco struck in turn.

Again the crowd roared at the sight of blood.

"Fast," said Zucco. "The fastest I have ever met. Slower and you would be screaming from the pain of a severed kidney."

Instead the blade had struck low to bathe Dumarest's thigh with a carmine flood.

A wound far less serious than it looked but he played up to it, limping, nursing the leg as he faced the other man, who now seemed too reluctant to attack and, suddenly, Dumarest knew the reason why.

"So you've guessed." Zucco edged forward, losing his smile. "Not that it will do you any good. In fact it will add spice to the combat. To know that you are without a defense. That your skill is useless and it is only a matter of time before you are reduced to a whimpering parody of a man. Here, in this arena, you've met your master."

A telepath.

Zucco's special skill which Shakira had mentioned. A man who could read thought and intention and act before they had been turned into movement. A fighter against whom there could be no calculated defense.

Dumarest inched forward, accelerated into a lunge, darted to one side, feinted again, heard the clash of metal and felt the burn of steel. A cut on his upper arm, shallow, harmless, but a demonstration of Zucco's power. Another followed, the point aimed at an eye missing to nick an ear, Zucco following the blow to cut again as Dumarest turned.

"Soon," he promised. "Then the game will be over. I shall cut deep and hard—try to guess where and when."

Thoughts Zucco could read and so direct his attack. A man facing a threat could avoid it in only so many ways but before action there had to be thought and Zucco would know the decision. As he would be able to anticipate the nature of any offensive.

"Come," he urged. "Why delay? The crowd are for you. They want you to win. Don't disappoint them. Even a whining coward would have the guts to try."

Taunts followed by others all of which Dumarest ignored. An old trick aimed at blinding him with rage but he had met it too often for it to have effect.

143

Why did Zucco want him to attack?

"Come," he said again. "It's time you made up your mind."

Time?

Time!

Dumarest stooped, snatched up a handful of sand, flung it at the other's face as he darted forward. A blinding shower rendered harmless as Zucco moved aside. Moving again as Dumarest followed the grit with a handful of blood. Then he was within reach, his knife a shimmering blur, cutting, slashing, a thin, high ringing filling the air as the blades clashed, parting to strike again in a fury of action.

Action too fast for thought, born of the reactive instinct honed by numberless combats and augmented by Dumarest's natural speed. The speed was too fast for Zucco to follow and he backed across the ring toward the tunnel where Valaban stood, Reiza at his side, Shakira a shadowy figure behind.

"No!" Zucco backed faster, face distorted with terror as he read the grim, unrelenting purpose in Dumarest's mind. "No!"

Steel clashed as he parried, a thin red line marring the smoothness of his torso, another gaping just below the throat to add its carmine stream to the smears staining the chest and stomach. Blood stained the shorts and laced the oiled flesh.

"No!" Zucco screamed as again he felt the ice-burn of shearing metal. A shallow cut to join the rest but the wound to his self-confidence was far deeper. "Dear, God—no!"

A man facing death, knowing it, feeling the terror he had so often induced in others. His nerve broke as again Dumarest sent his blade to cut a furrow in the oiled skin.

He would be flayed, crippled, maimed, blinded—things Zucco could read in in Dumarest's mind. A mind without mercy, cold in its determination, maintaining a single red image as his body moved on an instinctive level, robbing Zucco of his advantage.

Turning he ran toward the mouth of the tunnel, screaming as Dumarest reached him, gripped his hair, turned him to stand, face tilted upward, the point of his knife at the straining throat.

"Talk," snarled Dumarest. "Talk!"

Before he sent the blade upward, the point slicing through skin and fat and tissue. Driving up through the lower jaw, through the tongue, up into the palate, the sinus cavities, the brain itself.

A slow and lingering way to end.

"No," said Zucco. "Don't." He was helpless, his own knife lying where he had thrown it on the sand, already, in imagination, feeling the slow thrust of the threatening blade. "No," he said again. "It's not what you think. I—"

He broke off, rearing, eyes wide, the sudden convulsion racking his body causing his spine to arch in a bow, which snapped forward to send his head down, driving his throat hard against the needle point of Dumarest's knife.

CHAPTER TWELVE

Reiza said, "You murdered him! Murdered him—you bastard!" She faced Dumarest in the tunnel, radiating her fury. An emotion which distorted her face and made it ugly. "He was unarmed, helpless, at your mercy. Begging, even, I saw his face. And you killed him. Butchered him!"

"No," said Valaban. "He committed suicide. Shoved his own throat against the blade."

"Liar!"

"If you say so." Valaban shrugged. "What does it matter? The right man died."

"You filth! Jac was murdered!"

"Yes," said Dumarest. "He was. But not by me." He held out his clenched left hand, turning it, opening it to show the dart resting on his palm. A sliver of wood tufted at one end the point dark with blood. "This did it. I took it from his body."

Outside there was noise as the crowd, the entertainment over, moved back to work. Already Zucco's body had been removed, attendants racking the sand and hiding the soil of combat. But in the tunnel it was quiet, a silence broken only by the restless padding of the feline Valaban had treated. Recovered now from the gas and sensing the tension.

Dumarest allowed that tension to grow as he stood, saying nothing, the dart on his palm. Reiza had backed away to stand beside Valaban. Dim gleams from the shadows revealed where Shakira stood, watching. Aside from them the area was deserted.

Then Valaban gave a curt laugh. "So someone put a dart in him. I'd say, Earl, you had a friend in the crowd."

"A handy thing to have. But why did he wait so long?"

"Who knows? Maybe Zucco was moving too fast. Or you were figured to win. Or—hell, pick your own reason."

"I have." Dumarest tossed the dart into the air and watched as it fell to the floor. "Zucco wasn't hit earlier because he was too difficult a target. Whoever fired that dart had to wait until he came close. Almost here to the tunnel, in fact."

"But that's crazy! You had him at your mercy—why should anyone want to hit him then? You didn't need any help."

Moving forward Shakira said, "What you're saying, Earl, is that someone here fired that dart."

"Yes."

"Who?" Reiza was loud in her demand. "Who killed Jac? What kind of filth would murder a helpless man?"

"You, perhaps."

"Me?"

"A woman scorned," said Dumarest. 'You turned against me because you thought I'd been with Melome. Maybe you heard what Jac told me in the ring or maybe he'd told you earlier. To him you were nothing. You could have realized that and remembered what happened to Hayter and why. Or perhaps you were promised more than he could offer."

"I'm no harlot!"

"You helped him. You took me to Krystyna for the reading after he'd told her what to say. Things he'd learned in the sump when he amused himself with that wand." Dumarest's voice thickened with anger at the memory. "He acted too bold for him to be wholly what he seemed. Knew too much for a man in his position. In the ring, after I discovered the truth about him, things fell into place. But something didn't fit. There was no need for Krystyna to die."

"She was old," said Reiza. "It was a natural death."

"She was poisoned." Dumarest was blunt. "Someone gave her a snack with an added content. A generous gesture from someone she had reason to trust. A mistake, as was killing Zucco."

Valaban said, "No mistake, Earl. He was killed in order to save your life."

"No. He was killed to shut his mouth."

"That's ridiculous!"

"Zucco could have killed me at the first engage," said Dumarest. "He knew I was going to attack and how. He could have struck home but instead he merely parried. A good fighter, even an expert one, would never have taken such a chance. The job is to kill fast and have done with it. To do otherwise is to invite disaster."

"Are you saying Jac wasn't a good fighter?" Reiza snapped the question. "He was a champion."

Now he was dead; a thing Dumarest didn't mention. Instead he said, "Zucco was playing with me. As a sadist he couldn't help himself. He wanted to see me sweat, hear me beg. That's why, when he was cut, he didn't cut too deep. He wanted to savor every moment while keeping to his contract. From his point of view it was a good one. I was to be crippled but not killed."

"Why?"

"Isn't it obvious?" Dumarest met her eyes. "I would be helpless, drugged, neatly wrapped and stored for later collection. Zucco would have his fun, his revenge, you and control of the circus. A pity it didn't work out that way. From your point, that is, you would have made a fine pair."

"The best!" She drew in her breath, chest heaving. "He was right—I was always his woman!"

Dumarest shrugged.

"It's the truth!" Her voice rose with the need to emphasize the statement. Behind her, in its cage, the great cat ceased its pacing and halted, glaring with baleful eyes. "You were an incident, a momentary madness, just as he said. A novelty which quickly palled. You and that freak! Jac would never have looked at her. He was my kind of man."

"Then why did you help to kill him?"

"I didn't!"

"You helped the one who did. Who gave you that snack to take to Krystyna?"

"It was harmless! Val—" She broke off and turned to glare at the old man. "You!"

"Shut up, Reiza!"

"You gave it to me. Her favorite, you said. Bastard! You killed her!"

"As he killed Zucco," said Dumarest. "With a dart. One like that he fired at your cat. Remember?"

She screamed in a sudden convulsion of rage, rearing, seeming to arch her back, spitting like one of the cats she knew so

149

well. A reactive gesture as was the extension of her hands, the fingers curved into claws. The polish on her long, sharp nails gleamed like metal.

"Back!" Valaban circled, eyes wary, his left hand slipping beneath his tunic. "Get away from me, you bitch!"

"You killed Jac! Murdered him! For that I'll have your eyes!"

She exploded into action as a feline would attack, springing forward, hands outstretched, the rake of her nails furrowing the old man's cheek. He jerked free his hand as he gained distance, leveled the flat gun, fired as again she went for his eyes. The blast caught her in the chest. The second turned her face into a bloody jelly.

"Freeze!" The gun swung toward Dumarest, to Shakira, back to Dumarest again. "You saw what happened. She attacked me. I had no choice but to shoot."

"You still have no choice." Dumarest inched forward, the knife in his right hand lifting, circling so as to make Valaban turn toward him, his back to the cage holding the watchful cat. "But if you kill me the Cyclan will make you pay."

"So you know. Well, it makes it easier." Valaban lifted his right hand, the small tube it contained aimed at Dumarest's torso. "I won't have to kill you. The dart this contains will knock you cold for twelve hours. When you wake Tron will have you and I'll be rich."

"The circus," said Dumarest. "All of it. The help and backing of the Cyclan. Rejuvenation, maybe, the chance of a new life. What else did they promise?"

"Enough." The tube moved a little. "Don't try it. I know your speed. Drop that knife. Now!" Valaban relaxed a little as the blade hit the floor. "Good. You show sense. Not like that stupid cow." He glanced to where Reiza lay huddled. "She didn't have to die but maybe it's better she did. A clean start."

"Clean," said Dumarest and looked at the woman. His voice changed as he said, "But she isn't dead. She—"

He moved as Valaban turned his head, hurling himself forward, one hand hitting the floor, coming up with the knife he had dropped, throwing it in an overarm movement.

A bad throw; the blade spun, glittering, without true direction or force. A harmless distraction but Valaban responded to the threat of edge and point. He backed, slammed into the cage—and turned as sickle claws lashed through the bars in a blur of fur and fury.

Razor talons which caught his face just below the hairline, ripping down to strip the flesh from the bones, to leave a carmined skull in which rolled agonized eyes and the grinning parody of a smile.

Shakira lifted his glass and, looking at the wine it contained, said thoughtfully, "Who would have guessed the old man had so much blood?" Then, to Dumarest, he added, "I read that in a book once. Or something like it. It was a long time ago now and I wonder why I should remember it. But it seems apt."

Too apt for comfort and Dumarest tried not to remember the screaming thing lying in a pool of its own blood. The silence which came when severed arteries had ceased their spurting had signaled a merciful end.

"You knew," said Shakira. "But how? Zucco I could understand but Valaban? He seemed so harmless." He took a sip of his wine and smiling, said, "It would have been more logical to have suspected me."

"I did." Dumarest was blunt. "But you aren't that stupid. Only a fool or a sadist would warn a victim of his knowledge and Zucco was both. He couldn't resist having his little joke using Reiza and the cards. Valaban wanted Krystyna dead because she could lead me to Zucco and he would betray Valaban. Odd how both wanted the same thing."

"Zucco I suspected," admitted Shakira. "He was too ambitious."

"Which is why you wanted me to fight him. The only way you could defeat him—his telepathic ability had you cornered had you tried anything else." Dumarest took a sip of his own wine. "You took a chance there. I could have lost."

"As I told you, I'm an expert at assessing a person's skill. Zucco was a champion only because he'd never met a man of your caliber. A true survivor in every sense of the word. But Valaban?" Shakira shook his head. "He seemed so contented."

"A pauper in a small kingdom." The wine was rich and pungent and Dumarest held it in his mouth before letting it trickle down his throat. The combat was over but the battle had still to be won. Twelve hours, Valaban had said. How long did he really have? "He betrayed himself in small ways. No man who'd worked for the circus as long as he had would have so little knowledge. He'd know most of what had happened and all about those he worked with. And he was an expert with pheromones. It would have been easy for him to have arranged Hayter's death—maybe the price of Zucco's cooperation. And to have arranged the klachen's attack. Reiza's scarf was a deliberate plant to divert suspicion. He wanted me to concentrate on Zucco.''

"And all the time he was an agent of the Cyclan." Shakira finished his wine and said, "They must want you very badly, Earl.''

"They do.''

"So I gathered. The cyber who came looking for you was most insistent. Cyber Tron—Valaban mentioned him.''

"You can find him at the Dubedat Hotel." Dumarest met the other's eyes, holding them as he rose from his chair. Around him the office took on a new quietness as if the very walls could sense the mounting tension. "Are you thinking of selling me?''

"No, Earl!" Shakira lifted his hands. "No—I swear it!''

"Could you?''

"Elagonya no longer has power over you. I have kept to our bargain. Freedom from restraint, money," Shakira gestured to the bag lying on the desk, "and fortunately you are not in need of medical attention. Only Melome is left.''

She rose as they entered her room, running forward to catch Dumarest by the hand, her face radiant with smiles.

"Earl! You came! I knew you would!''

"And you know why.''

"Yes.'' A shadow touched her face, gone as soon as born. "Elagonya explained why you must do what you do and why I must not be a selfish child. To deny is not to love, Earl, and I love you.''

"In your fashion, Melome.''

"Yes," she agreed. "In my fashion as you love me in yours. Shall we begin?''

He sat and she took her place facing him, also cross-legged so they resembled two idols set as a pair on some ancient altar. Then she stirred, extending her hands for Dumarest to take.

As he closed his fingers around them he said, "You know what I need, Melome, please help me to find it. Send me back to that time in the past when I knew terror. The fear of discovery when I was in the captain's cabin. I must go back to that time. I must!''

To see the open book, to read it, to gain the coordinates of Earth!

152

To put an end to the long and painful search.

Music flowed from the recorder as Shakira touched a control, the air filling with the wail of pipes and the sonorous beat of a drum. Dumarest felt the hands he held grow chill as if the girl was withdrawing all but essential energy in order to power her song. One which came as it had come before, filling his mind, the room, the universe with its dominating cadences.

And again he was thrown on a mental journey back through time.

To feel again the stomach-gripping fear, the chill, the pain of terror.

A wind thick with knives and a sky blotched by the baleful eyes of a single moon. Snow on the ground and ice rimming the pond. A night in which too many would die and he knew that he would be one of them.

The blanket he wore was torn, thin, crusted with dirt. More dirt masked his face and rimmed his mouth, the coating marked with paths of mucous from his nostrils, wind-born tears from his eyes. A child, begging, knowing that charity was dead. To steal was his only hope of survival. To be caught was to know pain.

And he had been caught.

The hand which gripped his wrist forced it closer to the fire, the pot smoking above it. A container half-full of seething stew, thin, odorous, but containing the nourishment he had to have.

"A thief," said the man holding him. "Caught him reaching for the pot. Guess he thought I was asleep."

"His bad luck you weren't." The other's voice was thick with drowsiness. "He get anything?"

"No."

"Good. We won't have to slice off a foot so as to make it up. Just teach him a lesson and let him go."

Harsh times and harsh justice and the lesson wouldn't be easy to take. The terror mounted as his hand was forced closer to the fire, closer until he felt the burning kiss of flame, the searing of his skin, the agony which flowed from the spot.

One small against the possibility of what could happen if his captor chose.

A finger burned to the bone. A hand burned to the wrist.

"God! God! God, please God! Make him let me go!"

Then his free hand dipping, plunging into the soup, lifting from the seething liquid to splash the near-boiling wetness into his captor's face. Freedom as the man cried out and then the running, the hiding, the plunging of burned hands into the snow. The luck as a rodent, startled by his action, crashed from hiding to land against his chest.

"No," said Dumarest. "No."

"Earl?" Melome's face was a blur before him. "Do you want to stop?"

"The wrong time. Too early." Dumarest heard his voice, thick, mumbling. "Try again. Later. Later."

"You should rest." Shakira's voice held a genuine concern. "Take a glass of wine."

Sit and talk and waste the time that was left. To squander the precious minutes and lose the chance of learning what he had to know.

"Keep going."

"But—"

"Do it!" A burned hand, a night of fear and terror which had happened long ago. A thing he could live with and already it was fading. "Try again, Melome. Again."

And the pipe, the drum, the wailing song with its soaring cadences which held a rare and unusual magic. One which worked as he listened. As the girl changed, the room in which he sat.

One to turn into the round dial of an instrument set against a wall. The other into a cabin.

Dumarest felt his stomach churn as he listened to the sound of approaching footsteps.

They would find him and take him before the captain and he would be punished as they had said others had been. Taken and flogged until his bones showed through the lacerated flesh or sealed in a suit and evicted into space with an hour's air. Or put into the generator where invisible energies would rot his bones and send him blind and turn him into a thing of horror.

Threats whispered in idle hours. Tales of torments done and stories woven from sick minds and fevered imaginations. The fruit of loneliness and frustration to be showered on an ignorant boy.

He turned, seeking employment for his hands, a visible task to justify his presence in the cabin. An added defense should anyone look in. A duster was to hand and he used it, nearing the table, the book resting on it. A fat volume, the pages open, sheets bearing rows of the captain's script.

Dumarest looked at it as he plied the duster. Hearing the

154

footsteps outside the cabin fade into silence. Seeing the pages thin and vanish as the moment of terror ebbed away.

"Success," said Shakira. "There is nothing so satisfying. Come, Earl, let us drink to it."

The wine he served was rich and darkly red, the same as he'd produced before. Then it had reminded Dumarest of blood, now it held the acrid taste of defeat.

"It was success, Earl?" The circus owner's voice sharpened as he saw Dumarest's unfinished wine. "Melome said you had returned to the right time. She was sure of it."

"She was right."

"Then—"

"You want to share my knowledge. The bargain we made." Dumarest reached for a sheet of paper. "I went back and I saw the book. This is what I read."

He wrote and passed the sheet to Shakira who picked it up and held it before his eyes.

"The cargo we loaded on Ascanio was spoiled and had to be unloaded at a total loss," he murmured, reading. "A bad trip with no prospect of improvement so I took a chance and risked a journey to the proscribed planet. A waste of time—the place is a nightmare. God help the poor devils who lived here. Those remaining are degenerate scum little more than savage animals. Found a stowaway after we'd left, a boy who looks human. He claims to be twelve but looks younger and could be dangerous. Decided to take a chance and kept him but if he shows any sign of trouble I'll have to—"

Shakira looked at Dumarest. "Is this all?"

"Yes."

"But you were so sure there would be more."

"I was wrong." Dumarest gulped at his wine. "The book was a journal, not the ship's log. A private diary of events. And I could only look at it. I couldn't turn the pages. The coordinates could have been written plain on the previous sheet but I'll never know. Not even if I went back could I ever know."

"And you can't go back. Terror, relived, loses its impact. You could try for a dozen years and never again hit that exact period. But it lives in your mind. Your memory. Perhaps—"

"The facts remain," said Dumarest. He was curt. "I saw the book, remembered what it said, wrote it down. You have it in your hand. All of it. Useless rubbish!"

155

Words for which he had risked his life. Once they had him in their power the Cyclan would not be gentle. They would sear his brain with electric probes, test him with endless pain, tear him apart cell by cell in order to regain their lost secret. And time was running out.

"Wait!" Shakira lifted a hand as Dumarest rose to his feet. "Disappointment has blunted your natural shrewdness. The coordinates are lacking, true, but still you have won information. The name of a world, Ascanio. It must be relatively close to the proscribed planet. Earth? But why should it be proscribed? And by whom? And the rest? That about the boy who was found— you?"

"It has to be."

"A strange description. Malnutrition would account for your size, but why should he think you dangerous? Sit, my friend, take some more wine, let us consider this. You may have gained more than you realize."

Shakira brooded over the paper as Dumarest followed his suggestion. A few more minutes against what the other's fresh viewpoint could gain. Extra danger set against the possibility of winning gold from apparent dross.

"Proscribed," murmured Shakira. "Set apart. Outlawed. Banned. Incredible that a world should be so treated. But by whom? And how to enforce the proscription?"

Questions which hung in the air as he considered the matter. A silence broken by an imperious knocking at the door.

"Who is it?" Shakira's tone held anger though his face remained as placid as before. "I gave orders that on no account should I be disturbed." The paper fell to the table as the knocking was repeated. "Who is there?"

The answer stepped through the opened panel, tall, thin, glowing in a scarlet robe. One adorned with the Seal of the Cyclan.

"Cyber Tron." Pushed Shakira had fallen back to the support of the table. Now he stood, hands lifted, facing the intruder. "What do you want here?"

"You know the answer to that." Tron lifted his hand, the gun it held. One like that used by Valaban. "Do not waste time calling for help. Those you set on guard have been taken care of." The guard moved to point at Dumarest, the wide orifice aimed directly at his face. "You are to come with me. Unless you obey me implicitly I shall fire. The shot will not kill you but

156

your face will be ruined, your eyes. Even in the open a blind man cannot get far."

And in the maze of the circus it would be impossible. Dumarest froze where he sat, hands on the table, one close to the glass holding his wine. Across the board Shakira faced the cyber, hands still lifted in his pathetic gesture of appeal or surrender. An act? One to cover his betrayal? The face remained a mask and gave no hint as to the answer.

Dumarest said, "It seems you win, Cyber Tron. But I expected you earlier. What delayed you?"

"You will not move and you will not talk." Tron's face, like Shakira's, did not change expression but his eyes revealed his pleasure. "Disobey and I fire."

A good moment and he relished it; the prediction had been correct. Now, even though the agent had failed, Dumarest was held fast in the trap. One now sealed tight by his own presence.

"You will lift both hands and place them on your head," said Tron. "You will make no other movement." Then, as Dumarest made no move to obey, "Do it or—"

"You will fire. I know. You told me." Dumarest saw the tightening of the finger on the trigger and added, quickly, "To shoot me would be proof of your inefficiency. A blind man needs help—who will give it? Can you trust them? Could you watch them? It would be far more logical to keep me functional." Dumarest moved a finger closer to the glass of wine. A poor weapon but the only one available. "There is always the possibility of error should you fire. How can you be certain as to the charge? The damage it could do? And what of the trauma of the wound?"

Arguments to ease the tension and so lessen the immediate danger, but ones which he knew weren't going to work. Tron was too determined. Dumarest looked at the gun, knowing that before he could move it would fire. That it was only a matter of seconds before it did.

"Efficiency is a matter of adjusting action to the relevant situation," said Tron. "Your points are valid but negated by the paramount need to ensure your captivity. Therefore—"

Shakira screamed.

It was a sound like grating metal, a nail dragged over a slate, loud, shocking, totally unexpected. As the cyber turned toward him Shakira stepped forward, hands high, voice pleading.

"No! Don't! Please don't! I beg you not to do it!"

Words which masked action, even as he spoke the fabric of his blouse ripped open from neck to waist to reveal a hand. Holding a gun.

A laser which fired as Dumarest snatched up the glass and threw it as Tron fired at the same time. A blast which tore at Shakira's face and sent him turning as the cyber fell with smoke pluming from the ruined pattern of his insignia.

"Shakira!" Dumarest rose from his examination of the dead man. "How badly are you hurt?" He had tried to divert Tron's aim but knew he had failed. "Shakira?"

The owner remained turned away, hands to his face, leaning against the edge of the table. Something cracked beneath Dumarest's foot as he stepped toward him and he looked at the fragment beneath his boot. One of several lying scattered around; scraps of flesh-coloured plastic holding a limited flexibility.

Dumarest knew what they had to be.

"A mask," he said. "You wear a mask."

One shattered and ruined by the blast from the cyber's gun, but what other damage had been done? Shakira turned away as Dumarest reached him.

"Please. The mask is damaged, true, but I have another. In the bottom drawer of my desk. Be so good as to face the wall while I don it."

"I'll do that." Dumarest reached again for the shielding hands. "But only after I've seen what injuries you have."

A moment and they were exposed, ugly welts scored on flesh but harmless enough. The mask had taken the brunt of the shot, shattering like an eggshell but saving the wearer. One now revealed for what he was.

"You are disgusted," said Shakira. "I can read it in your eyes."

"No. You see what you expect to find. I'm concerned, not disgusted." Then, as the other made no comment, Dumarest added in a burst of sudden anger, "What kind of a man do you take me for? You saved my life—what the hell do I care what you look like?"

"You are kind. The other mask?"

"You don't need it."

"For you, no, but for others? And I must maintain the habit of wearing it. Help yourself to wine, Earl. I shall not be long."

It still held the color of blood and the acrid taste of defeat, but now a new dimension had been added, one of alien scope.

Dumarest sat, drinking, remembering how Shakira had looked when the last of the ruined mask had been discarded. The bald, rounded head, the protruding eyes, the noseless face, the mouth, the jaw—against him Elagonya was beautiful.

But there had been more than a distortion of the familiar, the visage had held inhuman facets as had the eyes as if an alien form of life had been so disfigured as to ape the human frame.

"Pour me wine, Earl." Shakira had returned, his face seemingly as it had been, but more stiff now as if the mask were an earlier model, made before he had recognized the necessity of falsifying a smile. "Thank you." He drank and set down his glass. "We each have secrets, Earl. Do we agree never to divulge them?"

"Of course." Dumarest looked at the dead cyber. "And him?"

"He will be disposed of."

"In the sump?" Dumarest guessed the answer. "He will be missed and others will come after him."

"When they do I shall tell them of the tragic accident which took so many lives. Valaban's, the cyber's, yours." Shakira picked up his glass and took a sip of wine. "A good story, my friend, and there will be those to swear to its truth. And they will not lie."

Primed and conditioned by the sensitives Shakira controlled. The powers he owned which could delude the test of machines. Dumarest relaxed even as he wondered why Shakira should go to so much trouble. He had been made a part of the circus and the circus took care of its own, but was that the real answer?

"More wine?" Shakira poured and sipped his own. "We have much in common, Earl, you and I. When I was very young I never guessed how different to others I was. My family was wealthy and kept me apart. I grew up attended by those I thought normal. It was only later, when I left home, I realized what a hell the universe could be."

He made the familiar gesture, hands lifting to hover as if in appeal or surrender, but now Dumarest knew it to be neither. The lifting of the hands and arms was to give clearance to the other hands hidden beneath the blouse. The armless appendages sprouting from the waist like vestigial limbs.

"But I found a solution."

"You bought the circus."

"More than that, Earl, I bought a home." Shakira sipped

159

again at his wine, his voice softened with memories. "The circus of Chen Wei," he said. "Once the name meant Golden Joy, or so I was told but Chen Wei could have lied. He often did. But for me the name was no lie. I had found the one place where I could be accepted for what I was. A haven against all those who despise the unusual and who want to hunt down and destroy the different. And I could do more. I could provide a home for others like Elagonya and Melome and even you, Earl. But the circus is not for you."

"And yet you could find happiness here. Melome loves you."

"She is still young."

"And you love something more. Your hunt. Your search for home. And I think I can help you to find it. Here." Shakira reached for paper and wrote on it, folding it before handing it to Dumarest. "A name and a world, Earl. One not too distant. The man is unusual and if anyone can help you he can. Go to him. Tell him I sent you. Tell him what you know."

Dumarest said, "Why are you doing this for me?"

"You saved my circus for me from Zucco. My home, Earl, my world. Can I do less for you?" Shakira lifted his glass. "A toast, my friend. To your success!" Then, as the glasses were lowered, he said with a sudden, raw urgency, "Find your world, Earl. Find Earth. And find it soon—we freaks must have somewhere to call our own!"

160

ANGADO

To: My mother with love.

Chapter One

Once, the place had been bright with the froth of make-believe; domes, minarets, spires, towers, soaring arches and sweeping promenades all blazing with variegated colors—a skillful illusion created with paint and plastic, lying like a jewel in the cup of rounded hills. The circus of Chen Wei was gone now, leaving only an expanse of torn and barren ground, a scatter of debris, the crusted surface of a fetid lagoon.

A monument to emotional waste, which Avro pondered as his raft circled the area. How many work-hours had been poured into its construction, operation and maintenance? How many more had been squandered by those visiting the circus for the sake of transient thrills? Time, effort, resources, skills all dissipated to the wind. Leaving nothing but a raw devastation. Time would heal the wound and soon the hills would seem as if they had never been touched. More waste. Under correct guidance things of lasting worth could have been constructed for the benefit of humanity. Testimonials to the efficiency of the Cyclan.

Instead the place was evidence as to its failure.

"Master?" The acolyte was deferential, the title more than an acknowledgment of Avro's superiority. "Would you care to go lower?"

"No." Avro had seen enough. "When did they leave?"

"Five days ago." Cardor added, "A week after the accident."

When Tron had died, and Valaban, and most important of all, Dumarest. Avro looked again at the place where it had happened, assessing, extrapolating, knowing the mental bitterness of defeat. Too late. He had arrived too late. A matter of days and his search would have been over, his mission accomplished. Dumarest, taken and helpless in his charge. Dumarest—and the precious secret he owned. One which had made Avro into an angel.

The cyber leaned back as the raft headed toward town. High above, a winged shape glided, others wheeling close. Small birds feeding on airborne seeds, mindless creatures operating on a plane of sheer instinct but, for a moment, he envied them. Remembering the freedom of the skies, the rush of wind, the thrum of pinions, the surging impact of alien emotions. Then he had known hate and fear and anger and, yes, even concern. He had known the burning flame of passion and, at the end, he had experienced death.

Watching him, Cardor felt a mounting unease. He was young, taken and trained by the Cyclan, yet still to don the scarlet robe which was the mark of a cyber. He might never wear it. Not all acolytes made the grade. Some continued to work in subordinate capacities but the majority quietly vanished from sight, erased by the touch of oblivion.

He said, "I did what I could, master. As I was ordered to do."

By Tron who had demonstrated his inefficiency. Who had escaped his punishment by extinction.

"Tell me again what happened."

Unnecessary repetition, every detail was clear in Avro's mind as the acolyte knew. As he also knew that, in making the demand, the cyber had put him on trial. The next few minutes would decide his fate.

"I arrived with Cyber Tron on Baatz fifteen days ago. We stayed at the Dubedat Hotel. He was in contact with an agent in the circus of Chen Wei. The man had reported that Dumarest was attached to the circus and could be captured. Cyber Tron visited the circus but neither Dumarest nor the agent was present. He made a second visit later. That is when he died."

"And you?"

"Obeying orders, I stayed in town. To meet you should you arrive and report on what was happening. When Cyber Tron failed to return I made inquiries at the circus. There I learned of the accident." Cardor paused, reliving the incident, recognizing its importance. "The owner, Tayu Shakira, explained what had happened. An animal had gone berserk, broken free of its cage and had run amok. A klachen. It—''

"I know what it is. Continue."

"Its keeper, Valaban, had been killed. Cyber Tron and Dumarest also. There were witnesses."

"Did you see the bodies?"

"No. But with Shakira's permission I tested the witnesses with lie-detectors. All responses were positive. They were not lying."

"But you did not see the bodies."

"They had been disposed of before I arrived. A matter of necessity, so it was explained. The scent of blood needed to be eradicated in order to prevent further upset among the beasts. And the bodies themselves were terribly mangled. But some things had been saved. Cyber Tron's bracelet and a gun he carried. I recognized them both."

Proof the cyber had died—but the others? Avro stared at distant, wheeling shapes. Valaban, certainly, the man must have died if Dumarest had escaped but, from the evidence, he had joined the others in death. A fact Avro found hard to accept; he did not want to accept. Yet to refute the evidence was to be illogical.

"How many witnesses did you examine?"

"Eight. Three actually saw the incident. The others all saw the bodies and three helped to dispose of them."

"And the owner?"

"He actually saw nothing. Cyber Tron must have contacted the agent direct."

"But you tested him?"

"I did. With his permission after I pointed out how ill advised he would be to make an enemy of the Cyclan. The findings confirmed what he claimed."

Which meant that he had not lied. And yet . . . And yet . . .

"Relate the evidence of those who saw the incident," said Avro. "Individually and in detail."

He sat immobile as he listened to the acolyte. The raft headed toward the sun and warm hues painted his face with red and gold and amber. Colors which accentuated the scarlet of his robe, reflecting brilliantly from the sigil adorning his breast. The Seal of the Cyclan, the symbol of his power. Yet despite the sunlight and the warm tint of his robe a chill rested about him. An aura emphasized by the skull-like contours of his face. One thin to the point of emaciation, the scalp shaven, the deep-set eyes meshed by lines. The visage of a living machine devoid of the capacity of emotion. A flesh and blood robot who could only know the pleasure of mental achievement.

Behind him the site of the circus fell away. The barren ground, the litter, the crusted lagoon. The pool in which the dead had been buried and, with them, the ending of a dream.

At night Baatz became a world of gaiety with bright lanterns illuminating the tiered buildings and the market itself turned into a playground. Here the venders, traders, merchants and entrepreneurs put aside business and joined with stallholders, farmers, shopkeepers, housewives, workers and the restless tide of transients that made up the population.

A time of drinking and dancing and merriment but one free of violence. The air saw to that, the invisible spores it carried from the vegetation clothing the surrounding hills. Exudations which calmed and reduced tension so that men laughed instead of quarreling and sought peaceful solutions instead of bloody settlements.

Like a scarlet ghost Avro moved through the town.

Cardor could have accomplished the task, as could others of his own acolytes, but he needed to do it himself. The woman who answered his knock frowned as she saw his face, became respectful as she recognized his robe. Even on Baatz the Cyclan was known.

"My lord!" Her head dipped in a bow. "This is an honor. How may I serve you?"

"A man stayed here." Avro's tone was the even modulation of his kind, devoid of all irritating factors. "Dumarest. Earl Dumarest. I have the correct address?"

"You have, my lord. He hired a room upstairs. In the back." She blinked sorrowful eyes. "Such a pity he died."

"You heard?"

"From the circus. They told me to sell his things and to let the room if anyone wanted it. Not that he'd used it much."

"Let me see it."

It was a box containing a narrow bed, a cabinet, a small

table, two chairs. A rug half-covered the bare wood of the floor. A jug held scummed water and a bowl had a chipped rim. Avro assessed this at a glance then he was at the cabinet, searching, the table, the drawers. They yielded nothing and he dropped to his knees and checked the underside of the bed, the chairs, finally stripping the cot and examining the bare, wooden structure.

Nothing aside from a few crumpled papers, some packets of dried fruit, a book, a folder of bright pictures, a deck of cards. These things he checked with minute attention, holding each of the pasteboards to the light, running his fingers over their edges. Finally he turned his attention to the room itself, scanning each wall, the ceiling, the floor bared when he moved aside the rug.

Again he found nothing and stood, thoughtful, trying to put a man into the chamber, trying to guess what that man would do.

Guessing, for he lacked data on which to base an extrapolation. The essential ingredient to promote his honed talent. Given a handful of facts he could predict the logical outcome of any event; without them he could only make assumptions. A man, alone on a strange world—how would he have safeguarded his secret?

Again Avro checked the room, looking for the fifteen symbols which would tell him all he needed to know: the sequence in which the biomolecular units of the affinity twin had to be assembled. The secret which would give the Cyclan galactic domination.

But he looked for it without success.

A failure he had expected, yet to have ignored the possibility of success would have been insane stupidity. An error equal in magnitude to that made by Tron. To have had Dumarest in his grasp and then to have lost him. Death had been a merciful punishment.

Avro looked once more at the room. A small, bare place, cold, featureless. One Dumarest had known as he must have known so many others. Moving on to leave nothing of himself behind. And yet there had to be more.

He found it at a local bank, the manager reluctant to cooperate, finally yielding to logical persuasion. To refuse Avro's demand was to ruin all hope of promotion.

"Yes," he admitted. "Dumarest did have money on deposit here. Quite a large sum as a matter of fact."

"Withdrawals?"

"None after the initial deposit."

"How was the credit registered?"

"The usual way." The manager added an explanation. "This is a transient world and we get all types. This bank is affiliated with others and we use the common system. When a deposit is made—" He broke off as Avro lifted a hand. "I see you understand."

"Give me the number of the account."

The deposit Dumarest had made had been registered in a pattern of metallic inks set invisibly beneath the skin of his left arm. Special machines could read the code and adjust the credit as necessary. A blast of flame would incinerate the limb had there been any tampering or forgery.

"Here." The manager handed over the desired information. "But no withdrawals have been made to date."

With Dumarest dead none ever would. More proof as to his extinction—would a man in need refuse to use the money that was his?

From the bank Avro went to the field where Cardor waited. The acolyte shook his head in a gesture of defeat.

"Nothing, master. The traffic is too great. It is impossible to gain detailed records of who traveled where and on what vessel."

"The circus?"

"Bound for Lopakhin."

Traveling in assorted ships, some members going their own way, others ready to disperse. All could be followed but nothing new would be gained. Dumarest was dead. All the evidence proved it. To deny the facts was to demonstrate his inefficiency.

Yet to accept evidence without checking was to do the same.

Avro said, "Take men out to the circus lagoon. Have it dragged. If bodies are found have them placed in cryosacs for later examination. Bones also. Nothing must be missed."

"Yes, master." The acolyte hesitated. "But all waste from the circus was pulverized before being pumped to the lagoon."

"Do as I order."

168

The tone of Avro's voice did not change but Cardor flinched as he bowed and hurried away. A mistake and one he must have recognized; no assumption could be regarded as proof. Yet it was a natural one for him to make, for what else was a dead body but waste? And he had been influenced by Tron who had demonstrated his weakness by his failure.

All this Avro considered as he made his way to the Dubedat Hotel. To waste a valuable resource was to be avoided and the young man could be salvaged. A period of intense training, exposure to what a true cyber could be, a final warning to stiffen his resolve and he could yet earn the right to don the scarlet robe.

A decision made and set to one side as he entered his suite. Byrne rose to greet him, Tupou at his side. Personal aides who have traveled with him.

To them both Avro said, "Total seal."

He moved on, into his chamber, the door closing behind him. A barrier the acolytes would protect with their lives. One enhanced as he touched the broad band of metal clasped to his left wrist. A twin to one Tron had worn; activated, it emitted a pattern of forces which formed a zone impenetrable to any prying electronic eye or ear.

Avro lay supine on his bed.

The hotel was luxurious, the bed soft, the ceiling decorated with intricate designs picked in red and yellow and vivid scarlet. Patterns which vanished as he closed his eyes and concentrated on the Samatchazi formula. Gradually he lost the use of his senses; had he opened his eyes he would have been blind. Divorced of external stimuli his brain ceased to be irritated, gained tranquility and calm, became a thing of pure intellect, its reasoning awareness the only thread with normal existence. Only then did the grafted Homochon elements become active. Rapport was immediate.

It was followed by chaos.

Avro felt the mental shock and twisted in his mind, screaming as his body lay immobile on the bed, dumb, soundless, incapable of movement. A husk that housed roiling insanity, a conflict of jarring discord, flashes of light, of color, of searing impossibility. A turmoil in which he spun like a leaf in a gale, helpless to do other than ride the storm, to wait for a period of calm.

It came with the echoes of rolling thunder yielding to a host of twitterings, whispers, murmurings, sighs. A shadowed darkness which slowly brightened to reveal a bizarre landscape composed of crystalline facets gleaming with a fire of splintered colors. A ball in which he stood with his feet resting on softly engulfing shadows.

Before him stood a mirror image of himself.

A shape as tall, as thin, as skeletal about the face. One wearing the twin of his scarlet robe. But the image was no reflection and he recognized it at once. Master Marle, Cyber Prime, the head of the Cyclan.

But how? How?

Normally communication with Central Intelligence was preceded by the illusion of bubbles moving in continuous motion with other bubbles all composed of gleaming light. An experience unique to himself; each cyber had a different experience. Then would come the actual contact during which information was absorbed from his mind as water was sucked by a sponge from a pool. An interchange in which orders were relayed as fast. Organic communication of a near-instantaneous speed. After would come the time of euphoria in which he drifted in a zone filled with the scraps of overflow from other minds.

Never before had he known this confusion.

"Avro?" Marle sounded as confused as himself. "Are you Avro?"

"Marle?" Avro caught himself, the evidence was before him. Incredible as it seemed they stood face to face. "A coincidence," he suggested. "We both established rapport at the same time and Central Intelligence has created this direct link. An improvement if restricted to special occasions."

"Perhaps." Marle was slow to agree. "What have you to report?"

"Dumarest is dead."

"Explain." Marle listened as Avro gave him the facts. "The lagoon?"

"Can only produce negative evidence. Anything recovered may, on examination, prove the death of Tron of which we have no doubt. The rest must be based on a valuation of other evidence. I regard it as conclusive.''

''Eye-witness accounts,'' said Marle. ''Irrefutable testimony substantiated by mechanical lie-detectors. And yet you were not satisfied.''

''I needed to be certain.''

''Of what? To check the lagoon was wasted effort if you believe the testimony. Time and expense used to no purpose. Could Cardor have lied?''

''No. His findings have been checked.''

''So he told the truth as he knew it. As others could have done.''

Avro caught the implication and stepped forward, noting, with vague detachment, that the figure he faced remained at the same distance.

He said, ''The possibility that a man could lie and yet not know that he lied is credible. Hypnotism could produce such a condition. But there were eight witnesses, not including the owner of the circus. All eight had seen the bodies and all swore as to the deaths. Also Cardor took steps to guard against such conditioning. I have checked the detectors and the results are conclusive. The men saw what they claimed to have seen.''

''Tron dead? Valaban?''

''And Dumarest. All three the victims of a klachen which had run wild.''

''And the animal?''

Avro hesitated. ''Dead, I think.''

''You are not positive?''

''No mention was made of it. The fate of the beast was not considered important.''

Against the greater loss that was understandable but it was an oversight which could not be forgiven. Avro revised his decision as to Cardor's fate. He would be questioned, tested, checked—then disposed of. Marle, by his question, had cost the man his life.

As, by his decision, he could cost Avro his.

As Avro watched, the figure before him seemed to blur, to dissolve into smoke which writhed and plumed to dissipate against the bizarre landscape. An illusion added to illusion, or reality which his limited senses could only convert to familiar terms. Then the return of the wind, the confusion, the mind-wrenching turmoil as the universe gyrated around him and his ears were filled with the thin, hopeless screaming of the damned.

"Master!" Someone was pounding at the door. "Master! Is all well?"

Byrne, his face anxious as Avro broke the total seal, Tupou behind him carrying wine. Ruby fluid which he gushed into a goblet and handed to Avro without a word. Liquid he drank without thinking then dismissed them both with a curt gesture. Alone, he sank on the bed and buried his face in his hands.

And heard the song of wind, the thrum of pinions, the thin, keen hiss of parting air.

Madness and he reared, looking at the walls, the ceiling, the familiar shapes of ornate furnishings. Things to be despised for their nonfunctional design but now objects of comfort.

What had happened?

Coincidence, Marle had said, or the figure he had taken to be the Cyber Prime. But it was a coincidence which must have happened many times before. Why had this been different?

Avro examined the problem with trained mental efficiency.

Central Intelligence was the sum total of the massed brains which formed the heart of the Cyclan. Living intelligences, released from the hampering prisons of fleshy bodies when age had made those bodies no longer efficient. Locked in sealed capsules, fed with nutrients, hooked in series, the brains rested in darkness and total isolation from external stimuli. An ideal state in which to ponder the problems of the universe. A tremendous organic computer of incredible complexity; with its aid the Cyclan would rule the galaxy given time.

But the tool had revealed a flaw. Certain of the brains had shown signs of aberrated behavior and had to be destroyed. Was the sickness continuing?

Was Central Intelligence going insane?

A possibility loaded with frightening implications, for if the brains could no longer be trusted then what of the Cyclan? And what would be the reaction of cybers denied their reward for dedicated service? The potential immortality granted at the end of their useful physical life?

"Master!" Byrne turned as Avro opened the door to his chamber. "Is all well?"

A question Avro dismissed with a wave of his hand.

"Go to the field," he ordered. "I want all details of every vessel movement from Baatz from the time Tron landed here. Names, cargoes, destinations, complements, operating velocities—everything." To Tupou he said, "Bring all the records of the examinations made by Cardor together with a complete record of all circus workers." A near-impossible task but one which had to be attempted. "When you have done that, relieve Cardor and have him report to me."

Effort and expense with little hope of reward but Avro was beyond counting the cost. If Dumarest was dead he must be certain of it. If, despite all the evidence, the man had managed to survive then he must know that too. The future of the Cyclan depended on it.

Chapter Two

From his seat at the table Helith Lam looked at the prospects in the salon. They weren't encouraging, the usual assortment of deadbeats and cheap riders, but he had a place to fill and Krogstad was getting ugly. The gambler thinned his lips at recent memory, seeing the captain's face in his mind's eye, the cruel, determined set of the mouth. The ultimatum had been brief.

"Up the take or quit the *Thorn*!"

Dumped on Cadell or Bilton or another of the small worlds forming the Burdinnion. Garbage dumps mostly with little trade, no industry, scant farming and a viciously savage native life. Once kicked off the *Thorn* on such a world and he would starve. Too old to sell his labor, too inexperienced to wrest a living from the local terrain, he'd last only as long as his money. And the captain, damn him, would leave little of that.

A bleak prospect and one he had to improve. A decent cut from the table would grant him a reprieve and he could pad the captain's fifty percent share of the profit from his own cut. But first he had to fill the vacant seat.

"Come on!" Lissek, seated to his left, was impatient. "You're letting the deck grow cold."

"It'll warm." Cranmer was cynical. "Why be in a hurry to lose your money?"

"That's right." Varinia touched a handkerchief to lips painted a lurid scarlet. "Why be in a hurry over anything? But why the delay?"

"We need seven," said Lam. A lie and one he justified.

174

"It makes a better game and adds spice. Also it brings in fresh money."

"You should have told that to Deakin before he got skinned." Yalin, a wasp of a man, rapped a finger on the coins piled before him. "Come on, man, deal!"

Lam obeyed; a moving game attracted attention but his eyes weighed those lounging in the salon. The monk was out; no Brother of the Universal Church would waste time and money at the table. The young married couple had other things to interest them; after they'd swallowed their ration of basic they would vanish into their cabin. The gaunt-faced seller of symbiotes was immersed in his books and the old woman with the artificial gems had already used up her luck. Which left only two others.

"Damn!" A raddle-faced miner swore and threw down his hand. "That decides it! I'm out!"

"And me." A pale youngster followed his example. "Varinia?"

"Stays," said Lam, then, softening his tone, added with a smile, "We need her to make up the number and to add a touch of beauty to the company. And I don't think she'll regret it. See?" The cards riffled in his hands, falling to lie face upward. "Four Lords—could you hope for better? Your luck is about to change, my dear."

"It had better." Her eyes met his in mutual understanding. "But who else will join us?"

"Our friends." Lam lifted his voice as he made the appeal. "Please, you two, accommodate us. A small game to while away the time." Then, as the younger of the pair turned toward him, "Angado Nossak, isn't it? I think we have met before."

"On the *Provost*," agreed Nossak. "You taught me a hard lesson. Maybe now's the time to put it to use."

He took a chair, gesturing for his companion to take another. A hard man, decided the gambler, looking at him. A brief glance but enough to take in the shape and build. Faded garments spoke of hard times and the shiny patches on the fabric showed where straps could have hung or accoutrements rested. A mercenary, he guessed, a professional guard or a hunter—now down on his luck and hoping to improve it.

A forlorn hope, as was Nossak's intention to use what he

175

had learned. Both prime fodder for the gambler's art and he riffled the cards, the rubbed-down skin of index fingers and thumbs reading the tiny marks a nail had impressed into the edges.

"Well, my lords and lady—" he inclined his head toward Varinia—"let us begin."

The game was starburn; a variation of poker with a seven-card deal and a double discard dropping the hand to the normal five cards. Lissek sucked in his breath as he scooped up his hand, a thin stream of purple running from the corner of his mouth. Saliva stained by the weed he chewed to ease his cough and steady his nerves.

"Give me three." He dropped five cards on the table. "Make them friendly."

So he had a pair. Lam glanced at Cranmer. Dealt him two cards, moved to where Nossak studied his hand.

"Three—no! Make it two." He watched Lam deal. "Earl?"

"I'll take one."

Dumarest watched as the deal moved on to the woman, his eyes on the gambler's hands. Smooth, ringless, the skin soft and supple. The result of applied salves, he guessed. He was certain as to why the index fingers and thumbs lacked any trace of the normal whorls and patterns.

A cheat and a desperate one; the risks he took were obvious. Chances he compounded as he returned to Lissek who threw down two cards for another pair. His original hand had been improved to one containing three of a kind, now, with luck, he could have built it into a full house or gained a healthy four. Cranmer shook his head after the final deal and dropped out. Angado pursed his lips and changed a single card. Dumarest shook his head and threw in his hand. The woman stayed. The gambler. Three rounds of betting and the game was over.

Varinia chuckled as she scooped in the pot.

"You know, Lam, I think I'm going to like this game."

One designed to build the pot and to ruthlessly squeeze the players. The extra cards and double discarding enabled good hands to be won and encouraged pressure-betting. If the dealer could manipulate the cards he would find it simple to clean up.

Lam could manipulate them and was clever despite his

desperation. He was using the woman as his shill, letting her win so as to cover his own involvement. Later, when she had grown too confident, he would clean her out.

"Raise ten." Angado threw coins into the pot. "This time I win."

Dumarest doubted it but made no comment. The man was his cabin mate, a temporary association born of chance. He owed the man nothing and his main concern was to remain inconspicuous. He'd left Baatz in a crate supplied by the circus, transported by discreet friends of the owner, shipped by a captain who wasn't too curious.

A journey ending with Dumarest in a warehouse. One he'd broken out of to take passage on a vessel heading toward the Burdinnion. Changing to the *Thorn* on Tysa. A ship like most in the region, catering to all trades, making short journeys, touching small and almost deserted worlds.

Now he had to make a decision. If Angado continued to play he would lose and could become violent, which would bring attention not only to himself but to the man who shared his cabin. But to beat the gambler at his own game would be to arouse a more direct interest.

And the captain was no fool.

Ships, even battered tubs like the *Thorn*, were valuable possessions and all took elementary precautions. A man who lied could be harmless but no harmless man had reason to lie. Dumarest had maintained his deception by giving only half his name but a deeper check would reveal things he wanted to keep hidden.

"You in?" Angado Nossak was impatient, sweating, hand tugging at the collar of his blouse. "God, it's hot in here. Where's the steward? I want some ice."

"Hot?" The gambler looked puzzled. "I've noticed no change." He looked at Dumarest. "You in or out?"

"In." Dumarest chipped into the pot. "No raise."

Varinia hesitated, glanced at Lam, then doubled Nossak's raise. Pressure which drove out Lissek and Cranmer. Nossak hesitated as he examined his hand, pulling at his collar and finally tearing open his blouse.

"I'm burning. Where's that damned steward?"

"Forget him." Varinia stared at the man. "You sick or

177

something?'' Her voice rose in sudden fear. "Hell, man, look at your face!''

It had broken out in lumpy protrusions. An attack shocking in the speed of its progression. The woman jumped up and backed from the table, others following, cards spraying from the gambler's hand as Nossak slumped over the table. Within seconds Dumarest was alone with the sick man in a circle of staring faces.

"Get the steward,'' said Lissek. "He'll know what to do. He's got drugs.''

"Drugs, hell!'' Cranmer was harshly aggressive. "Get the captain. That man's got plague!''

Captain Krogstad took five paces over the floor of the salon, turned, paced back to where he had started. Aside from himself, Brother Jofre and his first officer, the place was deserted. All the passengers were safely locked in their cabins and he wished Jofre was among them. But he knew better than to be hostile. It didn't pay to ride roughshod over the Universal Church.

He said, "Brother, you must see the situation from my point of view. As captain I am responsible for the ship and all in it. I cannot permit the possibility of contagion to remain.''

"You are assuming the sick man is a carrier of disease. That need not be the case.''

Krogstad was blunt. "With respect, Brother, you are not a medical man. I can't afford to take a chance on your diagnosis. If you are wrong—''

"Then the damage has already been done.'' The monk met the captain's eyes. "The ship has become infected and your duty is clear. All must be placed under total quarantine. You must send word to your world of destination for ships to monitor the isolation of the *Thorn* while in orbit. It will have to remain in that condition until such time as a clearance is granted.''

Which would take its own sweet time, as Krogstad knew. Time during which expenses would mount from feeding the passengers and crew, from medical fees and the charges made by the monitors. Costs which would eat into his reserves and could leave him ruined.

Fedotik, the first officer, cleared his throat.

"There is an alternative," he suggested. "The sick man can be kept isolated, evicted if he dies." Or even if he doesn't—who would be concerned over the fate of a single man? Something which would already have been done if it hadn't been for Jofre's presence. "I'm thinking of the best for everyone," he added. "As you must be. It is our duty to safeguard the welfare of the majority."

"Not at the expense of the minority." Jofre was firm. "I don't think isolation is the answer."

"What else can we do?" Again Krogstad paced the floor. "Quarantine would ruin us and once I send the word there can be no retraction. If—" He halted and snapped his fingers. "I have it. The sick man is not alone. His cabin mate is with him. If Nossak is diseased with a contagious illness then his companion must be affected. As yet he appears untouched. Which must be evidence of a harmless infection."

"The man could be a carrier."

Fedotik said, quickly, "We have considered the possibility and have a solution which we hope will meet with your approval. The ship is bound for Anfisa. We can make a diversion and land on Velor away from any habitable area." He saw Jofre's expression and added, "Not too far away, of course, and we can leave supplies. If the illness is harmless—as we are certain it is—then they will recover and no harm will have been done."

"And the ship will be safe," said Krogstad. "By the time we reach Anfisa we'll know for sure if any plague is on board. If there is more sickness the authorities will be notified." He spread his hands in mute appeal. "Two men against the ruin of us all. Brother, I beg you to accept the compromise."

One made only because of his presence. Jofre had no illusions as to the captain's motives. To evict the pair would be easier and cheaper than landing on Velor.

"When?"

"Two days."

"Can I see them?" Jofre listened to the silence which was his answer. "Talk with them?" A pause, then he said firmly, "At least let me check their supplies."

Things Dumarest stacked after the ship had gone, leaving him and the sick man on a rolling plain already touched by shadows. Low on the horizon a sullen sun threw long rays of gold and amber, orange and yellow light, which illuminated drifting cloud to swathe the sky in dying beauty. As the day died so did its heat and Dumarest worked quickly to build a fire, using dried grasses and lumps of peat which burned slowly and cast a somber glow.

"Earl!" Nossak woke to rear upright where he had lain. "Earl!"

"I'm here, Angado." Dumarest handed the man a canteen. "How do you feel?"

"I'm burning. My insides are like a furnace and I ache all over." He drank and fell back to lie in the shelter of the supplies. "So we got dumped, eh? I thought it was a nightmare. Well, I guess it's better than getting thrown into the void. What was it that hit me?"

Dumarest shrugged. "Maybe a virus of some kind or it could have been an allergy. No one seemed to want to find out. That fool Cranmer shouted 'plague' and that was it."

"So I got dumped and you with me." Nossak turned his head, face ugly with lumps now darkened with blotches. "I guess you had no choice, huh?"

"No."

"If you had? I mean, would you be here now?"

"No."

"At least you're honest. I'll have to remember that. Maybe . . ."

He fell back, lost in a sudden sleep which was close to a coma; fitful periods of unconsciousness that hit at any time and without warning. A symptom of his illness; the lumps were another. Blotched masses hard beneath the skin that covered his entire body. Some were crusted by the dried scabs of oozing secretions.

By the light of the fire and the stars overhead Dumarest checked the supplies. There was water, concentrated food, a small supply of drugs, a hand axe, a compass, some needles and thread, a length of fine wire, a knife. Dumarest compared it to the one he lifted from his boot then set it to one side. The rest of the bulk was made up of two large but empty plastic sacs and a bundle of clothing.

Dumarest piled most of them around the sick man, covering the whole with one of the plastic bags. Seated before the

180

fire he worked at the length of wire, fashioning lines ending in running loops. Stepping into the starlit darkness he set the snares, holding them with doubled ends of the wire set deep in the dirt. Back at the fire he ate a wafer of concentrate, washed it down with a sip of water and, knife in hand, closed his eyes.

He slept like an animal, hovering on the brink of wakefulness, starting alert as something threshed in the grass to one side. A small rodent, he guessed, which had become caught in a snare and he mentally marked the direction of the noise.

As the stars began to pale with the onset of dawn he heard a series of dull explosions to the north followed by a vivid lavender flash. He marked it with the knives dug into the ground to form a line of sight which he checked with the compass as the day grew brighter. When the plain lay revealed in sharp detail he went to check the snares, finding them all intact except one. It rested in a twisted mass among crushed grass stained with flecks of blood. Around it he saw the marks of spatulate paws.

An hour later it began to rain.

Angado Nossak was singing in a high, cracked voice, a melody that made little sense followed by a babbling string of words that made even less. Dumarest rose from his place beside the fire and crossed to the prostrate man. It was late afternoon, the rain had cleared the air leaving a brisk freshness now sharpened by the chill of approaching evening.

"Earl!" The babbling stopped as the man looked up, crusted lips parting in a smile. "Good old Earl. My friend. My faithful retainer. Did I tell you how you will be rewarded? For you a palace filled with nubile maidens, fountains of wine, tables groaning beneath the weight of assorted viands. Land and workers to tend your crops. On Lychen you will live like a king."

"Lychen?"

"My home world. The residence of the family to which I belong. Allow me to present Hedren Angado Nossak Karroum." His arm waved in a vague gesture. "The spoiled son of a decaying line. Yet there are those who hold me in high regard. Those who . . . who. . . ."

"Wake up!" The slap of Dumarest's hand against the

181

lolling cheek caused birds to rise with startled croakings from the plain. "Damn you, wake up!" Another slap. As the eyes opened to focus with bleared concentration Dumarest snapped, "Now listen to me! Listen, damn you! I'm giving you two days to get on your feet. Until the dawn after next. Call it thirty-six hours. Do you understand?"

"Earl, I. . . ."

"Keep awake!" Dumarest rose and gripped the plastic sac he had spread over the recumbent man. The rain it had trapped sloshed wetly over his hands to cascade down over Nossak's face and head; the deluge caused him to splutter but cleared his eyes. "Now listen!"

"Earl?"

"You're ill, dying, and I mean that. Unless you're able to travel the day after tomorrow I'm leaving you. That means you work to get well or you stay and be food for what's living out there." Dumarest jerked his head at the plain. "It's up to you. Personally I don't give a damn. I'd be better off alone."

"You mean it." Nossak struggled to focus his eyes. "You really mean it."

"That's right." Dumarest's tone matched his expression, cold, hard, unyielding. "Now hold still."

The drugs were in ampules fitted with hollow needles serving as strings. The first brought sleep, the second was loaded with wide-coverage antibiotics, the third held slow time; chemical magic which speeded the metabolism and stretched seconds into minutes, hours into days. Angado would wake thin, starving, but able to walk if luck was with him. If his survival instinct, bolstered by the grim warning, gave him the needed incentive. If either failed then he would die.

Dumarest covered the sleeping man with clothing, covered that with one of the plastic sacs and turned away. He'd done all he could and now it was time to ensure his own survival.

Far out on the plain birds rose with a sudden thrum of wings, and he studied them, eyes narrowed as he counted their number, the direction of their flight. A period of quiet and then another sudden uprush of winged shapes, closer and heading in his general direction. More came as the sun touched the horizon much closer than the others. Then nothing but silence and the brooding of watching eyes.

Out on the plain death was waiting.

Dumarest knew what it had to be. In such open country game was scarce and hard to bring down. The creature that had stolen the snared rodent had tasted blood and wanted more. It was only a question of time before the predator decided to attack.

For Dumarest it couldn't be too soon.

He had prepared the trap; ropes woven from strips of clothing now set to form a pattern of loops and barriers that would hamper quick movement if the beast loped over the area. The bait was made of food concentrates pounded and soaked in water thickly stained with his own blood. A compound smeared on a bundle of clothing set near enough to the smoldering fire for the heat to disperse the scent but not too close to frighten the beast away.

Now there was nothing to do but wait and he crouched, waiting, watchful, the small axe to hand, a knife resting in each boot. A man matching his patience against that of a beast, his ability to kill against a creature developed for just that attribute.

The fire dwindled, became a sullen, ashed ball, a shrinking, bloodshot eye. High above, the stars shone with an increasing brightness, a brilliant scatter of glowing points, sheets and curtains of luminescence interspersed with the fuzz of distant nebulae. Suns were close in the Burdinnion and always, toward the galactic center, the skies at night showed a blaze of luminescence, touching the plain with a soft, nacreous glow. Turning dried stems into wands of silver, drooping leaves into fronds of shining, filigreed silk until the frosted landscape stirred to the touch of a gentle wind that filled the air with a whispering susurration.

Dumarest thinned his lips as he stared into the empty spaces.

The wind would mask the approach he'd hoped to catch. The slithering rustle of a creature making its attack. One impossible to avoid and the only warning he would get. Now, because of the wind, his ears were useless and his vision limited. The beast could be behind him at this very moment, crouching, claws ripping into the ground as it sprang, those same claws reaching out to tear the flesh from his bones.

Dumarest dropped, an ear pressed to the ground, the other covered as he strained to catch subtle vibrations. He heard nothing but the beat of his own heart. A hand snatched a knife from his boot, drove it into the dirt, metal jarring against his teeth as he clamped them on the blade. A long, dragging moment then he heard it. A soft rumble, a rasp, a sound more movement than noise. Echoes transmitted through the ground and into the knife and by bone conduction into his brain.

A murmur which grew stronger, closer and then, abruptly, ceased.

Turning, snatching at knife and axe, Dumarest saw it limned against the stars.

A beast like a tiger, five feet long from head to the root of the tail, clawed paws extended, jaws gaping to reveal long, pointed fangs. A ruff of fur circled the neck to run in a line along the back. The tail, like a whip, bore a spined end. The back legs held razors.

Natural weapons which kicked at the ground to throw dirt pluming upward as the jaws closed on the clothing bearing the bait. The snarl of frustrated anger was a guttural roar of muted thunder, and shreds of fabric flew to either side as the beast vented its rage. Then it dropped the rags and stood, snuffing the air, head turning to where Nossak lay in drugged unconsciousness.

Dumarest acted before it could spring.

The axe spun from his hand, whirling to bite into the neck, the blade shearing through hide and muscle but missing the arteries. An attack which confused the animal by its sheer unexpectedness and it sprang to one side, head turning, jaws gaping as it scented the new enemy. One which came darting toward the creature, knives in hand, steel which stung and slashed at tendons and ligaments.

Dumarest moved back and felt the wind as a paw raked at his face. Then he was running, jumping high over the ropes he had set out. Behind him the animal snarled as the strands hampered its movement, a noose tightening to trap a rear leg.

Dumarest returned to the attack. The beast had to be killed, not frightened off to lurk hurt and dangerous on the plain. He darted forward as the animal reared, paws extended, jaws gaping. A lunge which placed him within range of the belly and he felt the jar and rasp as claws tore at his shoulders and back, the impact of the knife as it plunged deep to release a gush of blood.

He twisted as the free rear leg kicked out in a hammer blow which sent him staggering to fall beside the fire.

Rising, he snatched at the coals, threw them, ran toward the beast as sparks coated the snarling mask. His speed sent his face to press against the neck, his head rammed up hard beneath the lower jaw, his left hand rising to grip the mane as his right felt along the cage of the ribs.

To find the pulse of the heart. . . .

Stopped as he drove home his knife.

Chapter Three

Alive!

Avro leaned back in his chair, feeling his mind expand with the euphoria of relief. On the desk before him rested the reports and findings on which he had based his conclusions. They were not certain—nothing could ever be that—but the probability that Dumarest was alive was above ninety percent. And, for him, that was good enough.

The eye-witness reports had given him the initial clue—Cardor had been thorough on that if nothing else. The stories were too similar, not exact, for that would have been obvious, but certain facets had left unanswered doubts. The viewpoints seemed to be roughly the same and that was wrong. The relation placed the same importance on the series of events and that too hadn't quite fit. Yet all was explained if the speakers had, somehow, been influenced by one other. Told the story and been made to believe it to be true. And for them it had been true.

But none had remembered what had happened to the klachen that had run berserk in a killing frenzy.

A mistake and he wondered who had made it. The owner? It was possible but even if true it no longer mattered. Punishment needed to be extracted for Tron's death though it could have been accidental. The animal could have broken free. Could have killed the cyber and the agent, and Dumarest, recognizing his chance, had taken it.

Speculation of no value and Avro dismissed it. The proof was enough and he leaned forward to examine it. The correlated reports, the scraps regained from the lagoon; bones, fragments of clothing, the remains of four bodies, one of them a woman.

The report of a man who had been found drinking in a tavern and telling of a vicious fight in the ring of the circus. A combat Dumarest had won.

The dead man had aided the deception.

Avro picked up a fragment of clothing, gray plastic covering a hidden metal mesh—protection favored by travelers and known to be worn by Dumarest. But such clothing was common, especially among those visiting hostile worlds. Dumarest could already have replaced it if he was alive.

Avro was convinced he was.

His luck would have seen to that. The peculiar ability Dumarest seemed to possess which yielded favorable circumstances when they were most needed. A survival trait Avro had recognized and which must govern his every step in the pursuit of the quarry.

But, if Dumarest was alive, where was he to be found?

The answer lay in the mass of data resting on the desk; the ship movements, cargo manifests, destinations, reports culled from a thousand sources. Most was unrelated trivia but from the rest Avro had selected items which could form a pattern. One which would carry the image of truth.

Baatz was a busy world with traders and merchants coming from all parts to buy and sell in the market. But such could be eliminated; creatures of habit, they were known, their movements predictable. Others posed harder problems, gamblers, harlots, pimps, entrepreneurs together with free-traders and other vessels following no regular routes. Yet the apparent randomness took on a different aspect when the whole was considered. Transient though the population of Baatz might be, yet it followed certain laws similar to those dictating the migrations of birds and wild animals. The need of being at the feeding ground at the right time, the combination of holiday and carnival and the flux of tourists.

Few, like Dumarest, were unattached wanderers drifting from world to world without apparent reason. And those working on the field had grown to recognize the regular visitors.

Avro studied a thin sheaf of reports. A man resembling

Dumarest had taken passage on the *Sinden* a day after Tron had landed. Too soon—eliminate him. Another had left on the *Harrif* a day after the cyber had died. A gambler known to the field agent and expected back soon. Two men who had looked furtive, one who had hidden his face, another traveling with a giggling harlot, a somber individual who wore gray along with the mask of a clown.

A possibility Avro considered then discarded; even if Dumarest had chosen to hide behind conspicuousness the ship had been bound for Zshen. A long flight. Too long for a man needing to lose himself.

And there were other factors to be taken into account. Central Intelligence absorbed an astronomical amount of information from a host of cybers. Data of no obvious value but all taken and sifted through the organic computer to be correlated, aligned, evaluated and all possible connections checked and determined.

Information passed to Avro at his request.

He stared at the papers before him, remembering, wondering why, the last time he had established rapport, it had been as normal. There had been no bizarre landscape, no figure to greet him and exchange words as if face to face. No enclosed universe in which he had been thrust as if by a whim. Would it ever happen again?

He set aside that question as he returned to his task. With a handful of facts he could predict the logical outcome of any event. Training and talent which could not only show where Dumarest had been but predict where he would be and when.

On Nyne a warehouse had been damaged. Broken out of by someone locked within. An item of local news coupled with that of a broken crate. And crates of just that size had been shipped from Baatz after Tron had died. Dumarest could have traveled in one. And after?

The Burdinnion was close and a good place for a man to hide. Easy traveling, with journeys too short to do other than ride Middle. Natural time spent in a variety of ways all designed to eliminate boredom—and Dumarest had skill as a gambler.

Which ship and where headed?

Three had left Nyne at the relevant time. One, a private

charter, could be eliminated; such craft didn't cater to the casual trade. Another, heading toward Baatz, the same. The third, the *Solinoy*, had been bound for Tysa.

Tysa?

It held nothing but a farming complex fueling a stringent economy based on the export of medicinal drugs. A small, harsh, bleak world lashed by radiation and populated mostly by contract workers who had no choice but to stay where fate had dumped them. The last place a man would hide.

And yet?

Avro checked the data; the mechanism of his mind evaluated probabilities. Then he judged time and distance. A button sank beneath a finger as he reached a decision.

"Master!" Tupou answered the command. "Your orders?"

"Go to the field. Have my ship readied for immediate flight. I shall require full velocity. Have Byrne clear the suite."

"Yes, Master. The destination?"

"Anfisa."

It had to be Anfisa. The *Thorn* had left soon after the *Solinoy* had landed and the ship was bound for that world.

Avro intended to meet it.

Angado Nossak sucked at a bone and said, "Earl, I've never felt better in my life."

He looked it. The lumpy protrusions had gone as had a slight plumpness at the waist and jowls. The skin and eyes were clear. Sitting cross-legged before the fire he was the picture of health.

Dumarest said, "You were lucky."

"Sure I was lucky—I had you to look after me." Nossak sobered as he reached for another meaty bone from the heap stacked before the fire. "Though I had a bad dream, once. A nightmare, I guess. I seemed to hear you saying you were going to desert me."

"It was no dream!"

"It had to be!"

"Is that what you always say when you bump up against something you don't like?" Dumarest lowered the tunic he was working on with plastic and a hot iron; the knife included

189

in the supplies which he'd heated in the fire. "Pretend it doesn't exist? Call it a dream? Keep that up and you won't have to worry about growing old."

"I almost didn't." Nossak looked at his arms and frowned. "You gave me slow time, right?"

"That and other things."

"Drugs, sure, but what about the rest? I'm in too good a shape to have starved for over a month. We've no equipment or supplies for intravenous feeding so how did you manage?"

With blood mixed with water and fed into his stomach through a pipe made from the intestines of the predator. Fluids followed by raw, pulped liver and other soft meats.

Nossak gulped as he listened.

"Maybe I shouldn't have asked."

"Squeamish?"

"Let's just say I was never used to things like that."

"What were you used to?" Dumarest thrust the knife back into the fire. Stripped to shorts his body showed a pattern of bruises, marks left by the blow and rake of claws, the snap of teeth. Only the metal protection of his clothing had saved him from fatal lacerations. Now, slowly, he was doing his best to refurbish the garments. "Servants? Money? Adulation?"

"Let's forget it."

"No." Dumarest's tone brooked no argument. "I want to know. Someone tried to kill you and I got mixed up in it. They could try again. It would help to know why."

"Kill me? But I was sick, ill—"

"Poisoned." Smoke rose as Dumarest applied the hot metal, forcing molten plastic into the rents left by claws. "Nothing crude and it couldn't be detected but it exploded allergic reactions once triggered. Anything could have done it, the cards, the basic, the woman's perfume. What do you know about Cranmer?"

"Nothing. Why?"

"He yelled plague and scared the hell out of everyone. Stopped them thinking, too. A smart assassin would have thought of that. One way or another he wanted you dead. Why?"

"It doesn't matter." Nossak gnawed at the bone. "It happened. It's over. Forget it."

"You said that before."

"Then why not do it?"

Dumarest rose, standing upright, the early sun touching his skin and accentuating the bruises. He dressed, adjusting tunic and pants, slipping his knife into his right boot. The other, the one he had used to melt the plastic, he threw into the dirt at Nossak's feet.

"You'd better have that. The axe I'll take with a canteen, one of the sacs and half the snares. The compass too and some of the concentrates." Stooping, Dumarest lifted a joint of meat from where it had been set to cure in the smoke from the fire. "You can have the rest."

"You're going?"

"Yes."

"But—" Nossak rose to his feet, the bone falling from his hand. "You're leaving me? Earl, you can't do that!"

"Watch me."

"But why? What the hell have I done?"

"Nothing. You're a full-grown man now and can stand on your own. If you can't then too bad—I'm no nursemaid."

Nossak said, slowly, "It's because I won't talk, is that it? But what difference does it make? A man's business is his own affair."

"Not when it involves others. I'm here because of you, remember. I'd like to know why." Dumarest paused then said, flatly, "It's up to you, Angado. Or should it be Hedren? Or Karroum?"

"You know?"

"You babbled. Big promises, long names, great rewards. What's so special about being Hedren Angado Nossak Karroum?"

"The seventh," said Nossak bitterly. "Don't forget the number. And if you want you can stick a title in front. Lord Hedren—" He broke off and spat. "To hell with it. Why can't I have one name like you, Earl?"

"You can. Pick one. Angado. From now on that's it." Dumarest sat and picked up the bone the other had dropped. Handing it back he said. "Eat. We can't afford to waste a thing. Now why would anyone want to see you dead?"

"I don't know."

Dumarest sighed. "Just talk," he suggested. "Fill me in on your background."

It was much what he'd expected, an old and established family suffering from inbreeding and decay. The sharp edge which had originally lifted them to power and carved a position of authority weakened by petty rivalries and jealousy. Angado, the seventh to hold the name and title, had an ambitious cousin. One who had made him a tempting offer.

"Just to travel," said Angado. "A regular income paid as long as I stayed away from home. I could go where I liked, do as I liked, but only on that condition. So you see why the very thought of anyone wanting to kill me is ridiculous."

A fool—as he had shown at the card table; any child could have computed the logical outcome of such an arrangement. One fee paid to a skilled assassin and no more payments. No threat of the wanderer's return. No focus for any dissatisfied associates to use as the basis of a rebellion.

"Perotto is hard but fair," said Angado. "He made a bargain and will stick to it. I'd stake my life on that."

He had and almost lost. Dumarest said, casually, "Is Lychen your home world?"

"Yes, do you know it?"

"I've heard of it."

From Shakira of the circus of Chen Wei. The name of the planet on which he could find someone able and willing to help him to find Earth.

They headed out at noon, moving toward the north where Dumarest had seen the lavender flash. Behind them the fire sent up a thin column of smoke which he used to check their direction.

As it finally fell below the horizon Angado said, "Well, if they ever come looking for us, they'll never find us now."

"No one will come looking."

"I suppose not. Krogstad didn't strike me as the sort of captain who'd burn atoms unless he was paid." Angado shrugged and looked around. "A hell of a place."

The plain stretched around them on all sides. Flat, gently undulating, covered with thick grass, featureless.

192

Dumarest halted to sniff at the wind. It came from the east, a soft breeze which barely moved the tufted tips of the grass, and the odors it carried were the same as those all around. At a distance birds rose, wheeling, settling as he watched.

"Too far." Angado had misread his interest. "We'd never be able to bring them down." He grunted as Dumarest made no comment. "You ever hunted?"

"At times."

"Big game hunting?"

"Not if I could avoid it."

"There's a thrill to it," said Angado. "Pitting your wits and skill against something which could tread you into the ground if given the chance. Standing, waiting, finger on the trigger. Holding your aim and watching for that one moment to fire. It gets you, Earl. Like a fire in the blood." He frowned as Dumarest remained silent. "If you've hunted you must know what I'm talking about."

Dumarest said, "Did you hunt for food?"

"Of course not. It was for sport."

"Butchery, you mean. Killing for the pleasure of it. Standing in a hide and waiting for the beaters to drive the creature toward you. Waiting for it with a gun. What chance did it have?" Dumarest looked at his companion. "I've seen it. Spoiled bastards, rich, pampered, having fun. They don't see what they leave behind. The hurt beasts, wounded by too hasty a shot, dragging themselves away with their guts trailing after them. Some with broken legs or no leg at all. Animals blinded and left to starve. Hunting! Don't boast to me about hunting!"

"It wasn't like that."

"How do you know? You hired men to clean up the mess but did they do it? Did you check or were you too busy showing off your trophy?"

Angado said, "I'm sorry. I didn't know you felt that way about it. I guessed you were a hunter and you killed that beast—"

"For food and because it threatened us." Dumarest added, "There's a difference. By the time this trip is over you may recognize it."

193

They moved on over the plain, which was as featureless as a sea. Only the compass kept them on a straight line; without it they would have wandered in circles despite the guiding light of the sun. As it swung toward the horizon Dumarest looked for somewhere to camp. It had to be soon; Angado was showing signs of distress but refused to give in to his weakness. A stubborn man who insisted on gathering fuel for the fire and was reluctant to take his share of water.

"We ought to save it, Earl. Ration it."

"Ration it, yes, but not save it," Dumarest tried to explain. "It's best to store it in our bodies not in a canteen. The same with food. We need all the energy we can get and all the strength. If a chance comes we must be strong enough to take it."

"A chance?"

"For food, water, anything which could help us to survive. This plain can't go on forever. Drink up, now."

Later, when the stars glowed above, he studied the sleeping figure of the younger man. One maybe a decade younger than himself but centuries his junior in experience. A man cosseted when young, spoiled by fawning servants, convinced by his peers that he was not like the majority. The product of wealth and influence who had much to learn. With luck he would learn it before he died.

Dumarest wished they had never met.

Rising he looked toward the north hoping for more of the reports, the lavender flash. He saw nothing but the stars and a rising mist which blurred their light. One which thickened into a fog which closed around like a wall of growing darkness. From it, to the west, he heard a shrill screaming and he added more fuel to the fire.

"Earl?" The screaming had awakened Angado and he reared, voice anxious. "What's that?"

"A hunter at work."

"A predator? Like the one you killed?"

"Maybe."

"Do you think it will attack us?"

"It might."

Angado rose and came to sit with Dumarest at the fire. As he settled he said, "You don't like me, do you? On the ship it didn't matter, we were just passing strangers, but here it's different. You told me about the hunting but what else is wrong? My title?''

"You were born to it.''

"And so can't be blamed. Right? Any more than a slave can be blamed for being a slave. We don't use them on Lychen, you know. Contract workers, yes, but not slaves. In the old days we had them but not for a long time now.'' Angado held out his hands to the fire. "I guess that's what you'd call progress.''

"Would you?''

"What else? There's a difference between being a slave and being a contract worker. Workers are in it from choice.''

"Unless they owe money,'' reminded Dumarest. "Or were sold under sentence.''

"Sure—but you aren't saying a man should get away with crime? And even they get treated well; food, shelter, clothing, some amusements. It can't be such a bad life.''

"Would you want it?'' Then, as Angado made no answer Dumarest said, "For most it's a life sentence. The food, the shelter, the clothing, all has to be paid for and the company sets the price. A few amusements and the worker is back where he started and often worse than before. It takes a rare type to buy himself free.''

"Maybe, but it's still better than slavery. That's why I said we'd progressed on Lychen. We gave that up a long time ago.''

"Most civilized worlds are against the use of slaves,'' said Dumarest. "Especially those with a high technology. But it isn't because of a liberal attitude toward freedom. That's just the reason they like to give to cover the real motivations.''

"Which are?''

"Two. The first is fashion. Once it becomes unfashionable then a slave owner is at a disadvantage. He will be ostracized, derided, made to feel socially inferior. His business will suffer and he'll be hit where it hurts. Once he feels the pain in his wallet he'll join the rest as a matter of survival. He'll free his slaves and begin charging them for what he'd been supplying for nothing. An advantage he'll be quick to recogonize.''

Angado nodded. "That's one reason. The other?"

"A matter of economics. Slaves make bad workers and who can blame them? The higher the technology the less productive they are and the greater the risk of damage to expensive equipment. In the end, to be efficient, you'd need an overseer for each worker. If the overseer can do the job why go to the expense of keeping a slave?"

"Because you can—"

"What? Beat them? Force them to work? Make them obedient? That may be true but you can't force anyone to be clever or loyal or even trustworthy. And what incentive can you give a slave? Freedom? Do that and you lose valuable property. You can kill them, sure, but you'd be hurting yourself in the long run. So it comes back to economics. The only real—" Dumarest broke off, listening, as another thin screaming echoed through the night. "It's made another kill. Good."

"Because now it won't be hungry and so will leave us alone?"

"You're learning."

"More than you think. What were you going to say just then? About slaves. The only real reason anyone would want to own them."

Dumarest hadn't said that but he answered the question.

"Power. Real power. Wealth and influence doesn't make you strong, it only shows how weak others can be. You can bribe them to obey but, if they've any guts, they can always tell you to go to hell. But a slave has no choice. He jumps when you give the word or you have him flogged, burned, tortured, maimed. Power like that can be a drug. Some can't live without it."

Perotto for one as Angado knew. Larsen for another and he saw their faces painted against the mist. Both of equal age, his cousin old enough to be his father. Older than his years, his face seamed with lines of determination, eyes hard beneath thick brows. Had he gone back on his word? Larsen might have dropped the hint with his cunning serpent's tongue, but surely Perotto would never have agreed. Had Larsen acted on his own? If . . .

"Angado, you'd better finish your sleep."

"What?" He blinked at Dumarest. "Sorry, but I was thinking," he said. "Family business."

Of which Dumarest could have no part and yet if it hadn't been for his companion he would be dead by now. Could still die—how long could they hope to survive in this wilderness?

Chapter Four

Halting, Dumarest threw back his head and sniffed at the air. Like a dog, thought Angado dispassionately. Like the animal he'd become as they made their way over the endless plain. Sniffing for scent, looking for sign, surviving where no ordinary man could have lasted. A trait he envied while knowing he could never hope to emulate it.

He stumbled, feeling the jar in knees and hips as he fought to regain his balance. The pack he carried was a monstrous hand pressing him down, a load full of trivia which Dumarest refused to discard. He turned to look behind, seeing their trail wending over the rolling plain toward a featureless horizon, one which faded, vanishing, as gusting wind flurried the long grass and resettled it in a new pattern.

The trail they left was as transient as that made by a boat on an ocean. Their progress apparently measured by inches.

He lunged forward, cursing the pull of the grass which hampered his stride and sapped at his energy. Strength too low for the task; the scant food failing to replace that used and, now the food was gone, hunger was turning into starvation.

"Steady!" Dumarest was at his side, a hand firm on his arm. "Take a rest."

"But—"

"Do it!" Dumarest softened his tone. "Rest now and we can keep going until twilight. Be stubborn and you'll collapse after a couple of miles." His knife flashed as he hacked free a bunch of grass. "Here, keep busy with this. Something to fill your stomach." He illustrated running a

strand between his teeth to remove the husk and pulp.
"See?"

"Can we live on it?"

"No, but it'll give you bulk and some moisture." And
give him something to do as well as taking his mind off
present difficulties. Dumarest added, "There's a run over
there. The sun's low enough to shade it and with luck we'll
get something to eat."

He moved off before Angado could comment, one hand
delving beneath his tunic to reappear with a scrap of food
concentrate wrapped in a cloth. Sweat had soaked into the
fabric, adding his own body odor to that of the ripening
wafer. Carefully he set it at the place he had noted; one
where small tunnels through the grass joined to form a
junction. Snares would have created a warning scent and an
unusual sight image and Dumarest didn't want to wait
longer than necessary. Taking up a position facing the sun,
the wind in his face, he poised the knife in his hand and
stood, waiting.

A living statue dark against the sky. Angado watched,
running strands of grass between his teeth. The gain was
small but his mouth welcomed the opportunity to chew and
swallow and the moist pulp held a refreshing tartness. More
gratifying was the opportunity to rest and he eased the ache
in back and legs, bones and muscles.

The pack was a nuisance. The need of the sacs had been
demonstrated; spread at night they collected condensed dew
and twice the fruit of an intermittent rain. But most of the
rest was useless; clothing they would never wear, empty
containers, voided ampules. . . . discarded rubbish . . . stuff
which swirled in his mind and created a sudden complexity
of dancing patterns.

Angado started, aware that he had dozed, fighting the
sleep which clogged his mind. The sun was lower than he
remembered but the dark silhouette against the sky was as
before. Then, as he watched, Dumarest exploded in a sudden blur of motion. A flash as the knife left his hand, a
darting forward, a stoop then he was upright again and
coming toward him the creature he had caught impaled on
the blade of the thrown knife.

A thing little larger than a rat, which he skinned, filled

the pelt with the guts, head and feet, then split the remainder into two segments one of which he handed to Angado.

"Eat it."

"Aren't we cooking it first?"

"There's more energy in it raw." Dumarest bit, chewed, blood rimming his mouth. "We may get something else later on."

Another rodent, a twin of the first, which Angado turned on a crude spit over the smoking fire. It was stringy and, lacking salt, flavorless, but it was hot and something to chew and a filled stomach restored his optimism.

"I could get to like this kind of life," he said, poking at the fire. "But not without a gun and a few comforts. A sleeping bag, some emergency rations, a radio to summon help if anything went wrong." The smoldering eye flared as it fed on a morsel of fat. As it died Angado said, in a different tone, "How much longer, Earl?"

"As long as it takes."

"How far, then? Damn it, you know what I mean. There has to be someone around. A settlement, a town, civilization of some kind. Even a farm. We just can't wander on forever."

The truth, but they could wander until they died, and, for Angado, that would mean the same thing.

Dumarest said, quietly, "A world's a big place. Any world. Even the residents never get to see all of it and it takes a long time for even them to spread. A planet can be settled, no riches found, the community dwindle to a string of farms. Natural increase will take care of things in time but that means a few thousand years at least. The planets which are heavily populated are old or rich or usually both."

"And, in the Burdinnion, such worlds don't exist." Angado looked at his hands. They were clenched into fists as if he wanted to fight and defeat the truth Dumarest had given him. "Krogstad," he said. "The bastard! He didn't intend for us ever to be found. He as good as killed us."

"We're alive," reminded Dumarest.

"Because of you, not him." Angado drew in his breath, fighting to master his anger. "I'll find him," he said. "If I ever get out of this I'll hunt the bastard down. And when I

200

meet him—" He looked again at his hands. "We'll do it together, Earl. You've the right to be in at the kill."

"Maybe, but I've other things to do."

"You'll let him get away with it?" Angado thought he understood. "I'll do the paying. Perotto can't refuse me funds to gain revenge. He—" He broke off, looking at Dumarest's face, remembering. "You still think he tried to kill me?"

Dumarest said, "That's your problem, not mine. As for the rest if I ever run into Krogstad he'll regret it. But I'm not chasing him."

"You don't want revenge? On Lychen we'd—"

"Is Lychen a vendetta world?"

"Not exactly, but we have pride."

"The old families," corrected Dumarest. "The established clans. Only the rich can afford the type of revenge you're talking about. Only the stupid would pursue it. Families locked in strife, killing each other, using assassination, anything, just to level the score. After a while even the cause of the quarrel is forgotten but the killing goes on."

"And pride remains."

Dumarest said, dryly, "Which, no doubt, is a great comfort to those who bury the dead."

He leaned back, running strands of grass between his teeth, watching Angado's face, illuminated by the glow from the fire, harden from what it had been and not just through loss of underlying fat. The journey was forcing him to face reality; pressure accentuated by Dumarest's talk; deliberately provocative stands taken on subjects the younger man had taken for granted. A means of engaging his mind and testing his attitude. Inflexibility would have shown the man to be brittle and liable to break in an emergency. As it was the black-and-white presentations had helped to soften the monotony of the journey.

Angado said, "Earl, those reports you heard and that flash. On the night we landed."

"Yes?"

"I've never seen anything like them while I've been on watch. Have you?"

"No."

"Yet we're heading toward them. Why? They could have been a natural occurrence."

"I doubt it."

"But you can't be sure."

"No." Dumarest added, "We've talked enough. Will you take the first watch or shall I?"

"I'll take it."

Angado watched as Dumarest settled then turned to look at the surrounding emptiness. The rolling plain of featureless grass now silvered by starlight into a desert of snow, of frost, of uncaring indifference. Later, when tossing in restless sleep, he dreamed of lying on it forever, his skull grinning at the skies.

The next dawn it rained and they lunged forward through wet and hampering grass. Noon brought sun and thrusting winds. Night came with hunger and tormented rest. A pattern repeated with variations over the next three days. On the fourth they reached the end of the plain.

It ended abruptly as if a giant knife had slashed the terrain from side to side in a cut which reached from left to right as far as the eye could reach. A division which proved the plain to be the summit of a plateau rearing high above the ground below. Dumarest halted well clear of the edge, one ornamented with wheeling birds, graced with the susurration of wind.

"God!" Angado, more foolhardy, had dropped to thrust his head over the edge. Turning he waved. "Look at this, Earl! Look!"

From the edge the ground fell sharply in a precipitous slope broken by rocky outcroppings, clumps of vegetation, tufts of grass and clinging vines. An almost sheer surface ending in a mass of scree far below.

"A mile!" Angado drew in his breath. "We must be a mile high at least."

Rising, Dumarest shaded his eyes and studied the terrain beyond. An expanse of raw dirt, trees, rocks, stunted bushes ran to the far horizon. Nowhere could he see signs of habitation. The edge on which he stood could run in a ragged circle and to follow it would mean being trapped on the plain. To descend would be easy and it was important they choose the right place.

He checked the compass and again looked ahead seeing nothing more than before. The instrument could be faulty or distance had compounded small, initial errors. He looked at the sky. The sun was rising and wind droned against the cliff. A blast that carried seeds and dust, leaves and debris which spun as it rode the thermals, fluttering like broken fans.

Without the compass they would have wended toward the right and, for lack of checking sightings, they must have done just that.

"Left," he said to Angado. "We'll move left and hope to find something."

They spotted it at noon, a thread of smoke, a glitter which flashed and vanished from among a clump of trees.

Angado squinted at it, puzzled, shaking his head.

"I can't make it out. There're no houses that I can see and it certainly isn't a town. The smoke must be from an open fire—but the glitter?" He grunted as it came again and quickly vanished. "The sun reflected from a window? A mirror? What?"

"Water," said Dumarest. "That's a camp of some kind. They've got a bowl of water, washing in it, maybe." He checked the direction on the compass. "That's where we'll make for."

"Sure." Angado sat down, relief had brought a sudden weakness. "All we have to do is climb down this cliff."

Dumarest examined it again, finding the surface no different from what it had been before. He checked a probable line of descent; from the edge to an outcropping to where tufts of grass could provide a series of holds, to where a narrow ledge supported a clump of tall, bamboo-like vegetation.

Opening the packs, he sorted out the clothing, the ropes he had made.

"Weave more," he told Angado. "Make them tight and strong."

He set the pace, slicing the clothing with his knife, plaiting the strands, making sure they would hold. When the rope was long enough to reach the ledge he tied it around his waist.

"Hold it fast," he warned the younger man. "If I slip ram it against the ground with your foot and throw your weight against it. Keep it tight—too much slack could jerk you over when it tightens."

"What about the other stuff?" Angado looked at the discarded litter, the sacs and painfully carried items. "You dumping it?"

"This is just a test run. Hold fast now."

Dumarest slipped over the edge, feeling dirt crumble beneath his weight, dropping until his foot hit the rocks he had spotted. More dirt plumed down over him, grit stinging his eyes. Angado's face looked anxiously through a mist of dust.

"All right, Earl?"

"Get back! Watch that rope!"

His lifeline if he should slip but Angado's death together with his own if the man was careless. Dumarest waited then resumed the descent. Grass yielded beneath his weight to reveal crusted stone traced with roots. A second tuft held and he paused to examine the face of the cliff. It was rotten, eroded with wind and weather, turning to dust beneath his touch.

He inched lower, hoping that rock would provide a firmer surface, brushing aside the tall shoots as he reached the ledge bearing the bamboo. Tall poles a couple of inches thick covered with thorned leaves which dewed the back of his left hand with blood. Behind them, hidden by the foliage, gaped the open mouth of a cave.

Suddenly it filled with vicious life.

It came with a rush, a thing gleaming with chitin, mandibles open, faceted eyes reflecting the sun as if they had been rubies. A centipede-like insect three feet long nine inches thick, multiple legs covered with cruel spines which ripped and tore at Dumarest's arm as the mandibles reached to close on his throat.

Closing on his left forearm instead as he swung it up to block the attack.

The creature doubling to drive its sting into his face.

Dumarest felt the rasp of the body as he jerked his head aside, kicking so as to drive himself out and away from the ledge. Spinning, dropping, he reached for his knife, lifting it as the insect scrabbled at his arm, the sting slamming against his shoulder. Acid stung his cheek as he stabbed upward, the blade digging deep into the armored body. A blow with little result and he freed the knife and slashed instead, the keen

204

edge cutting deep before the sting, crippling, cutting again to lop off the last few segments of the writhing body.

Hurt, maimed, the creature twisted, raking Dumarest with mandible and spines, then reared up to catch the rope and run up it. Halting, it began to tear at the plaited strands.

"Angado!" Once weakened, the rope would break and he would fall a mile to end as a bloody pulp on the scree. "Up, man! Up!"

A shout followed by a jerk which sent Dumarest crashing hard against the face of the cliff. Above him the insect slid down the rope, the upper half of its body twisting to take a new hold, to send the entire creature scuttling down toward Dumarest's head.

A moment and it was on him, mandibles tearing at his scalp, legs ripping at his eyes. Instinct drove the knife upward to cut, slash, stab at the ruby eyes, cut away the threshing legs. Ichor oozed from the lacerated body to dew him with odorous slime. Then, as Angado hauled at the rope, the thing fell away to drop, spinning, to the ground below.

"God!" Angado dropped the rope to help Dumarest as he climbed over the edge. "Your face! What the hell happened?"

His face tightened when, later, Dumarest told him. Water from a canteen had washed away the ichor and slime and an ampule of drugs had ended the pain from the acid-burn of bites and scratches. But nothing could have saved his eyes and the lacerations on his brows told how close the sting had come.

"A thing like that living in the cliff. You were lucky, Earl. But maybe it was a loner."

"No."

"It could have been. A freak of some kind." Angado wanted to be convinced. "Or maybe they only lurk near the edge."

Dumarest said, "It had a lair behind that clump of bamboo. My guess is that we'll find others like it wherever there is cover. Other things too—the cliff is riddled with holes and they can't all be natural. And don't forget the wind."

"What has that to do with it?"

"It blows from the ground out there to the cliff and it brings all sorts of things with it. Spores, seeds, insects, eggs, birds—anything which gets caught winds up here. Food, and where there's food there will be predators. I just happened to run into one.''

Angado walked to the edge and looked over. The sun, now in its descent, threw golden light over the slope, painting it with a false warmth and gentleness.

Returning to where Dumarest sat, he said, "Aside from the insects could we climb down it?''

"With luck, maybe, but we'd need a hell of a lot of luck.'' Dumarest met his eyes. "With what I figure is lurking on the face it's impossible.''

"So we're stuck up here.''

"That's right. We're stuck—unless we can find another way down.''

That night they saw lights, faint glimmers far in the distance, blooming to die as if born from a struggling fire that sputtered and fumed and roared into new and angry life.

"A camp,'' mused Angado. "I guess you're right, Earl. It has to be a camp.''

"Maybe more than that.''

"Hunters, maybe, or—'' Angado blinked. "What?''

"Those reports I heard and the flash. The noises could have been sonic bangs high up and going away from us. If they had emanated at ground level we'd have run into them on the journey. The flash could have been from an Erhaft field.''

"Lavender?'' Angado shook his head. "A field is blue.''

"Normally, yes, but the air could have colored it.'' Dumarest paused then added, "Or there could have been another reason. Do you know anything about generators?''

"You're talking about a malfunction in the phase effect resulting in a spectrum drop.'' Angado smiled with a flash of white teeth. "We studied chromatic analysis of the Erhaft field during my last semester at university. The Daley-Ash University of Space Flight,'' he added wryly. "I guess you could say I know something about generators.''

"You surprise me.''

"Why? Because I act the dilettante?'' Angado shrugged. "I had an ambition when a child and tried to achieve it. I wanted to be someone who could do things. A doctor or an engineer, healing and building, even be an expert on something so I'd be respected. Family pride," he said bitterly. "A defense against family pressure. So I went to university and studied until I was told to stop wasting my time."

"So you called it a bad dream and ran from it? The necessity of having to make a decision?"

"Call it that." Angado was curt. "A family can be a prison, Earl. You live by rules not of your making. You conform to ideals established before you were born. Play along and everything's fine. Step out of line and—" His hand slapped the ground as if he were squashing an insect. "End of ambition. End of career. End of any pretense of freedom. So I sold out. Can you blame me?"

"That isn't my business. Could what I saw have been a ship?"

"It could and you know it. You've known it from the first." Hope animated the younger man's face. "That camp! If it was a ship you saw and the field was showing phase malfunction then it must have made an emergency landing. Which means—" He rose and stared at where they had seen the fire. "It's still here, Earl. Still here. A way out of this damned trap!"

"If we can get to it."

"What?" Angado slumped. "I'd forgotten. That blasted cliff. How the hell can we get down it?"

"Tell me."

"What's there to tell? We can't climb down. We can't slide or—" He broke off, shaking his head. "No. The terminal velocity would be too great. Even with air-drogues we'd never make it and that's assuming we can find material to build sledges and a slope shallow enough to try it. I must have been crazy to think about it. So what else is left?"

Dumarest said, "How about flying?"

"Hang gliders?" Angado was quick to assess the possibility. "No. It could be done but we haven't the materials. The wing would have to be strong and so would the covering. If either went we'd be dead." He frowned and said, "But maybe a kite? Two kites, big ones, one for each of us? Earl, how can we build a couple of kites?"

"From bamboo," said Dumarest. "That can be got from the ledge. I'll go down at first light and get it, it'll be safe enough now. The sacs will serve for covering and we have

207

wire to lash things tight. Ropes, too—we'd better get on making what we need.'' He glanced at the sky, the stars were misted with cloud. ''We want to be ready when the wind starts to blow.''

The kites were box-shaped, twice the height of a man, following aerodynamic principles learned by Angado at the university. Dumarest checked the lashings, using the handle of the axe to twist them tight, the flat to test for security. The plastic sacs, opened out and cut to shape formed the major part of the covering while broad strips of various materials from the clothing provided the rest. Empty containers, voided ampules, the rubbish Angado had resented carrying—all went into the final construction. Proof of Dumarest's knowledge of the wild where even a pin was an item of inestimable value and a battered empty can an object beyond price.

''Catch hold!'' He threw the end of a rope at Angado. ''Pull!'' He jerked his own end as the man obeyed. ''Again! Once more! Good! That should do it!''

The final rope and he knotted it firmly in place before attaching it to his harness. Each checked the other and both looked grotesque with thick rolls of material bound around shins, thighs, heads, hips, arms and chest. Padding to absorb the shock of impact when they landed.

If they landed, thought Angado grimly. If the wind didn't smash them back against the cliff and the kites provided enough support to break the speed of their fall. If the ropes didn't break. The coverings rip free. The bamboo framework shatter. The scree not too hard or spiked with hidden rocks.

Doubts which didn't seem to affect Dumarest.

He said, ''When the wind hits the cliff it turns up and back on itself like a cresting wave. I've been studying how grass acts in the thermals. Throw it out far enough and it doesn't come back. Once the wind catches your kite keep it heading out. If it doesn't, pull it back and try again. Got it?''

Simple instructions but not so easy to follow despite the guidelines attached to the framework. In theory the kites could be guided to a certain degree. But now, facing the acid test, Angado wasn't so sure.

He said, ''Earl, I've been thinking. Maybe—''

''Now!'' snapped Dumarest. ''Now!'' Then, as Angado hesitated, ''Damn it, man! Move!''

The whip-crack of command which he obeyed, lifting the kite and running with it to the edge, muscles cracking beneath the strain. A moment of teetering then the wind took over, catching the kite, lifting it, jerking Angado off balance and off the edge of the cliff to leave him dangling in his harness.

Dumarest watched then followed, knowing the impossibility of following his instructions, knowing too they had been given for the other's benefit. The gamble was risky enough without adding an utter helplessness to the equation. Angado had been lucky, the wind which had caught him had been kind, Dumarest's wasn't so cooperative.

He grunted as the wind veered, slamming him against the cliff, the kite jerking him away again, a clinging vine trailing from his boot. He kicked free as again the wind gusted, the kite bobbing, dropping, soaring upward in a complex motion which blurred his eyes and filled his mouth with the taste of vomit. Weakness he ignored as he fought vertigo, tugging at his line to shorten the distance between himself and the kite, hanging, swaying like a pendulum beneath it as the wind roared past his ears.

The sound was too loud—he was falling too fast. He tugged at the guidelines, discarding them as the kite refused to respond. Instead he threw his body in a widening swing, forcing the kite to react to his movements. It tilted, straightened, was captured by the uprushing air. The roaring died and, suddenly, he drifted in calm.

The cliff was well to one side, a soaring wall of blotched and mottled dirt and stone. The other kite was closer to the wall and, like his own, acted as a parachute. Larger and they would have lifted their burdens but it was enough they had carried them clear and lowered them slow.

Five hundred feet above the ground one of the ropes snapped with the sound of tearing paper.

Dumarest swung, hanging on the single remaining rope, his weight pulling the kite to one side, tilting it, forcing it to lose height and lift. The roaring started again in his ears and he gripped the rope, climbing up it, catching the inner structure of the kite and hanging from it as the ground rushed up toward him. A moment of strain with the force of the wind fighting against his arms, muscles burning, cracking with the effort to hold on, then a sidewise swoop and the sudden jarring rasp as the kite slammed against the wall of the cliff.

A glancing blow, repeated, the third time shattering the structure and leaving nothing but a mass of splintered bamboo, shreds of plastic, wire, frayed and disintegrating rope.

From it Dumarest rolled, falling through a clump of bushes, over thickly tufted grass, to half-fall, half-slide over the fan of scree. To come to rest in a cloud of dirt among a scatter of stones.

"Earl!" Angado came running. He had landed safely and close. Now he knelt, turning Dumarest over, the anxiety on his face turning to relief as he sat upright. "Are you hurt?"

"I don't think so." There was no blood, no ache of broken bones, just numbness and the promise of bruises. The padding had done its job. "You?"

"Fine."

Dumarest nodded and climbed to his feet. The padding made movement awkward and he cut it away, leaving the scraps where they had fallen. Stretching, he took cautious strides. Luck and experience had been with him. One had thrown him into the bushes the other had made him fall like a baby or a drunk, not fighting gravity, yielding to it instead, muscles lax and supple.

"We made it!" Angado drew in his breath as he stared at the towering wall of the cliff. "By God, we made it! All we have to do now is get to the ship. Which way do we head, Earl?"

Dumarest looked at his wrist compass, the face broken, the dial twisted, the interior useless.

Chapter Five

Brother Dexter straightened from the fire feeling the nagging twinge in his back grow to a sudden fire, one accompanied by a moment of giddiness so that he stood immobile in the smoke now rising from the coals. The effects of age as he knew, familiar but now growing more frequent. Soon he would have to yield his place to a younger man and be content with simple, routine duties, but not just yet. Not when there was still so much to be done.

The sin of pride; his lips quirked as he recognized it. The justification for hanging on and, by so doing, denying others the opportunity to fulfill themselves. They could do the work as well as he and probably far better. Lloyd, Kollar, Boyle, Pollard, Galpin—any of a host of others—they had been chosen for this mission and he had insisted on being its head. But now, feeling his age, he wished he hadn't been so importunate.

The pains eased a little and he stepped back from the fire. A tall, gaunt figure, bare feet thrust into plain sandals, his body wrapped in a cowled robe of brown homespun, the fabric held by a cord belting the waist. The garb of all monks of the Church of Universal Brotherhood. Sometimes called the Universal Church. Sometimes just the Church. The name was unimportant only the work they did. The work and the creed they preached and carried to wherever men were to be found. The simple doctrine that no man is an island. All belonged to the *corpus humanitatis*. That if each could look at the other and remember that *there, but for the grace of God, go I* the millenium would have arrived.

He would never see it. No monk now alive would ever do

that. Men bred too fast and traveled too far but it was
something to live for. A purpose to his existence.

One which now could be near its end.

"Brother!" Lloyd came toward him, face anxious, the
stubbled skull framed by his thrown-back cowl. "I saw you
stagger," he said. "For a moment I thought you would
collapse."

"A momentary dizziness caused by the smoke." A possibility and so not wholly a lie. And to increase the other's
concern would not be kind. "The others?"

"At their duties. Brother Kollar is with Sadoria."

"Any improvement?"

"None." Lloyd hesitated, scraping at the dirt with a sandal.
"Kollar thinks he will die."

And, with the engineer, would go their only hope of
repairing the *Guilia*. Dexter looked at the ship where it had
come to rest. A good landing; Ryder, though a hard captain,
knew his job, but even though the vessel appeared undamaged its heart was dead. The generator which alone could free
them from the prison they were in.

Dexter added more damp leaves to the fire, stubborn in his
refusal to yield to incapacity. The smoke plumed thicker,
rising in a twisting column to be caught by the higher winds
which shredded it and carried it toward the soaring wall of the
escarpment. A cliff which alone would be an attraction for
tourists if ever it could be tamed. If Velor could be tamed
with it. But even if both were done, tourists were few in the
Burdinnion and the chance of rescue was remote.

Negative thoughts which dulled the day and Dexter turned
from the fire, his face resolute. If they could do nothing else
the monks must radiate a calm serenity and the conviction
that all would be well. A duty owed to the captain, the crew,
the other passengers the *Guilia* had carried. A hard bunch but
each had their inner secrets, their private fears. All the need
for consolation. To provide it the monks had set up their
portable church manned now by Boyle.

Before him, through the mesh dividing the booth, he could
see the taut, strained face, the eyes wild, the brow dewed
with sweat. Sforza Bux, small in more ways than one, now
trembling with emotion as he eased his soul.

The litany of sin was all too familiar; an outpouring limited by the capabilities of the human condition, but magnified by an uneasy conscience.

". . . cheated, Brother. I looked at the bottom card and knew Ranevsky couldn't have held four aces so I upped the stake and forced him to call. But I shouldn't have won and shouldn't have taken the money because it was wrong to cheat. And I found some berries yesterday which I didn't turn in. I ate them instead and that was cheating too of a kind. I wasn't even hungry."

A man wanting to be clean and decent but trapped in the conditioning imposed by his environment. Wanting to rid himself of guilt and make a clean start and doomed to fail no matter how often he tried. But he tried—that was the important thing. And, trying, yielded himself to the power of the Church.

"Cheating is a sin," said Boyle. "It is tantamount to lying and a partner to theft. It is dishonest and unworthy and lessens those who yield to it. In the situation we are in it is even more heinous for unless we have mutual trust we are less than beasts. Think now of the sins you have done. Assess them in your mind. Void them with words of requital."

After a moment Boyle threw a switch.

"Look into the light of forgiveness," he said gently. "Bathe in the flame of righteousness and be cleansed of all pain, all sin. Yield to the benediction of the Universal Brotherhood."

The pale face of Sforza Bux shone with reflected color as he stared into the benediction light. A swirling kaleidoscope of shifting hues which gave his features an ethereal quality. The light was hypnotic, the subject subservient, the monk a trained master of his craft. Under his suggestion the suppliant relaxed to slip into a deeper trance. One in which he underwent a stringent penance; time encapsulated to provide a subjective torment of being robbed, cheated, denied and yet accepting all to find a final absolution.

Later he would be given the bread of forgiveness and, if on too many worlds too many suppliants came to kneel before the benediction light for the sake of the food alone, it was a fair exchange. For all who so knelt were conditioned against the act of murder.

* * *

213

Captain Ryder was short, square, his face creased with a mesh of lines, the pattern marred by a deep scar running over one cheek. Surgery could have removed it but he retained it for the bonus it gave to his appearance. Dealing with the scum he met in the Burdinnion every little bit helped.

Now he scowled at the two men standing before him. Both looked like hell, clothing worn, chafed, showing rents. Faces almost identical in their marks of privation. But, instinctively, he sensed the elder of the two was the leader.

To Dumarest he snapped, "How the hell did you get here?"

"We followed your smoke."

"I don't mean that. We registered no ship since we landed. That's over two weeks ago—closer to three. If you had a camp why didn't you answer our beacon?"

Dumarest said, "What good would it have done? Would you have come for us?"

"No—but you could have come to us. Your ship—" Ryder broke off then said, questioningly, "You do have a ship?"

"No."

"Then what the hell are you doing here?"

"We're all that's left of a survey team," said Dumarest quickly. "Five of us were dropped on the plateau together with equipment and supplies for six months. That was a month ago. The Tziak-Wenko Consortium. You may know of them."

Ryder frowned and shook his head.

"Based on Chalowe," said Dumarest. "A new and ambitious outfit. They send out teams to make a survey and then figure if it's worth developing the area. We picked this dump." He spat in the dirt. "For me you can keep it."

"Trouble?"

"Three days after landing. A storm first then we got hit by predators. They killed two and hurt the other so bad he only lasted three days. The radio was smashed, the supplies spoiled and scattered, we were lucky to stay alive. Then we saw you land and headed toward where we figured you'd be." Dumarest held up his wrist and displayed the ruined compass. "If you hadn't made smoke we'd never have found you."

"That was the monks." Ryder jerked his head to where

214

they stood before the church. "God knows why they bother. There's no one around to see it. I guess they hope to keep up morale. Six months, you say?"

"That's right."

"So your ship won't be back for another five."

"At least. That's why we'd like to take passage with you. How bad is the damage?" Dumarest added, "We saw you land and spotted the color of your field. Phase malfunction, right? How long will it take your engineer to effect repairs?"

Ryder said, curtly, "Why don't you ask him yourself?"

Sadoria lay in his cabin, a place ornamented with illustrations in vivid color depicting an age-old act in countless variations. Obscenity somehow enhanced by the presence of the monk who sat at the side of the cot. Like all monks, Brother Kollar had trained in basic medicine but he had pursued his studies further than most. Under his hands the writhing figure of the engineer eased a little but his droning babble never ceased.

"Traumatic shock induced by drug abuse," explained the monk. "In a sense his brain has been short-circuited and the censor divorced from the speech center. At this moment he is lost in a world of violent hallucinations and, inevitably, his psychosomatic reactions will result in a total degeneration of all faculties." His hands moved a little, touching the throat, the nerves of the neck. "I am trying to induce a somnolent period so as to give him hypnotic therapy."

"Will it cure him?"

"No, but it will help his pain." The monk met Dumarest's eyes. "It's all I can do, brother."

Outside the cabin Angado halted in the passage and shook his head. "That poor devil! If ever that happens to me—"

"Forget him." Dumarest was impatient. "I want the truth now. Can you repair this ship?"

"I could try."

"Anyone can do that. Can you repair it?"

"I'd have to examine the generator first. I guess the captain would give permission for that."

"We'll find out. Let me handle it. Just don't volunteer information. If I ask a question you signal an answer; one blink for yes, two for no. Got it?"

"Yes, but—"

215

"When this ship leaves we have to be on it. Making a deal may not be easy. If the captain ever finds out we were dumped and why it'll be impossible." Dumarest glanced along the passage. "Get to the engine room. I'll meet you there with Ryder."

He was in the control room with his navigator and the steward. They, together with the engineer, formed the entire complement of the *Guilia*. Normal for the kind of vessel it was; a free-trader with each crew member sharing in the profits and all doing a double stint for the sake of a larger cut. The engine room reflected Sadoria's personality, a place thick with grime and plastered with lurid pictures. Only the generator looked clean.

Ryder frowned as he saw Angado kneeling beside it. He'd already removed one cover and was at work on a second.

Dumarest said, watching his eyes, "How does it look so far? Bad? I thought it might be. Can you do anything with it? Good." He looked at the captain. "Do you want us to go ahead or would you rather wait for rescue?"

A loaded question. The radio beacon signaling the position of the vessel and calling for help emitted a wide-range broadcast but one now dampened and blocked by the bulk of the planet. Even if picked up there was no certainty of response. Rescue was determined by the possibility of recompense and, if too much trouble, was rarely attempted.

Ryder said, "If you can repair it go ahead."

"And?"

"We'll talk about that when it's done."

"Before it's done," said Dumarest. "Passage for the both of us to your next world of landing and—"

"When it's done!" snarled Ryder. "What's the good of haggling over something until we've got it?"

He stormed away, a man living on his nerves, one too close to bankruptcy to have the patience to argue. Rescue would ruin him but without it he was stuck on a hostile world. Dumarest was his only chance but he hated to admit it.

"He'll pay." Angado looked up from the generator. "He'll have no choice."

"There's always a choice," said Dumarest. "Promises can be broken and a fee given can always be taken back. But if I

216

press him hard then ease off he'll be too grateful to hold a grudge. He'll give us passage and what he can afford. It won't be much but he won't resent giving it." He looked at the exposed interior of the generator. The components seemed undamaged but one unit showed a shimmering rainbow effect where it faced the others. "Is that it?"

"If I said it wasn't?"

"You'd be a liar. Phase malfunction is confined to the similarity units. A burn-out would have left a deposit. An overload the same but in a different sector."

"And power-pulse feedback?"

"The regulator takes care of that."

"And if it doesn't?" Angado didn't wait for an answer. "You're dead, that's what. Or drifting. You know a lot about generators, Earl. Where did you study?"

On ships and helped by a man long dead. Dumarest saw his face pictured on the shining surface of the generator units, multiplied by conduits, flat planes, distorted by convex swellings. The face of the captain of the first ship he had ever seen. One in which he had stowed away to be found, threatened with eviction, saved by an old man's kindly whim.

"Earl?"

"It doesn't matter." Dumarest squeezed shut his eyes and shook his head to clear it of fogging memories. "How long will you be?"

"As long as it takes." Angado smiled as he gave a remembered answer to the question. "As you told me on the plain."

"Days? Weeks?"

"It's a matter of synchronization. That and balance of similarity. Nine nines is as good as we're ever going to get and we can't reach that without specialized equipment, which isn't here. Seven nines is good. Five nines is the least we can get away with. I'll have to use a mirror-reflection phaseometer and I'll need help to compute the trial-and-error readings. The first I can rig from what's available. The second?"

"I can manage that."

"Good," said Angado. "Let's get to it."

It had been raining and the streets of Anfisa held an unaccustomed shine. A gleam in which the drooping pennants showed like smeared patches of oily hues and the rounded

217

domes with their spike ornamentations were reflected in a profusion of altered shapes so that the town seemed to be haunted by bizarre creatures of some undersea forest.

An association Avro didn't make as he stood at the window looking toward the distant field, the spot where his ship was resting. Where it had rested for days now after a journey in which three of the crew had died and two others had suffered irreparable damage to hearts and kidneys.

That sacrifice had been unnecessary and stood as a silent accusation.

What had gone wrong?

The *Thorn* was behind schedule and no message had been received to give the reason. Accident? Damage? A burst engine causing the vessel to drift helplessly in space between the stars?

Madness?

The possibilities were endless and to speculate a waste of mental energy. It was time to search out facts and to be more determined than before. The factor could have been careless or hiding the truth for reasons of his own. The *Thorn*, on a regular route, would have gained friends and backers who needed to protect their investment.

Avro saw a touch of scarlet in the street below. The flash of color vanishing as it was spotted. Minutes later Byrne knocked and entered the chamber.

"Master!" The acolyte bowed. "I have—"

"News? What of the *Thorn*?"

Impatience displayed with an interruption; behavior so alien to normal procedure as to cause the acolyte to stand mute. A silent reproof Avro recognized as he knew the reason. Time had been wasted—Byrne could have been about to tell him what he had demanded to know. The interruption was a blatant display of inefficient conduct.

He said evenly, "You may report."

"Yes, Master." This time there was no bow. "I have gathered all available information from the field as you ordered. Nothing new has been gained but Cyber Ishaq arrived on the *Panoyan* as I was questioning Amontabo, the Hausi agent. Cyber Ishaq waits outside."

He was too young, too ambitious, too eager to make his mark. Avro studied him as he walked forward to make his

218

greeting, the bow almost perfunctory as if he resented the older man's superior rank. Yet, superficially, he was deferential.

"I was ordered to report to you and place myself at your disposal," he said. "It meant terminating my association with the Matriarch of Lunt. However, as I assured her, a replacement will be provided. I understand you are here to meet the *Thorn*."

"That is so." The information would have been relayed to Ishaq from Central Intelligence—but why hadn't he been told of the man's coming? Avro added, "The ship is behind schedule. No reason has yet been given to account for the delay."

"I can provide it. The vessel is under quarantine."

"Quarantine?"

"It is now in closed orbit around this planet." If Ishaq took a mental delight in displaying his superior knowledge he didn't show it. "The information has been kept secret for obvious reasons. The suspicion of plague would create a panic and affect the financial welfare of this world."

"How do you know this?"

"A radio message was picked up by one of our monitoring stations. A monk of the Church, Brother Jofre, was informing his superior of an incident that happened during flight. A sudden illness followed by the forced abandonment of two passengers. The superior must have informed the appropriate authorities." Ishaq paused then added, "It was something they dared not ignore."

The Church had friends in high places and the Cyclan had long known of the net of communication built on the super-radios incorporated into every benediction light. A system not to be compared to the efficient working of Central Intelligence but good enough for the activities of the monks.

Why had Jofre radioed ahead?

Had it been an act of revenge against Krogstad for his high-handed action or a genuine concern for the people of Anfisa? A question now without relevance; the *Thorn* was in quarantine. The ship and all it held isolated and beyond reach.

Avro said, "The passengers who were evicted. Was Dumarest one of them?"

"That has not been determined. Nor has his presence on the vessel."

"You doubt the probability?"

"The fact. It has yet to be verified."

The truth as Avro knew; no probability could be regarded as certain and his own convictions were not enough. If Dumarest was on the *Thorn* he was safely held. The ship was now a prison. But if he hadn't been on it or was no longer on it—what then?

Wait?

If Dumarest was free then delay increased the risk of losing him. Yet to contact the *Thorn* direct would be to reveal an interest it was better to keep hidden.

Amontabo solved the problem.

The Hausi was thick-set, strongly built, his dark cheeks slashed with the livid scars which were the castemark of his Guild. A man who never lied, but that was not to say he always told all of the truth. A dealer, go-between, agent, proxy—the Hausi performed a variety of needed roles. And Amontabo knew of the power of the Cyclan.

He bowed as he entered the chamber, first to Avro then to Ishaq. No accident, he had taken the trouble to discover who was senior. His words, when he spoke, were carefully aimed between the two.

"My lords, it has been an honor to have served you. I only trust the information I was able to gain will be of value. Of course, there were difficulties, a matter of certain arrangements which had to be made—closed beam radio with double scrambler is not something used every day."

"You will be paid," said Ishaq.

Avro, more discerning, said, "All expenses will be met as promised together with the agreed fee. In addition certain advantages will come your way." Commissions, fees, advantages, opportunities to partake of certain profits—the Cyclan could be generous when it chose. "Your report?"

"Negative, my lord. Dumarest is not on the *Thorn*."

"Are you positive?"

"Captain Krogstad listed each and every member of his crew together with all passengers. Most of the passengers and all of the crew are known. Of the rest none fits the description you provided. The man you are interested in is not on the ship."

Ishaq said, "Was he ever?"

Amontabo shrugged, shoulders lifting, hands rising, palms upward in a gesture which was an answer in itself.

"Assuming the man was on the ship and is not there now the conclusion is that he must be one of the two men dumped on that planet," said Avro. "What is its name?"

"Velor, my lord." The Hausi added, "A harsh and barren world."

"There is no need to elaborate. Concentrate on the men. What is known about them?"

"One, younger than the man for whom you are looking, is known to the gambler who has seen him before. His name is Angado Nossak and he was the one who fell sick. The other could have been a mercenary or a miner. Five people swear to that impression."

"His name?"

"Earl, my lord. The younger man was heard to call him that and he was so registered."

Earl! Earl Dumarest! Avro felt the mind-opening euphoria of the proof of his prediction. He had been right. The quarry he hunted had been exactly where he had said it would be.

Ishaq said, "There is no doubt?"

"None, my lord. Krogstad uses a lie-detector as a check against possible trouble. Most vessels in the Burdinnion follow the practice. With worlds so close and markets available the temptation to steal a ship is high."

And so the precaution, the risk Dumarest had been forced to take. A small one; who would be looking for him so far from Baatz? Who would have questioned the sworn testimony of his death?

The answer was reflected in the window Avro faced; his own shape limned against the darkening sky. An unanswerable demonstration of his efficiency; if it hadn't been for Krogstad's action Dumarest would have been taken and on his way to interrogation.

And now?

Avro knew the answer to that too—the hunt must go on.

Chapter Six

The generator was stubborn. Stripped, cleaned, reassembled, it held the beauty of functional design but remained inert. Before the Erhaft field could be created to swathe the *Guilia* in its blue cocoon and let it traverse the void at a velocity far greater than that of light the similarity components had to be aligned to near perfection. Not true perfection, that was impossible, but 99.9999999 percent of perfection, the nine nines which was the aim and dream of every engineer.

Angado didn't even try to get it. Instead he aimed for the lowest workable alignment of five nines. It took a week to achieve it. Another two before the *Guilia* completed its journey to Yuanka.

They landed in a storm of wind and dust; minute grains of sand and dirt which eddied like a fog and settled in a gray coating over the town, the field, the warehouses along the perimeter. Within seconds the *Guilia* was a copy of the other vessels standing on the dirt, a gray ghost standing like a shadow among the roiling dunes, detail lost in the diffused sunlight of a dying day.

Ryder was blunt. "You're fools to stop here," he said to them both. "Stay with the ship. I can use a good engineer, a handler too." His eyes moved toward Dumarest. "And from what I've seen you'd make a good assistant to your friend."

"Thanks for the offer," said Dumarest. "But no thanks."

"You?" Ryder grunted as Angado shook his head. "Well, I guess you know your own business, but take some advice. Watch yourselves—Yuanka is a bad world on which to be stranded. If you are then mention me to a few of the captains.

222

Some of them know me. All of them could use a good engineer.''

"We'll remember that," said Dumarest. "And thanks again." He held out his hand. "The rest of the fee, Captain? We'd like to leave with the monks.''

They alone were disembarking, loaded with bales, bundles, assorted supplies. Brother Dexter smiled his appreciation when Dumarest offered to help, frowned when he added a stipulation.

"Robes? You both want robes?"

"Just the loan of a couple," said Dumarest. Then added, as explanation, "For protection against the wind. Also it'll be easier to wear them than carry them."

And, robed, they would merge among the monks, becoming members of the party. A thing Dexter realized even as he nodded to Pollard to supply the garments. Normally he would have refused the request; the Church took no part in deception practiced by others, but neither did it refuse needed help. And here, on Yuanka, the Church needed all the help it could get.

The wind caught them as they trudged from the ship, dumping their goods and leaving monks to guard them as they went back for more. Three trips and they rested, faces grayed by the dust, eyes stinging, nostrils blocked. As they waited, backs to the wind, the *Guilia* headed again into space, spurning the dust and dirt of the planet for the clean emptiness between the stars.

"Ryder's a fool." Angado shouted over the wind. "That generator's shot and needs replacing. He didn't even wait to hire another engineer."

A replacement for Sadoria now lying in a shallow grave on Velor.

Dumarest said, "He knows what he's doing."

"Like hell he does. He didn't even wait for passengers or cargo.''

An assumption which displayed Angado's ignorance of free-trader operations. Ryder was impatient but neither crazy nor a fool. He would have contacted the field-agent by radio, have learned there were no passengers or cargo bound for his next world of call, and have decided not to waste time. A gambler risking that the generator would hold and that he could get profitable commissions if he beat other vessels.

Things Dumarest didn't bother to explain; the problem at hand was enough.

To Dexter he said, "Where is this stuff to be taken? Where is the church?"

"We have it with us." Brother Dexter gestured at the bales. "We have none established here on Yuanka as yet but the authorities have given us permission to stay."

"And build?"

"Yes. Beyond the field. In sector nine." The monk pointed to where the wind fluttered a tangle of pennants; strips and fragments of cloth and plastic adorning a sleezy collection of hovels. "Over there, I think. In Lowtown."

On every world they were the same; the repositories of the stranded, the deprived, the desperate. Dumping grounds for the unwanted and differing only in the degree of filth, stench and squalor they displayed. Shacks made of rubbish; mounds of dirt roofed with discarded sheets of plastic, hammered tin, cartons, the remains of packing cases. Huts fashioned of any scrap material to hand. The home of vice and crime, of degeneracy and poverty.

The monks' new home.

Brother Dexter set to work as soon as the wind eased and by the time it had died the church had taken shape. A tent firmly held by stakes, ropes and pegs. One containing space for a communal kitchen, a dispensary, accommodation for the monks and the all-important cubicle containing the benediction light. The portable church now incorporated into the main structure but with its entrance outside. Even before it was finished the line had begun to form.

"Patience." Brother Galpin, young, trying hard to practice the virtue he preached, held up an admonishing hand. "Give us time to get established."

"You have food?" The woman was in her thirties and looked twice as old. A shawl was draped over rounded shoulders and hugged to her hollow chest. "Please, Brother, you have food?"

"And medicine?" Another woman, almost a twin of the first, thrust forward, her face anxious. "My man is sick, dying, medicine could save him. You have medicine?"

"Some. Antibiotics and—"

"You will dispense it?" The woman's voice rose with

kindled hope. "Give it free? We can't pay and my man is dying!"

"And my child!"

"My brother and . . ."

"Food! I'm too weak to work!"

"Give me . . . Give . . . Give . . ."

Brother Galpin retreated from the sudden clamor, the outstretched hands and avid faces. A man beyond his depth and almost overwhelmed. He hit one of the ropes holding the tent, tripped and would have fallen if Dumarest hadn't caught his arm.

"Back!" He confronted the mob, face framed by the thrown-back cowl of his borrowed robe, blazed with a harsh determination. "Back, all of you! Get about your business!"

"But, Brother—"

"Come back tomorrow." Dumarest glared at the speaker, a thin runt of a man with a face like a weasel. "If you want to stay you can work. Grab a shovel and start clearing away this grit. We need a trench running over there. A wall built just here. Who will volunteer?"

"I'd help but I'm sick." The weasel-faced man coughed and spat blood. "See? My lungs are gone. The mines did that. I need medicine or I'll die."

"And me! I need it more than him. He's lying, anyway, that blood came from a bitten cheek." Another man, stocky, his face bitter, thrust the other to one side. "Help those who need it most, Brother. My wife is dying. You can save her."

"Maybe." Dumarest looked at him. "Name?"

"Worsley. Carl Worsley. You want help I'll arrange it. But my wife—"

"Get the help," said Dumarest. "The quicker we get settled the sooner we can start helping." He added, "But your wife needn't wait. Bring her as soon as you can."

She was thin, emaciated, with huge, luminous eyes. Her hair, once rich and dark with the sheen of natural oil, hung dull and lank over bony shoulders and shriveled breasts. Her cheeks, hollow, held the flush of fever and when she breathed her chest echoed to a liquid gurgling.

Looking at Dumarest, Brother Kollar shook his head.

"No!" Worsley had seen the gesture. "No, she can't be beyond help! Dear God, no!"

225

"I'm sorry." Kollar had seen such scenes too often but always he felt the pain as much as those more personally involved. "The tissue degeneration is too far advanced for anything we can do. I can ease her pain and give her hypnotic conditioning but—"

"What's that?"

Dumarest said, "She will be in a subjective world in which there will be no pain, no fear. Suggestion will give her as much happiness as she could hope for and the trance will last until she no longer needs it."

"Until she dies, you mean?" Worsley clenched his fists as Dumarest nodded. "You thinking of passing her out?"

"No, but if she was my wife I wouldn't hesitate."

"You? A monk? Why, you bastard I—"

"I'm not a monk," said Dumarest sharply. "And watch your mouth. You came here begging, remember. Pleading for what help could be given. Well, that's it. All of it. Did you hope for a miracle?"

"I . . ." Worsley swallowed, his eyes filling with moisture. "I thought, I'd hoped—God! Dear God don't let her die!"

A useless prayer and he knew it. Surgery could save the woman; cryogenic storage while new lungs were grown from fragments of her own tissue. Her body laved with selected antibiotics, strengthened with intravenous feeding, bolstered with supportive mechanisms. A long and tedious process even with the aid of slow time but she would live.

All it took was money.

Money Worsley didn't have. What no one in any Lowtown had. The stench which filled the air was the reek of abject poverty.

The dust storms were intermittent and happened only when strong winds blew from the northeast after a dry period. The grit they carried was abrasive, fretting the thin coverings and opening roofs to the sky. Even as the church was being constructed men were busy patching their hovels.

Watching them Angado said, "They remind me of bees. Always working, never still, yet what they do can be wiped out in a single day. As a hive is robbed of the honey it may have taken months to store. Yet they go on doing the same old thing again and again." He glanced at the church. "Like our friends the monks. Preaching, giving aid, comfort, food when they have it. And for what?''

"Do they need a reason?''

"They claim to have one.''

"A goal,'' said Dumarest. "They want to change the way men behave. Those who preach peace have always wanted that. And, always, they have failed.''

As the monks on Yuanka would fail. As they would on all bleak and hostile worlds. Jungles in which to be tolerant was to be dead.

Dumarest narrowed his eyes as he studied the men Worsley had gathered. Volunteers all, but some had subtle differences from the majority. They worked but accomplished little and seemed too interested in the area leading toward the heart of Lowtown. Watching for something, he guessed, or waiting for someone. He had a good idea of whom it might be.

"It looks good.'' Angado nodded toward the church. "Big and clean and it stands out a mile. A nice position too, it can be seen both from the field and the town. Brother Dexter knows his stuff. I'll bet this isn't the first time he's set up a church. Brother Lloyd was telling me something about him. Old, stubborn, but clever.''

A man shrewd enough to have selected the best spot available and surely he must know what could well happen? Dumarest turned as the monk came toward them. Dexter was genial but firm.

"It is time you returned your borrowed robes,'' he said. "Brother Kollar reported the incident in the infirmary. I do not blame you but your attitude is not ours. A suppliant could have gained the impression that we terminate the lives of the sick placed in our care.''

"I told Worsley I wasn't a monk.''

"He may not have believed you.''

"It may be as well for you if others don't either.'' Dumarest glanced at the men who seemed to be waiting. "There could be those who don't welcome your presence here. They might hesitate to object if they think you stronger than you are.''

"Eight instead of six.'' Dexter shook his head. "You mean well but I must insist. Our foundation here must not rest on deception. Your robe, please.'' The old monk turned to Angado who had stood quietly by, listening. "And yours also. We are on this world by sufferance of the authorities and dare not risk the possibility of a misunderstanding. You both lack the training necessary to follow the philosophy of the Church."

"Peace," said Dumarest. "But that's something you have to fight for."

"To achieve," corrected the monk. "The robes?"

"Are they really that important?"

"The garments, no, what virtue lies in a piece of cloth? But as a symbol of what we are and are trying to accomplish—"

"The credo," Dumarest met the old monk's eyes. "There," he said softly, "but for the grace of God, go I. The thing you want all to remember; the rich, the whole, the comfortable when they look at the sick, the poor, the deprived. But it works both ways and, at times, you could forget that. The sick and maimed and hopeless you feel so concerned about look at the spoiled and pampered, the strong, the ruthless. They can see the benefits of being cruel and arrogant, and they too could think that there, but for the grace of God, they could be. And they might want to alter things a little. Correct the balance in their favor. Could you blame them if they tried?"

"The Church can never condone violence."

"Just accept it and preach that others should do the same? To be meek? To believe that to bend the head is to avoid the kick in the rear? How much punishment do you expect people to take?"

"There are worlds even now where criminals are maimed as a punishment for their crimes," said Dexter. "Once such things were common but now are rare. Soon that barbarism will vanish. As will other things." He held out his hand. "The robes, please. A monk, above all, must practice humility."

Angado watched as the monk moved away, the robes over his arm. Beneath his own he had worn clothing similar to Dumarest's, a knife thrust into his boot, the axe dumped with them riding in his belt.

He said, "You were hard on him, Earl. Why? Dexter does his best and isn't a bad man."

"He's too good for this world." Dumarest gestured at the huddle comprising Lowtown. "And for any other like it.

228

He's a fool. He's done his stint in the past and should now be taking things easy.''

"Monks never do that."

"They should."

"They can't. That's what dedication is all about. It was unfair you talking to him the way you did. Brother Dexter's not stupid, he knows human nature as well as anyone, but he has to keep doing what he believes in." Angado paused then added, "As you would in his position. But then I suppose you'd run classes in unarmed combat and teach suppliants to use a knife. All in the name of peace."

"No," said Dumarest. "Survival."

"Kill or be killed." Angado shook his head. "God, but you're hard. People don't live like that, not even in this slum. They share a common misfortune and make the best of it. Brother Dexter and the other monks know that. That's why they're so against violence. Once it starts who knows where it will end?"

Dumarest shrugged, not answering. He looked at the sky then to where a knot of men had gathered to the far side of the church. Among them he noticed those he had spotted earlier. All looked toward the heart of Lowtown.

To Angado he said, "Find Worsley and bring him to me."

"Why do you—"

"Do it! And don't get involved no matter what happens. Remember that, don't get involved."

"Trouble?" The younger man looked around. The monks had gathered in front of the church, Dexter still holding the reclaimed robes. "I can't see anything."

"It hasn't happened yet. Well, I tried to warn him but he wouldn't listen."

"Who?"

"Brother Dexter," said Dumarest. "He's due a visitor."

He came as such men always did, confident, smiling, enjoying the moment, the pleasure to come. A man middle-aged, middle-sized, his face bland, his clothing good and clean but not too obviously expensive. Heavy rings glinted on his fingers and his hair, thick and dark, framed prominent cheekbones and deep-set eyes.

He wasn't alone. At his side trotted a smaller version of

himself, thinner, older, the sharply pointed nose and darting eyes betraying the questing, curious nature of the man. Two others, big, stocky, followed at the rear. Both carried staves a yard long and, Dumarest guessed, loaded with lead.

Worsley said, "That's Gengiz. The small one is Birkut. He keeps the accounts and tallies the score. The two big ones are his bodyguard."

"The take?"

"A zobar a person a week."

"How much is a zobar?"

"The price of half a day's work at the field—if you can get it."

"And if you don't pay?"

"You know the answer to that."

"I know," said Dumarest. "But he doesn't." He gestured toward Angado. "Tell him."

"You pay or your shack gets ruined. Your things get stolen. Your food spoiled. After that you start getting hurt." Worsley was bitter. "He calls it insurance. He'll even lend you the premiums but, after a while, if you still don't or can't pay, he collects."

"Nice," said Dumarest. "Just think of all the good things that money would have provided. Your wife's sick—she would have liked the soup and drugs you didn't get because you avoided trouble and paid."

"I paid," said Worsley tightly. "But I didn't like it. And you're wrong about one thing, mister. My wife isn't sick—she's dead. And to hell with you!"

He strode away and Dumarest looked at his companion.

"You see?"

"See what? I—"

"The reality of that garbage you were spouting. The rubbish about people sharing a common misfortune and making the best of it. You live in a jungle and you'd better realize it. You can't stop violence. All life is a continual act of violence. In order to survive you have to fight every step of the way and keep on fighting. Against disease, starvation, thirst, heat, cold, nakedness. Against the parasites wanting to feed off you. Lice and insects and ordinary predators. And against scum like Gengiz."

"He should be stopped."

"Maybe, but not by you. It's none of your business."

"But—"

"Forget it."

Dumarest held a broom, a pole tipped with a wide fan of bristles, and he used it as he followed Angado as the man moved toward the group of monks. Curious, he wanted to hear what was being said. Dumarest had already guessed.

"So you see, brothers, what the position is." Gengiz had made the preliminary spiel, his voice soft, devoid of threat, almost gentle as he urged cooperation. "In order to maintain the peace we must abide by the rules and as Mayor it is my duty to see that everyone complies. As intelligent men you can see that. As you can see that to patrol the area requires men who have to be paid. A form of tax per head of the population takes care of that. It is small, a zobar a head a week, but in your case—well, perhaps we could discuss it in private?"

Dexter shook his head. "That will not be necessary."

"It would be best."

"No. We have permission to establish our church here. That permission was granted by the authorities. The tax you mention is unlawful."

Gengiz said, softly, "Brother, answer me one thing—have you ever been in this situation before?"

"Many times."

"And must have learned from your experience. Now, if we could go somewhere to be alone?"

Seclusion where the mask could be dropped and the naked threat revealed. Pay or suffer. The structure of the church damaged, monks beaten up, suppliants threatened, stores and supplies ruined or stolen. Even a demonstration could be given—a broken arm or shattered kneecap a hint of what was to come if refusal continued.

Things Dexter knew, as he realized that to yield was to destroy the aim of the Church. To bow to the threat of violence was to condone it. To pay the levy Gengiz demanded was to buy peace at too high a price—yet to refuse was to invite harsh retribution.

Dexter looked at the sun, the sky, aware of the monks at his back, of the watching faces all around. The moment of truth he had known so often before; the hardest thing for any

231

monk to take. Those who served the Church could not be weak in either spirit or body yet that strength had to be sublimated to the greater ideal. To be meek. To be humble. To trust that, by example, they would give rise to a protective concern.

"Well?" Gengiz was becoming impatient. "Have you nowhere we could be alone?"

"There is nothing to decide. Therefore no good purpose would be served by further conversation."

"I see. Birkut!"

The small man stepped forward as Gengiz and his bodyguard moved away. A toady, basking in the reflection of the other's power, as poisonous as a serpent. His voice held an oily note of subtle menace.

"The Mayor is being kind," he said. "He understands your problems and is eager to accommodate you. Think it over. Discuss it with the others. It could end as a matter of a percentage—a share of donations." His smirk was as oily as his tone. "You have until sunset."

Chapter Seven

Yuanka's sun was a sullen ball of smoldering ochre edged by a flickering corona of orange. Colors which combined with the murk in the atmosphere to produce a purple haze as sunset drew near. In it the perimeter fence surrounding the field showed as a misty web topped by lamps which, later, would illuminate the mesh with a vivid glow.

The fence encompassing Lowtown was less obvious but just as restricting. Dumarest looked at the cleared strip encircling the area, the deep ditch dug beyond it, the huts set at strategic points. Those controlling the planet had taken precautions against the danger residing in the hungry and desperate.

"Nice." Angado had accompanied Dumarest. "Try to break out and they'll gun down anyone reaching the ditch. I'll even bet they've got a curfew."

A gamble he would have won. As Dumarest led the way to where a plank bridge crossed the ditch men stepped from a hut at its end.

"Hold it!" The officer, like his men, wore a uniform and was armed. "It's late—you got business in town?"

"Nothing special." Dumarest glanced toward the field. "Just wanted to check on the chance of getting a berth."

"Leave it until tomorrow." The officer rested a hand on the pistol holstered at his waist. "Curfew runs from an hour before sunset to an hour after dawn. You should know that."

"We've been helping the monks," said Angado. "Do you police inside?"

"Hell, no." The officer echoed his contempt. "You scum take care of yourselves."

In more ways than one.

233

Dumarest heard the shout of pain as he neared a hovel sprouting like an ugly growth at the edge of the cluster. A man answered it as it came again.

"Steady! Hold still, you fool! Damn it, Susan, get help!"

A woman burst from the door and stared at them with wild eyes. She was gaunt, dressed in rags, an ugly blotch marring one cheek. Flecks of blood stained her hands and naked forearms.

"Please!" She looked from Dumarest to Angado. "My man! He's hurt bad! Jacek is trying but needs help! Please!"

Inside the gloom was thick, relieved only by the guttering light of a wick floating in a cup of oil. On a heap of rags a man lay writhing, another kneeling at his side. Like the woman, his hands and wrists were stained with blood.

"Hold him!" he snapped after one glance at the visitors. "Grab him tight."

Dumarest said, without moving, "What's wrong with him?"

"He tripped and fell into a bed of feathers." Jacek's tone was sarcastic. "That's how he got that face."

The nose was broken, the lips split, the chin caked with blood. The eyes were puffed and the forehead bruised. Whoever had beaten the man had done a vicious job.

"Gengiz?"

"His boys. Breck fell behind on his payments. They warned him once but he still couldn't find the cash. So they worked him over. Smashed his face, cracked some ribs and twisted his arm out of its socket. I'm trying to get it back."

The hard way, working with strength but little skill. Dumarest gestured him aside, took his place, examined the injured limb. The dislocation was severe, the joint badly swollen. The injured man groaned as Dumarest moved his hands.

"How long?"

"Since noon. I had to wait for Jacek to get back."

Angado said, "Couldn't you have sent for trained help?"

"Medics won't come into Lowtown. They'll treat you if you can get to them but first they want paying." Breck was patient despite his pain, talking as if to a child. "I can't pay. If I had money I wouldn't be in this mess."

The woman said, "Can you help him? If you can for God's sake get to work."

"Hold his legs, Jacek. Angado, you hold his other arm.

Keep him turned on his side." Dumarest picked up a mess of rag and wadded it into a ball. "This is going to hurt," he warned. "But it'll soon be over. Just try to relax. Take some deep breaths. Got anything to bite on?"

"Here." The woman thrust a stick between Breck's jaws. "Don't hurt him too much, mister."

Dumarest placed the wadded ball between the upper arm of the injured man and the torso, setting it high beneath the armpit to act as a fulcrum. Checking its position he adjusted the limb then, without warning, thrust down hard on the elbow.

Breck strained, biting into the wood, a low, animal-like groan coming from his throat. Sound Dumarest ignored as he fought the pull of muscles, maintaining the leverage as he felt the swollen joint. A moment as he rammed the heel of his hand against the spot, then he felt the joint slip back into place.

"Good." He rested a hand on Breck's sweating forehead. "It's all over," he said. "Just relax now."

"It hurts."

"The pain will go but it'll be sore for a while." Dumarest ripped rags into strips and bound the arm and shoulder in a constricting web, tying the arm hard against the chest. "That'll help the ribs, too." He looked at Jacek. "The next time anyone gets into trouble take them to the monks."

"I did my best."

"I know, but you lack training. They've had it." Dumarest added, "I guess you know how to take care of his nose."

"I should." Jacek's own was twisted across his face. "I've had to fix mine often enough. The rest of the cuts too. It was just that shoulder which beat me. A neat trick that; you using the arm itself as a lever." He paused then said. "Not that it'll do much good."

"Gengiz?" Dumarest shrugged. "A few of you could get together and take care of his boys."

"There'll be others." Jacek's tone reflected his loss of spirit. "There are always others."

Angado said, "What happens if he still can't pay? Will they kill him?"

"Not unless they have to. There are mines to the north and

a ready market for workers. Deliver a volunteer and collect a bonus. Gengiz has a habit of delivering volunteers."

Dumarest looked at the interior of the hovel. "Maybe a man could do worse."

"I'm not signing a contract!" Breck struggled to sit upright on the rags. "Once they get you they never let go."

"You'd eat," said Dumarest. "You and your woman. What better have you got here?"

"I'm free!"

"Sure," said Dumarest. "I'd forgotten. Maybe Gengiz has too."

He moved to the opening and stepped out into the thickening purple haze of the dying day. After a moment Angado joined him, falling into step alongside as Dumarest moved along the littered path. In the shadows rodents scuttled and, from a shack, came a snatch of discordant song.

As it died Dumarest said, "You gave Breck money, right? It was a mistake."

"It was my money."

"It was still a mistake. Now he's not as desperate as he was. He'll pay and buy his way out of trouble. But it'll return and he'll be back where he started."

"I've given him time, at least. His shoulder will heal and maybe he can find a job." Angado looked at his companion. "Would you pay, Earl? If Gengiz makes his demand will you meet it?"

"I might."

"Then how can you blame Breck and those like him for doing the same?"

"I'm not blaming them," said Dumarest. "They can do as they like. It's none of my business. But if I was starving and had a woman depending on me and she was starving too and some thug came and tried to rob me—well, who knows?"

They reached the end of the path, turned left, moved into a cleared space formed by the junction of crossings, headed up a slope to where the church rose against the sky.

Before it, silhouetted against the brightly colored plastic, two men were beating a robed figure to the ground.

It was a scene from nightmare, the men tall, broad, their clubs the yard-long weapons carried by Gengiz's guard. The monk was crouched, hands lifted to protect his face, body bowed as if he were a suppliant accepting a merited penance.

A stagelike vista broken as Angado yelled and ran forward.

"Stop that! Stop it! Leave him alone!"

A command obeyed only momentarily as the men turned at the shout, clubs lifted, contemptuous of the new arrivals.

Dumarest said, sharply, "Angado! Leave it!"

An order ignored if heard and he ran in turn, passing the other, heading to where he had left the broom leaning against the fabric of the church. Set far to one side of where the men stood over the monk he was ignored. As he snatched it up Angado came to a halt.

"Back off!" His breath was ragged, his voice hard but shaking a little. "You filth! Beating up a monk! Is that the best you can do?"

He was talking instead of acting, a mistake repeated by the thugs.

"Listen to the insect." The man on the right hefted his club. "Doesn't all that big talk frighten you, Rayne? Maybe we should get down on our knees and beg his forgiveness."

"Maybe we should, Kay." The other thug played along. "For all we know this thing could be his father." His foot kicked at the monk. "I've heard they have some strange ideas of how things should be done."

"We could make them show us, eh? If—"

Rayne broke off as Dumarest came running toward him, broom in hand, the wide fan of bristles aimed at his eyes. Spines which circled to avoid the sweep of his club and dug into cheeks and forehead. Lifting as Dumarest reversed the pole to send it rising sharply between the thighs to smash against the groin. As the thug doubled, retching, the end of the pole slammed into his throat, rupturing the larynx and filling the windpipe with blood and congested tissue.

As he fell Angado lunged at the other man.

He had his knife in his hand, the point slanted upward, thumb to the blade as he had seen trained fighters do in a dozen arenas. A hold, stance and motion designed to deliver a killing thrust. But he was slow. Slow!

Dumarest saw the lifted club, the practiced response of a man who had made violence his trade. Held like a sword the weapon gave him the advantage. Before he could drive the knife home Angado would be dead.

Dumarest yelled, throwing the broom as he yelled, the sound shocking in its harsh timbre. As the thug slowed his advance the pole, hurtling like a spear, glided between his legs causing him to stumble, to fall helplessly on the lifted blade of Angado's knife.

As the thug twitched, spilling his life in a carmine flood, Dumarest said, bitterly, "Well, I hope you're satisfied."

"It was him or me, Earl."

"It needn't have been either. You shouldn't have interfered."

"They were beating up a helpless man. A monk!"

"That makes them special?" Dumarest shrugged as Angado made no answer. "Well, it happened, let's get him inside."

Pollard had taken the beating but he wasn't the only one in the infirmary. Dexter lay on another cot, supine, his eyes closed, hands lying limp at his side. A bandage made a white swath across his forehead.

"Concussion," explained Kollar. "A cracked clavicle and a badly bruised elbow. In that he was lucky."

"When?"

"About thirty minutes ago. Two men arrived and demanded to see him. Brother Dexter guessed what they wanted and ordered us not to interfere. After the attack they left and we brought him inside. Then they returned and Brother Pollard went out to remonstrate with them. The rest you know."

Dumarest said, "You stood by while they beat up an old man?"

"We had no choice."

"You could have gone out there. Shouted. Gathered a crowd if nothing else."

"No," said Angado. "They couldn't. They were under orders and had to obey." He looked at the limp figure lying on the cot, at the groaning shape of the younger monk. "Gengiz cheated. He gave them until sunset. The attack took place before then. Brother Dexter must have thought they came to talk. In any case he would have wanted to avoid a battle."

Taking the beating himself. Willingly offering his own body as a sacrifice. A waste—the men who'd attacked him

238

had lost the meaning of shame as had the man who'd sent them.

"It's the way of the Church," said Angado, "to follow a policy of nonviolence no matter what the cost. If the church here is to succeed then others must protect it. Those who value it and find comfort in its teachings. Once a congregation has been established there'll be no need for the monks to prove themselves. They'll have been accepted. After that the rest will follow."

"Until it does?" Dumarest didn't wait for an answer. "Never mind. I wanted us to stay out of this but now we have no choice. You took care of that. Those thugs are dead and others would have seen how they died. Now we're both marked men." He looked at the monk. "Find us two robes. Large ones."

Kollar shook his head. "I'm sorry, but Brother Dexter made it clear—"

"Look at him now," snapped Dumarest. "Do you want others to join him? But if your conscience troubles you let's do it this way." He spoke directly at the unconscious monk. "Brother Dexter, do you object to us using a couple of robes?" He waited, listening, then looked again at Kollar. "You see, he didn't object."

"But—"

"Get them!" Dumarest looked at the injured men then at Angado. "Violence," he said bleakly. "It's everywhere. The strong bearing down on the weak with demands and threats. Scum like Gengiz or some puffed up lordling or a faceless bureaucrat all issuing their orders. Pay or be punished. Obey or suffer fines, imprisonment, execution. Well, to hell with them. There's only one way they can be stopped." He looked at the robes Kollar had fetched. "Good. Now, Brother, go outside and bring in those clubs."

As Dumarest had expected the clubs were weighted with lead. Long, slender wands with the vicious capacity to shatter a skull or snap a bone. He hefted one, sent it whining through the air, lifted it in a curve, sent it darting forward to halt an inch from Angado's chest.

"Fast," he said. "See?"

"What are you trying to tell me?"

"When you decide to act don't hesitate. That's the mistake you made out there. Don't waste time in talk. Attack, do it fast and don't be gentle. A hurt man can hit back, a dead one can't. Now hit me with your club." Dumarest shook his head as Angado lifted the weapon, his own reaching out to jab hard against the other's chest. "Not like that. It leaves you too open. Thrust as I did."

Angado was slow. Dumarest swept aside the club and jabbed again. The next attack was faster, the club circling to avoid the parry. Dumarest knocked it far to the opposite side, jabbed, stood waiting.

"Earl, I—"

"Don't talk! Act! Kill me before I kill you! Move, damn you! Move!"

Hard practice within the body of the church, sweating inside the hampering robes, learning how to compensate for the heavy material. As they moved the axe fell from Angado's belt, Dumarest picking it up and thrusting it beneath his robe. Finally he called a halt.

"That's enough. We'll rest for a while."

"Do you think I've improved?"

"You're better." Angado was still slow but had lost his initial hesitation. Dumarest said, "You killed a man tonight. Was he your first?"

"There was another. We had an argument and he came for me. It was an accident, really, he had a gun and I grabbed at it and it went off and shot him in the chest. A laser. The stink of burned flesh stuck in my nose for days." Angado paused then said, "I suppose you find killing easy."

"No," said Dumarest. "It's never that."

"But you intend to kill again."

"You've left me no choice—I told you why. Gengiz has to dispose of us as a matter of pride. He's got a good thing going here and others know it. Once he shows weakness they'll try to take over. So we have to go. As we can't avoid it we have to meet it. Pick our own time and place."

"But why the robes?"

Dumarest shrugged, "It gives us an edge—who's afraid of a monk?"

They rested, dozing, waiting for the dawn. The best time to attack when the guards would be sleepy and Gengiz unaware.

In the infirmary Brother Kollar kept vigil over the sick, two of the other monks sleeping, the third standing awake in case of need. Dumarest started fully alert as a hand touched his shoulder. In the dim light he saw the strained face of Brother Galpin.

"Something is wrong," whispered the monk. "There are people outside."

"Suppliants?"

"No. I think they intend to rob us."

Thieves working under Gengiz or others eager to seize an opportunity. The dead thugs, untouched where they lay, no longer served to keep the vultures at bay.

Dumarest rose, stretched, looked at the translucent roof of the church. The stars, paling, had left a blurred glow and he sensed it must be close to dawn. Others knew the best time to attack.

They could be heard working at the wall to one side. A rasp of metal against the stubborn plastic the sound like the ugly grating of teeth. Dumarest crossed to it, knelt, listened, looked to the other side.

Angado said, "Wouldn't they break directly into the storeroom?"

"If they knew just where it was," agreed Dumarest. "Or if that's all they wanted."

"You think they're after us?"

"Gengiz knows we're in here. We killed his men. Now he has the chance to kill us and wreck the church at the same time. If monks die we'll be blamed. Either way he can't lose."

"The church eliminated and used us as an example of what happens if anyone steps out of line." Angado drew in his breath. "We shouldn't be here, Earl. Nor wearing these robes. The monks don't deserve this."

"If you're tired of life just strip and walk outside." Dumarest was curt. "If you're not just shut up and listen."

The grating had grown louder, a sound impossible to miss and one sure to attract attention. Dumarest moved to the far wall where, dimly, he could see the vague outline of shadows.

"Here," he whispered to Angado. "They're coming through here. Remember what I told you."

"Are you going to attack without warning?"

"I thought you'd learned."

"Sorry. I wasn't thinking."

"Don't think," advised Dumarest. "Just act. Hit hard and fast." He shifted the grip on his club. "Here they come!"

The wall opened like a flower, petals of plastic parting to reveal a cluster of shapes, men who ran forward, metal glinting in their hands.

The first went down, choking, vomiting from savage thrusts to throat and stomach. Others follwed them as the clubs whined through the air to land on shoulders, backs, skulls. Victims of a ferocious and totally unexpected defense. Monks did not fight, yet monks seemed to be everywhere; in the dark interior of the church only the robed figures could be seen.

Calm followed the violence, a period that Dumarest knew would be followed by a more calculated attack. One which, surprise now lost, would give numbers the advantage.

He blinked as a vivid beam of light streamed from outside to illuminate the scene.

It came from where Gengiz stood at a distance from the structure, a powerful flashlight in one hand, a laser in the other. The pale light of dawn gave him a somber appearance, accentuated by his scowl and the weapon in his hand.

He fired as Dumarest watched, the beam searing plastic, burning a hole high and to one side.

"Drop those clubs!" The laser fired again adding a second hole to the first. "Drop them, I say!"

Again the laser vented its energy, closer this time, and Angado grunted as he slapped at the smoke rising from the edge of his robe.

"Your last warning! Drop those clubs!"

"Earl?"

"Do it!"

His own club followed Angado's to the floor, his eyes narrowed as he assessed the situation. The attackers had dropped at the signal of the firing, hugging the ground to give Gengiz an open field. The man himself stood too far away to be reached by a thrown knife even if the blade could travel fast enough to beat the speed of his finger. The clubs were gone.

"Raise your hands," said Dumarest quietly. "Walk toward Gengiz. Stumble a little as if you're hurt. Beg if you want but do what he tells you."

Angado threw him a glance then obeyed. He was a good actor. Dumarest followed him, stooped, one leg dragging, a hand clutching his chest.

"Please!" Angado turned his raised hands palms outward, the fingers spread to demonstrate his defenselessness. "Don't hurt me. I had nothing to do with this. Look, I've got money, I'll pay—"

"Shut up!" The muzzle of the laser remained aimed at his stomach. "Move over to one side. Faster." The gun signaled the direction, the beam of the flashlight searing into Angado's face. "You're not a monk. I know you. You killed my boys. You and—" The beam of the flashlight moved to Dumarest. He was crouched even lower, one hand pressed to his stomach, lurching as he moved forward. "Hold it!" Gengiz snarled as he recognized the face in the vivid light. "You're the other one. But why the robes? What the hell's going on?"

"Money," said Dumarest. "The monks had it. We wanted it. Now we've got it. If you hadn't arrived we'd have got away. The guards wouldn't argue with a couple of monks breaking curfew. Not now it's after dawn."

"Money?"

"Sure. A lot of it. Show him, Angado."

Dumarest moved as Gengiz turned toward the other man, flashlight and laser shifting targets. Both jerking back as, too late, he realized the mistake he'd made.

The distance was too great for a knife even if he could have snatched it from his boot, but the axe had extra weight. Dumarest tore it from his belt, lifted it, threw it with all his strength as Gengiz turned. Smoke and flame spurted from his robe as the laser fired then Gengiz was down, the axe buried in his skull, blood and brains making a red-gray patina on his face.

"Hold it!" Dumarest yelled at the men coming from the church. "He's dead! You want to join him?"

He faced them, the laser he'd scooped up steady in his hand, searing the ground inches from the boots of the nearest man. Firing repeatedly until the men ran in panic, leaving them alone with the damaged church, the staring monks, the uncaring dead.

Chapter Eight

This time it was different; instead of the bizarre landscape with the solitary figure of the Cyber Prime there was a vaulted hall, a dais holding three thronelike chairs occupied by figures adorned with legalistic robes. A tribunal seated as if in judgment, faces dimmed and blurred in the flickering light of flambeaux. But if the scene was different the shock was the same.

Avro drew in his breath and looked at his hands. Air filled his lungs and the hands were his own as were the feet, the arms, the robe which clothed his body. One now lying as if dead in his cabin on the ship resting on the surface of Velor.

What was happening to him?

Rapport was never like this and, since the time when he had apparently spoken to Marle, it had been as always. The contact, the exchange, the euphoria which yielded ecstasy and which resulted from electromagnetic stimulation of the pleasure center of the brain.

A thought which startled him—was it true? And why should it have come to him at all?

"Cyber Avro you may speak." The central figure lifted a hand, let it fall back to the arm of the chair, to grip it with long, spatulate fingers. "Your report?"

One which could have been transmitted with the speed of thought now having to be vocalized.

Avro was brief, ending with the finding of the grave. "The body was in the final stages of dissolution. Little remained but a skeleton and identification was impossible."

"The size?"

"Fitted the characteristics of both men dumped from the

Thorn.'' Unnecessary detail—he had said that identification was impossible. Inefficiency compounded as he added, ''The bones had been badly fretted but fitted the structure-scale relevant to the search. More could have been learned had we discovered the grave sooner.''

''Obviously.'' The tone was dry. ''Continue.''

''The grave was on the site of what had been a camp. Radiated heat from the colony of scavenger beetles which had congregated on the spot registered on our instruments. The immediate terrain showed signs of having been stripped of fuel, and ash was found beneath a layer of sand. To one side, also beneath windblown sand, was found what could have been the landing spot of a vessel. Tests in the lower soil-strata confirm the size and weight of an object which could have been a ship.'' Avro paused, seeing again the glinting mass of chitin from the insects attracted to the water and food held in the body. The bones which first had seemed to be fashioned from tiny, mobile gems, turning gray and dusty as the scavengers fled from the light. The landing spot had been a ragged scar. ''Tests revealed radiation levels in the local soil consistent with the generation of an Erhaft field.''

''Your conclusions?''

''A vessel landed. A man was buried. The vessel departed.''

It was not enough and Avro knew it but there was reason for his brevity. Before him the seated figure stirred, those to either side remaining as motionless as before. Were they nothing but a part of the illusion? An addition to the flambeaux, the dais, the thrones, the vaulted chamber?

It had to be illusion—but the central figure?

It stirred again and Avro caught the impression of a host of faces blurring one into the other to form a montage at once familiar and strange. People he had known, cybers long gone to their reward, now the brains forming Central Intelligence. Was this the product of some dreaming mind toying with the creation of new frames of reference? The fruit of a whim?

Of madness?

''Brevity is always to be desired,'' said his inquisitor. ''But brevity, carried to the extreme, verges on stupidity. Which vessel? What man? Elucidate.''

''The vessel is unknown,'' said Avro. ''Working on the assumption that it could have been in distress, a wide search

245

was made in order to determine if any radio signal had been received. The results were negative. The settlements on Velor lay to the far side of the plateau—I have described the terrain.''

"And?"

"The man is also unknown. The probability that it is Dumarest is in the order of fifty percent. Two men were dumped," he explained. "Either could have died."

"Or," said the central figure, "it could have been someone from the vessel."

The obvious and Avro felt again the sickening sense of failure he had once known as a boy when new to the Cyclan. Even as he watched the dais blurred, the chamber, both becoming the bleak room in which he had sat for initial testing and tuition.

"You." The man who had sat on a throne now stood behind a desk, warmly scarlet in his robe, his face one Avro would never forget. Cyber Cadell, coldly unforgiving, relentless in weeding out the unsuitable. "Come here and tell me if these are the same."

Three blocks of plastic rested on the desk before him, all apparently identical. Avro stared at them, checking shape, color and size.

"Well?"

"Master, they are the same."

Cadell said nothing but his hand turned over the blocks. The lower side of each was colored differently from the rest and no color was the same.

"Master! I—"

"You jumped to a false conclusion based on insufficient data. I did not say you were not allowed to touch them for a complete examination. A fault. Repeat it and the Cyclan will have no further use for you."

The room dissolved, became again the vaulted chamber, but Cadell remained, his face replacing the blurred visage of the inquisitor.

He said, "The ramifications of the problem are such that any prediction would be of such a low order of probability as to be almost valueless. The dead man could have come from the vessel; a passenger or a member of the crew. He could have been Dumarest or his companion. The grave itself need

246

have nothing to do with either the ship or the man you are hunting. Coincidences do happen."

Another test? Avro remembered the bleak room, the blocks of plastic, the same cold, watchful eyes of the tutor. It was tempting to accept the suggestion; coincidences *did* happen, but he knew this was not one of them. A conviction on the intuitive level as strong as that which told him Dumarest was still alive.

But where? Where?

Ryder had cheated; the fee he'd paid over and above passage for work on the generator had been made up of cash and a pair of heavy bracelets ornately designed and studded with gems. The design was genuine but the metal was dross thinly plated with gold, the gems glass.

"Fifty zobars." The jeweler had the visage of an old and weary bird of prey. "Fifty—and I'm being generous."

Angado said, "You're robbing us."

"Did I ask you to come to me? Am I making you stay?" The jeweler's shoulders lifted as if they had been wings. "Try elsewhere if you want but you'll get no better offer. Ladies here demand items of genuine worth and the poor cannot afford costly baubles. To sell them I must wait for a harlot with a bemused client or a lovesick fool eager to impress his mistress. Fifty zobars. That's my final offer."

One raised to sixty as they reached the door, doubled when Dumarest added the laser Gengiz had used.

Outside he headed for the baths. The robes had been discarded but the taint of violent exertion remained as did the stench of Lowtown. Both vanished in clouds of scented steam, icy showers, hot-rooms inducing a copious sweat. A nubile girl led them to a private cubicle.

"Here you can rest, my lords. If you should require a massage I shall be happy to attend you."

Angado said, quickly, "No. Just leave the oil. We'll manage the rest."

"As you wish, my lord." Her tone was flat, devoid of emotion, but her eyes held a worldly understanding. "Some wine, perhaps? Stimulants? If there is anything you should require just press the bell."

The button which gave access to a host of pleasures and all at a price.

Dumarest relaxed on the couch, sweat dewing his naked body, hanging like pearls on the cicatrices marking his torso. Old scars long healed to thin, livid welts. Angado touched them, his fingers smooth with oil, pressing as they followed the line of muscle. His own body, unmarked, wore a halo of mist generated by the heat and illuminated by overhead lights.

"Hold still, Earl, you've a knot there!" His fingers probed, eased, moved on with skilled assurance. "I learned massage in the gynmasium at the university. Most students were short of funds and we saved by each treating the other. The instructors insisted we intersperse bouts of study with althetic pursuits so there were plenty of strained joints, pulled muscles and the like to take care of." His hands roved over the shoulders, the chest, the stomach. "These scars, Earl. The arena?"

Dumarest rolled over to lie on his face.

"The arena," said Angado. "None on your back so you had to be facing your opponent. And the way you fought showed skill. The way you taught me, too." His oiled thumbs ran up the sides, dug into the declivities alongside the spine. "But I'll never be as good as you are. Nor as fast." His hands fell to his sides. "That should do it. You want to rub me?"

"Call the girl."

"No." Angado mounted his own couch. "I'll do without." He lay silent for a while then said, "I've only seen two other men scarred like you. One was a fighter and I saw him in the arena on Rorsan. Kreagan, I think he was called, a big man, moved like a cat. A left-hander as I remember. He fought and won and afterward I bought him wine. He got a little drunk and started to boast. Said he could take on any three ordinary men at the same time. He also claimed there was nothing to match the excitement of facing an opponent. He said it was better than going with a woman." He turned on his couch to face Dumarest. "Was he right, Earl? Is it like that?"

"For some, maybe."

"And you?"

Dumarest said, "What happened to your friend?"

"Kreagan? He died shortly afterward. But—" Angado

248

broke off. "I see. Fighting isn't a game and it isn't like going with a woman. Make one mistake and it's your last. Right?"

"Yes." Dumarest looked at the floor beneath the couch, one set with a variety of colored squares. Turning he looked at the ceiling with its mass of abstract designs. Patterns designed to soothe and induce a restful somnolence. One negated by Angado. He said, "Who was the other man?"

The one with the scars? A monk. Brother Lyndom. He was old and was giving me tuition. We went swimming one day and I saw his body. It was horrible. All seared and puckered as if burned and torn. Later I learned that he'd been tortured on some world where he'd gone to set up a church but when I asked him what had happened he just laughed and said he'd run into a swarm of angry bees. I guess that's why I respect monks. I wanted to be one once, but that was before I learned I had no real choice in determining my future. And perhaps it wasn't in me. I'm too much of a coward to face what they put up with."

"Most are." Dumarest reared to sit upright then threw his legs over the edge of the couch. "Where's that oil?"

It was warm, scented, slippery beneath his hands as they moved against the other's body. His fingers, stronger, if lacking the fine skill an expert would possess, dug deep into fat and muscle.

As Angado relaxed he said, "Was the monk with your people on Lychen?"

"That's right."

"What happened?" Dumarest filled his palms with more oil. "What made you leave home?"

"It's an old story. My father married late and was old when I was born. He died in a crash and my mother with him. My uncle took over until I became of age. By then Perotto had become the real head. I tried to take over but couldn't manage." Angado stirred beneath Dumarest's hands. "Maybe I should have fought harder but I didn't know how. So I compromised."

"And?"

"I drifted. Just traveled around. What else?"

"There's no harm in that." Dumarest slapped a thigh and began to knead Angado's back as he turned over to lie prone on the couch. "The trouble is it doesn't get you anywhere. Ever think of going back?"

"To Lychen? No. That was the deal."

"Deals can be changed. Don't you ever get homesick?"

"No. Do you?"

"Often." Dumarest moved his hands up to the base of the neck and probed at the tension he found there. "So where will you go? There's not much here on Yuanka."

"I guess not." Angado lay silent for a while, speaking as Dumarest lowered his hands to the shoulders. "You saved my life," he said abruptly. "I'm not forgetting that."

"So?"

"You don't have to be stranded here. We could travel together. I've always wished I had a companion and we seem to get along. Just as if you were my older brother." He forced lightness into his tone. "I've always wanted an older brother. As a kid I was always alone and after my parents went—well, uncle did his best but it wasn't the same. Anyway, I owe you."

The truth and Dumarest didn't argue. "It takes money to buy passage."

"You don't have to tell me that." Angado twisted his head to look upward, smiling, confident he would get his own way. "We've been robbed and cheated but it doesn't matter. I've got money. As much as we need. All I have to do is get it. Earl?" His smile widened as Dumarest nodded. "Then it's a deal. Good. Let's be on our way."

Credit Debutin had branches scattered throughout the Burdinnion and that on Yuanka occupied a prominent position on the main plaza. Dumarest waited outside as Angado entered, looking at the shops ringing the area, the familiar figure standing outside the casino. Brother Lloyd, somber in his robe, a bowl of chipped plastic in his hand, was busy collecting alms.

A good position, as he knew; gamblers were superstitious when it came to luck. A coin on entering could placate the goddess of fortune and if you were successful another was her just tribute. Even losers dropped a coin in the bowl in the hope of bettering future chances.

250

"Earl!" Angado came from the bank, his face drawn. "I don't understand it," he said. "I just don't understand it."

"No money?"

"No, but—"

"Leave it." A cafe stood to one side and Dumarest led the way toward it. At a table he ordered a pot of tisane and waited until it had been served and poured before looking at his companion. "No money," he said. "Did they tell you why?"

"Yes, but it's crazy. The account's been stopped. I can't understand it. The arrangement was plain; I can draw at any branch of Credit Debutin against the family account. Five thousand ryall a month. That's Lychen currency," he explained. "It's converted to local."

"How many zobars would that be?"

"Over ten thousand." Angado met Dumarest's eyes. "I told you I had money."

Dumarest said, "Have you an account? A credit balance?" His right hand moved toward his left forearm checking as he halted the subconscious gesture. "Any money at all?"

"Only what we split." Angado looked helplessly at the tisane. "I can't understand it. Perotto gave me his word and there's never been any difficulty before. Just my name, thumbprint and code number and the cash is handed over." His hand clenched, slammed down on the table with force enough to send tisane slopping from the cups. "What the hell's going on?"

The waitress came from within the cafe, attracted by the noise, frowning at the mess. Dumarest dropped coins on the table. "For your trouble," he explained. "Would you bring me a sheet of notepaper? Nothing special, a leaf from a book will do."

The paper was thick, rough, jagged down one edge. Dumarest placed it on the table before Angado.

"Write me a promissory note. It's a gambling debt for five hundred and date it before we were dumped. No," he amended. "Earlier than that. Before you took passage on the *Thorn*."

"When I was on Tysa?"

"That'll do." Dumarest took the paper when Angado had finished. He folded it, opened it, dropped it on the ground and trod on it. Picking it up he scuffed the sheet and stained it with tisane. Folding it again he tucked it under his tunic and rested it beneath his armpit. "How did they treat you in there?"

"The bank?" Angado scowled. "Like dirt!"

"I want the truth."

"They were cold. Hostile, even. They just said there was no account and no funds for me. I argued but got nowhere. The instructions had been revoked and no money would be paid."

"Did they check you out? Your thumbprint or—"

"No. Nothing. They just weren't interested. I can't understand it. Perotto swore that—what the hell's gone wrong?"

"Think about it," advised Dumarest. "Now let's see if I can cash this note."

The man behind the counter was snobbishly supercilious. He picked up the paper with caution, nose wrinkling at the odor of human perspiration, unfolding it as if it could bite.

"Yours?"

"It's mine." Dumarest leaned over the counter thrusting his face toward the other. "A bearer promissory note, right? You pay whoever presents it. I'm presenting it."

"I meant was it issued to you?"

"It's a bearer note." Dumarest let impatience edge his tone. "What the hell does it matter who it was issued to? I've got it. Check it out and give me the money."

"If you'd like to wait? Come back later—"

"Now!" Dumarest looked beyond the man. "You the boss here? If you can't handle the job maybe I'd better speak to someone who can."

He relaxed as the man hurried away to confer with others. The note was genuine, drawn on the Credit Debutin, carrying Angado's signature, code number and thumbprint. Those details could be checked against the computer data in the bank. He straightened as the cashier returned, another man at his side. One who waited until they were alone.

"Mister—?" He shrugged as Dumarest made no answer. "No matter. I'm the manager here and I'm afraid I have bad news for you. This note of yours cannot be met."

"You mean it's a fake?"

"No, I'm not saying that. It seems genuine enough and

normally I'd accept it but there are no longer funds to meet it."

"He's broke?"

"Not broke—dead. The account has been closed." Frowning the manager added, "It's odd. You're the second man who's come in asking about that account. The other claimed to be the person himself."

"Maybe he was."

"Impossible. The report from head office was most explicit. That's why no money can be paid against that note. Of course you can make due representation to the estate for settlement but that will take time. My advice to you is to sell it. You'll have to take a loss, naturally, but—"

"Sell it? Who the hell would buy junk like this?"

"At a quarter face value?" The manager met Dumarest's eyes. "I would for one—the Karroum own most of Lychen."

Chapter Nine

Angado had gone when Dumarest emerged from the bank, the monk seated in his place. Brother Lloyd looked tired, grateful for the tisane he had been given. As Dumarest approached he looked up and began to rise from his chair.

"Sit down." Dumarest dropped into the space facing him. "Did he leave word?"

"Yes. He's in there." The monk gestured toward the casino. "He said to be sure and tell you where he had gone."

A fool unable to restrain his impatience and seeking novelty to pass the time. Dumarest helped himself to some of the tisane and leaned back in his chair as he sipped the fragrant brew. Thoughtful as he reviewed the situation.

Angado was a liability and yet it was hard to think of him as such. A danger; those who wanted him dead would try again and to be close was to invite disaster. A man now without assets and only one proven skill. Yet he held potential value; the resources of his House and Family. Wealth, influence, power—things Dumarest could use in his search for Earth and that search could begin on Lychen where Angado belonged.

He stood at a table, face flushed with excitement as he watched the bounding progress of a ball. One which bounced at the edges of ranked divisions to hover and finally come to rest.

"Red. Even. Eighteen." The croupier's voice was a drone. "Place your bets."

Angado had lost. He lost again. As he went to put more coins on the board Dumarest caught his arm.

"We need to talk."

"You're back! Good!" Angado smiled his pleasure. "One more turn and I'll be with you."

"Now!"

"One more turn."

He played and lost and ordered wine as he led the way to a table set in an alcove flanked with mirrors. The girl who brought it was young, enticing in her slit gown, smiling as she saw her tip.

"Anything else, my lord?"

"Food. A plate of delicacies. The best."

"No food." Dumarest was harsh. "Not yet." Then, as Angado made to protest, he added, savagely, "Do as you like after we've spoken. Now we have things to settle. Why didn't you tell me you were rich?"

"I'm not. I told you about the arrangement. Anyway, what does it matter?" Angado sipped, drank, refilled his glass. "Drink up, Earl, enjoy yourself. We can afford it."

"No."

"Why not? You got the money, didn't you?"

"A quarter of face value." Dumarest stacked coins on the table. "Your share. All you're going to get. If you want to squander it go ahead. It's your money."

Looking at it Angado said, slowly, "What are you telling me?"

"You're dead. Officially dead. No cash and no credit. Your notes won't be met. From now on you make your own way." Dumarest picked up his glass, lifted it in a mock toast. "Freedom, Angado. Let's drink to it—you can't afford to waste the wine."

He watched as Angado obeyed, the truth swallowed with the ruby liquid, cold realization dampening the euphoria of alcohol. As yet life to Angado had been an adventure, one padded by the cushions of wealth, now those cushions had been tweaked away and he was going to get hurt.

Dumarest said, "Think of Lowtown. Remember it. That's where you could wind up unless you're careful. Bear it in mind, the dirt, the stink, the decay." The grinding poverty, the pain, the desperation. An alien world to one accustomed to riches. A hostile one to a man arrogant with the memory of wealth. "Do you still feel hungry?"

Angado shook his head, remembering the cost of the wine, the loss at the table.

"What are you going to do?"

"Get back to Lychen. There has to be some mistake. Perotto will correct it. He—"

"Wants you dead!" snapped Dumarest. "And you're a fool not to see it. Remain a fool and you'll die alone. I mean it."

"You'll leave me?"

"I've no time for a man who refuses to help himself. You're dead, Angado. It's only a matter of time before you're in the ground. That's just what will happen when you meet Perotto unless—" He broke off and waited for the other to recognize the obvious.

"I've got to get back home," said Angado. "But without Perotto suspecting I'm back until I'm ready to face him. You'll come with me, Earl? Help me?" Anxiety tinged his voice as Dumarest remained silent. "You won't regret it. I swear to that. I'll give you anything you want."

The gratitude of princes—but first it had to be earned.

Larbi Vargas was old, wizened, his face seamed with a mesh of lines as if it had been leather unoiled and left too long in the sun. Only his eyes were young, holding a shrewd brilliance, one which matched the razor-edged keenness of his mind. An entrepreneur, an agent, a go-between. A man like a spider sitting in a web of information. One drifting in the dim region lying in the strata between law and lawlessness, order and chaos. Men like him existed on every world and Dumarest had known how to track him down. To Angado he was an alien form of life.

Now he watched as the preliminaries were completed; the small cakes eaten with wine. The pleasantries. The handing over of scarce resources.

"You are a man after my own heart," said Vargas. He wiped a crumb from his lips. "Too many who come to me are impatient. They neglect the niceties of civilized conduct but you, obviously, are aware of ancient traditions. Some more wine?"

"Thank you, no."

"You?" Vargas sighed and lowered the bottle as Angado

256

shook his head. "Your problem is a common one, my friends. How to escape a hostile world? Money is the answer, the key to all things. How to get it? That is a harder problem. Theft is difficult and dangerous but desperate men are willing to accept risks. If you are such something could be arranged. No?"

"No."

"Then let us examine other prospects. Work at the mines is available but only for those willing to sign a contract. They pay is low and expenses high. I would not advise it. A party left last week for the northern hills to hunt kulighin. A beast as large as a man," he explained. "Vicious, cunning, valued for its hide and certain glands. Always some die on such a hunt and reward is never certain. But your stake is large enough to buy you a place in such a party if you can match it with experience and would be willing to take a lower share."

"Too long," said Dumarest. "We want something fast. Passage on a ship heading to Lychen. One needing an engineer would be ideal."

"Every vessel operating in the Burdinnion needs engineers," said Vargas dryly. "Which is why all ships carry them. If you were a captain would you trust your life and ship to an unknown? Someone lacking the years in which to have gained experience and without documents to prove his ability? Of course," he added, "such documents could be provided."

In time and with money they couldn't spare. Things the old man knew but he worked in his own way and to press him would lessen his desire to cooperate.

Now he said, "For one of you there is no real problem. If you just want passage away from Yuanka and are willing to do what is asked and spend what you have on bribes there are several ships on which I could arrange a passage. The *Warton* bound for Lorne. The *Koura* bound for Balaban. A handler who can run a table and show a profit would be accepted." His eyes rested on Dumarest. "And there would be no need for him to pass through the gate."

An extra bonus and an essential one for any wanted criminal.

Angado said, quickly, "We must travel together."

"Then your choice is limited. The *Audran* leaves tomorrow at dawn. They carry a cargo of mikha and need men to

257

tend them. For the right price the captain will allow you to work your passage.''

"To where?"

"Haroun." Vargas shrugged as Angado shook his head. "The choice is yours but I suggest you take it. Haroun is less hostile than Yuanka."

"The mikha?"

"A low order of life similar to leeches." Vargas added, with the hint of a smile, "They need to feed on human blood."

At dusk a wind began to blow from the south carrying an acrid dust which caught at the nostrils and stung the eyes. As the purple haze deepened to night the wind ceased to leave a dusty film over the town. One stirred by pedestrian boots into flurries which rose to settle in new configurations.

"A hell of a world." Angado turned from the window of the room they had hired. "And a hell of a deal Vargas gave us. How much did you pay him, Earl? Whatever it was it was too much. Turn thief," he sneered. "Join a bunch of suicidal hunters. Feed parasites. He had to be joking."

Dumarest made no comment, lying supine on one of the two narrow beds the room contained, looking at the cracked and stained ceiling. One typical of the rooming house with its sagging roof, creaking floors, dingy walls. At night parasites crawled out to feed.

"Earl?"

"He wasn't joking. We're taking his offer."

"I'd rather steal!"

"Then you do it alone." Dumarest sat upright and stared at the younger man. "Vargas will set it up for you if you pay. Find a location, arrange to dispose of the loot, even put you in touch with help if you need it. To him it's just a matter of business. To you it will be your life."

"If I'm caught."

"You'll be caught. People living on worlds like this have learned to take care of their property. And they aren't gentle with those who try to take it. Both hands amputated, blinding, hamstringing—most likely you'll be sold to the mines to work until you die. That needn't take long."

"But to feed parasites!"

258

"Most do it all their lives." Dumarest rose from the cot. "Maybe we can find the captain in a tavern; if not I'll go to the ship. But first we'll get something to eat."

The food was poor, as cheap as they could find, as everything they had eaten since leaving Lowtown had been cheap. As had the wine, the accommodation, yet still the money dwindled away. Cost was relative; what would keep a man a week in Lowtown would barely buy a snack on the plaza, yet to return to the sprawling slum was to commit suicide. Gengiz had had a brother who had sworn revenge.

Things Angado thought of as he spooned the redolent stew into his mouth. He wasn't hungry but Dumarest had insisted that he eat; good advice from a man who too often had never been sure when he would be able to eat again. A trait nurtured by poverty as were so many others and Angado wondered if he would ever be able to master the basic techniques of survival. Not the ability to maintain life in the wild, that was a matter of learning how to best use available resources, but to master this new and frightening environment. How would he have managed without Dumarest? His money would have been squandered, thrown away on gaudy trifles, on food which gave bulk but little nourishment, on high-priced comfort which, compared to his normal life style, would have been hardship.

It would have been better to have died as Perotto had intended. Perotto! At the thought his hand tightened on the spoon.

Dumarest, watching, said, "Relax. He can wait."

"Can you read my mind?"

Just his hands, his face, the lack of focus in his eyes. Signals he had learned to read when facing gamblers in the salons of a hundred ships. As he had learned to read other signals, more important, those worn by men intent on taking his life.

Tables or the arena. Money or blood. It was all the same.

Neary, the captain of the *Audran*, was a human wasp; thin, vicious, with a hatchet-face and cold, hostile eyes. He sat alone in a corner of a tavern close to the field, a bottle standing before him, a plate of flat cakes smeared with a sickly paste at his elbow.

To Dumarest he said, "I've been expecting you. Vargas said you might be along. Got the money?"

"We've money."

"Then sit. Have some wine. A cake." The captain hammered on the table and snapped at the girl who answered the summons. "Bring wine, girl. A flagon of your best for me and my friends." He looked at Dumarest. "He'll pay."

"Like hell he—" Angado fell silent as Dumarest gripped his arm.

"He'll what?" Neary had caught the objection. "You don't want to buy the wine? Is that it?" His head thrust forward like that of a snake. "Well?"

"I meant that I'll pay, not him." Angado swallowed his anger, realizing the mistake he'd made. One born of ignorance—never before had he needed to beg favors from a captain. "Get the wine, girl. A big flagon and your best."

It arrived as drums began to pulse and a dancer spun on the cleared space before the tables. One artificially young, paint masking her face, the lines meshing her eyes. Her body needed no artifice, mature, full-brested, hips and belly rotating in an age-old enticement. The clash of metal merged with the sonorous beat of the drum; coins hanging from her costume more suspended from her ears, her throat, her wrists and ankles. Twinkling discs which caught and reflected the light so as to bathe her in shimmering brilliance.

As she froze to a sudden, abrupt immobility at the end of her performance those watching yelled their appreciation and flung coins at her feet.

"Nice," said the captain, pouring the wine. "But I've seen better. On Elmer and Hakim especially. They start them young on those worlds." He drank and pursed his lips. "Did Vargas tell you what our cargo is?"

Dumarest nodded.

"They'll need feeding," said Neary. "If they don't they'll go comotose and sporifulate. If that happens they won't be worth the atoms used to move them. Lost profit always makes me angry. Need I say more?"

"I get the picture."

"And your friend?" Neary grunted as Angado nodded.

"Good enough. It'll cost you two hundred." He paused for a moment then added, "Each."

"We don't have to dodge the gate."

"So?"

"So we can afford to haggle." Dumarest reached for the flagon and poured all goblets full. "How many mikha are you carrying? A full load? I thought so. You know how much blood they're going to need? I see you do." He lifted his goblet. "Your health, Captain. Now let's start talking sense."

The drum began to pulse again as they left the tavern, the deal made, the wine finished. Angado staggered a little as he stepped into the open air; with Dumarest doing the talking he'd had nothing to do but sit and drink. Now he halted and stared at the field.

"Why not go aboard now, Earl? Neary wouldn't mind."

"We've things to do." Dumarest led the way back into town. "We need plasma," he explained. "It'll eke out our blood. Some frozen whole-blood too. We can get it at the infirmary."

"Why couldn't Neary?"

"He'd have to pay," said Dumarest, patiently. "This way he gets paid."

Together with free labor to handle the cargo. Angado smiled as he thought about it then lost the smile as he tripped and almost fell. Standing beside Dumarest, motionless, he heard a soft scrape of boots.

"Earl—"

"Be quiet!"

Dumarest had heard it too; the grate of soles on the grit deposited by the wind. It came again from a point behind and was echoed from a point ahead. The sounds of wayfarers making their way home or crewmen heading for the field and their vessels. But few roamed the streets of Yuanka at night and crewmen had no reason to creep through the darkness.

"Thieves," whispered Angado. "At least two of them. Waiting for us, Earl?"

If so they wouldn't wait for long and there would be more than two. Dumarest sniffed at the air and caught the scent of sweat and wine coupled with another, unmistakable odor.

261

The stink of Lowtown and, smelling it, he knew the danger they were in.

"Move." He touched Angado on the arm. "Slowly. Stagger and make noise. Pretend we're together. If anyone comes at you don't hesitate. Hit out and run."

Dumarest crossed the street as Angado began to sing, the noise covering the rasp of his own boots. Shadows swallowed him as, staggering, the younger man lurched down the street talking as if to a companion.

"Good wine, eh? And that dancer was really good. I'd like to know her better. Have her dance just for me." A pause then, "Why not? My money's good. I bet she'd agree if I asked. Damn it, Earl, let's go back and put it to the test. Five hundred. I'll give her five hundred if—" A rattle as Angado walked into a garbage can. "What the hell is that?" And then, louder, "Who the hell are you?"

They came running from either end of the street, four shadows which solidified into men. Shapes which carried lengths of pipe which whistled as they cut through the air.

As the bottle Angado had snatched from the garbage whistled to land with a soggy impact on the pale oval of a face.

Dumarest was running before he hit the ground, his hand moving, the knife it held giving it heft and weight, the pommel smashing against a temple to send a second attacker down. A third followed, screaming, hands clutching his groin and Dumarest turned to hear the gong-sound of beaten metal as the pipe the remaining man held slammed against the garbage can Angado had lifted to use as a shield. One blow and then the pipe fell and the man was running to vanish in the darkness.

"Come on!" Dumarest ran, halting as a whistle broke the silence, turning to head back in the opposite direction. "Quick!"

The four would not have been alone. Others would have been placed as lookouts, the whistle a signal from one of them. Hunting packs followed a pattern the same if animal or human. To surround, to run down, to attack, to kill and then to feed.

Dumarest slowed as he reached the mouth of an alley, speeded as he found it innocent, slowing again as he neared the end of the street. Another crossed it forming a junction restricting his choice to a right or left turn.

As the whistle came again from behind, louder, more imperious, he headed toward the left, Angado following.

To the men waiting with flashlights and guns and nets which caught them both like flies in a sticky web.

Chapter Ten

The cell was a box ten feet long, eight wide, eight high. One fitted with a double bunk and primitive facilities. The door was a barred grill, the window another. Through it Dumarest had seen the dawn come to lighten the sky, the blue shimmer as the *Audran* had headed into space. At noon a guard took them to an office.

It was as bleak as the cell, holding little more than chairs, a desk, the terminal of a computer. The official seated at the desk was old, tired, heavy lines marring the contours of his face.

"Be seated." Inspector Vernajean gestured at chairs. "I think this can be kept informal. But before we begin do either of you have any complaints as to how you have been treated?"

"No." Dumarest had a bruised cheek, Angado a cut lip and a welt on his forehead. "None at all."

"Good." Vernajean relaxed a little. The injuries could have been accidental but the older of the two had the sense not to make an issue of them. "Last night we received reports of prowlers in the Voe district of the city. A patrol was sent to investigate and you were apprehended. Apparently you were running from the scene of a crime. Other men were also seen but managed to elude arrest. Well?"

Dumarest said, "It was a coincidence."

"Explain."

"We were making our way from the field and heard someone cry out for help. There were too many for us to handle so we ran to get assistance. That's when you caught us."

"Can you describe the men?

"No, it was dark."

264

"How many were there?"

"About six."

"Four attacking two others?" Vernajean didn't wait for an answer. "In a way you were lucky to be caught. The patrol disturbed men who had been waiting for you. Scum of Lowtown who had broken curfew as had the others. Does the name Birkut mean anything to you?"

"I've seen him."

"And Yuli?"

"No."

"Gengiz's brother. He's sworn to kill you but you know that. He's taken over and maybe he's getting impatient. That attack could be repeated and the next time you needn't be so fortunate. You appreciate my position?"

Angado said, "We were attacked and had to fight for our lives and all you worry about is your position? How about doing your duty? If you know who was responsible then go after them and make them answer. Why are—"

"Shut up!" Dumarest didn't look at his companion. "He's young," he said to the inspector. "Still learning. He doesn't realize that Lowtown is what it is because you want it to be that way."

"What other way can it be?" Vernajean shrugged. "Men without money, without hope, growing more and more desperate. An abscess ready to burst and spread infection all over the city. It has to be drained."

By using men like Yuli to rule and bleed malcontents into the mines. A ready source of cheap labor for the installations which provided the wealth of the planet. But, for Yuli, the price of cooperation was the death of those who had killed his brother.

"The monks have spoken for you," said the inspector. "We have no wish to antagonize the Church but—" His gesture completed the sentence. "And there is another thing. Without a job or funds you are not allowed within the city during curfew. If you should be picked up by a patrol and found to be deficient then you can be fined or sentenced to the mines. I tell you this so as to make you aware of your position."

"Thank you," said Dumarest.

"Position?" Angado was less gracious. "What position? If

265

it hadn't been for your damned men we wouldn't be here now!"

"If it hadn't been for them we could be dead." Dumarest rose to his feet, facing the inspector. "Can we go now?"

"Yes. Your property will be returned at the desk outside." Vernajean rose in turn. "A last word to the pair of you—do not stay on Yuanka too long."

Outside Angado swore with savage bitterness.

"They robbed us! The bastards took half our cash!"

"But left half."

"We should complain. Go back and make a formal accusation."

Dumarest said, "You heard what the inspector said. He was warning us. Leave Yuanka or wind up in the mines or dead. Maybe some of those officers in there want to see us that way."

"So they robbed us to force us to the brink and over." Angado looked bleak. "How do we get out of this hell-hole? Steal? Gamble? Try our luck at the wheel? Put all of our money on a single turn?" His laugh was brittle. "What have we to lose?"

Everything, but that was the nature of a true gamble. To risk life itself on the throw of dice or the flip of a coin and yet, as Dumarest knew, the need to win was often the surest way to lose.

Yet there was more than one way to gamble.

The place had the familiarity of home; the smell, the sounds, the sight of the ring, the tiered seats, the cubicles in which men sat with blank faces or sported with artificial gaiety. The environs of the arena in which men faced each other with naked steel to maim and kill for the sake of gain.

The promoter was curt. "It's fifty for show, as much if he lasts five minutes, a hundred more if he wins." He looked at Dumarest standing black-faced, vacuous, a seeming moron. "Does he know what it's all about?"

"He knows." Angado, primed, acted the part of an entrepreneur eager for a profit, uncaring how he got it. A cynic who shrugged as he added, "You won't be disappointed. He's good and has scars to prove it. Fifty, you said?"

"When he's due to climb into the ring." The promoter

ignored the outstretched hand. "Gives you a chance to place your bet," he explained. "Of course, if your man doesn't make good, you do."

"Medicals?"

"We've a doctor but you pay his fees." The promoter glanced at his watch. "The prelims are all arranged; first and third blood stuff. Your man'll feed a main event."

"For fifty?"

"You can double it if you bet right." The promoter sharpened his tone. "You want it or not?"

"I'll take it." Angado obeyed Dumarest's signal. "Doubled, eh?"

"Sure, if he makes a good entry. That's settled then. He'll face a prime contender."

To be hacked, slashed, maimed and slaughtered to provide a bloody spectacle. Dumarest had seen such too often; men driven to the ring by desperation, unskilled, untrained, trusting to luck and the mercy of their opponents. Ending as things of carmined horror, dying to the frenzied yelling of the crowd.

Dumarest could hear them from where he sat, imagine their faces, avid, feral, features taut with sadistic pleasure. Men and women converted by their blood-lust into mindless, reactive beasts. Thrilling to the sight of blood, of pain, the stink of fear.

"Earl?" Angado had heard the shouts and seen some of the men coming from the ring. Youngsters, mostly, many with gaping wounds. Some having to be supported, others making their own way to where the doctor worked on a bench covered by a stained, plastic sheet. "Earl, are you sure you want to go through with this?"

"We've no choice."

"To hell with the money. We can work in the mines, try hunting, anything. This is butchery."

Sport seen from a different angle and he no longer felt the vicarious pleasure he had when seated in a place close to the ring. Enjoying the combat, the near misses, the cuts, the hits and scores, the deaths while comforted by the knowledge that he would remain unharmed.

Dumarest said, "Make sure the odds are right. I'll stumble when entering the ring, look vague, act stupid. Easy meat to anyone who knows his stuff. I might even take a cut. Give me a couple of minutes to decide then make the bets.''

"You're good," said Angado. "You have to be. And fast, I know that. But I still don't like it.''

"Do your part and I'll do mine.''

"Yes, but—" Angado broke off as someone screamed from the medical bench. A hoarse, animal-like sound of sheer agony. "God!''

The scream came again, the doctor's voice rising above it, harsh, commanding.

"Help me, someone! Hold this man still! Hold him, damn you!''

Angado gripped sweat-slimed shoulders, fighting the explosion of muscles as he forced them back on the bench as others gripped threshing arms and legs. The man was young, face contorted with pain, intestines bulging through the slit abdomen. Blueish, greasy coils stained with blood and lymph, one slashed to show a gaping mouth.

"Keep him still!'' Air blasted as the doctor used a hypogun to drive anesthetic into the bloodstream directly through the skin. He'd aimed at the throat and the effect was immediate. As the patient slumped into merciful unconsciousness the doctor sewed the slashed intestine, coated it, sprayed it, thrust it and the others back into place. More sewing, spraying and sealing and the job was done. "Next?''

"Will he live?'' Angado lingered as a couple of porters carried the man away.

"He should.'' The doctor was middle-aged, hard, coldly proficient. "Thanks for your help. You running a contender?''

"Yes.''

"Tell him not to be heroic. It's better to drop and grandstand than to end up cut all to hell. Cheaper too.'' The doctor raised his voice. "Who's next?''

A man with a slashed face, an eye gone, the nose and lips slit. He was followed by another clutching at the ripped fabric of his shorts, thick streams of blood running between his fingers and staining his thighs. A third had a small hole on his torso and coughed and spat blood from a punctured lung.

A winner—in the clash and flurry of edged and pointed steel the one who stayed longest on his feet gained the prize. But even winners could be hurt.

Angado moved back to Dumarest, his façade cracking, sweat dewing his face. The smells were making him gag and the cold indifference of others to pain made him feel alien and vulnerable. In this madness Dumarest was a consolation. A rock of security.

One who seemed asleep.

He leaned back against the wall, muscles relaxed, eyes closed, his breathing deep and even. A man devoid of tension, sitting easily, resting so as to conserve his energy. To Angado it seemed incredible, then he realized that Dumarest was not asleep at all but had deliberately thrown himself into a trance-like state of detachment. One which suited the pose he had adopted, that of a moronic intelligence unable to imagine the consequences of failure and willing to be guided by a sharper mind.

"It won't be long now." The promoter paused, taking time during the interval to check on the next events. Known contenders were safe enough but ring-fodder sometimes grew apprehensive and needed encouragement. "I've picked an easy one—old, slow, too gentle for his own good. Abo hates to see a man hurt. A fault, but one in your favor." He glanced at Dumarest. "He need anything? A pill, maybe?"

"I can handle it."

"See that you do." The promoter jerked his head as a roar came from the crowd. Naked women, fighting with clubs, had given rise to yelled appreciation. "Better get him ready."

He bustled away and Dumarest rose, stretching. As always he felt the tension, the anticipation which crawled over his skin like multi-legged insects. Warnings of danger which even the shower could not wash away. Cleaned, oiled to prevent a grasping hand gaining a hold, he donned shorts and reached for his knife.

"Not that one!" An attendant called from where he stood before the passage leading to the ring. "We provide the weapons. Hurry up if you're ready!"

Sound exploded from the crowd as they reached the passage, a shrill, yammering roar which caused the partition to quiver.

"That was a killing!" The attendant sucked in his cheeks. "The crowd always like to see a man go down. Right. You're next!"

"The money." Angado was insistent. "I get paid or he doesn't show."

"It's here." The attendant handed over the cash. "Happy now?" He didn't bother to hide his contempt. "Damned leech!" Then, to Dumarest, "Right, friend. Off you go."

To the head of the passage, the open space, the watching crowd, the ring, the man who waited to kill him.

Dumarest tripped as he entered the auditorium, clumsy as he climbed into the ring to stand beneath the glare of overhead lights, the knife they had given him hanging loosely in his hand. One an inch longer than his own, not as well honed, not as well balanced, but the ten inches of edged and pointed metal could do its job. It glittered as it caught and reflected the light, a flash which caught the eye and attention of a woman in the third row. One aging beneath her paint, her costume designed to accentuate her charms. The jewels she wore were no harder than her eyes.

"That man," she said. "What do you know about him?"

"Nothing." Her companion was indifferent. "Just fodder for the ring. Forget him."

A thing not easy for her to do. Narrowly she watched as Dumarest moved, noting his build, the scars, the lean suppleness of his body. A man who was more than he seemed to be and her own experience doubted his artifice. Too often she had acted the innocent in order to gain an advantage and such maneuvers were not restricted to women.

"A thousand," she said. "I want to back him for a thousand."

"To win?"

"Please don't be tiresome. Just do as I ask."

"No." He was definite. "It would be a waste of money. Abo isn't due to go down yet. Another few bouts and then, when his reputation is at its peak, the odds will be right for a killing."

"You could make one now. That man will win."

"He won't be given the chance." The man ended all argument. "Here's Abo now."

He bounced into the ring, the idol of the crowd, a winner who seemed set to go on winning. He smiled with a flash of white teeth, brown skin oiled, glistening beneath the lights.

The tight mat of his hair was thick against his skull, the arms long, corded with muscle. He moved like a cat, restless, poised and balanced on the balls of his feet. An animal, fast, quick, dangerous, he basked in the shouted adulation of women, their screamed invitations.

Promises of their beds and bodies if he would only kill . . . kill . . . kill!

And kill he would despite the rules which stated that a man down should be left alone and given the chance to yield.

"Attention!" The voice over the speakers was flat, emotionless. "A fight to the finish between the defender Abo and the challenger Earl. To your corners." A pause during which tension mounted. "Ready?" Another long, dragging wait then, like a cracking whip, "Go!"

And the third man entered the ring.

He was always there, always waiting, an invisible shape dressed in sere habiliments with bony hands ready to collect his due. Death who could never be avoided, now present by invitation.

A presence Dumarest ignored as he did the crowd, the lights, the ring itself. They blurred into a background framing the object of his concentration. The tall, lithe, man before him. One armed with a knife. One intending to kill.

And the killing would not be merciful.

Dumarest could tell it from the sadistic grin, the stance, the feline movements, the twitch of the eyes. A man playing cat and mouse in order to please the crowd. Eager to give them what they wanted; blood, pain, fear, the long-drawn agony of the final end.

A man who knew he could deliver. Success had augmented his natural skill; easy kills rubbing away the edges of hesitation. Now he moved slowly forward, blade extended before him, point out, edge upward, light glinting from the honed steel. His free hand made inviting gestures.

"Come closer," he said. "A shallow cut and you go down. Scream a little and writhe as if you're in pain and then it's over. Easy money for a scratch. Why make it hard, eh?"

Dumarest said, "I've got to last five minutes. I need the fifty."

"A cut you go down, get up and hit my blade. Plenty of noise and movement. Then another little cut and down you go

271

again, this time to stay. A good deal, eh?'' The purring voice hardened a little. "Take it while you've got the chance."

A gamble in more ways than one. A cut would enhance the odds against him and so up the take, but Abo could cut too deep; to trust him would be suicide. A risk Dumarest would never normally have taken but the man wanted to gain popularity, a quick and easy win would work against that and, to cooperate now, would be to gain a later advantage.

"Right," he said. "But be careful."

They closed, blades flashing, ringing, darting like the tongues of serpents, Dumarest saw the lance of Abo's knife, its slashing, backhand sweep, and moved sideways away from its edge as it sliced into his side. A shallow gash barely more than a scratch and far less serious than Abo had intended. Dumarest clapped his free hand over the wound, masking it, enhancing the flow of blood with the pressure of his fingers. Staggering, he retreated to a halt, gasping, at the far side of the ring.

A pretense to gain time, to allow Angado to place his bets, but looking at Abo he knew he had made a mistake.

The man had more than luck and skill to help him win.

Knives were not always what they seemed. A blade could have inbuilt weaknesses and snap under pressure. Or the hilt could be hollowed to contain various vapors which could be spurted through holes in the guard. Abo's blade held indentations which held a numbing paste.

Dumarest cursed his stupidity but he was trapped in a game over which he had no control. There had been no chance to examine the weapons. None to take elementary precautions and, had he fought to avoid being cut, the odds would have fallen too low.

Now only speed could save him.

He met Abo's rush with a flick of his hand, the blood it had held flying to spatter on the smiling face, the cruel eyes. An attack followed by his own rush and the air shook to the thin, harsh ring of steel, the crowd roaring as Dumarest sent his blade home in a vicious slash which would have spilled Abo's guts had he not twisted to take the edge on his hip.

A cut followed by another, a third, deep gashes which laced the torso and marred the smooth brown skin with a patina of blood.

Backing, Abo fought back. He was quick, skillful, alert now to the real danger. The smile gone now, replaced by a snarl as he turned into an animal fighting for its life. Matching the one Dumarest had already become.

Time became meaningless, the universe itself diminishing to a matter of cuts, parries, dodges, feints, thrusts, attacks, ripostes. As life became a matter of crippling cuts, weakening blood loss, of speed and instinctive action unhampered by the slowing need for thought.

Abo lunged, missed, received a slash which crippled his left arm. Spinning, he brought up his edge, the blade halting as Dumarest blocked the motion with the barrier of his forearm against the other's wrist. A moment of strain then they parted, Dumarest seeing his target, aiming for it against the growing numbness.

Feeling the jar of metal against bone as a sun burst in his eyes.

It was a flare of light so intense as to be a physical pain and Dumarest stepped backward, hands lifted, feeling the ice-burn as steel cut into his body. A blow repeated as he moved blindly to one side and he tasted blood in his mouth and the pain as metal scraped over bone. A thrust which had penetrated a lung, another searing into his bowels, a third tearing at his liver in a storm of edge and point to send him down.

To lie blinking on the floor of the ring as vague images replaced the blackness—the lights, a shadow standing tall against them, one smeared with blood, grinning in the rictus of impending death, but still standing, still upright.

Abo enjoying his victory.

"Earl!" Angado was at his side. "You're hurt! How badly—God!" His voice rose as he called for help. "Get him to the doctor! Fast!"

Dumarest sagged in the rough hands which grasped and carried him. Pain was something not to be ignored, an agony which filled every crevice of his being. The pain and the knowledge that, at last, he had reached the end.

It happened and, in the arena, it could happen to anyone at any time. A slip, a moment of carelessness, a touch of overconfidence and, when least expected, death would reach out its waiting hand. He had seen it happen to others and now it had happened to him. The luck which had served him for so long had at last run out.

"Earl!" Angado was pleading. "For God's sake—Earl!"

A voice like a whisper in the darkness echoed by others, one stronger than the rest.

". . . internal injuries and there is profuse hemorrhaging . . . needs extensive medical care but it'll be costly . . . cryogenic sac . . . move to the institute . . . need to waste no . . . must hurry . . . hurry . . . hurry . . ."

The doctor pronouncing the sentence of death, his voice becoming ragged, lost in the encroaching gloom. Death by inaction. Death from reasons of poverty. Death because he couldn't pay for the treatment necessary. Death, smiling wider now as he always smiled, coming closer . . . closer. . . .

"No!" Dumarest forced open his eyes fired by the spark deep inside of him, the urge to survive which gave him a transitory strength. Darkness still clouded his vision and obscured shapes but one, close to his face, had to be Angado.

"Earl! Those bastards fired a strobe-laser into your eyes. There was almost a riot from the crowd. All bets are off."

Which is why he was lying on the bench with the doctor treating him with basic remedies. Stanching wounds and killing pain while knowing he could only stave off the inevitable.

"My arm!" Dumarest lifted his left forearm. "Get a banker-machine. Money, you understand? I've money."

". . . hang on and and maybe I can get something arranged. A loan or—"

"Money!" Dumarest snarled in impatient anger. "Listen to me! Get a banking machine and do what's necessary. Do it." He sank back, blood welling to gurgle in his throat, to drown him with his life's fluid. To spray in a carmine fountain as he coughed and spat and said, while he was able, "I've money, damn you! Credit! Use it and . . ." He felt himself beginning to fall into an eternal oblivion. "Angado—I'm relying on you!"

Then there was nothing but the endless spinning tunnel of darkness and, at the end, the single point of a glowing star.

Chapter Eleven

Avro screamed; a shout which illuminated the shadows of his sleeping mind. A challenge hurled at the wind, the sky, the male hovering before him on spread wings. An aggressor, young, ambitious, fired by the biological need to perpetuate his genes. One screaming his intent as Avro screamed his warning but knowing, even as he screamed, that this time it wouldn't be enough. And to strike first was half the victory.

Wind gusted around him as he launched himself from the peak with a thrum of wings. Pinions which threshed the air as he fought to gain height, to turn, to hurl himself at the challenger, arms extended, fingers spread, feet lifted to deal a devastating kick. One which missed as the other twirled aside, to kick in turn, to register a blow which sent Avro spinning.

Whirling as he was attacked again with feet and hands, toes and fingers ripping at his wings, adding to the strain they already fought to overcome.

The penalty of age when the body grew too gross and the great pectorals, the deltoids, began to weaken. A time when lift was slower, agility less, vulnerability a growing menace.

The moment of truth for an angel who refused to yield his nest, his women, his position in the community.

A thing Avro knew from the instinct buried in the body and brain of the host he dominated as he knew that to fold his wings and fall would be to signal his peaceful withdrawal from the conflict. An act which would save his life and leave him to fly alone as long as his wings would carry him. To join the flock of other aging males who had been forced to yield to younger blood. Tolerated and even cared for as long as they recognized the victor's right.

But Avro was too new to this body and its way of life. Too entranced by the novelty of emotion and conditioned by the subtle knowledge that, for him, death in this body would not mean extinction. So he fought until the blood ran from a dozen wounds and his wings were in tatters. Fighting on until he began to fall, to continue to fall despite his struggles, wheeling in circles to the rocks below, the wheeling becoming a tumble, a drop, a sickening plunge to the jagged teeth waiting to smash out his life.

An impact which was the hammer-blow of extinction, filling his eyes with a flash of vivid light.

One which lingered as he jerked upright on his bed to sit, fighting for air, hands clasped over his eyes.

"Master!" Byrne calling from beyond the door attracted by his screaming. Concerned by it also; it was becoming too frequent. "Master?"

"All is well." Avro lowered his hands. "Enter."

He stood upright as the acolyte came into the room his face masked, hands steady. The chamber was as it had been when he'd retired for the sleep which should have refreshed him but had not. And the pressure at the back of his skull seemed to have grown worse.

To the aide he said, "You have something to report?"

"Nothing positive, Master."

"Have the electroencephalograph scans arrived from the ship?"

"They are on your desk, Master."

"That will be all."

"Yes, Master."

Avro stared after the aide as Byrne bowed and made his way through the door. Insubordination was out of the question: an aide was trained to obey, but obedience could be tinged with more than a desire to please. Had his use of the title been all it seemed? Normally to address a cyber as "Master" was a recognition of superiority and an admission of dependency but overuse could make its own point. One of accusation or even of contempt. Had Byrne, by what could be regarded as zealous courtesy, shown his disquiet?

He was a spy, of course, as Tupou was a spy, as all

acolytes were spies. Eyes and ears to see and listen and a mouth to report. Had he told Ishaq of the screaming? Had the cyber reported the incidents to Central Intelligence? Had he received secret orders in turn to watch and assess and, if necessary, to restrain his nominal superior?

Avro lifted his hands and pressed them against the back of his skull. Why had Marle ordered Ishaq to join him? Why had rapport altered so strangely? Why did he so constantly dream of his life as an angel?

What was happening to him?

Part of the answer was in the electroencephalograph scans sent from the ship.

Seated at the desk Avro studied them, checking one against the other with quick efficiency. The variations were minor but unmistakable and when combined with other records from other examinations left no doubt. Even so he double-checked before leaning back to stare at the tinted panes of the window.

They were diamond-shaped, made of various hues, the sunlight streaming through them forming a tessellation of mauve, orange, red, blue, amber, emerald which flowed over the floor, the desk, the scattered papers on the surface. A transient beauty which Avro ignored as he stared at the window, the sun, the endless expanse of the dried sea bed beneath it. On it men and machines crawled in a constant search for nodules of manganese and other valuable minerals. The only source of wealth on the world and one controlled by a combine who had reason to be generous to the Cyclan.

Janda, a world as hostile as Velor, was set in the mathematical center of a sphere in which Dumarest would be found if he was still alive.

Closing his eyes Avro saw it again; the open grave, the metallic sheen which broke into rippling motion, the fretted bone revealed as the insects scuttled from their feeding place. Dumarest or some other? How to be sure?

Yet on the answer depended his life.

Avro glanced at the scans, again conscious of the pressure within his skull. One not born of imagination but of harsh reality. The Homochon elements grafted within his brain showed unmistakable signs of change. Normally quiescent until stimulated by the Samatachazi formulae they lay incorporated in the cranial tissue; a sub-species of reactive life akin to a beneficent growth which enhanced telephathic contact and made rapport possible. Now, those within his brain were growing.

Swelling like a bomb which would rip his skull wide open.

He would be dead long before that could happen and insane long before he was dead. His only hope was to have his brain removed from its bony casing and placed in a vat forming part of Central Intelligence. There the Homochon elements could grow as they normally did once the transfer had been made and his intelligence would not be affected. But, to gain the final reward, he must redeem his past failure and capture Dumarest.

Find him, capture him and deliver him to Marle. And do it before it was too late.

Angado said, "Home, Earl. Lychen where I was born. Now I'm back I wondered why I ever left."

He wore soft fabrics touched with vibrant color; reds overlaid with green trimmed with gold piping. A costume which once had suited the lanquid dilettante he had been but which now no longer belonged to the lean body and hard face. Something he spotted in the reflection carried by the window before which he stood and he turned, smiling, arms lifted in a gesture of greeting.

"Cousin! How wonderful to see you! In truth there were times when I thought we should never meet again. I was desolate as I am sure you would have been at the concept. Have you wine? A comfit? Something to ease the endless burden of this tiresome round?" His arms fell, his tone hardening as he looked at Dumarest. "Well?"

"Is that how you used to talk?"

"To Perotto and his cronies? At times, yes. It amused me to see their contempt."

"Is that all?"

"No," admitted Angado. "The spoiled sons of rich families tend to act the fool until it is no longer acting. To go into raptures over a trifle, to swear vengeance on a slight, to vow undying feality to a friend—" He shook his head in disgust. "How little they know of real values. You've taught me a lot, Earl."

Dumarest said, dryly, "I hope enough for you to stay alive."

"I'll be careful." Angado spun in an elaborate pirouette. "A fool left Lychen and a fool has returned. One concerned about his finances and for no other reason. He'll be apologetic, gracious, swearing it's all a mistake and promising retribution—but I'll remember Yuanka."

"And remember a man can smile and murder as he smiles."

"I shan't forget." Angado hesitated then said, "There's a lot I shan't forget, Earl. I—"

"You don't owe me."

"I can't agree. If it hadn't been for you I'd be stuck on Yuanka."

"If it hadn't been for you I'd be dead." Dumarest rose from the deep chair in which he'd been sitting. "We each helped the other. The slate's clean."

"But your money!"

"What good is money to a dead man?"

Dumarest moved from the chair and crossed the room to stand as Angado had done before the window. It gave on a wild and rugged scene; bleak rocks, cracks, slimed stone the whole dominated by the sheet of water which dropped from above so close it seemed it could be touched. A waterfall of stupendous proportions falling to the floor of the chasm far below. Mist filled the crevice, hiding the upthrust teeth of stone with shifting rainbows, clouds of drifting spume. The roar of the impact was the deep, prolonged note of an organ.

One muted by the treble glazing, absorbent padding, the very shape of the rocks molded with cunning skill to reflect and minimize the noise.

"My grandfather built this, Earl." Angado had come to stand at Dumarest's side, his voice quiet, brooding. "I think he wanted to leave his mark and chose to build a challenge against nature itself. Beauty turned on beauty to enhance the total effect. At times, standing on the balcony, I've felt what he must have done. The utter insignificance of a man when compared to the universe. How futile all our striving seems. We're like rats fighting to garner corn we'll never be able to eat. Denying others for the sake of greed and, in the end, what does it all amount to?"

Dumarest said, "How many know that I'm here?"

"Does it matter?"

"How many?"

"A few. Servants, of course, and some others. Those of
the ship would have talked and to deny your existence would
have been stupid. You're a friend. Someone I met while
traveling." Angado's eyes were direct. "In my circles it is
considered impolite to be too curious about such associations.
You'll be safe here, Earl."

"Why do you say that?"

"You talked. Back on Yuanka when you'd been sedated
prior to treatment you said enough for me to know you were
looking for something and something was looking for you.
My guess is you're afraid of the Cyclan." Angado paused
then, when Dumarest made no comment, added, "It's your
business, Earl, but as I said you're safe here. Just eat and
sleep and laze around and leave the worrying to me."

"Thanks."

"Forget it. We're friends, aren't we?" Angado frowned as
he noticed the time. "It's getting late and I don't want to
offend my hostess. Wynne is a wonderful person but can be
too punctilious at times. I'd like to take you with me, Earl,
but it's better left for another time. I can learn more from her
if we're alone."

"She might think the same."

"She might," Angado agreed. "But I'm no longer the man
she used to know."

He left with a lift of his arm, smiling, his step light as if
already he was fitting into his part. One which might delude
those who had known him if they didn't look too close.
Alone Dumarest roamed the apartment. It was large, a collection of rooms adorned with various works of art; carved
blocks of crystal, vases shaped in erotic patterns, tapestries
depicting scenes of bizarre fantasy. Decoration reflecting the
imagination of the man who had built a cave in the side of a
cliff simply to stare at a moving sheet of water.

Seen from the balcony it was awesome.

Dumarest felt the wind of its passing, the moisture from it
which dewed his face, heard the deep, sonorous note from its
impact against the rocks far below. A hypnotic sound as the
water itself held a dangerous attraction. The fall seemed
static; a curtain made of shimmering crystal, adorned with

transient gleams of reflected light. Beauty which masked the power of it, the crushing, destroying force born of relentless gravitation.

Leaning against the rail Dumarest looked below. A master-mason had cut away the rock to leave the balcony suspended over the chasm and he stared at the roiling mist rising from the depths. At night the mist was illuminated with colored glows but was now a mass of white and gray, twisting, turning, rising like innumerable fountains. Hands which reached and arms which invited and he felt the attraction of it, the urge to throw himself over the rail into its embrace.

An impulse he resisted, stepping back to lean his shoulders against the wall as he looked upward at the summit of the fall. No rock had been allowed to remain to break the smooth outward curve, one enhanced by skilled adaptation, and Dumarest appreciated the artistry behind the concept. Here was nature as it should be, complete, perfect, a living example of a poem or a piece of music. Art in its purest form with all irritations carefully erased. An ideal—nature was not and could never be like that. As no life could be all harmony. As no death could be a gentle release.

Dumarest had met death too often; the small death when he had ridden Low, lying doped, frozen and ninety percent dead in caskets designed for the transportation of beasts. Risking the fifteen percent death rate for the sake of cheap travel. Another kind of death, more traumatic, when the host-bodies he had occupied when using the affinity-twin had ceased to exist. Real, physical death softened only by the knowledge that it was only the body which was dying and not himself. Yet the pain had been real, the fear, the helpless terror of an organism that struggled to survive.

And he had met death beneath Abo's knife.

A death as real as any he would ever know for the agony had been present, the bleak realization of final extinction, the oblivion into which he had fallen. A darkness which had encompassed the universe and no death, no matter how exotic, could do more. Only the prelude could be extended but when death came, it came, and for him it had come on a small world in a dirty ring circled by avid, hungry faces eager for the spectacle he provided.

But did the dead ever dream?

Looking at the waterfall Dumarest remembered the dream he had had, or had it been a vision? A sea as wide and vast as any ocean could ever be. A sun which had drawn vapor from it, to condense into droplets, to fall as scattered rain on hills and plains and mountains. To be lifted again, to fall, to end in rivers which returned to the sea. A cycle repeated endlessly for all time.

Did the ocean care what happened to its substance? Did the drop of rain know from where it had come and to where it must go?

Was conscious life nothing but a temporary awareness of individuality?

A shadow touched Dumarest and he felt a sudden chill, one vanishing as the cloud which had covered the sun moved on beneath the pressure of wind. An incident which broke his introspection and he straightened with a sudden resolve. There had been too much thought of dying—now he needed to find life.

And it was time to look for the person on Lychen he most wanted to find.

An elevator rose from the apartment to the upper surface, one circled by spiral stairs which he used for the sake of exercise. A long climb which sapped at his weakened reserves and Dumarest sat on a bench as he surveyed the area. To one side sprawled a hotel holiday complex; something of recent construction that, he guessed, would never have been allowed by Angado's grandfather. Lawns surrounded it dotted with flower beds set in a riot of vivid colors. A long observation walk reached out over the head of the falls invisible from below. The body of massive timbers supported a mesh of lighter beams forming a protective barrier. Flags surmounting the structure streamed in the wind.

A breeze which carried a fluttering scrap of paper to rest against his boot.

"Please, sir, may I have my drawing?"

She was about eleven, tall, well-made, with strong white teeth showing between generous lips. A girl now solemn though the hazel eyes held the hint of laughter, her round face stamped with determination. She wore a long striped dress bound with a wide sash at the waist, the ends falling on her left side to a point below the knee. In her left hand she held a sketching pad and a sheaf of pens.

"My drawing, please."

"May I look at it?" Dumarest stooped to grasp it, holding it until she nodded. "Did you do this all by yourself?"

"Yes."

It was an animal, brightly colored as no real beast could ever be; the body red, the snout green, the tail blue to match the paws. A creature of fantasy yet in true proportion, the colors blending to form a pleasing whole.

"That's Ven," she said. "He's a sort of mole but I like Ert better, he's a bear."

Dumarest looked at the pad she held out for his inspection. Again the creature was colored in bright hues and was standing upright like a man. Another creature of fantasy and, like the first, it bore the stamp of a real talent.

"May I?" Taking the pad he turned the sheets, pausing as he saw a round, pitted, silver disc. One in close proximity to a circle bearing a cross, A drawing which could have depicted a moon—and the crossed circle was a symbol of Earth. "Did you think of this all by yourself?"

"Of course. I intend to be an artist when I grow up and an artist must be able to compose a picture."

"I'm sorry." Dumarest forced himself to be casual. "I meant did you see these designs anywhere? In an old book, perhaps? A painting?" Hope died as she shook her head. "Are you sure?"

"We haven't any old books. Mummy says they smell. Grandfather has some but he keeps them locked away." She held out her hand. "May I have my pad now, please."

"Of course." Dumarest closed it and looked at the cover. "No name?"

"Of course I have a name. Everyone has a name. I am Claire Jane Harbottle. My pad, please." Taking it she said, "You don't look well. You should walk around and get the air. My nanny says it is very healthy on the platform. Goodbye, now."

She ran off with a rustle of fabric, a girl oddly demure in formal garments, yet full of life and vitality. She would make her mark if her talent was allowed to flower and, if nothing else, she had given him good advice.

Dumarest rose and wandered between the flower beds as he followed a sweeping path which would bring him back to the observation platform. The wind stung his eyes, gusting, the flags streaming to fall and hang in limp abandon, to flutter again in varied hues, to droop and hang again. An odd pattern for such a place and Dumarest wondered at the vagery. A thought swallowed by another of far greater importance.

Had the girl merely dreamed up the notion of a pitted sphere and a circle barred by a cross or had she actually seen them somewhere? A decoration of a nursery wall, a painting, an illustration in a book—something seen and forgotten to rise to the forefront of her mind when triggered by the need of artistic expression. If so her grandfather could be of help—but would Lychen hold two people who could solve his problem? Did both know how to find Earth?

A stone turned beneath his foot and he stumbled, catching his balance, annoyed at his lack of attention. He had wandered among a collection of statues, tall figures simply clad and wearing haughty and disdainful expressions. Some had been adorned with flowers, others with cruder additions many displaying a ribald sense of humor. They fell behind as Dumarest lengthened his stride and headed toward the platform. If the girl was still around he wanted to learn more from her. Or from the person she would be with.

He heard the scream as he reached the foot of the ramp, a high shriek followed by words.

"Claire! Come back, Claire! For God's sake, child, come back!"

Wind had caught a picture, wafting it to catch against an upper timber and with grim determination she was going after it. Dumarest saw the small shape climbing doggedly up the framework, to grab at the paper, to miss as it blew to a farther point. To grab again as the flags stirred and wind blasted in a sudden gust.

One which thrust at the exposed shape, catching the striped dress, billowing it, using it as a sail to push the small figure off its perch.

To send it toppling from the framework into the air, the sweep of the waterfall, the long drop to the rocks below.

Dumarest moved as the woman screamed again, this time in horror, not warning. He stooped, hand lifting weighted

284

with his knife, eyes judging time and distance, the movement of the sash over the timbers. His arm swept in a wide circle, steel glittering as it left his hand, thudding broadwise through the sash and into the wood beneath. A spike which held her suspended, twisting in the wind which caught her hair, her dress, the sash around her waist. Before it could slip free Dumarest had the girl cradled in his arms.

Chapter Twelve

Edelman Pryor was seventy years old and looked it. He wore
drab garments and walked with a shuffle but still had a sharp
mind and intelligence. His home matched the man, old,
decaying, full of dust and forgotten corners yet retaining a
staid dignity—demonstrated by the decanter, the wine, the
courtesy with which it was served.

"Your health!" He lifted his glass to Dumarest. "And my
thanks for what you did. If I had money you could take it all.
The girl is precious to me." He sipped and added, "We are
not related in blood, you understand, but she is kind enough
to call me her grandfather. When young she used to stay here
with her mother."

"Her father?"

"At the time was busy on other worlds. Now he is home
where he belongs. Why didn't you want him to know what
happened?"

"Would it help if he did?"

"No. He would give you his thanks and anything you might
ask but—"

"It would be a memory he can do without." Dumarest
tasted his wine not surprised to find it thin and acid. "The
governess will say nothing for her own protection and the girl
is wise beyond her years. Even her mother needn't be told."

"The dress?"

"Only the sash was damaged. An accident." Dumarest
shrugged. "To the young such things happen all the time."

But the incident had been of value, giving him an introduction to the old man, one arranged by the governess who had
been too relieved to argue. Now, sitting in the dim chamber,

sipping the weak and acid wine, Dumarest waited for the courtesies to end.

"You're a friend of young Angado," said Pryor. "I heard of his return. I hope for his sake he has learned caution during his travels. Are you close?"

"We traveled together."

"And are staying with him?" Pryor sipped his wine as Dumarest nodded. "Well, he could do worse. And your own reason for coming to Lychen?" He blinked when he heard it. "An interest in antiquities? Books, maps, old logs? What appeal could such things have for a man like you?"

"The same as they have for yourself." Dumarest set down his glass. "I learned something today and saw items of interest. A drawing of a moon and a symbol I recognized. Things which could have been seen here in your house. Perhaps in the books you keep locked away."

"From a curious little child who was into everything she saw." Pryor chuckled and finished his wine. "There's no mystery about it. I collected the books for a client and the things you mention could be found within them. One at least held symbols and pictures and charts of some kind. I must confess they held little appeal but they did represent a profit. As did the maps and logs and other items I bought for later resale. As a dealer, you understand, specializing in the abstruse and rare. In fact one of my acquisitions is to be seen in the museum; a plaque inscribed with what must be a hymn of praise to an ancient god. One called Apollo. You have heard the name?"

"No."

"A pity." Pryor was disappointed. "I loaned it to the museum for the duration of my life but I expect it'll stay there for as long as they want it. Or until someone is willing to pay the demanded price. But if you are really interested in ancient things then I may have something which could interest you." Rising, he went to a corner and rummaged in a cabinet, returning with an object in his hand. "Here."

It was squat, grotesque, a female figure with swollen belly and huge, sagging breasts. The face was blurred, the nose a rounded knob, the eyes deep-set pits of blankness. Three inches high the depiction was wholly engrossed with female sexual attributes.

"I've had it for most of my life," said Pryor. "It's very old and must have been an object of veneration at one time. Some say it is a fertility symbol but I'm certain it must be more than that. The representation is that of the mother-figure and so could have associations with the very source of human life. If so it is an ideal depicted in stone. Primitive, crude, but unmistakable."

And to him of high value—why else should he have kept it so long? Dumarest studied the figurine, sensing the raw power of it. A woman. A mother. A female born to breed. Naked, unashamed of the attributes which made her what she was. The epitome of every male consumed with the desire to gain the only immortality he could ever know—the children which would carry his genes.

"Erce," whispered Pyror. "Once a man told me she was called Erce."

Mother Earth, a name Dumarest had heard before. One appropriate to the figure; turned, it would be Earth Mother.

Earth Mother?

"The man who told me that told me more," Pryor reached for his glass, found it empty, refilled it with a hand which created small chimes from the impact of the decanter with the rim. A quiver which sent ripples over the surface of the wine. "It's nonsense, of course, as anyone can see, but an interesting concept in its way. You may have heard of it. Some profess to believe that all life originated on one planet. All the divergent races on one small world. Logic is against it. The numbers are of no importance, natural increase would account for that, but how to account for the diversity of color? How, under one sun, could people be white, black, brown, yellow and all the shades between? They would be affected by the same climatic conditions, the same radiation, water, air, food. How to account for the different germ plasm?" He drank and wiped droplets from his lips. "As I said it's just an interesting concept. The image itself yields a certain tactile pleasure which you may enjoy. The story, of course, is nothing. An exercise in logic, you might say. No intelligent man would give it a moment's credence."

And only a fool would have mentioned something he took such pains to deny.

Pryor was old but no fool and the figure meant more to him

than he admitted despite his protestations. A gift for a service rendered, the most he could offer, and yet one it hurt to lose. The talk had been a cover for his emotions, the code by which he lived enforcing the gift as a matter of honor. As it would regard rejection as an insult. Dumarest must accept it or make an enemy and, on Lychen, he had only one friend.

Quietly he said, "I am honored. I have seen an object like this once before. On a far world in a commune of those who claimed a common heritage and held a belief close to that you spoke of. They call themselves the Original People." He saw the clenching of a thin hand, the sudden spatter of spilled wine. Without pause he continued, "To them the figure was sacred. They kept it in a shrine."

"So?"

"I think it a pleasant custom." The hand and the spilled wine had been enough but if Pryor knew of the Original People or subscribed to their beliefs the secrecy shrouding them would block his tongue. A thing Dumarest knew and accepted. "I receive this figure from you as a valued gift," he said. "But gifts should be shared and I return it into your keeping. To be guarded until such time as I choose to send for it. It is agreed?"

"I don't understand." Pryor frowned, cheeks flushing with a dawning anger. "Are you refusing—"

"No!" Dumarest was sharp. "That is the last thing I intend. Let me explain. The plaque in the museum is yours, agreed? They are displaying it for you. Safeguarding it. I am asking that you do the same with my figure. I have reason for the request which I am sure you will appreciate." His voice deepened, took on the echo of drums as he said, "From terror they fled to find new places on which to expiate their sins. Only when cleansed will the race of Man be again united."

The creed of the Original People and Pryor gulped, his eyes startled, veiling as he stared at Dumarest's enigmatic face.

"I see," he said. "I—yes, we understand each other. It will be an honor to do as you ask. But I feel at a loss. It is not right that you should leave this house without some token of my appreciation." Pryor gestured with a thin hand. "Look around. Choose. Anything you wish will be yours."

"This." Dumarest rose and picked up his wine. "I choose

what this glass contains." He drank and added, "The wine—
and the name of the man for whom you collected old books."

It was late when Dumarest returned to Angado's cavelike
home and the apartment was deserted aside from servants
who remained discreetly invisible. One answered his summons,
a man who stood with quiet deference, eyes widening as
Dumarest asked his question.

"A study, sir?"

"Something like that. A room with books and maps. Surely
there are maps?"

"I can't be certain, sir. There was a clearance when the old
owner died and the present master has been long absent. Also
changes have been made." A lift of his hands emphasized his
inability to be precise. "But if maps are present, sir, they
could be in the desk."

"And that is where?"

In a room barren of windows lit by lamps shielded by
decorated plates of tinted transparency. One with a soft carpet
on the floor and erotic paintings on the ceiling to match those
writhing on the walls. A library of a kind but one which
would have held a bed rather than books. Now it held neither—
just a chair, a display cabinet holding small artifacts, a desk
which dominated the room with its massively carved and
ornamented bulk. The top remained closed beneath Dumarest's
hands, the maps it may have contained beyond his reach.

A small irritation and one he ignored as he returned to the
main salon and stood before the wide window watching the
play of colored illumination streaming upward from the mist
at the foot of the waterfall. In it the curtain of water became
an artist's palette alive with vibrant hues; reds and greens,
blues, oranges, dusty browns and limpid violets, shards of
gold and streamers of silver, changing, blending, forming
transient images which dissolved as soon as recognized. A
magic reflected by the rock wall facing him across the chasm,
the stone taking on a strangely disturbing aspect as if the
stubborn material had softened and become the door to new
and alien dimensions.

From behind him a woman said, "It's beautiful, isn't it,
Earl?"

She was tall, slim, wide shoulders adding to the hint of

290

masculinity accentuated by the close-cropped silver hair which framed a broad face and deep-set eyes of vivid blue. A woman who moved with a boyish grace, no longer a girl, the maturity of near middle-age giving her a calm assurance. Her mouth, wide, the upper lip thin, curved into a smile, revealed neat and even teeth. She wore a masculine garb of pants and blouse, her femininity displayed in the fine weave, the intricate pattern of complex embroidery. Her voice was deep, resonant and Dumarest thought of the sound of fuming water.

"My lady?"

"So formal," she said. "So cautiously polite. Lhank said you were that."

"Lhank?"

"Lord Hedren Angado Nossak Karroum. When there are so many names it helps to use initials." Her laughter rose in genuine amusement. "Don't look so startled. I have a key, see?" She lifted it swinging from her fingers. "You were busy when I arrived. What did you think of the den? Lhank Five had some peculiar attributes and had a liking for the bizarre. Lhank Six was something of a prude and Lhank Seven—well, you know about him."

"And nothing about you."

"Nothing? He didn't mention me? His old and trusted friend?" Again her laughter drowned the murmur of the waterfall. "Wynne Tewson. At times I like to think that he left Lychen because of unrequited love. Now he has returned and with a new friend. A hero." Her eyes narrowed, became appraising. "There are many who will envy him."

Dumarest said, "The key you have in your hand—will it fit the desk?"

"What?" She frowned as he explained. "The desk in the den? What the hell is it doing there? Now if it was a bed maybe we could use it. Did you know that as the lights change color the paintings take on new and various forms? Speed the illumination and you get a kind of stroboscopic effect; one minute the walls are full of coupling shapes, the next a crowd of goggling voyeurs. Old Lhank certainly had imagination."

"The desk?"

"Is just that, a desk. Put in the den to get it out of the way. I can't open it but even if I could it holds nothing of value.

Why are you so interested." She blinked as he told her. "Maps? You are interested in maps?"

"Just of this area. This world. I like to know where I am."

"Yes," she said. "That I can imagine. But there are other ways to find out aside from maps. How about a personally conducted tour? I've a raft waiting and we could take a ride. Go to the Steaming Hills or look at the Pearls of Toria. If you're really interested in old maps we could even pay a visit to Chenault."

The name Pryor had given him, the same as that Shakira had mentioned back in the circus of Chen Wei. The man Dumarest needed to find—but without leaving a trail others could follow.

Casually he said, "Is that why you are here? To take me on a conducted tour?"

"No. I came to bring you a message. Lhank wants you to join him."

"Do you always do what Angado wants?"

"Angado?" She smiled with a secret amusement. "Is that what you call him? How touching. Such a sweet name."

"He chose it."

"Of course. He would. His mentor called him that when he was young. The monk—did he tell you about Brother Lyndom? He had a great influence on his charge and it would have been better for Angado to have joined the Church. That or the Cyclan, but he lacked the application for that. For either, if the truth be known, an inherent weakness of character—why else should he have run away? Would you have done it, Earl? Given up the leadership of a great House and gone roving?"

"Perhaps, if the reason were strong enough."

"Such as?"

Dumarest said, meeting her eyes, "Unrequited love?"

"No!" She was emphatic in her denial. "Never that! You'd abduct the girl, fight for her, rape her, even, but never leave her."

"I was talking about love," he said. "Not lust."

"And love is sacrifice? Is that what you mean?" She thought about it for a moment then said, "You should be right. Maybe I misjudged Angado. Certainly he seems different now, more adult, more confident. He tries to hide it but it's there."

She had noticed, had others? Dumarest said, "He wants me to join him, you said. Why and where?"

"To give him moral courage, perhaps." The small mounds of her breasts lifted beneath her blouse as she shrugged. "Or to show you off to his friends—the hero with whom he battled against incredible odds and managed to survive. Give it a week and it will be you whose life he saved. Give it another and the whole thing will be forgotten. No novelty lasts long on Lychen." Her eyes moved past him to settle on the shifting lights beyond the window. "Boredom, Earl. Why are we always so bored?"

"You know the answer to that."

"Too idle, too rich, too spoiled. The cure?"

"You know the answer to that too."

"Work. Fill every minute of every hour with unremittent effort. But what if you can't work? Or don't want to work? Or there is no work to do?"

Dumarest said, "Some people are fat. They are fat because they eat too much. It's as simple as that."

"And we're bored because we're lazy—it's as simple as that. Or is it?"

"Lazy," said Dumarest. "Or afraid. No matter what reason you choose to blame, the cure lies within yourself."

"As it does with those who are too fat." She looked down at her slender figure. "Would you like me if I were fat, Earl? Great bulges here and here and here." Her hands moved to breasts, belly and buttocks. "Masses of flesh, quivering, bouncing, sagging, grotesque. The thought is disgusting. I'll never grow fat." She sucked in her stomach the action making her even more like a man. "Let's get out of here."

"To where?"

"Didn't I tell you? To the party, of course. But first we take a ride."

The raft was a work of art, small, gilded, the controls and body shielded by a transparent canopy which could be rolled back into the sides of the vehicle. Wynne handled it with skillful ease, rising with a velocity which sent air gusting in a muted roar as the hotel complex beside the head of the waterfall fell away to become a model touched with silver light.

"Scared?" Turning she shouted above the wind. "Or do you like the taste of danger?"

"No."

"No what? You're not scared or—"

"I don't like the taste of danger and, yes, I am scared." His hands closed on her own, his strength mastering hers as he adjusted the controls. The raft slowed in its climb, steadied, began to drift toward the east. "If you're trying to prove something you've made your point."

"Which was?"

"To show me how well you can handle a raft, perhaps." His hands moved a little and she gasped as the vehicle veered and, suddenly, began to fall. As it leveled Dumarest added, "We can both handle a raft."

"And we both can be scared."

"Which makes us human."

"And honest." She looked at him, starlight touching her hair, adding a sheen to its silver smoothness so that from where he sat she seemed to be haloed in a nacreous luminescence. "Are you honest, Earl?"

"As much as you, my lady."

"My name is Wynne. I would like you to use it." As he remained silent she said, "Please."

"Wynne." He smiled as he repeated the name. "Wynne. I would guess, my lady, that the name is appropriate."

"Don't be so damned formal!"

"Am I right?"

"Yes, I guess you are." She smiled in turn, the quick anger forgotten. "I usually get what I want in the end." She looked over the edge of the raft at the waterfall to one side and far below. "Spoiled," she said. "Old Lhank must have been mad to have tried to improve on nature. It's too smooth, too pretty. Like a painted harlot skilled in deception." Her eyes moved to Dumarest as if inviting comment then, as he remained silent, she said, "To hell with it. Let's find something more amusing."

The raft lifted with a sudden savage velocity, darting forward to throw Dumarest back, wind blasting at his face and hair. In it the woman's silver crop took on a life of its own, each hair seeming to stand out with individual vibrancy. A fuzz which dominated her face, enlarging her head so that, for a moment, she seemed grotesque.

Then, as she touched a control, the transparent canopy rose to a halfway position, forming a windscreen which protected them from the blast. Above the droning, organlike note from above, her laughter rose high, brittle-edged.

"Do you like it, Earl?"

A child enamored by a toy and demanding praise. He studied her profile in the starlight, recognizing her willfulness, her need to hold attention.

"Earl?"

"A souped-up raft," he said. "I've seen them before. Helped clear away their wreckage too. Overstrain the antigrav units and they can fail. Sometimes the generator can fuse. There are better ways to commit suicide."

"Old man's advice," she sneered. "You're too young to give it and I'm too young to take it. Hold on!"

The speed increased, auxiliary burners flaring to add their thrust, turning the raft into a rocket which lanced on a tail of flame across the sky. One which ended over the loom of hills shrouded in luminous smoke.

"The Steaming Hills," she said. The canopy lowered and Dumarest caught the scent of acrid vapors. "By day they look like bones hiding in drifting mists. At sunset and dawn the mist becomes a sea of blazing hues, but at night the trapped energies are released and they are what you see now."

A place of enchantment and drifting glows. Light and shadow in which bizarre shapes took form to change and vanish and reappear in a different guise. A moving, living chiaroscuro of incredible complexity and stunning beauty.

"There is a game the courageous sometimes play," she said. "Couples take their rafts to a certain height then cut lift and make love. The trick is to finish before the raft hits the ground." Her eyes were brooding as she stared at the luminous smoke. "Sometimes I think that those who don't return are the lucky ones."

Dumarest said nothing but moved closer to the controls.

"Think of it," she breathed. "The rush, the urgency, the race against time—all sauce to add piquancy to the experience.

295

Have you ever done anything like that, Earl? Would you dare to try?

"No."

"Why not? Afraid? Or don't I appeal to you enough?" She faced him, eyes direct as they searched his own. "Would you be willing if I were other than what I am? Bloated? Broad hipped? A breeding machine for children? Or would you rather—"

"No!" he said again, his tone sharp. "Leave it at that."

"But—"

"Love isn't something to be timed. If it's worth having at all then, while it lasts, time has no meaning. And I'm too old to play childish games."

"And too young to need such stimulation." She smiled and reached for the controls. "Let me show you the Pearls of Toria."

They stretched across the plain round lakes of limpid brightness, a cluster which formed a giant necklace of pendants and ropes edged with a soft vegetation and gentle banks. The result of an ancient meteor strike which had created a host of isolated aquatic worlds.

Landing, Wynne jumped from the raft and ran to the edge of a pool shot with streaks of varied color. Stripping, she stood naked, slim, lithe, a column of nacreous whiteness, then dived into the pool to leave a widening circle of ripples.

Before they reached the shore Dumarest had joined her.

The water was cool, refreshing, the luminous trails made by darting fish disturbing drifting organisms. Tiny motes which blazed with light to the impact of larger bodies. Like an eel the woman twisted, swam, glided through the water to touch him, to dart away, to return with extended hands. A game in which he joined feeling the smooth sleekness of her, the muscle beneath the skin, the hard, tautness of her body.

One which lay beside him when, exhausted, they had climbed on the bank to sprawl on the sweet scented grass.

"Earl!"

He turned to look at her, seeing the silver sheen of her hair, the direct stare of her eyes, the message they held. One repeated by her body as she moved, small breasts signaling her femininity, narrow hips and waist belying it, the slender

296

column of her thighs parting to leave no doubt as to her sex and her need.

"Earl! Earl, for God's sake!"

Then she was on him, straddling him, engulfing him, lips seeking his, closing on them, teeth nibbling as her nails raked his flesh. Moving with a fevered determination to drain him and, her own need satisfied, to slump against him.

"A man," she murmured. "My God, but you're a man!"

She caressed him until again time ceased to have meaning and she lay against him warm and sleek, the silver crop of her hair against his shoulder, the nails of her fingers scratching like kitten claws over his torso.

"Happy, Earl?"

"You've made me so."

"That's nice." She snuggled closer to him then, turning over, looked at the stars. "I hate them, Earl. All those bright points. Those suns with all those worlds. Every time I look at them I'm reminded of the fact I'm a failure. Scared to move away from the familiar into the strange. Living a more and more constricted life. . . . At least Angado had guts. He took a chance and—" She turned her head to look at Dumarest. "No," she said. "He didn't take much of a chance. Paid to stay away—for him it was just a holiday. But he came back and he brought you with him. For that I thank him if for nothing else."

"I thank him too."

"For me?"

"Yes, Wynne." Dumarest made the name sound like music. "For you."

"Darling!"

In the pool a fish jumped in mating frenzy, the trail of its passage a golden streak of flame.

Chapter Thirteen

The party was dying and Angado was bored. A condition he shared with others but while their ennui was a cultivated pose or the genuine result of too few things done too often his was the product of comparison. Spall prating about the hardships of poverty—after experiencing Lowtown his complaints were both trivial and ridiculous. Plaskit and his talk of personal combat—a man who would never dare risk his skin against an armed opponent. Or even an unarmed one; his talk was based on long-distance viewing and the safe slaughter of helpless game. Crixus who spoiled the air with words appertaining to the idealistic existence to be found when living close to nature in the wild. Deakin Epstein, Spencer—all fools unconscious of their folly; posturing, gesticulating, making sly allusions, asking pointed questions.

The women were as bad, each in their own way acting a part, jealous, spiteful, vicious even as they made overt invitations. Angado remembered Dumarest's advice about those who could smile and murder as they smiled. The majority, no, they lacked the elemental courage. Some, perhaps, driven by whim or the pursuit of novelty. Only a few fitted the bill and of them all Perotto was the most ruthless.

"See how our young friend fits so easily back into his niche, Juan? Almost it seems as if he has never left us."

At his side Juan Larsen, sycophant, aide, a living echo of his master, nodded and smiled with thin lips. His tone was as acid as his words.

"Men are like the birds, Luigi. Some find the strength to leave the nest of their own volition. Others have to be helped. Some need to come crawling back to the only haven they can find. A pity. The Seventh Lord of the Karroum would, I thought, have had more pride."

Angado shrugged, remembering the part he was playing, the pose he needed to maintain.

"Pride and hunger make poor bedfellows, Juan. Blame my return on the accountant who forgot to continue my agreed allowance."

"He will have cause to regret it for years to come." Perotto turned to his friend. "You were a little hard, Juan. Angado has not had an easy time. In fact he was lucky to survive at all. A fascinating story, you must hear it soon, but one now we can put behind us. In any case it would be enhanced by the presence of his friend. One who still has not arrived, I see."

"Earl will be here soon. I sent Wynne to bring him."

"Wynne?" Perotto raised his eyebrows. "Wynne—ah, I see. A fine woman and she would have made you a good consort. A good wife too, once she had proven her ability to continue the Karroum line. Maybe that was your trouble, Angado. A man should not live alone. A woman at your side would have eased both body and mind."

"Or driven him insane." Larsen was blunt. "Not all men share your taste, Luigi."

"True, but who is to condemn? One likes cake another bread and who is to say which is right? But the head of a House has obligations and—well, never mind that now. Wynne, you say?"

"Yes, Wynne Tewson." As always Perotto made him feel small, inferior, and Angado fought to maintain his calmness. A battle partly lost as he snapped, "You know damned well who she is."

"Who and what," said Perotto. "It is obvious why your friend is so late in joining us. You made a bad choice of messenger, Angado. You should have sent another to pick up your friend. By now they are probably over the Steaming Hills or sporting in the Pearls of Toria. Not that it matters. We must be tolerant of such things. To be otherwise is to act the barbarian." Smiling he added, "And to be jealous is to act the fool. Don't give your friends the pleasure of seeing your discomfiture."

"You are mistaken."

"Of course. I often am." Perotto turned and signaled to a servant bearing a tray laden with goblets. The wine was smooth, subtle in its hidden potency, but Angado gulped it as if it had been water. Watching him Perotto said, "I think it time for our surprise, Juan. Will you fetch the box?"

As Larsen turned and walked away Angado said, "Box?"

"Merely a container for something rare and rather strange. The product of a new confectioner who has set up business on Schenker. A trader brought me a sample and you may find his wares amusing." Perotto took the box Larsen had fetched. "That will be all, Juan."

Angado reached for more wine as Perotto lifted the container. One made of finely carved wood inset with a tracery of metal and stone, gold and silver merging with emerald, ruby, amethyst, sapphire, amber, the clear sparkle of diamond, the somber hue of opal. The lid opened beneath his touch to reveal a compartmented tray filled with small mounds of rich darkness decorated with a dusting of minute pellets of a thousand hues.

"Chocolate." Angado was disappointed. The wine had made his head spin a little; boredom had sent him to the anodyne of alcohol too often during the evening. Now he looked at his cousin. "Ordinary chocolates."

"Far from that, Angado. Once tasted they can never be forgotten. For a discerning palate the effect is incredible. Here!" Perotto touched a chocolate with the tip of a finger. "Try this one."

"Aren't they all the same?"

"Far from it. Each contains within itself an entire new world of titillation. In fact I can't resist their promise." Perotto lifted the chocolate he had urged Angado to take, placed it within his mouth, closed his lips and sighed with audible satisfaction. "Magnificent!"

He had eaten and it would be safe to do likewise and courtesy demanded the acceptance of the gift. Angado picked a chocolate, placed it within his mouth, bit down and was suffused with a sudden plethora of flavors. There was peach and apple and chard and a touch of grize and a hint of orange and the tang of grape and of embra and lemon and . . . and . . . and . . .

And a sharp, overwhelming thirst.

His goblet was empty but the servant was already making his way toward him. The wine accentuated rather than washed away the flavors, joining with them to tease his palate and to wake memories of the recent experience. One amost duplicated as he ate another sweet. Almost—as Perotto had said there were differences and now he tasted blood and leather and the sweat from hides and horn and more subtle exudations from a hundred living things. Tastes which aroused strange stirrings and sent his hand again to the refilled goblet, the goblet to his mouth, the wine to his stomach.

Close to him a woman laughed with a thin, vicious chittering.

"Drink deep, Lord Karroum, it will help you to bear your loss. But don't worry, your friend will return."

"Unless Wynne kills him."

"A good sleep and he'll be as good as new and think of the fun you'll have scolding him."

More laughter and more wine to drown the sound and another chocolate and still more wine. And more laughter and too many grinning faces and walls that moved and air that stank.

And a floor that rose to hit him in the face to the sound of ribald cheers.

Dumarest heard the noise as the raft settled to land, the yelling incorporating a name which sent him jumping over the side and into the rooom before Wynne had time to kill the engine. Angado lay where he had fallen, face down on the carpet, a ring of shouting partygoers laughing and deriding his condition. They scattered as Dumarest burst through them to stoop over the fallen man.

"Don't worry about him, Earl." A tall, young, languid man smiled as he reached out to touch Dumarest's arm. "I may call you that? It's much better to be on friendly terms, don't you think? I'm Yip Zaremba—you can call me Yip. Or anything you like as long as it's nice. But don't worry about your friend. He's just drunk too much. Once he's sober he'll be all over you unless—"

He staggered back, blood dripping from his lips as Dumarest lashed the back of his hand against the simpering mouth. To Wynne who had joined him he snapped, "Get some water. Salt too. Hurry!"

301

"Earl—"

"Do it!"

Angado sagged in his arms as Dumarest lifted him, bending him over a table which he swept clear with a brush of his arm. A woman screamed as he snatched feathers from her ornate headdress then fell silent, watching as Dumarest forced open Angado's mouth with the fingers of his left hand, standing behind and beside him as he was thrust the bunch of feathers down the exposed throat.

"Earl?" Wynne had returned with a jug of water and a container of salt. "Shall I mix them?"

He nodded, busy with the feathers, feeling the limp body in his arms begin to jerk and heave. A moment then vomit sprayed from Angado's mouth to spatter the table with regurgitated wine, food, blobs of nameless substance.

"Now!"

Wynne poured as Dumarest kept open the mouth, wiping it clean with his hand before bending Angado over again, using the feathers as before, again causing the limp man to empty his stomach in a liquid gout.

"More."

"Earl, is it—"

"More!"

Angado struggled as the water entered his mouth, pushing at Dumarest with weak hands, barely aware but conscious of his discomfort. As Wynne emptied the jug Perotto came through the crowd to watch as Dumarest clamped his arms around the young man, jerking to constrict the stomach, again flooding the table with a now almost clear fluid.

"What's going on here? What are you doing? If the man is ill a doctor should be summoned. This conduct is inexcusable."

"He was drunk." Zaremba thrust himself forward, caked blood on his mouth. "I went to help and this boor struck me. A matter of jealousy it seems. I—" He broke off, backing as Dumarest turned toward him. "That is, I mean, well, they seem to be friends."

"Of course!" Perotto beamed, extending his hands in a gesture of welcome. "You must be Earl. I should have recognized you from Angado's description. Still taking care of him, I see."

"Someone has to."

302

"And you are best suited for the task. We must talk, you and I. Later perhaps? Before you leave?"

Dumarest nodded and led Angado to the windows, the cool air outside. A fountain cast a crystal shower into the air, droplets illuminated with subtle glows, mist that flowed as if made of silk. Light that showed the area deserted, sound that masked his voice.

"All right, what happened?" Dumarest frowned as he listened. "Chocolates?"

"They were harmless. Perotto ate one before my very eyes."

"One?"

"Yes, just the one." Angado frowned, thinking. "It didn't seem to make him thirsty but when I ate one I had to gulp down some wine. The same with the others but the one he ate didn't affect him at all." His face took on a deeper pallor as he realized the implication. "Poison?"

"I doubt it. Just something to get you drunk but all kinds of accidents can happen to a man who can barely stand. Or perhaps he merely wanted to make you look a fool. Lord Hedren Angado Nossak Karroum the Seventh—crawling and puking on the floor. Who would respect you after that?"

"Who will now?"

Dumarest said, "You were ill. A blockage in the windpipe or a constriction of the epiglottis—there is no need to go into detail. You've had it before and I recognized the signs. How did you get on with Perotto?"

"What?" Angado blinked, then shrugged. "He put the blame on a clerk. The allowance will be resumed together with that owing and with an increase. He was most apologetic and promised it will never happen again."

"Do you believe him?" Then, as Angado hesitated, Dumarest added, "You were reported dead. Did he explain that?"

"Of course. A message from the *Thorn*. He had it all to hand, Earl. The answer to every question I might ask. Once, I would have swallowed every word but not now. I've learned to be mistrustful." Angado gave a wry smile. "It seems I've still a lot to learn."

"We all make mistakes."

"I make too many. You warned me but still I acted the fool." Angado swayed and would have fallen had not Dumarest

303

caught his arm. "Those damned chocolates," he muttered.
"Earl!"

"Drink water and bring it up." Dumarest half-lifted Angado
to the fountain. "Wash out your stomach. Quick now!" He
watched as the other obeyed. 'Better?"

"I feel awful."

"Sick?"

"Queasy and my head aches like hell. That's just what I
feel like."

And looked. Dumarest studied the pale face, the sweat
dewing cheeks and forehead, the color of the eyes. Any
poison would have been eliminated unless it was a subtle
variety which had passed immediately into the bloodstream. A
possibility but one he discounted; the death of Angado must
not be too obvious.

"Get home," he said. "Get to bed. Call medical aid.
The hotel should have a resident doctor. Can you manage on
your own?"

"If I have to. Why can't you come with me?"

"I've an appointment to keep," said Dumarest. "With
Perotto."

He sat in a room which echoed his dignity; a chamber rich
in leather, wood, intricate carving and expensive fabrics. The
chair behind the wide desk was like a throne and he occupied
it as if he were a king. One who lifted a hand in regal
greeting as Dumarest stepped toward him.

"Earl, be seated." Light blazed from the gemmed ring he
wore as he gestured toward a chair. "My apologies for
having kept you waiting but some affairs cannot wait. The
penalty of duty, you understand. To be the head of the House
of Karroum demands the sacrifice of all personal inclinations."

"A sacrifice you are willing to make," said Dumarest,
adding, as he saw the other frown, "as Angado was not."

"He was too young. He is still too young and I am not
talking of chronological years. His mind is unable to accept
the concept of total dedication. The need to sublimate all
private needs and desires for the sake of the greater good.
Words." Perotto gestured, the light again blazing from his
ring, one Dumarest studied as the hand was lowered. "How
little they mean. Dedication, devotion, duty—labels, some

would say, for outmoded concepts, yet without them what of the House of Karroum?"

"Ruin," said Dumarest. "Devastation."

"For the House and all connected with it. Entire families made destitute because of a youthful whim or brash inexperience. I do not intend that to happen."

"There are ways to prevent it."

"Many ways," agreed Perotto. "What is Angado to you?"

"A friend."

"And?"

Dumarest said flatly, "I'm broke. Stranded here on Lychen and totally dependent on Angado's charity. If he should turn against me or fall sick or die I'd be sleeping in the fields and living on dirt. That's why I acted as I did out there; my concern was to keep him alive. Once I get a stake he can sweat in his own juice: I wasn't born to be a servant."

"The price of friendship," murmured Perotto. "The price of two High passages? Three?"

"To do what?"

"To persuade Angado to leave this world and never to return. I've made him an offer—you can see that he accepts it."

"Three High passages." Dumarest looked at the room, the rich furnishings, the items of price. "A low price for what you have here. Five would still be low but a little more attractive. Paid in advance?"

"In your hand when you board. Of course there could be more if your powers of persuasion are too strong to resist. Fifty times as much if you can convince me Angado will never return to Lychen."

"Fifty?" Dumarest pursed his lips in a soundless whistle. "My Lord, you are generous."

"But hard to convince."

"You shall have positive proof. My word on it." Dumarest rose from his chair. "Now I must see how my friend is faring. A sick man needs a break from routine and there are other worlds aside from those in the Burdinnion. Interesting worlds, some a little dangerous, perhaps, but what is life without risk?"

Perotto said, "How will you travel?"

"To the waterfall? Wynne will take me."

"She has already taken Angado. I'll arrange for a raft." Perotto reached for an intercom then withdrew his hand as he changed his mind. "No. I'll take you myself. Work has made me stuffy and it'll be a chance to clear my head."

Outside dawn had broken, the day brightening as the raft moved east. Perotto sat beside Dumarest, the driver a hunched and silent figure at the controls. The air was clear, deserted aside from minute flecks wheeling over the top of the waterfall: birds scavenging the hotel complex, many settling to perch on the rails of the observation platform. Close to the entrance to Angado's home Wynne's raft lay empty on the grass.

She met them as the elevator sighed to a halt, turning to lead the way into the main salon. The door to the balcony was open, cool air wafting into the chamber together with the deep organ-note from the chasm, until it died to a muted drone as she closed the portal.

"Angado sat out there for a while," she explained. "I tried to get him to eat but he wasn't hungry so I made him take a shower and go to bed. The last time I looked in on him he seemed to be asleep."

"How is he?" Perotto sounded genuinely concerned.

"As well as can be expected."

"I've been thinking of what must have happened. Some fools at the party must have slipped drugs into his wine. A combination which caused a syndromic shock. Maybe it was triggered by the confections he ate. A special blend of exotic flavors that I thought would amuse him." Perotto shook his head in self-reproach. "I should have remembered his delicate stomach. Even as a child he had to be careful of what he ate. I blame myself for what happened."

"It wasn't your fault." Wynne glanced at Dumarest. "Do you want to see him?"

"Not if he's sleeping."

"He might be awake. I'll check." She left the room to return, shaking her head. "Still asleep and I guess it's best to leave him that way. One thing, Earl, I managed to find the key to that desk. You know? The one in the den. It's open now if you want to check what's inside."

Perotto frowned. "Desk?"

"Earl wanted to examine some old maps. The kind of thing Chenault is so fond of." Smiling she added, looking at

Dumarest, "I never did get to take you to him—well, we didn't have the time. Tomorrow, perhaps. If you find anything interesting he'll be able to explain it to you."

"The den," said Dumarest. "You know, I've forgotten where it is."

"Just down the hall and—" Wynne broke off, shaking her head. "How could you have forgotten so soon?"

"Maybe I've had other things on my mind." His eyes held hers, their message plain. "Come with me. You can show me that trick with the lights you mentioned. Perhaps I could learn something."

"I doubt it." Her smile was inviting. "Come on, then. I won't be long, Luigi, when I come back I'll make some tisane. You like tisane, Earl?"

"I'd like anything you make."

He followed her from the salon, a man eager to get her alone, to recapture the experience of the night, its joy and pleasure. Coming close to her as she paused before a door ending a passage, his left hand rising to rest against her back, his head lowering to touch her cheek with his lips.

As she relaxed he jerked open the door with his right hand, pushed with his left, slamming the door after her as she staggered through the opening. A second and he heard the thud of her falling body.

"Wynne?" Perotto called out as Dumarest neared the salon. "Wynne, is everything all right?"

He was standing beside the wide window facing the waterfall. He was not alone.

Chapter Fourteen

As a man Avro had never known physical pleasure. The operation performed on him when young had seen to that; one deft stroke of the scalpel had turned him into a living, thinking, unfeeling machine. But now he rode the crest of a giddy intoxication born of mental achievement.

Dumarest caught, trapped, safe in his hand.

The man the Cyclan had hunted for so long and who had escaped so often, leaving dead cybers to mark his success, now the living proof of his own efficiency. The key to his own survival; soon now he would be safe in his vat joined in a gestalt of his own kind.

A moment he relished, extending it as he saw Dumarest catch the scarlet of his robe, spinning, halting the movement of his hand toward the knife in his boot, lifting it instead to his chin. A casual gesture of outward calm to mask the tension within and a warning of the true nature of the man. One who had assessed the situation in a flash, recognizing the futility of violence, gaining time by talking while apparently relaxed.

"Cyber Avro. This is a surprise. I never thought to see you again."

"Did you think the Cyclan so foolish as to believe the report of your death?"

"It was worth the chance."

"Negated once you used your credited funds."

"Of course." Dumarest touched his left forearm with the fingers of his right hand. Watching as eyes followed the gesture, dropping the hand slowly to his side. "You learned I was on Yuanka and traced me from there. And found an ally,

I see. A willing accomplice. What is his price? The death of his cousin?''

Perotto said, "Where is Wynne?"

"Enjoying the sleep she meant for me. Your idea or hers? Or did you set the trap?'' Dumarest looked at the cyber. "My guess is that you were the guiding mind."

"You knew." Perotto gnawed at the subject like a dog with a bone. "About the gas. But how?"

Small items adding to form an uneasy whole, the sum triggering the instinctive reaction of a man determined to survive. A shallow answer and Avro knew there had to be more; the trait he was certain Dumarest possessed and which gave him the thing known as luck.

Dumarest said, "She was too friendly on too short an acquaintance and too eager to show me the sights. Time gained for you to feed Angado that filth. Not just something to make him puking drunk; such sights must be common in this society. Nor to show his friends what a weakling he is; they already knew that. You wanted to arouse their disgust and win their sympathy. Left alone he would have vomited then climbed to his feet. He would have stunk and staggered and he would have had an overwhelming desire to talk. He would have babbled and revealed his innermost nature. Become maudlin, sentimental, affectionate, amorous—and we both know he has a dislike of women."

"That is no secret."

"As Zaremba demonstrated when he tried to stop me helping Angado. He knew you wanted him shamed."

"That bothers you?" Perotto sneered. "You? A common traveler? A sycophant? A criminal? A man willing to take money to kill a friend who trusts him? Do you deny that?"

"A trap to get the man wanting him dead into admitting it," said Dumarest. "You want him dead. That's why you're helping the Cyclan. That's why you used Cranmer." He looked through the window at the waterfall. "He almost got away with it."

"He was a fool."

"Just as you are. As any man is who works with the Cyclan. Do you imagine you can use them and then forget them? And what of your own danger? How can they allow you to live now you know so much? Soon you will begin to wonder why I am so important to them. What makes me so valuable." Dumarest paused then added, "Side with me and I'll tell you."

Information which could kill; had killed for the existence of the affinity-twin must not be divulged. Perotto was as good as dead and Avro could appreciate the skill Dumarest was displaying. Attempting to drive a wedge between himself and the other; dividing so as to rule.

He said, "You waste your time. Killing me will gain you nothing. The apartment is sealed and men are stationed outside. As an intelligent man you can recognize the inevitable and yield. Do not force me to use this." Avro lifted his hand and displayed the weapon he had kept hidden in his wide sleeve. One which would vent a cloud of stunning vapor at the pressure of his finger.

Perotto said, "He is armed. His knife—"

"Leave it." Avro knew of Dumarest's speed. "If he reaches for it I will fire."

To stun and render unconscious but not to kill. He was too important to the Cyclan for that, which meant Perotto would not be armed with conventional weapons; Avro could never trust his aim. An advantage Dumarest assessed as, again, he rubbed thoughtfully at his chin. The cyber was making the basic mistake of talking when he should have acted. A need to mentally gloat, perhaps, but a weakness which had yielded information as to the trap he had closed on his victim.

One from which he had to escape or die.

Dumarest moved to one side, away from the door at his rear, checking distance and opportunity. Perotto faced him on one side, Avro, gun leveled, stood before him and the window. Ready now to shoot or summon help—and once he fired and the gas took effect the thing would be over.

"I yield," said Dumarest quickly. "You are correct—I have no choice. There is no need to use the gas. It would be inefficient. I'd have to be carried and the elevator is small. It would be better if I walked. It would give you greater credit; my capture would be yours alone."

The truth and Avro knew it. The reason he had insisted on facing Dumarest leaving Ishaq and his men on the surface. A matter of pride if not of perfect judgment but what could go wrong?

310

His vision blurred as, suddenly, a pain filled his skull. Pain and the realization of the mistake he had made.

Now! He must correct it while there was still time. Now! The gun aimed as he fought a rising nausea, finger tightening on the release. Now!

"No!" The voice filled the chamber as Angado threw himself into the room. "No!"

He had waited outside, listening, an ally in reserve, now acting with speed which emulated Dumarest's own. A small, round tray left his hand, spinning across the room to strike Avro's wrist and send the vapor-gun to the floor. The cyber followed it, twitching, hands clutching at his head. Then Angado was close to Dumarest, stooping, snatching the knife from his boot, lunging toward Perotto with the blade lifted to strike.

"You lied to me. Cheated me. Wanted me shamed. You filth! You stinking filth! Die, you bastard!"

Words instead of action and time given for Perotto to spring to one side, to lift the hand adorned with the heavy ring, for something to spurt from it and land with a thin, waspish drone against Angado's skull.

As he fell Dumarest was moving.

He dived forward, low, rising as Perotto turned toward him, shoulder catching the underside of the hand aimed at his face and throwing it upward as he struck. One blow smashed into Perotto's stomach and sent him doubling forward. Another dropped him to the ground. A third sent him to sprawl, gasping, face upward as Dumarest fell to his knees beside him. As the ringed hand swung toward him he grabbed it, aimed the ring at the orifice of the gaping mouth, squeezed to release the darts held within the gemmed casing.

Two of them sang as they buried themselves deep into the soft inner tissue of the throat, creating a black crater of destruction, filling the body with toxic poisons as it filled the mouth with blood and pain.

"Earl!"

Angado was dying. The dart which had struck his head was buried deep above the left eye, already into the bone, the brain beneath. Dumarest knelt beside him, reaching for the throat, resting his fingers against the carotids.

311

"Earl! I—"

"Easy." Dumarest's voice was warmly reassuring. "Just relax, Angado. This is just a dream. A bad dream. When you wake you'll forget all about it. It's just a dream."

"No." Angado swallowed and then, incredibly, managed to smile. "It's real and I know it. As I want you to know something, Earl. I love . . . I . . ." He writhed beneath Dumarest's hands, sweat dewing his face, his throat. "You, Earl. I love . . ."

He stiffened and lost the smile as he lost the power of speech and the one became the rictus of death as the other grew into a silence which filled the world. One broken by the muted drone of the waterfall, the faint, insectlike scrap of a moving hand.

Avro reaching for his gun.

It lay beneath the wide window and his fingers touched it as Dumarest reared upright, closed on it as he moved forward, twisted it to aim as he approached, fired as, holding his breath, he dived toward the door.

Opening it as green vapor closed around him, falling through it into the open air of the balcony, clutching the rail as the wind tore the clinging mist from his face and body and his lungs burned with the need for oxygen.

Seconds dragging into minutes then he breathed and breathed again of the cool, damp, life-giving air.

Avro lay slumped on the floor, his breathing shallow, his gaunt face relaxed in the sleep the gas had created. A man felled in the moment of victory by the pain which had turned his mind and body into a rebellious mechine. Dumarest checked he was helpless then snatching up his knife returned to the balcony and hung dangerously over the rail.

Beneath him the rock had been cut away in a smooth concave sweep devoid of any trace of hand or foothold. That above was as formidable; a carved overhang moist with condensation pearling the near-mirror finish. Only the sides were left.

Dumarest moved to the right, stepped up to balance on the rail and, extending his arm, quested along the stone. He found nothing and moved to the other side, this time probing with his knife. The point found a crack, slipped into it, held for a moment then rasped free.

Back in the apartment he went into Angado's bedroom, found sheets, ripped them into strips to form a rope, lashed one end around his waist. On the balcony he tied the free end to the rail and, mounting it, tried again. This time the knife held and he swung from the rail on its support. His left hand found a hold and he heaved, boots scrabbling for purchase. A few inches and he rested before moving again. Farther out this time, a little higher, the knife coming free to find a new hold. Up and along again to halt as the rope tightened at his waist.

The moment of decision as wind tore at his hair and the roar of falling water echoed in his ears.

To free himself from the rope was to risk everything on his ability to climb to the upper edge of the chasm. avoid the men waiting there and make his escape in some way. To return to the apartment was to reenter the trap Avro had constructed; a sealed place from which there was only one exit and that guarded by watchful men.

Taken, he would be held, questioned, his mind probed to the last cell. He would be stripped of all knowledge then discarded as so much useless gargage. To attempt to climb was to risk falling to the rocks below. A quick death against one of long-drawn torment.

A choice made for him as rock crumbled beneath his boot and the knife slipped free to send him falling to halt with a jerk at the end of the rope. Thrusting the blade back into his boot he climbed hand over hand back to the balcony.

On the floor Avro stirred; a crippled spider tormented by savage dreams. From the room of bizarre decorations came the rolling echo of drums as Wynne Tewson pounded feebly at the door.

She was pale, lips almost bloodless, eyes marred by a yellowish tinge. The silver helmet of her hair was mussed and a bruise showed livid on her left cheek. She fought against Dumarest's arms as he dragged her into the bathroom, stripping her before holding her beneath the stinging shower. As she dried herself, shivering from the icy spray, he searched her clothing, pocketing the keys he found.

"You bastard!" Dressed, she glared at him. "You smart, know-it-all bastard!"

313

"Shut your mouth."

"Lying to me. Kissing me—then shoving me into that gas. And then what? Woke Angado, I suppose and used him to help you. Now you want me to do the same. Well, you can go to hell!"

"You'll go first." He grabbed her arm and dragged her into the main salon. "Over the edge and down to the rocks." He pointed at the open door of the balcony. "You want that?"

"You wouldn't—"

"What have I to lose?" He was curt in his interruption. "Men are waiting on the surface to take me. If they do it's my life. You tried to trap me—why the hell should I consider you? Make your choice. You help or you go over." He pulled her toward the opening. To where the roar of falling water filled the air. "What's it to be?"

A choice that was no choice at all. She looked at the water, his eyes, the mouth that had grown cruel.

"I'll help, but what can I do? This place is like a prison."

With men waiting outside on guard. By why did they wait? How long had they been ordered to stand by before taking action? Who would give the order for them to move in?

Avro stirred again and Dumarest guessed the answer. One verified as he stripped off the scarlet robe to reveal the mechanism clipped inside. A small transmitter which, when activated, would bring the others crashing in. The gas had worked too quickly for the cyber to have used it—a failure that gave Dumarest a chance.

"It won't work." Wynne stared as Dumarest donned the scarlet robe. "You'll never pass for a cyber."

"Maybe not."

"What happened to him?" She glanced at Perotto lying in a pool of blood that had drained from his mouth. "Did you do that?"

"He killed Angado."

"So you killed him?"

She shivered as he nodded, knowing he would kill her with the same lack of compassion if she thwarted him. As he would kill anyone who presented a threat or who had done him injury. An attribute she had sensed when lying in his

314

arms. Even when sharing a mutual passion and, remembering it, she felt a sudden desire.

"Earl! Earl, you can trust me!"

Dumarest ignored her, cutting free the rope still hanging from the balcony, dipping a portion of it into the carmine pool beside Perotto's head, winding it around his skull to form a blood-stained bandage which covered most of his face. With talc from the bathroom he whitened his features and stooped for the robe to sweep the floor.

Scarlet identified a cyber, one hurt, his face almost invisible beneath the bandage and the drawn cowl.

"Earl?"

He said, "The way out is by the elevator or the stairs. The stairs will be guarded so we'll use the elevator. I'll lean on you and you'll explain to anyone who asks that I was hurt by the man I came for. He's still downstairs gased and helpless."

She was bitter at his rejection. "Then what? We take wings and fly?"

"One thing at a time. First we get out. Unless we do that the rest doesn't matter."

"Not to you," she agreed. "But I'd just as soon stay here."

"As a corpse?" Dumarest stepped close to her, the knife glimmering in his hand. Steel as hard as the determination stamped on his face. "I'm fighting for my life, girl. Remember that. Cross me and you'll be dead. The same if you betray me. The same if you don't cooperate. Now let's get going."

The elevator sighed down and to a halt at Wynne's signal. It held a man who went down beneath the smashing impact of Dumarest's knife, the pommel a hammer throwing the man into unconsciousness. Blood would have betrayed the deception; the missing man could prove an asset. Dumarest dragged him from the elevator before locking the woman to him with his left arm, his right hand with the knife slipping close to prick her flesh through the clothing.

"He was sent to stand guard over Dumarest," he said. "If anyone should ask that's what you tell them. Volunteer the information if they are suspicious but don't go into too much detail."

"Dumarest?"

"Just do as I say." She winced as the point dug deeper. "Up now."

The door slid shut and the elevator moved upward. As it came to a halt Dumarest sagged even more, throwing his weight against the woman, twisting to hide the blade he held against her.

"Master!" The acolyte was concerned, stepping forward as he saw the figure in the scarlet robe. "Master, are you hurt?"

"A head injury." Wynne answered the question. "Please step to one side."

Tupou obeyed, checking the empty elevator, stepping toward it.

"The man is guarding Dumarest." Wynne spoke quickly, conscious of the knife at her side. "Inform your master that he is ready to be taken."

His master? Ishaq had his own aides but Tupou was assigned to Avro. A thing the cyber would have known if not the woman, but why hadn't he ordered her to summon aid if he was hurt? Expecially when his acolyte was so close.

Dumarest whispered, "Tell him to report to the other cyber." He had seen the glow of the scarlet robe. "You will attend me until Dumarest is taken. Hurry!"

A matter of efficiency which the acolyte could appreciate. Avro was in no immediate danger but the quarry must be taken at all costs. And, if there was doubt, Ishaq could settle it.

He came forward, impatient at the delay, the need to accede to Avro's decision. The operation had been badly conducted; too much time had passed since Dumarest had entered the trap. He should now be safely contained. As it was he had managed to hurt Avro and done who knew what else?

"Wait." He called after the pair now moving toward the woman's raft. "Cyber Avro. A moment."

One in which the masquerade would be exposed and what would happen to her for having aided the deception? Wynne felt the sudden rising of panic.

"No!" She twisted away with desperate strength, breaking Dumarest's hold tearing herself from the blade at her side.

"He isn't Avro! He's the man you want! Dumarest! He's Dumarest!"

The betrayal he had feared. Now only speed could save him. Dumarest straightened, running toward the raft, his hand diving into a pocket and finding the keys he'd taken from Wynne's clothing.

A precaution justified as she called. "He can't get away. It's locked. I've—" Her tone changed as she discovered the theft. "Get to the other raft. Chase him. Move, damn you! Move!"

Orders followed as Ishaq gestured obedience. Dumarest reached Wynne's vehicle as the cyber and his men climbed into their own, the woman with them, eager to demonstrate her loyalty.

It lifted as Dumarest fumbled with the keys, finding the right one almost too late, jerking the raft up from beneath the shadow of the other. A beam struck the rear edge and metal flowed from the point of impact. More as the laser quested for the generator to wreck it and bring down the raft. Shots which ended as Dumarest sent it darting forward to hover over the waterfall, hanging poised as the other vehicle came up behind him, men leaning over the rail ready to jump when given the chance.

As it drew close Dumarest hit the controls.

Fire streamed from the rear of his raft; the roaring torch of the auxiliary burners Wynne had demonstrated during the night. Livid flames bathed the other raft with their fury. Searing those it contained like ants in a blowtorch. Sending them to fall into the chasm of the waterfall as Dumarest rose toward the sky, to freedom, to the man who could tell him how to find Earth.

A Selection of Legend Titles

☐	Eon	Greg Bear	£4.95
☐	The Infinity Concerto	Greg Bear	£3.50
☐	Wolf in Shadow	David Gemmell	£3.50
☐	Wyrms	Orson Scott Card	£2.95
☐	Speaker for the Dead	Orson Scott Card	£2.95
☐	The Misplaced Legion	Harry Turtledove	£2.95
☐	An Emperor For the Legion	Harry Turtledove	£2.99
☐	Falcon's of Narabedla	Marion Zimmer Bradley	£2.50
☐	Dark Lady	Mike Resnick	£2.99
☐	Golden Sunlands	Christopher Rowley	£2.99
☐	This is the Way the World Ends	James Morrow	£5.50
☐	Emprise	Michael Kube-McDowell	£3.50

Prices and other details are liable to change

ARROW BOOKS, BOOKSERVICE BY POST, PO BOX 29, DOUGLAS, ISLE OF MAN, BRITISH ISLES

NAME..

ADDRESS...

....

....

Please enclose a cheque or postal order made out to Arrow Books Ltd. for the amount due and allow the following for postage and packing.

U.K. CUSTOMERS: Please allow 22p per book to a maximum of £3.00.

B.F.P.O. & EIRE: Please allow 22p per book to a maximum of £3.00

OVERSEAS CUSTOMERS: Please allow 22p per book.

Whilst every effort is made to keep prices low it is sometimes necessary to increase cover prices at short notice. Arrow Books reserve the right to show new retail prices on covers which may differ from those previously advertised in the text or elsewhere.